BEFORE YOU

WERE
GONE

SHEILA BUGLER

C **CANELO**CRIME

First published in the United Kingdom in 2021 by Canelo

This edition published in the United Kingdom in 2022 by

Canelo
Unit 9, 5th Floor
Cargo Works, 1–2 Hatfields
London, SE1 9PG
United Kingdom

A CIP catalogue record for this book is available from the British Library.

Print ISBN 978 1 80436 181 8
Ebook ISBN 978 1 80032 164 9

Look for more great books at www.canelo.co

Printed and bound in Great Britain by Clays Ltd, Elcograf S.p.A.

1

This book is dedicated to a very special group of women who all live in the same little corner of SE London: Anna Pattenden, Bridget Morrison, Helen Cunningham, Moira Cuthbert and Ursula Gaffney. I love you all and am so lucky to have you in my life. And remember girls, what happens in Brighton, stays in Brighton…

One

It happened on the last day of her trip. Emer was on the London Underground, travelling back to her hotel to pick up her bags before heading to the airport. The Tube was packed, just like every other time she'd travelled on it, and she was squeezed into a corner near the door, trying not to inhale the smell of bodies.

She had her earphones in, listening to her latest music crush, Lana Del Rey. Lana's haunting voice, singing about big American skies and empty landscapes. Immersed in the music, Emer closed her eyes and tried not to think about her mother, or the row they'd had on the phone earlier.

She should have expected it. If she'd thought about it for more than a few seconds, she'd have realised Ursula was never going to approve of Emer's plans to move to London. Because if Emer was living in London, how could Ursula continue to control every aspect of her daughter's life?

Let's face it, Emer. It's not as if you're going to get the job, is it? I'm sure the only reason you got called for an interview is because you're Robert's stepdaughter.

Then, when Emer had pointed out that although her stepfather was quite well-known in Ireland, it was unlikely many people in London had ever heard of him:

That's so typical of you. You're never able to give Robert the credit he deserves. He has achieved so much, and he works so hard – every single day – to keep you in the manner you're accustomed to. And what thanks does he get for that? His ungrateful stepdaughter, spending his money on a trip to London for an interview for some job she hasn't a hope in hell of getting because she hasn't worked for so long she's practically unemployable by now.

Besides, we all know the real reason you've gone to London. It's nothing to do with any job. You've gone there chasing after her, haven't you?

The train came out of the tunnel at Barbican, and Emer's phone beeped with a text.

> Despite what you think, I'm not trying to be
> difficult. I simply want what's best for you. Is
> that so hard for you to understand?

Emer deleted the text, without replying.

It had been raining when she left the hotel that morning and she'd put on a jacket. She regretted that now. It was too hot on the Tube, but she was packed in so tight, there was no room for her to take off the jacket. She pulled down the zip and flapped her T-shirt a few times, for all the good it did. Not for the first time since coming to London, she wondered how people did this journey every day of their working lives.

The Tube stopped at Moorgate and she looked up at the map, counting the stations to Victoria. Twelve more stops. She'd read somewhere that the average time between Tube stations was three minutes. Which meant she had thirty-six more minutes stuck inside this burning furnace trying not to inhale the stink of body odour and wet clothes.

At Liverpool Street, the carriage emptied out and Emer grabbed a free seat before anyone else could take it. Like everyone else on the train, she surreptitiously scanned her fellow passengers while, at the same time, avoiding eye contact at all times.

Eleven stops. Thirty-three minutes. A group of Italian tourists were standing by the door, talking loudly to each other, their voices cutting through Lana's singing. Emer had lived in Italy for a bit, teaching English, and she listened out for the familiar phrases, regretting how quickly she'd forgotten the language after she left.

There was a girl in the group, tall and dark haired and so shockingly, perfectly beautiful it took all of Emer's self-control not to stare. As the train slowed down and entered Tower Hill station, the group prepared to get off the train, gathering their bags off the floor and reassembling once more by the exit.

Emer dragged her eyes away from the Italian bomb-shell, focusing on a woman standing a few feet further along the carriage. She was reading a book and, although Emer twisted her neck, she couldn't quite see the cover. The woman had short, bleached blond hair and she was wearing the most amazing, hand-painted silk dress. Emer knew the dress was silk, and knew it was hand-painted, because she'd done little else last summer except browse images of hand-painted silk dresses, trying to find one she wanted to get married in. Before her wedding plans were cancelled when Nikki walked out on her.

Emer lifted her phone, thinking she'd take a photo. She still held out hope of getting back with Nikki. That hope was the only thing keeping her going. If that happened – when it happened – then *this* was the dress she wanted to get married in. She switched the camera on and was getting ready to take the photo, when the woman looked up from her book.

The shock of recognition was instant. The eyes. She'd know them anywhere. But it was more than that. The shape of her nose, the way she tilted her head sideways as she stared back at Emer.

Memory after memory slammed into her. So many memories she was drowning under them. Her throat closed and she couldn't breathe. She clawed the collar of her T-shirt, pulling it away from her neck as if that might help. A buzzing sound inside her head blocked out Lana's voice and all the other noises around her.

Somehow, she became aware that the train had stopped and the woman in the dress was putting her book into her pale pink leather rucksack and was stepping off the train.

'Stop.' Emer's voice was hoarse and the word was no more than a whisper. Forgetting about the plane she had to catch, she stood up and pushed her way through the crowds of people getting onto the train.

On the platform, a blast of air hit her as the train sped away to the next station. Looking around, Emer tried to locate the woman, but there were too many people and she couldn't see her amongst the crowd. She started to think she'd made a mistake, remembering all the other times, too many to count over the years, when she'd seen someone and thought – for a split second, sometimes longer – that the person was Kitty.

But this was different. She could feel it, a certainty deep inside her. The woman she'd just seen was Kitty. No doubt about it.

A memory from earlier. Sitting across from the two women interviewing her. Ursula's voice screeching inside her head, telling her she was useless and unemployable and a waste of space. Her voice blocking out everything else until Emer had found it impossible to focus on the questions she was being asked.

A flash of blond hair at the end of the platform. Emer pushed her way through the crowd, following the woman as she disappeared into the tunnel that led up to the exit. She walked with a faint limp, easy to miss if you didn't know to look for it. The result of an accident when she was four years old. She'd fallen off a pony at the horse fair and broken her leg. Ever since, she'd walked with a slightly lopsided gait.

'Kitty!'

Several people turned to look at her, but not the woman limping into the tunnel. She was moving faster now, as if she'd heard her name and didn't want to be caught. As if she knew the person calling out to her was the same person who'd spent the last twenty-three years blaming herself for what had happened the day Kitty died.

Two

Two months later

Gordon's Wine Bar on London's Embankment. A nineteenth-century, candlelit underground haven. This was where Dee had come on her first date with Billy, her dead ex-husband. Over the course of their ill-fated marriage, they'd spent many more nights here. Drinking wine and talking shite with people Dee had once considered her closest friends.

Today was her first time back in the wine bar since she'd left London three years ago. She'd worried it might feel overwhelming to be here again. But as she'd walked down the steps into the cave-like space below, it had felt a little like coming home. She'd spent so long trying to move past her divorce and everything else that had driven her from London, she'd almost forgotten there had been a long time – most of her adult life, in fact – when she'd been happier here in the city than anywhere else.

It was late afternoon when she arrived. Late enough to order a glass of wine without feeling guilty; early enough to find a free table. Her drink ordered, she settled at one of the wooden tables and waited. And waited. Forty minutes later, her glass empty, she was still waiting.

By now, the buzz she'd had since leaving the TV studio had faded. She'd been recording a ten-minute slot for a frothy, early evening programme that most people Dee knew would never watch. She'd been asked to come on the programme to discuss the government's plans to reduce the flow of immigration into the UK. Following a series of articles she'd written on immigration, Dee was increasingly asked to comment on the issue in different media. This had been her first TV appearance, and she'd been nervous as hell. But the young man and woman presenting the programme were great fun, and Dee had enjoyed herself more than she'd expected. At the end, they'd asked if she'd like to come back another time and she'd said yes straight away.

She checked her phone for messages but, so far, nothing. She was trying to decide whether or not to order another glass of wine when a young woman came into the bar and, after scanning the room, approached Dee's table.

'Emer?' Dee stood up, smiling.

'Dee? Oh thank goodness. I'm so sorry. I got on the wrong Tube and ended up heading east instead of west. I didn't realise until I looked up and saw I was already in Mile End. I might not know my way around London, but I know Mile End is nowhere near here.'

'Well you got here eventually,' Dee said. 'Sit down and let me get you a drink. What would you like?'

'Soda and lime, if that's okay?'

At the bar, Dee ordered another glass of wine for herself, along with the soda and lime. As she carried the drinks back to the table, she took the opportunity to take a good look at the woman she'd come here to meet.

Her name was Emer Doran. She was Dee's cousin but, until today, the two women had never met. And probably never would have, Dee reflected, if Emer hadn't contacted her last week out of the blue. She'd sent an email, saying she'd just moved to London and asking if Dee would like to meet up. Emer's father and Dee's father were brothers who had fallen out when Dee was a child. Her father had always refused to talk about his brother. As a result, Dee knew very little about her uncle and his family, who lived in Ireland in the same town Dee's father had lived in until he emigrated to England in the sixties.

'I'd never have guessed we were related if I'd passed you on the street,' Dee said, putting the drinks on the table and sitting down. 'You don't look anything like my dad's side of the family.'

'I'm more like my mum, I guess,' Emer said.

Unlike Dee, who had inherited her father's height and stockiness, Emer was like a delicate doll. With porcelain skin, pale blue eyes and a dancer's body, she couldn't have looked less like Dee if she'd tried.

'I'm so glad you got in touch.' Dee took a sip of her wine, thinking about all the other things she wanted to say. This should be a big moment for her. Since her father's death five years earlier, Dee had resigned herself to never getting to know his side of the family. When she was younger she'd tried to convince her father to rebuild his relationship with his brother, but he'd always refused. After his death Dee had made a few attempts to contact her uncle, but without any luck.

'I should have done it a long time ago,' Emer said. 'It doesn't seem right that we don't get to see each other just because of some stupid argument our fathers had years ago.'

'I know your parents separated,' Dee said. 'Our mothers kept in touch a little, I think. Before she died, my mum gave me your mother's address and telephone number. I called her a few times, even wrote to her at one

8

point, but she made it very clear she didn't want anything to do with me.'

'I'm so sorry,' Emer said. 'I had no idea.'

'It doesn't matter,' Dee said, although she'd been upset at the time. After her father's death, the need to connect with his remaining relatives had been strong. But over time, she'd grown to accept that the reunion she longed for was unlikely to happen.

'So,' she said. 'You've just moved to London?'

'A three-month contract,' Emer said. 'I'll be heading home again when it's finished.'

'What do you do?'

'IT project management. It's not the most interesting job in the world but it pays well, and when the chance came up to spend a few months in London, I thought, why the hell not? Once I was here, it made sense to reach out to you and see if we could meet up. I've read some of the stuff you've written, Dee. It's really good.'

'Thanks.' Dee's face flushed at the compliment. She would never tire of people telling her they liked what she wrote.

'On your website it says you're writing a book,' Emer said. 'That's impressive.'

'You've done your homework,' Dee said. 'I feel embarrassed you know more about me than I do about you.'

'You don't mind, do you? I was interested to know more about you, that's all.'

'Of course I don't mind,' Dee said. 'There's not much point having a website if no one's going to look at it, right?'

'Exactly.' Emer smiled, and Dee realised it was the first time she'd done so since she'd got here. She seemed nervous. Which was normal, Dee supposed. Meeting up

9

like this for the first time was a weird situation for both of them.

'Anyway,' Dee said. 'Enough about me. Where are you living in London? How did you get into working in IT project management? Do you like it? Are you in a relationship? What sorts of things do you like doing?'

Realising too late she was turning this into an interview, not a conversation, she stopped with the questions.

'Sorry,' she said, smiling. 'I didn't mean to give you the third degree. I'm excited to meet you, that's all.'

'It's fine,' Emer said, 'To tell the truth, Dee, I'm not great at talking about myself. I'd love to know more about the book you're writing. Looking into a double murder, right?'

'It was one of those stories that captured the public imagination,' Dee said. 'I happened to be in the right place at the right time, and I got to write the inside story. Later, a publisher got in touch with a proposal for a book. It seemed too good an opportunity to pass up.'

In fact, several publishers had tried to sign Dee up and she'd been in the lucky position of getting to choose which publisher she wanted to work with.

'You got to solve the case,' Emer said. 'I read all about it. You don't need to be modest, Dee. It was amazing.'

'Well.' Dee took a sip of wine, uncomfortable with the way the conversation was going. She might be good at taking compliments about her writing, but anything above that always made her squirm. 'I can tell you what's not amazing – trying to write a book.'

'What do you mean?'

Dee frowned, trying to find the right words to explain it.

'It's such a different format to anything I've done before. It's longer, of course. And you have to think about structure and form in a way you don't have to do so much when you're writing a piece for a paper or magazine.'

'I'm sure you'll get there,' Emer said.

'I hope so. And now I really am done talking about myself. I'm a journalist and I'm used to being the person asking the questions, not answering them.'

'I'm not very good at talking about myself,' Emer said. 'Sorry.'

'There's something I wanted to ask you,' Dee said, 'if that's okay?'

'Sure.'

'It's about Eamon, your dad. Are you still in contact with him?'

'I'm afraid not,' Emer said. 'He left us a few months after Kitty died. You know about that, right?'

Dee nodded. Her mother, who occasionally relented and answered Dee's questions about the Dorans, had told her about it. Emer's older sister, Kitty, had drowned when she was eleven years old.

'He left and he never bothered to keep in touch,' Emer said. 'I don't even know if he's alive or dead.'

'That must be hard.' Dee thought of the relationship she'd had with her own father. He'd been a great dad, loving and interested in his only child without ever being overbearing. Dee had loved him fiercely and still missed him terribly.

'I've got used to it,' Emer said. 'Mum says we're better off without him, and I guess she's right. I have a stepdad, Robert. He's been pretty good to me.'

'Well I'm glad to hear that.'

They were silent for a moment. Dee was searching around for something to talk about when Emer started speaking.

'I hope you don't mind, Dee. There's a reason I got in touch with you. I need your help.'

Something shifted inside Dee. She'd been excited about today, looking forward to taking the first steps towards being reunited with a part of her family that she'd never known. But now it seemed the only reason Emer had contacted her was because she wanted something.

'Of course.' Dee took a sip of her wine. 'Whatever I can do. Just tell me.'

'It's about Kitty,' Emer said.

'Kitty – your sister?'

Emer nodded.

'The thing is, Dee. I think she might still be alive. I want to ask if you'll help me find her.'

Three

Dee drained her glass.

'I'm going to need another drink for this. Can I get you something?'

Emer shook her head, holding up her barely touched soda and lime.

As she waited at the bar, Dee ran back over everything she knew about her cousin, which wasn't a lot. She knew Emer's life hadn't been easy. First, she'd lost her sister in a terrible accident. Soon after that, her father had abandoned her. Maybe both those tragedies had damaged her more than she realised. Because, clearly, the poor girl was damaged if she believed her sister could still be alive.

'I thought Kitty drowned,' Dee said, when she sat back down. 'Are you telling me that's not what happened?'

'I know how mad it sounds.' Emer smiled. 'You must be wishing you'd never agreed to meet me, right?'

'Wrong.' Dee reached across the table and squeezed the young woman's hand. 'I'm glad we've found each other, and I'm happy to help if I can. I'm just not sure how.'

'Will you at least hear me out?' Emer said, pulling her hand away. 'Before you decide I'm a certified nut job?'

'Of course.'

'Right.' Emer paused. 'Sorry. It's not easy, you know? It wasn't the first time, you see. I was only ten when it happened. So when I told people that I'd seen her, no one believed me. They tried to convince me I'd made it up. Over the years, I accepted that maybe I had. Until two months ago. I was in London for a few days and I saw her on the Underground.'

'You said this had happened before?'

'They never found her body,' Emer said. 'Did you know that? Sorry. Why would you? Our fathers had stopped speaking long before then. Anyway, the day itself is a blur. I remember we'd had a row and Kitty went to a different part of the beach to get away from me. Our mother was with us, but she was reading magazines and she'd made it clear she didn't want us disturbing her. I wasn't worried, at first. We were always having silly rows, they never meant anything. I don't know how long it was before my mother started panicking. She said she'd seen Kitty at the edge of the water earlier. I remember her running up and down the beach, calling Kitty's name. Kitty couldn't swim, you see. She'd always been scared of the water so I didn't know why she'd gone in that day.

'The problem was, there was no one else around. We weren't on the main beach. We'd gone to a quiet part, away from the crowds, because our mother didn't like crowds. When she couldn't find Kitty, we had to go through the dunes onto the golf course. There were three men. I remember that. My mother was crying and begging them to help. Even then, I didn't understand, not really. I thought Kitty had run off. She did that sometimes, you see. She didn't really get on with our mother. They were always rowing and sometimes Kitty would disappear for hours.'

Emer paused and took a sip of her drink.

'I thought it was my fault. We'd had a row and, because of that, Kitty was gone. Because she couldn't swim, everyone assumed she'd drowned. I did too, at first. There were people out searching the coast. But later that evening, something happened.'

'What?'

'We were on holiday at the time. In Lahinch, a seaside town in the west of Ireland. We were staying in a hotel. At some point, someone must have sent me to bed. I was lying in the room by myself, trying to understand what had happened. I couldn't accept what they'd told me. Kitty hated the water. Why would she have tried to go in? I kept thinking someone had made a mistake and if they just looked a little harder, surely they'd find her.

'Then the door opened. I thought it was my mother, coming to check I was okay. But it was Kitty. She said she'd come to say goodbye. I asked her where she was going and she said she couldn't tell me. I begged her to stay. She told me she was sorry, and then she left.

'I tried to stop her. But she'd always been faster than me. I remember chasing after her along the hotel corridor. It was like one of those dreams, you know the ones where you're chasing someone but you can't catch up with them no matter how fast you run?'

Which is exactly what it sounded like, Dee thought. She'd had similar dreams herself in the months after her ex-husband's death. Grief was a bastard that messed with your mind in all sorts of ways.

'There was a fire escape at the end of the corridor. There was a staircase the other side of the door. We weren't allowed to go there, but I knew that's where she was. The door was open, but before I could follow her, my mother found me and took me back to my room. The next day, she convinced me I'd been sleepwalking and had imagined the whole thing. But I never forgot it,

Dee. And then, when I saw that woman on the Tube, it all came back to me and I haven't been able to think about anything else since.'

'Okay.' Dee drank some wine while she tried to work out the best thing to say. 'Tell me about the woman. Did you speak to her?'

'I didn't get a chance. She was getting off the Tube when I saw her. I ran after her, tried to call her back, but she didn't stop.'

'It must have been an awful shock,' Dee said, 'after all this time. But Emer, it's not uncommon to see someone who reminds you of another person.'

'I know that,' Emer said. 'And I know there's every chance I got it wrong. But I need to make sure. What if I wasn't dreaming that night? What if Kitty's still alive?'

Dee didn't bother pointing out all the reasons that was impossible. Like how unlikely it was that an eleven-year-old child could fake a drowning and disappear all by herself.

'You're a journalist,' Emer said. 'You've got experience investigating things, trying to find the truth. If Kitty really is out there, I can't think of anyone better placed to find her.'

'Well, I'm flattered you've got so much trust in me,' Dee said. 'But even I can't work miracles. Finding a woman you saw once on the Underground? I wouldn't know where to start.'

'There's more,' Emer said. 'I followed her when she left the station.'

Dee drank some more wine.

'Keep talking. I'm listening.'

'Outside the station, she got into a cab before I could catch her. So I did that classic thing you see in films. I jumped into the next cab that came along and followed her. She didn't go far. A few minutes later, her cab pulled up outside a pub and she went inside. But by the time I'd paid my own cab driver and gone into the pub, there was no sign of her.'

'So you made a mistake,' Dee said.

'Or she knew I was following her and she was hiding from me. I asked the barman if he'd seen her but he told me no one matching that description had come into the pub. He was lying.'

The poor girl was delusional, Dee thought. She needed counselling, not a journalist.

'You checked the toilets?'

'Of course,' Emer said. 'I know what I saw, Dee. She walked into that pub and when I followed her a few minutes later, she wasn't there. The only possible place she could have gone was behind the bar and into the back area that's not open to the public.'

'Did you get the name of the pub?'

'It was in a place called Wapping,' Emer said. 'Near Tower Bridge and Limehouse. I've googled it obsessively ever since.'

'I know Wapping,' Dee interrupted. 'And I know most of the pubs there as well. Which one?'

'It's called the Town of Ramsgate.'

'Right.' Dee grabbed her bag and stood up.

'Where are you going?' Emer asked.

'You mean where are we going,' Dee said. 'To Wapping, of course.'

'So you believe me?' Emer said, standing up as well.

'I don't know what I believe,' Dee said. 'But I know there's only one way of finding out for sure if that woman is your sister. We're going to the Town of Ramsgate now and we're going to find out who she is.'

'Hang on.' Emer put her hand on Dee's arm. 'She can't see me. That's why I need you. If she sees me, she'll try to run away again. If that happens, I may never get to find out if she could be Kitty.'

'You can stay outside.' Dee walked up the steps from the cellar bar into the searing London sunshine. On the news the other night, they'd said it had been the hottest summer on record. Something so blindingly obvious she'd wondered, at the time, why anyone had considered it a newsworthy fact. Midway into September and, so far, the heat had shown no sign of abating. She headed towards the Tube station but changed her mind. The thought of being stuck beside so many other sweaty, overheated bodies didn't appeal to her. Besides, what was the point of getting paid ridiculous sums of money for taking part in fluffy TV shows if you couldn't treat yourself every now and then?

'We'll get a cab,' she told Emer. 'Follow me.'

She led her cousin around the corner onto Savoy Place, where she hailed the first black cab she saw and gave the driver the name of the pub in Wapping. Dee didn't know if this was a sensible idea or not, but she knew it was the quickest way to prove to Emer that the woman she'd seen on the Tube couldn't be her dead sister. While the cab crawled through the early evening London traffic, Dee got Emer to tell her everything she remembered about the woman.

'Kitty had a condition called heterochromia,' Emer said. Then, when Dee frowned, 'Her eyes were two different colours.'

'Like David Bowie?'

'Not exactly. Bowie had something called anisocoria, which is when a person's pupils are two different sizes. Heterochromia affects the iris, not the pupil. In Kitty's case, it meant her left eye was blue, her right eye was green.'

'I'm guessing the woman you saw had the same condition?'

'She did, but it wasn't just that. I'm not stupid. Six people in every thousand have heterochromia. It was more than the eyes. It was everything about her. Not her hair, which she'd dyed. Kitty's hair was brown and she'd always worn it long. This woman's hair was blond − Marilyn blond − and cropped short. But her face, the way she walked. I forgot to tell you that. Kitty had a slight limp, and so did this woman.'

Dee refrained from pointing out that this, too, was hardly proof the woman was Emer's dead sister. It was clear Emer had convinced herself Kitty was still alive. Until Dee could prove otherwise, Emer wasn't going to change her mind.

Fifty minutes later − because in London that's how long it took to travel four miles by car during rush hour − Dee and Emer were climbing out of the black cab onto a quiet, cobbled street lined with leafy trees and yellow-brick converted warehouses. The Town of Ramsgate was situated at the end of a particularly impressive warehouse conversion that, Dee was pretty sure, had once counted Cher as one of its celebrity residents.

'Okay,' Dee said. 'So you're going to stay out here while I go inside and ask if anyone knows a woman with bleached blond hair and two different coloured eyes?'

'One green, one blue.'

'Got it.'

The pub door was closed, but when Dee peered through the window, she was able to see the people inside. Behind the bar, a tall, striking, eighties-era Annie Lennox lookalike was pulling a pint of Guinness.

'Is that her?' she asked, stepping back from the window to make room for Emer. 'Short blond hair, working behind the bar.'

Emer looked through the window for a long time, without speaking.

'Well?' Dee said. 'Is it her or not?'

'Yes.'

'You don't sound too certain.'

'It's her. One hundred per cent.'

She certainly didn't sound 100 per cent convinced, Dee thought, as she pushed open the door and walked inside. The door swung shut behind her and she waited for her eyes to adjust after the bright sunshine. The pub was a long, narrow room with the bar running down one side. Original stained glass panels on wooden partitions separated the space into cosy snugs. It had been updated since Dee's last visit, sometime around the millennium, but it was familiar enough to trigger a host of memories.

At this time in the afternoon, it was quiet. Dee walked through the pub slowly, scanning the faces of the few drinkers, pretending she was looking for someone. At the back, there was a tiny beer garden that overlooked the banks of the River Thames. It was busier out here than inside, afternoon drinkers taking advantage of the sunshine. Again, Dee made a show of scanning the faces before going back to the welcome cool inside the pub.

'Excuse me,' she said, approaching the woman behind the bar. 'I wonder if you can help me.'

'I can try.'

She was beautiful. The contrast of her eyes – one green, one blue – enhanced her exceptional good looks. She was the sort of woman who'd turn heads wherever she went and Dee understood why she'd captured Emer's attention on the Tube that afternoon.

'I'm looking for directions,' Dee said. 'I'm meant to be meeting a friend but I think I've come to the wrong pub, and now I can't get the map app working on my phone.'

'Where are you trying to get to?'

'I think it's called the Captain Kidd?' Luckily, Dee knew the area well enough to know several other pubs close by.

'You're not far,' the woman said. 'Ten minutes, maybe? A bit of a walk in the heat but most of the street's pretty shaded at this time of the day.'

'Ten minutes is fine,' Dee said.

As the woman gave directions to a pub Dee already knew how to find, she started thinking about how she was going to get Emer to see the sad truth – that her sister was dead and wasn't here in London, or anywhere else.

'You got that?' the woman said.

'Absolutely,' Dee said. 'Thanks so much. You've been really helpful.'

'A pleasure.' The woman smiled again. 'Hope you're not too late meeting your friend.'

'Me too.' Dee paused. 'I'm sorry. You look really familiar. Do I know you from somewhere?'

The woman's body stiffened and the smile disappeared.

'Definitely not,' she said. 'I never forget a face, and I'm sure I haven't seen you before. Good luck meeting your friend.'

She moved along the bar and started collecting glasses. Dee waited for a moment, until it became clear the woman wasn't going to engage with her, and walked back outside.

'So?' Emer asked. 'What did you think?'

'Well she looks nothing like you,' Dee said. 'Although that doesn't mean much. Sisters don't always look alike. And she doesn't have any trace of an Irish accent, either.'

'People can learn new accents,' Emer said.

'Perhaps,' Dee agreed. 'But apart from the eyes, there's really no reason to think she could be Kitty. I'm sorry, Emer, but I really think you need to let this go. There's another pub a bit further along, why don't we go there and have a drink?'

But Emer was peering through the pub window and didn't answer.

'She's not there,' she said. 'Where could she have gone? The only way out of the pub is through the front. If she'd come out this way, we'd have seen her.'

'She's probably just nipped to the loo,' Dee said. Then, realising Emer wasn't ready to let this go, 'Okay, come on. Let's go back in there, both of us, and ask her who she is and if she recognises you.'

She pulled open the door of the pub for the second time that afternoon and went back inside. The first thing she noticed was that there was a different person working behind the bar, and there was no sign of the woman who'd been here a few minutes earlier.

'I'll get us a drink,' she said, but she was speaking to herself. Emer was still standing outside, just visible through the tinted glass window.

A man was serving behind the bar now. Tall and thin, he bore more than a passing resemblance to Jarvis Cocker.

'I'm looking for the woman who was serving a few minutes ago,' Dee said, when she approached the bar.

'She's gone home. Her shift's finished for the day. Can I get you something to drink? If not, I've got other customers to serve.'

Not actually true, Dee observed. Apart from two solitary men with drinks already in front of them, she was the only person standing at the bar.

'Any chance you could tell me her name?' she persisted. 'She's the image of someone I used to know.'

The man leaned forward, pushing his face close to hers.

'She's a private person. And she doesn't like strangers sticking their noses into her business. So why don't you do us all a favour and sling your hook before I call the police and get you arrested for trespassing?'

'It's not trespassing if I'm in a public place.'

'It is if I tell you to leave and you refuse.'

Fair point. Recognising he wasn't going to back down, Dee left before he could follow through with his threat.

'She doesn't want to speak to me,' Dee told Emer when she went back outside. 'There's not much we can do about that, I'm afraid.'

'So we just walk away and forget all about her?' Emer said.

It was the sensible thing to do. But Dee had never been very good at being sensible. She didn't think the woman was Emer's sister. The idea was ridiculous. But her journalist's instinct had kicked in. The woman inside the pub was hiding something, and Dee wanted to find out what that was.

'Come on,' she told Emer. 'I'm taking you up the road to a different pub.'

'What about Kitty?'

'Leave Kitty with me for now,' Dee said.

'But if she's refusing to speak to you, what can you do?'

'I might know someone who can find out who she is.'

'You mean you'll help me?' Emer said.

'Of course.' Dee linked her arm with Emer's as they started walking. 'You're my cousin, aren't you?'

She glanced back at the pub. Just in time to catch a movement in one of the upstairs windows. The blond woman was up there, watching them. She stepped back from the window when Dee saw her but, as she walked away, Dee imagined she was still there, her eyes boring into Dee, watching to make sure she wasn't coming back.

Four

Two months earlier

She is running down a corridor, looking for Kitty. The murmur of voices travels up from the ground floor, muffled by the thick carpets and the layers of space between them. They told her that Kitty's dead, but how can she be dead if Emer's just seen her?

She'd been lying in her bed, eyes wide open staring into the darkness, wondering how it could be true – how could her sister have drowned without anyone noticing a thing? And then, like a miracle, the door had opened and Kitty was there. Not dead. Coming into the room and sitting on the side of Emer's bed. The weight of her body pressing into the mattress, her breath hot against Emer's cheek as she leaned down and whispered to her.

'I did something really bad, Emer. And because of that I have to go. I can't see you again.'

Emer's bare feet fly over the carpeted corridor as she calls her sister's name, over and over, louder and louder.

'Kitty! Kitty!'

She turns the corner and sees Kitty. She's at the fire exit, pushing open the door that leads to the steps they're not allowed to use. Their room is on the top floor of the hotel and they usually get the lift. If the lift is busy, they take the stairs – but the big, curved staircase with its red carpet at the front of the hotel, not these ones at the back which are for emergencies only and if you go there on your own no one can see you so it's not safe.

When she sees Kitty's face, she stops running, because Kitty is crying and she never cries. Emer's the crybaby who cries at everything and should try harder to be more like her sister because she's a big, brave girl. But Kitty doesn't look big and brave now. She looks sad and lonely and it makes Emer feel sad and lonely looking at her.

'Go back to your room.'

Kitty sounds angry, but Emer's not going to go back to her room because everyone thinks Kitty's dead and if this is a joke it's not very funny.

Emer starts to run towards her, but someone grabs her and lifts her off the ground. She sees her hands, reaching out in front of her, trying to pull Kitty back, but she's already too late.

Kitty is gone.

–

The same dream, always. The details so familiar it had become impossible, over the years, to separate the dream from what had actually happened. There were times she could almost believe that's all it had ever been: a dream. It would be so much easier if that's all it was. If she could let go of what she believed had happened that night and move on with her life. And she'd tried. God knows, she'd tried. When Nikki had first threatened to leave, Emer had promised she'd change. She would accept, once and for all, that Kitty was dead. And she would focus, instead, on the life she had with Nikki. But she hadn't been able to keep the promise. The memory of her sister in the hotel that night continued to haunt her. Her belief that Kitty was still alive remained as strong as ever. And because of that, Nikki had left, and now Emer was living back in Ballincarraig with her mother and stepfather.

She could hear them now. Talking in the kitchen of the big house that Robert O'Brien had bought for his new wife as a wedding present. The house, a converted coach inn, was one of the finest in the town. Ursula never tired of telling people how, when she was a little girl passing the house on her way to school each day, she'd dreamed of living here eventually. She refrained from adding that the only reason the house had come on the market was because of the town council's plans to build a municipal dump on the land behind the property. Or that these plans were mysteriously rejected by the same town council a week after Robert, then head of the council, had purchased the house.

'She's never going to get a job if she lies in bed until lunchtime, is she?' Her mother's voice, deliberately loud so Emer would hear her. 'I'm sick and tired of her using Kitty as an excuse not to do something with her life. I never liked Nikki, but I don't blame her for not wanting anything to do with her.'

This was followed by the rumble of Robert's voice. Emer couldn't catch what he said, but she could guess the gist of it. He would be quietly telling Ursula not to worry so much, that Emer would be 'grand' and all she needed was a 'bit of time to work out what she wants to do with her life'.

Sure enough, a moment later, Ursula was off again, telling Robert that what Emer needed was a bit of discipline, not a stepfather who spoiled her instead of telling her to get her act together and grow up.

Again, Emer couldn't hear Robert's response, but she heard the heavy tread of his footsteps on the stairs a few minutes later, followed by a knock on her bedroom door.

'Come in, Robert.' She sat up in the bed, pulling the quilt around herself.

'Sorry to disturb you,' he said, standing in the doorway. 'Ursula was wondering if you fancied a trip to the shops? She wants to buy you some new clothes.' He smiled. 'She seems to think a new wardrobe will improve your chances of getting a job.'

Dear old Robert, Emer thought. Always trying so hard to maintain peace between his wife and her daughter.

'Only my mother would think that buying new clothes is going to suddenly make everything better.'

'She's upset,' Robert said. 'You can't blame her for that, Emer. First you head off to London without telling her where you've gone. And then you come back with all this business about seeing Kitty. You're not stupid. You must have known how this would play out.'

'I thought she'd be happy I was showing some initiative for once,' Emer said. 'She's the one who's always on at me to do find a job.'

'Not in London, though.'

'Why not?' Emer said. 'I thought she'd be delighted to get rid of me.'

'She's already lost one daughter,' Robert said. 'The last thing she wants is to lose you too.'

'She wouldn't be losing me if I moved to London. It's hardly the other side of the world, is it?'

'Try not to be too hard on her, Emer. Losing a daughter the way she did, that's not something any parent gets over. And, well, we both know there's a lot of uncertainty around what actually happened the day your sister drowned.'

'She blames me, you mean. My mother thinks what happened to Kitty was my fault.'

'Can you blame her?' Robert said quietly. 'She tries not to, but it isn't easy. You were the last person to see Kitty alive. Your mother thinks... Well, it doesn't matter what she thinks. The point is, you need to be a bit more understanding, that's all. Do you remember when you were a little girl and you used to come into the office with your mother during the summer holidays?'

Emer remembered. Back then, her mother had been working as Robert's PA. During the summer holidays, there'd been no one at home to look after Kitty and Emer, so Ursula used to take them into work with her. Long, boring days when they'd been forced to sit at a desk with nothing to do for hours on end.

'We used to have those young women working with us,' Robert said.

'The work experience girls,' Emer said. A steady stream of older teenage girls, working on an apprenticeship scheme set up by Robert back in the eighties and still running today.

'Those girls,' Robert said, 'they'd never worked in an office before. Most of them had never even made it to secondary school. It took a lot of patience to skill them up and get them to a standard where they were employable. But I put the effort in because it was worth it. That's why the scheme is still running. Because people see how much it helps.'

'And your point is?'

Robert smiled.

'My point is that a little bit of patience pays dividends. I know your mother can be difficult, but she means well. And she does love you, in her own way. So come on, what do you say? Hop out of bed, get dressed and let her take you shopping. And maybe stop all this nonsense about seeing Kitty in London. It's not fair on your mother.'

She wanted to tell him to get stuffed, that it wasn't nonsense. She knew what she'd seen, and if her mother didn't like that there was nothing Emer could do about that. But she'd always found it hard to say no to Robert. Something he knew and used to his advantage whenever he wanted her to give in to her mother.

'Give me fifteen minutes to shower and get dressed,' she said, 'and then I'll be right down.'

'Good girl.' He smiled and her spirits lifted, as they always did, when she made him happy.

She was ready in under ten minutes. Which gave her five more before she had to leave the bedroom. Her laptop was open on the desk beneath the window. An old colour photo filled the screen; two girls, their smiles wide and bright and so happy her throat ached.

They could have been twins. Everyone said so. Except for the eyes. Emer's were blue; Kitty's, of course, were two different colours – the left one was blue, the right one was green. Two sisters, and then there was only one.

Sometimes, when the memories came, she tried to resist. Now, just for a moment, she let them in. Image after precious image, snapshots of the first ten years of her life. Playing with Kitty in their tiny back garden. Fighting over a Barbie doll that Kitty had stolen from her and refused to give back. Cuddled up together in the same bed, whispering to each other late into the night. So many memories, all of them ending abruptly one night in a hotel corridor.

I did something really bad, Emer. Kitty's voice, whispering, her breath hot against Emer's cheek. *And because of that I have to go. I can't see you again.*

Closing the photo, Emer quickly checked her emails – still nothing from Nikki – and opened her internet browser. When she started typing, the words appeared automatically on the screen. Remembered by her browser because she'd typed them so often: *Kitty Doran, Lucy Ryan, Ballincarraig.*

The results were almost instant. Thousands of links to thousands of different stories about the two girls. And there, midway down the first page, the story Emer was looking for.

> Father of missing girl, Lucy Ryan, found
> dead in family home.

She clicked on the link, like she'd done countless times over the last few days, and saw Lucy's face smiling out at her. The same photo that had accompanied the many news stories Emer had read over the years. And beneath it, a more recent photo of Lucy's sister, Maeve, standing outside the hotel she now ran. The story was three months old. Robert and Ursula had gone to the funeral. Emer had thought about it but, in the end, the thought of seeing Maeve again was too much. So she'd taken the coward's way out and stayed away. And every day since, she'd gone onto the internet to read about her old friend.

She opened a new tab on her browser and checked Instagram and Twitter. Last month, she'd finally plucked up the courage and followed Maeve's social media accounts. So far, Maeve hadn't followed her back. As each day passed, it seemed less likely she ever would. Maeve's Instagram account was private, but her Twitter account wasn't. Emer scrolled through Maeve's tweets, mostly promoting the hotel she ran, searching for any mention of what had happened in Ballincarraig twenty-three years earlier. But there was nothing. There never was.

Based on her social media presence, it seemed that Maeve had found a way to put the past behind her and get on with the rest of her life. Emer knew social media didn't always give an accurate portrayal of a person's life, but she couldn't help feeling Maeve was managing to cope better than she was.

Five

Two months later

The hotel was on the riverfront, with sweeping views of the Thames from the restaurant, where Dee was enjoying a substantial breakfast. She wouldn't normally stay somewhere this fancy, but she'd been paid well for her ten-minute appearance on the TV programme and had decided to spoil herself.

The last time she'd stayed in London had been with Ed Mitchell, the man Dee had briefly thought she was in love with. Booking this hotel had been a way of proving to herself she could have a good time without him. Unfortunately, every time she let her guard down her mind started to imagine what it would be like if he was here with her. Because Ed would love a place like this, with its views and its good coffee and its fancy breakfast menu. She could just picture him reading the menu, that little frown line between his eyes while he tried to choose between Eggs Benedict and a Full English.

Thankfully, before she got to the bit in her daydream where they went back upstairs after finishing their breakfast, Dee's phone started to ring. The caller was Louise, Dee's cousin on her mother's side of the family. The only person who called Dee this early.

'How was it?' Louise asked. 'Did they tell you when the programme will be aired? The kids are so excited their auntie is going to be on TV. They think this means you're famous.'

'I hope you've set them straight then,' Dee said.

'What about Emer? Did you meet her? What's she like?'

'Yes, I met her,' Dee said, 'and she seems very nice.'

'Nice?' Louise snorted. 'So you didn't like her then.'

'That's not what I said.'

Dee looked out the window at the river and the people hurrying along the waterfront. So many people. She thought of the view from her house on the beach in Eastbourne. An uninterrupted stretch of shingle, sea and sky. She was missing it already. Strange to think she'd spent so many years living here, in the city, not ever planning to leave. Now, she couldn't imagine how she'd ever lived so long in this overcrowded metropolis.

'So what was it then?' Louise said.

'It's complicated,' Dee said. 'I'll tell you about it when I see you. Any chance you're free for a coffee or a walk over the next few days?'

'Maybe,' Louise said. 'Although not tomorrow or Saturday. I've got a meeting in Worthing tomorrow. Then Saturday's pretty full on with the kids' activities. Let's see if we can fit something in on Sunday?'

'Only if you've got time,' Dee said. 'Otherwise, don't worry. We can catch up next week.'

'Great. I've got to go now. Just dropped the kids off and I've got a session with Pete before work.'

'Pete?'

'My PT. Catch you later. Bye!'

She hung up before Dee had a chance to ask what PT stood for. Deciding she was probably better off not knowing, she directed her attention back to her laptop, open on the table. A faded colour photo of two girls filled the screen. Gap-toothed and smiling, their arms draped over each other's shoulders. A row of nondescript terraced houses in the background. The similarity between the two girls was impossible to miss, although if you looked closely enough, you could see that the taller girl had two different coloured eyes.

The girls were Emer and Kitty. Emer had emailed the photo last night.

> One month before Kitty disappeared. Also,
> you might want to read up about Lucy Ryan.
> She was Kitty's best friend.

Emer had included links to several archived stories about Lucy Ryan, along with a Facebook friend request which Dee had accepted.

Picking up her phone again, she scrolled through her list of contacts until she found the name she wanted. Leonard Mann, a journalist Dee had got to know the previous year, when she was investigating a murder that had taken place outside her house in Eastbourne. The victim, a young woman, had been at the centre of another murder that had happened in London ten years previously – a murder Leonard had covered extensively at the time.

Dee dialled the number, and waited.

'Dee Doran, as I live and breathe. What a pleasant surprise.'

His voice hadn't changed, still sounded as if someone had sandpapered his throat. A little frailer, perhaps, than when she'd first got to know him. Not surprising, given everything that had happened to him since then. His girl-friend and his oldest friend both killed in the same tragic event eleven months earlier. Dee knew that the loss of his girlfriend, in particular, was something Leonard was still struggling to come to terms with.

'Hey Leonard. How are you?'

'Getting by. Good days and bad days, as you'd expect. But the good days are becoming more frequent, which is something. I hope you're calling to tell me you're coming to London soon and you'd like to buy me that pint you still owe me.'

'Actually,' Dee said. 'I'm in London at the moment. I was wondering if you'd like to meet up. There's something I want to run past you.'

'You know I quit working?'

'I quit myself a few years ago,' Dee said. 'Remember?'

He laughed, but it rapidly turned into a cough that went on for the best part of half a minute.

'If you quit,' Leonard said eventually, 'how come I keep seeing your bloody name and photo every time I open a newspaper these days?'

'You know what they say,' Dee said. 'Once a hack, always a hack.'

'You telling me you want to talk to me about a story?' Leonard said.

'Maybe,' Dee said. 'What do you say?'

She had to wait for his answer while he broke off to cough some more.

'Can't shake this bloody cough,' he said. 'Doctor told me it would get better if I gave up the fags, but she's a fool. It's got worse since I stopped.'

'You stopped smoking?' Dee was impressed. The only time she'd seen Leonard without a cigarette in his mouth was during his girlfriend's funeral. Even then, he'd lit one up the moment the service ended.

'I always promised Roxanne I'd stop,' he said. 'Never kept the promise while she was alive. The least I can do is keep it now. Just hope she's watching over me so she knows I did it eventually.'

'Good for you,' Dee said.

'Maybe. Fags and booze were two of the few pleasures I had left. Now it's just the booze. Been drinking like a bastard since I gave up the fags. Can't seem to help myself. Speaking of which, you said something about buying me a pint?'

'If you can spare me some time?'

'Time's all I've got these days, love. Too much of it. Just tell me where and when, and I'll be there.'

After checking out of her room, Dee spent the morning in the hotel lobby, working on her book. By early afternoon, she'd achieved her daily word count and was ready for a break. Which was good because she was meeting Leonard at the Town of Ramsgate in just under an hour. Gathering up her bags, Dee left the hotel and allowed one of the uniformed doormen to help her into a waiting taxi.

There was a different person working behind the bar today, a woman in her mid-twenties with multiple piercings and short hair dyed bright blue. Dee ordered a glass of white wine for herself and a pint of London Pride for Leonard.

It was too early for the post-work drinkers, and the woman behind the bar seemed more than happy to chat.

'How long have you been in the UK?' Dee asked, picking up on her strong Australian accent.

'Couple of months,' the woman said. 'Saving to continue my travels. Another nine months and then I'm back home to Oz. I finished uni last summer and haven't been able to work out what to do with the rest of my life. So I've done the classic Aussie thing of travelling while I get my head sorted.'

'And is it sorted?' Dee said.

The girl grinned.

'Not by a long shot. All I want to do when I go back is save so I can do more travelling.'

'How long have you worked here?' Dee asked.

'Ever since I arrived in the UK. Nick – that's the landlord – is a friend of a mate of mine back home. Nick was looking for someone to help out during the summer months, so here I am. I got lucky, I guess.'

'I've never been to Australia, but it's definitely on my bucket list.' Dee took a sip of her drink. 'Decent wine. My name's Dee, by the way.'

'Josie,' the woman said. 'Good to meet ya, Dee.'

'I think I may have met Nick,' Dee said. 'Was he working here yesterday afternoon?'

'Tall, lanky bloke with glasses?'

Dee nodded. 'That's him, yeah. Was that his girlfriend working here with him?'

'Girlfriend?' Josie laughed. 'Not sure his husband would be too happy to hear you thought that!'

'My mistake.' Dee smiled. 'They seemed to know each other quite well. I guess I just assumed...'

She trailed off, hoping the girl would finish her sentence for her. She wasn't disappointed.

'Could have been Annie,' Josie said. 'And you're right to pick up on the vibe between those two. They go way back. Friends from school, I think.'

The pub door swung open and Leonard appeared. Dee barely recognised him. He'd always been a thin man, but he'd lost so much weight since she'd last seen him, he was practically a skeleton. When he greeted her with a hug, it was like being embraced by a corpse.

'Bloody hell, Leonard. I thought people put on weight when they stopped smoking.'

'Food's overrated,' Leonard said. 'See you've already got my order in. Thanks for that.' He took the pint glass and lifted it to his lips, doing his best not to spill any before it reached his mouth. Not an easy task with a badly shaking hand. Thankfully, the shaking abated after a few more sips of beer.

Watching him, Dee felt a pang of guilt. She knew what loneliness and grief could do to a person. She should have made more of an effort to stay in touch with Leonard.

'Decent boozer,' he said, finally relinquishing his hold on the pint glass and setting it down on the bar. 'I used to come here a lot back in the day. Had a few mates working for *The Times*. This was their local after Murdoch moved them all to Wapping. Come to think of it, isn't there a beer garden out the back? Any chance we could sit out there? I could do with a bit of sunshine.'

They found a table outside and, once they were settled, Dee got down to the real reason she'd got in touch.

'I see Roxanne everywhere I go, you know,' Leonard said, when she'd finished speaking. 'It's bloody killing me, truth be told. I've lost count of the number of times I've walked into a pub or a supermarket and thought I've seen her. Day before yesterday, I saw a woman at a bus stop. I was so sure she was Roxie, I kept going back, trying to pluck up the courage to speak to her. Only it wasn't her. Of course it wasn't her. It never is, because how could it be? She's dead. But even though I know that, it doesn't stop me seeing her all the time. It's torture.'

'I remember the same thing after both my parents died,' Dee said. 'It's like there's a part of our minds that refuses to accept what we already know to be true.'

'So if you know that already, what the hell are we doing here today?'

'I know the woman can't be Kitty,' Dee said. 'Obviously. But there's something not right about her. Yesterday, as soon as I tried to find out who she was, she disappeared. And when I asked the barman about her, he got quite aggressive.'

'So bloody what?' Leonard said. 'People have all sorts of reasons for not wanting strangers sticking their noses into their private lives. Maybe this woman's got an abusive ex-partner, or she's got a criminal record, or she's one of those Instagram influencers who don't like face-to-face contact. Could be all sorts of reasons she didn't want you asking questions about her.'

'There's something else,' Dee said. 'Emer sent me some information about another girl. Her name's Lucy Ryan. According to Emer, Lucy and Kitty were best friends.'

'And?'

'Lucy is the real reason I can't let this go,' Dee said.

'Go on, then.'

She'd sat up late yesterday evening, reading all the stories about Lucy Ryan. The more she read, the more she knew there was something here. She wasn't sure, yet, what it was. But her gut instinct told her there was a story

40

here. And if Dee had learned one thing in all her years as a journalist, it was to never ignore that instinct.

'Lucy Ryan came from the same town in Ireland as Kitty Doran,' Dee said. 'Ballincarraig. She disappeared in 1997, three weeks before Kitty drowned. There was a lot of press speculation at the time that Lucy's father had killed her and disposed of her body, but he was never charged with anything. Lucy's body was never recovered and, even now, no one knows what happened to her.'

'And you say this kid and Kitty were pals?'

'Best friends, apparently.'

'Could be a coincidence,' Leonard said.

'Two girls, friends, from the same small town, both gone within a few weeks of each? One missing. One presumed dead, although her body was never found. Coincidence? Maybe. My ex-husband, Billy, he used to say that coincidences are just a pattern we can't see.'

'Still doesn't mean the woman working in this pub is your dead cousin.'

Dee looked at the river. So much life out there. So much death too. She wondered how many people had drowned in the Thames over the years, disappearing into its murky depths and losing their lives just like Kitty.

'Penny for them,' Leonard said.

'Sorry.' Dee smiled. 'Lost in my memories.'

'Tell you what.' Leonard held up his empty pint. 'How about you get me another one of these and then we can decide what we're going to do.'

'You mean you'll help me?'

'I can't see the harm,' Leonard said. 'It's not as if I've got much else to occupy myself these days. Besides, I get the impression you're not going to let this one go, are you?'

'Emer's my dad's niece,' Dee said. 'The one remaining connection I have with him. I want to help her. Even if it turns out to be nothing...'

'Which it will.'

'I know. But I have to do something. I'm scared if I don't do this for her, she won't want to see me again. I don't want to lose her before I have the chance to get to know her.'

Six

Two glasses of wine and several pints later, they had a plan. Leonard was going to start visiting the pub a few times a week, ingratiating himself with the bar staff and finding out what he could about Annie.

'I doubt I'll find anything interesting,' he told Dee, 'but if you think she's worth investigating, that's good enough for me. And if a bit of digging helps your cousin to finally accept her sister's dead, then all the better.'

He finished what was left in his pint glass.

'All right, Dee. Lovely as this has been, I've got plans for the rest of the day. I need to be heading off.'

By now, Dee was feeling decidedly woozy. Wine in the afternoon was never a good idea. After saying goodbye to Leonard at Wapping station, she decided to walk to London Bridge station, where she could catch a train to Eastbourne.

With her rucksack on her back, she headed west, following the river as it wound its way through the city. She called Emer along the way to give her an update.

'You really think it could be her?' Emer asked.

'No,' Dee said. 'I'm sorry to sound so blunt, but I think you need to prepare yourself for that.'

'If that's what you think, why bother helping?'

'Because I told you yesterday that I would. So that's what I'm going to do. I know how important this is to you.'

'Thanks, Dee. I really appreciate it.'

'It's a pleasure,' Dee said. 'Actually, I was wondering if you fancy meeting for a quick coffee?'

'Not now,' Emer said. 'Sorry. First day in my new job. I'm already crazy busy.'

'Where are you working?'

'The City,' Emer said. 'Isn't that what you guys call your financial district?'

'That's where I am right now,' Dee said. In fact, she was just south of the City, but she knew it was only a short walk from the river to the City of London with its narrow streets and glass and concrete buildings rising up to meet the clear blue sky. 'I'm happy to hang around until you're finished? It would be lovely to see you before I go back to Eastbourne.'

'I'll be working really late,' Emer said. 'It's always like this on short-term contracts. I could be here for another six hours. That's why I need you, Dee. I'm going to be working flat out. How about I give you a ring tomorrow and maybe we can sort something out the next time you're in London?'

'Okay.' Dee was disappointed, but told herself it was to be expected. Today was, after all, Emer's first day in her new job. She was probably doing all she could to prove herself. 'And hopefully you can come down to Eastbourne soon. My house is right on the beach. If the weather stays like this you'll be able to swim in the sea.'

'Sounds great,' Emer said. 'Sorry, Dee. I really have to go. Catch you soon, yeah?'

Dee had planned to spend the time on the train getting some writing done. After a period when she couldn't get any work, her career was taking off again. A recent story she'd written, exploring the links between two murders sixty years apart, had been picked up by one of the national papers and she'd barely paused for breath since. Alongside regular writing jobs, she'd also been busy doing interviews for radio and TV. She'd signed the publishing deal and her agent was also in talks with a radio production company to do a six-part series about the two victims.

Suddenly, everyone seemed interested in what Dee had to say. It was exhilarating to be in demand again, and she wanted to make the most of it. The sudden upsurge in work couldn't have come at a better time. It had kept her from slipping into the dark place she'd been in after she'd first moved back to Eastbourne. Most importantly, it had kept her mind off Ed Mitchell and their recent, failed relationship.

But this evening, as the train left the city and took her through the rolling green Sussex countryside, Dee couldn't focus on work. Her mind kept going back to the two little girls in the photo Emer had sent her. Opening Facebook, Dee clicked on Emer's profile, but there were almost no posts. Not surprising, Dee supposed. Given Emer's age – around thirty – she probably preferred other social media platforms.

Shutting down Facebook, Dee opened the Word document she'd created the previous day. Here, she'd made notes based on everything Emer had told her about her sister's disappearance. Early on in her career, Dee had learned to always take notes, even for stories she might never write. Because you never knew when something you thought wasn't a story might suddenly become one.

Using these notes now, she opened her internet browser and typed in 'Lahinch' '1997' and 'Kitty Doran'. Then she sat back and started reading.

On the morning of Sunday 27 July 1997, Ursula Doran took her two daughters, Kitty and Emer, to the beach. Mrs Doran and her daughters were on holiday, staying at the Aberdeen Arms Hotel in the seaside town of Lahinch in Co. Clare. The girls' father hadn't come on holiday with the family. He'd stayed behind to work, and had planned to join them later.

Rather than go to the main beach, Mrs Doran took her daughters to a quieter stretch of beach, near the estuary where the river Inagh flowed into the sea. She claimed she'd chosen this location because it was less busy. What she didn't realise, she said, was that the currents in the water here, where the river met the sea, were treacherous. Like many other holidaymakers before and since, she'd ignored the signs warning people not to swim and had decided this was the perfect place to spend the morning.

While Mrs Doran settled down to read a stack of magazines, her daughters started building sandcastles. At some point during the morning, the sisters had an argu-ment and Kitty went for a walk, leaving Emer to play by herself. By the time Mrs Doran went looking for her daughter, she had disappeared.

Two days after Kitty disappeared, the shorts she'd been wearing were washed up on a beach six miles further along the coast. Despite an extensive search that went on for weeks, her body was never recovered. This wasn't an unusual occurrence, apparently. The unpredictable nature of the currents made it a difficult – sometimes impossible – task to work out where a body might end up. There was no mention, in any of the articles that Dee read, about Emer's potential sighting of her sister later that same evening.

According to Emer, her parents had separated shortly after Kitty's death. Hardly surprising, Dee thought. A tragedy like that would put unbearable pressure on a relationship. Even so, it was strange Eamon Doran hadn't kept in touch with his remaining daughter after he left. Dee made a note to ask Emer about this the next time they spoke.

By the time the train was pulling into Eastbourne, Dee had gathered as much information as she could on the events surrounding Kitty Doran's disappearance that summer's morning twenty-three years ago.

Outside the station, as she scrolled through her phone while she queued up for a taxi, Dee noticed she had a new voicemail. The mobile signal was intermittent on the journey from London and she often missed calls when travelling on that route.

She dialled her voicemail and listened to the message:

'Dee? It's me. Hope you're having a lovely time in London. There's something I need to speak to you about. Any chance I could pop over tomorrow morning for a coffee and a chat?'

Dee's spirits plummeted as she listened to the message again. The caller was her neighbour, Ella. From the tense tone of Ella's voice, it was clear that whatever she wanted to tell Dee, it wasn't going to be good news. For the last six months, Ella's partner, Tom, had been dropping increasingly frequent hints about leaving Eastbourne and moving back to Ireland, where his family lived. Dee had done her best to ignore the hints, unable to contemplate a life without Ella, Tom and their son Jake. Now, she knew with a dark certainty that the moment had finally come.

They were leaving. And the truth was, Dee didn't know how she would be able to cope when Ella told her that's what they'd decided.

Seven

Two months earlier

The claustrophobic atmosphere in the house was becoming unbearable. Ursula's suffocating personality shaped every conversation, every nuanced exchange that took place under her ever watchful eyes. It was exhausting and, Emer was pretty sure, emotionally damaging. She didn't know how Robert put up with it. Yet, somehow, her stepfather never seemed bothered by his wife's excesses. He was too besotted, even after twenty years of marriage, to see her as anything but perfect.

Nikki had never liked coming here. She'd quickly decided that Emer's mother was toxic and, after her first few visits to Ballincarraig, Nikki had refused to come back. She could never understand the ties that bound Emer to Ursula. The guilt that made it impossible for Emer to break free of her mother's oppressive personality.

This evening, Ursula was in particularly poisonous form. Snipping at Emer every time she opened her mouth, watching her plate like a hawk to make sure she wasn't overeating. They were having dinner in the large dining room at the front of the house. The room was far too big for three people, but Ursula insisted on eating every meal in here. Another of her affectations that Emer couldn't stand. The kitchen, at the back of the house, had been extended last year to include a large dining area that, as far as Emer could tell, was for show only.

'I hear Dr Kennedy is looking for a new receptionist,' Ursula said, looking pointedly at Emer. 'Is that something you might think about applying for?'

'I hadn't really thought about being a receptionist,' Emer said. 'The thing is, Ursula, I'd rather hoped with a history degree I might get something better than a job as a receptionist in a doctor's surgery.'

It had been Ursula's idea for Emer to call her by her name, instead of 'Mum'. On the morning of Emer's eighteen birthday, Ursula had sat her daughter down and told her she had something important to talk to her about.

'*Mum* doesn't feel right now you're an adult. People are always telling me I look far too young to have an eighteen-year-old daughter. Think what fun it will be if you start calling me Ursula instead. People will think we're sisters.'

All of this, Emer remembered sourly, delivered without a trace of irony.

'The problem is,' Ursula said. 'You haven't been very successful at finding anything better, have you?'

Emer didn't say anything, because her mother was right. University had been a safe space for a few years. The first time in her life she'd lived away from home, out of her mother's overbearing presence. When she'd finished her degree, she had already fallen in love with Galway and couldn't bear the thought of leaving and starting again somewhere else. Instead of looking for jobs related to her degree, she'd worked in various bars around the city, telling herself she would get a 'proper' job eventually. Then she'd met Nikki, fallen head over heels in love and the idea of leaving Galway became harder than ever. Because how could she leave the only place she'd ever felt at home in? 'You could consider it, at least,' Ursula continued. 'I'm sure Robert would be more than happy to put in a good word for you. In fact,' Ursula looked across the table at her husband, 'why don't you call him after dinner? You know Emer won't do anything unless we push her. And we both know she refuses to listen to a word I say. I'm only her mother, the woman who gave birth to her and devoted my life to taking care of her, but apparently that's not enough for her.'

Emer rolled her eyes, but didn't bother responding. This was a favourite tactic of Ursula's – to speak about Emer as if she wasn't in the room. It drove Emer mad, but she'd learned a long time ago that the best thing to do was ignore it completely.

'It's not a bad idea, Emer,' Robert said. 'Brian Kennedy's a decent fella. And working in the surgery, you'd find out all sorts of stuff about people. Might be a bit of fun. You know, a lot of our apprenticeship girls did their work experience at the surgery. It helped quite a few of them to find permanent jobs later on.'

'I haven't heard back from the job in London,' Emer said. 'That might still happen.'

'If they were going to offer you the job,' Ursula said, 'they'd have done so by now.'

'Your mother's worried about you,' Robert said, before Emer had a chance to respond. 'She just wants to see you happy and settled. It's what we both want.'

'It's not just that,' Ursula snapped. 'We've got your reputation to think about as well, Robert. You're a high-profile figure, possibly the future leader of this country. Your speech next week in the Dáil is focusing on job prospects for our young people. What's it going to look like if your own stepdaughter can't even find a job? You have your reputation to consider, and I will not let Emer's laziness jeopardise that.'

And there you had it. The real reason her mother pretended to give a damn about Emer's life. Because she was terrified Emer might do something to thwart her single-minded ambition to become lady of Steward's Lodge, the official residence for Ireland's Taoiseach. Ever since seeing a documentary on the house a few years ago, Ursula had become obsessed with living there one day. An obsession fuelled by her husband's steady rise up the ranks of Fine Gael.

So far, there was little evidence that Ursula's ambition wouldn't be fulfilled. Robert O'Brien was the party's bright shining star. A successful businessman, he'd built a reputation as someone with integrity and empathy. In politics, he'd cleverly aligned himself with the emerging ideology of the new Ireland, becoming an outspoken supporter of causes such as gay marriage, divorce and the recent abortion referendum.

Robert's political ambitions, coupled with his money, had been an attractive option for Ursula after her husband disappeared. Boring, respectable Robert had offered her all the security and financial comfort her first husband had failed to provide. There had been times, plenty of them, when Emer had wondered if her mother had had a hand in her father's sudden disappearance. Because there was no doubt Ursula had benefitted hugely from being newly single and being able to choose a partner better suited to giving her the lifestyle she believed she deserved.

There were advantages to living with Robert, of course. He was kind and never seemed to lose his temper or get angry. The biggest change, however, was Ursula's attitude to her remaining child. While she didn't become kind or loving, her cruelty abated. She didn't lose her temper the way she used to and, since she'd moved in with Robert, she had never once hurt Emer physically. Emer suspected her mother's behaviour had improved for the benefit of her new husband, rather than Emer herself, but that hardly mattered. The important thing was that after they'd moved in with Robert, Emer was able to finally feel safe.

'Would you like some more chicken?' Robert's voice dragged Emer back to the dining room, the sun streaming through the windows and the tiny portions of food on the plate in front of her.

'She's not even finished what's on her plate,' Ursula said, before Emer had a chance to answer.

Ursula's obsession with portion control and calorie counting was another reason Emer hated living here. Ursula had been vigilant to the point of obsessive when Emer was younger, making sure her only remaining child didn't become overweight. Almost, Emer used to think, as if being fat were a worse crime than being dead.

She knew the food on her plate wasn't enough to fill her up, but she couldn't face the sharp comments if she admitted that. Instead, she shook her head and told Robert she was fine.

'You should start dating again,' Ursula said. 'Robert, who was the lovely woman you were talking to last week? The equal marriage campaigner. We should introduce her to Emer.'

'I don't want to start dating again,' Emer said. 'And if I did, the last thing I'd want is for my stepfather to set me up with someone.'

'I just think you can do a lot better for yourself,' Ursula said. 'Nikki was a fly-by-night. I suppose she hasn't bothered to stay in touch since she moved away?'

'I got an email from her last week actually,' Emer lied. 'She's loving her new job.'

The truth was, she hadn't heard a word from Nikki since they'd broken up and Nikki had moved to London. Emer had called, sent text messages and continued to send emails. But, so far, Nikki hadn't replied to anything she'd sent her.

'She wasn't right for you, Emer,' Ursula said. 'I knew it the first time I met her. Now she's gone, hopefully you'll find someone a bit steadier to settle down with. I'm still hoping to be mother of the bride one day, you know. I've got that dress I bought for your wedding. You haven't seen it yet, have you? It's really rather gorgeous. Pale blue with a striking hat. I could try it on for you later, if you'd like.'

'She does look very lovely in it,' Robert said.

Emer didn't doubt it. At sixty, her mother was still a strikingly beautiful woman. With sharp cheekbones, piercing blue eyes and the posture of a professional ballet dancer, it was no wonder she'd turned so many heads when she was younger. Emer knew her mother worked hard to maintain her good looks but, as Ursula herself had said on more than one occasion, she could only work with what she'd got. It was just that, in Ursula's case, what she'd got was a lot more natural beauty than most women could ever dream of.

'Can we not talk about it now?' Emer said. 'Please?'

'I told you we couldn't rely on her, Robert,' Ursula said. 'You'll have to come up with some other ideas for getting the gay vote.'

'Jesus...' Emer put down her knife and fork. 'Do you hear yourself? This is my life we're talking about.'

'Well it just so happens that your life, and the choices you make, affect all of us,' Ursula said. 'Take this business in London, for example. You're still obsessing over it, aren't you? That's the real reason you're spending your days lying around in bed instead of getting out there looking for work, or trying to get your girlfriend back. Because you've convinced yourself that the woman you saw was Kitty.'

'I didn't *think* she was Kitty,' Emer said. 'She *was* Kitty.'

'No.' Ursula shook her head. 'The only reason you keep insisting your sister is still alive is because you can't cope with the guilt of knowing she might still be here if it wasn't for you.'

'That's not true,' Emer said, but even to her own ears, the assertion sounded weak.

'Can we talk about something else?' Robert said. 'This endless raking up the past isn't helping either of you. Whatever happened that day on the beach, there's nothing either of you can do to change it now.'

'This isn't about me,' Ursula said. 'Can't you see that, Robert? If she goes around the place telling people her dead sister is still alive, the press will start digging into our personal lives and that's not good news for any of us.' She turned her attention back to Emer. 'This nonsense has got to stop, once and for all. I will not have you ruining things for Robert, after all he's done for you. He doesn't deserve that.'

'We both know this has nothing to do with Robert,' Emer said, 'and everything to do with your own greed. You'd rather be the Taoiseach's wife than learn the truth about your daughter. I know what I saw that day, and I'm not going to pretend it didn't happen.'

'Like the last time?' Ursula said. 'Or the time before that? Or one of the many other times you thought you'd seen her?'

'This is different,' Emer said.

'How?'

'It just is. I know what I saw. Do you remember Dad's brother, Frank? His daughter's an investigative journalist. I bet she'd be interested in something like this.'

'No!' Ursula pushed her chair back and stood up. 'Don't you dare! Your sister drowned that day in Lahinch. I wish to God it wasn't true. I'd give anything – anything in the world – for her to still be alive. But she isn't. She's dead, and the sooner you accept that the better for all of us. As for contacting any member of Frank's family, I forbid it. Absolutely.'

'How do you plan to do that, exactly?' Emer said. 'In case you hadn't noticed, I'm an adult. You can't stop me doing anything.'

But Ursula wasn't listening. She'd already left the room, slamming the door so hard that Emer felt the vibrations where she sat.

'I'm sorry,' she said, a moment later. 'I didn't mean to upset her.'

'You sure about that?'

'I think so.' Emer blinked hard to get rid of the tears threatening to spill out of her eyes and roll down her face. 'Do you think she's right, Robert?'

'About what?'

'That what happened to Kitty was my fault.'

'Emer, love. How can I say whose fault it was? I wasn't there that day. I didn't see how Kitty ended up in the water. You're the only one who knows the truth about that day.'

'The problem is, I can't really remember,' she said. 'I don't remember having a row with Kitty. But Ursula is convinced that's what happened.'

'If that's what she thinks,' Robert said, 'she must have a reason for it, don't you think?'

'I guess.'

Robert was silent for a moment, as if he was trying to think of what to say next.

'Well whatever your mother thinks,' he said eventually. 'I'm always here for you, Emer. I hope you know that. Tell me a bit more about this cousin. How do you know about her?'

'I knew Uncle Frank had a daughter,' Emer said. 'She contacted us after he died, and again after her mother died. Do you remember that?'

'I do,' Robert said. 'I also remember your mother wasn't very keen on the idea of keeping in touch with her. There was an awful lot of bad blood between those brothers, you know. She felt it was better not to get involved with any of that.'

'I've googled her a few times,' Emer said. 'She's a really good journalist. I was thinking, because she lives in England, I could contact her and ask her if she'd look into it for me.'

'Let's talk about it in a bit,' Robert said. 'I'd better find Ursula first and check she's okay. Can I leave the tidying up to you?'

Emer knew if she said anything she'd start to cry. So she nodded her head, willing him to leave quickly so she could be by herself.

In her bedroom, she opened her laptop and checked her emails, like she'd done every day since Nikki left. And, as on all of those other days, there was still no email. She shouldn't write again. She knew it was a bad idea; but knowing something and doing it were two different things.

> Hey Nikki
>
> Hope you're settling into London life and the new job is everything you could wish for. Life here is pretty much the same as ever. Except now everyone is convinced I'm a certified loony after seeing that girl in London. I'm sure you think that too, and I'm wondering if that's why you haven't replied to me. Sorry. I probably shouldn't have said anything. It's just difficult, because I'm used to telling you everything.
>
> I'm sorry (see? You said I never apologise and now I've just done it twice in one email!). I know I messed up, Nikki. And I'll do whatever it takes to make things better. I promise. Can we talk sometime? Please?
>
> Love you,
> Emer x

She sent the email, then regretted it as soon she had. But it was too late to do anything about that now. She spent the next twenty minutes scrolling through Nikki's social media accounts. Lots of photos of Nikki with her new flatmates, her new work colleagues, living her shiny new London life that didn't include Emer. When she couldn't bear it any longer, Emer shut down the laptop and started to get ready for bed. It was still early but she couldn't face going back downstairs for another – inevitable – confrontation with her mother.

She was in bed, reading a book, when Robert knocked on her door.

'You got a few minutes?' he asked.

'Sure.'

'I'm sorry about earlier,' he said. 'I know your mother can be difficult sometimes.'

An understatement if ever she'd heard one, Emer thought.

'She means well, though,' Robert said. 'Surely you can see that, Emer?'

'We've had this conversation so many times,' Emer said. 'Do we really have to do it again now?'

The truth was, it didn't matter how her mother behaved. Robert would adore her no matter what she did. He never tired of telling people how he'd known, from the first moment he ever set eyes on her when she came to his office for a job interview, that she was the only woman for him. Except back then, Ursula was married to Emer's father. Robert had had to wait another eight years before finally getting what he wanted.

'Let's agree to disagree then,' Robert said. 'Besides, your mother wasn't the reason I wanted a chat. When you came back from London, the first time you told us about seeing the woman on the Underground, you said it wasn't like the other times. Can you explain why not?'

'I know it sounds crazy,' Emer said. 'And I can understand why you're finding it hard to believe me. But those other times, when I thought I'd seen her, it was only for a moment.'

'Not always,' Robert said. 'What about that girl you saw in Dublin a couple of years back?'

'Aoife O'Malley,' Emer said, remembering the woman she'd seen on Grafton Street one afternoon. She'd been so sure the woman was Kitty that she'd confronted her on the spot. 'But the moment I spoke to her, I knew I'd made a mistake. This just feels different, Robert. For one thing, if the woman in London wasn't Kitty, why did she run away when I tried to speak to her?'

'Maybe she didn't hear you?'

'No.' Emer shook her head, remembering the way the woman had speeded up when she'd called out her name. 'She heard me, all right.'

'Well in that case,' Robert said, 'I'd like to help.'

'What do you mean?'

He was carrying a mug, which he held out for her to take.

'Cocoa. Do you remember how you used to love it?'

Emer took the mug, breathing in the rich, familiar smell.

'Thank you.'

'So what do you think?' Robert said.

'Do you believe me?'

'I believe you think you saw Kitty,' Robert said. 'And I believe it's possible – although, I'll admit, not very likely – that maybe your sister didn't drown that day. I've been having a think about the night she drowned. That story you've stuck by all these years about seeing her in the hotel that night?'

'It's not a story,' Emer said. 'It's what happened.'

'Mind if I sit down?' Robert said.

Emer nodded, and he pulled out the chair by her dressing table and sat down heavily.

'That's better,' he said. 'My old legs aren't any good for standing these days. Emer love, I know what grief can do to a person. I think it's perfectly possible that you imagined seeing Kitty that night. You were only a child. How on earth were you meant to process the fact that your sister had drowned – that she was dead and never coming back? No, don't look like that. Hear me out. It sounds to me as if you're never going to rest until you know whether or not that woman could be Kitty. Am I right?'

'Yes.'

'Then let me help you. But not the way you want. Involving your cousin – some journalist we don't know anything about – that's not the way to go about this.'

'What do you suggest?'

'I'll hire a private detective,' Robert said. 'Someone who's really good. Throw a bit of money at the problem.'

Emer smiled. 'Your solution to everything.'

'Because it's usually the best solution. So, what do you say?'

'You think a detective might be able to track her down?'

'I think it's worth a shot. You said you followed her?'

'To a pub in east London.'

'Okay.' Robert nodded. 'Tomorrow morning, we'll sit down in my office, you can tell me everything you remember about her, and I'll take it from there.'

'I'll pay you back,' Emer said. 'Whatever money you spend, I'll give you back every penny as soon as I can.'

'You'll do no such thing. I want to do this for you, Emer. So let me. Please?'

For the second time this evening, Emer's eyes filled with tears.

'That's so kind, Robert. Thank you.'

'My pleasure,' he said. 'And maybe we'll say nothing to Ursula for now. No point upsetting her until we know the truth, is there?'

He said good night and left her alone to drink her cocoa. She was suddenly exhausted. She climbed into bed, hugging the mug of cocoa to her chest. Letting the warmth seep into her body, soothing her. A few minutes later, she put the mug down and switched her light off. The last thing she saw before she drifted into sleep was her sister, running away from her down a long corridor.

Eight

'Canada.' Dee repeated the word, as if doing so might help her make more sense of it. But it was just as incomprehensible the second time round.

'Toronto,' Ella said. 'It's such a wonderful opportunity, Dee. There's no way Tom could turn it down. I always thought we'd never leave here, but this job is too good for him to pass up.'

'It's so far away.'

'But you can visit,' Ella said. 'Think about that. You could come and have the most amazing holidays. We'll have a huge house. The company's paying for all our travel and accommodation. Besides, it's not as if it's forever. Two years, that's all.'

But it wouldn't be just two years. They would never come back. How could they? Tom's career would go from strength to strength out there. Jake would start school there. He'd have friends and a new life. The first years of his life here in Eastbourne would soon fade. He would forget about Dee and what she'd meant to him, what they'd meant to each other.

From the little bits of information Dee had been able to retain through the fog of shock, the Toronto film industry was booming. Tom was good at his job as a set designer, and Dee knew he'd already outgrown the industry here in the UK and Ireland. Moving somewhere bigger was the logical next step. As Tom had said time and again. He hadn't been looking for work in Canada. Hadn't even considered it, apparently. Then this job offer had come up and the opportunity was too good to turn down. He'd accepted it and, in less than four weeks from now, they would be moving.

Dee felt a sudden flash of hatred for Ella's partner. If he'd never come back into their lives none of this would be happening. But then Jake would have grown up without knowing his father, and Dee wouldn't have wanted that, either. Besides, Tom was a good man, and no matter how much she didn't like it, Dee couldn't begrudge him doing what he thought was right for himself and his family. Which meant she'd have to find a way to accept this.

'It's brilliant,' she heard herself say. 'Like you say, a great opportunity. And Jake will love it.'

'You really think so?' The relief on Ella's face was painful to observe.

'I really think so.' Dee twisted her mouth into something close to a smile.

'Promise you'll come and visit?'

'Promise.'

Ella jumped up, crossed the short space between their chairs and threw her arms around Dee's neck.

'Thank you,' she said. 'Thank you so much, Dee. You don't know what it means to me that you're okay about this.'

'Okay is pushing it,' Dee said, returning Ella's hug. 'But I'll get used to it.'

Because she didn't have a choice. Then, before that thought had time to set up home inside her head, she extricated herself from Ella and stood up.

'This calls for a proper celebration,' she said. 'Lucky for you, I keep a bottle of Prosecco in the fridge in anticipation of any reason to celebrate.'

The Prosecco tasted like vinegar. Dee managed to swallow a few sips before giving up. Somehow, she got through the next forty minutes, smiling when required and making occasional comments, pretending she was interested in whatever Ella was talking about. While all the time her heart was cracking into thousands of tiny pieces.

'You still okay for this evening?' Ella asked, as she was leaving.

'This evening?'

'It's Friday,' Ella said.

Every Friday, Dee and her neighbours got together for pizza and a chance to catch up and celebrate the start of the weekend.

'Of course.' Dee frowned. 'I've totally lost track of the days this week. Tell Jake and Tom I look forward to seeing them later.'

She couldn't do it. She'd call later and make an excuse. Tell them she had a headache or something. She gathered up the empty glasses and the bottle, pouring the remains of the Prosecco down the sink. Moving on autopilot. Refusing to stop and think about what Ella had just told her, knowing if she did that she'd fall apart.

She'd known Jake since he was a tiny baby. Back then, Ella had been living alone in the mobile home next door to Dee's house. They were only two properties on this lonely stretch of beach between Eastbourne and Pevensey Bay. The two women had become friends. Dee already had a family of sorts – her cousin Louise, and Louise's two children Ben and Daisy. But they lived the other side of town and Louise was so scarily competent she had never needed Dee in the same way Ella had.

The three of them – Dee, Ella and Jake – had formed a special bond. Not having children of her own, Dee knew the love she felt for Jake was the closest thing she'd ever get to having that feeling other women spoke about so reverentially. When Jake was two years old, Ella was reunited with his father, Tom, who had moved into the mobile home with Ella and Jake. Foolishly, Dee had allowed herself to believe they would continue living there.

Any time she pictured her future, her neighbours were always there. Jake would grow older and Dee would be there to witness every stage of his life. She would be part of it. Driving him to school and picking him up whenever his parents couldn't do it. Being a confidante during his teenage years. Watching him grow and become a young man. It was this vision of her future that had given her the strength to break up with Ed Mitchell. She'd convinced herself she didn't need him, that having Ella and Jake in her life was enough.

Then, just like that, this imagined future had been rewritten. And that hurt. The urge to pick up the phone and call Ed was overwhelming. She picked up her mobile, her thumb hovering over his name as she imagined telling him about Tom's job. She knew he'd understand immediately how she felt. Just as she knew, even after all this time, he would come over if she asked him to. And he would do and say all the right things to make this news seem bearable. No. She couldn't do it. She'd made her decision six months ago, and she was going to stick to it. Ed Mitchell was out of her life and that was all there was to it.

She needed to do something, though, to distract her mind. Putting her phone down, she sat at her desk, opened her laptop and scanned the last few chapters of her work in progress. The story was coming together, but writing it had proved harder than she'd expected. Like she'd told Emer, writing a book required a different discipline to writing for newspapers. Plus, she'd now reached the part where she had to decide how much to say about Graham Reed, the young man wrongly accused of one of the murders Dee was writing about. She knew she had to deal with 'the Graham problem', as she'd started calling it, but she kept putting it off. Mainly because every time she tried to write about him, she got distracted by thoughts of Graham's nephew, Ed Mitchell.

'God damn you, Ed,' she muttered to herself. 'Why can't you get out of my head and stay out of it?'

Ed didn't answer. Which was just as well, because if he had, Dee would have really started to think she was losing the plot.

She read back through the notes she'd written, expecting to hit the same brick wall again, when suddenly she realised how she could do this. Writing about someone like Graham was what Dee did best – which was unpicking a mystery, digging into people's lives and motivations, working out why bad things happened to good people. Because whatever way you looked at it, what had happened to Graham Reed was tragic. A young man with learning difficulties who had been falsely accused of a brutal murder, and then killed in a misplaced act of revenge by a gang of local thugs.

Dee spent the next two hours bringing Graham's story to life, exploring his personality, his strengths and weaknesses and – finally – the tragic circumstances leading up to his death. When she was finished, her fingers ached from typing and her body was crying out for a coffee.

She made coffee and, while she drank it, she read over what she'd written, making the odd tweak but generally satisfied with her work. In two hours, she'd written 3,000 words. One thousand more than her daily word count. Which meant she could stop there for today and not feel bad about it.

Still needing to keep her mind occupied, she carried the laptop onto the deck outside. The deck ran along the entire length of the back of the house, overlooking the shingle beach and the English Channel. This was where Dee liked to sit whenever she needed to think. The clear, uninterrupted views of the ocean, the growling of the waves as they rolled in and out over the shingle, the squalling of seagulls overhead, and the tangy flavour of salt in the air – all of it helped calm the endless swirl of noise from too many thoughts competing for her attention.

Going back through the stories she had bookmarked, Dee pulled out two faded photos – one of Kitty Doran and one of Lucy Ryan. She organised her screen so that the two photos were side by side, both girls smiling out at her. Two girls. Friends. Both missing.

Dee had read through everything she could find about Lucy's disappearance and Kitty's death. She hadn't found a single thing that indicated any connection between the two events. But surely someone must have suspected the disappearance of two young girls was more than just a coincidence?

It was time to call Emer, and ask her what she knew about Lucy Ryan.

Nine

June 1997

'Don't be such a sissy.'

'I'm not being a sissy,' Lucy said. 'I don't want to do it, that's all.'

'Why not?'

Lucy pulled a face, the one she always made when she didn't want to answer a question.

'Why not?' Kitty persisted.

'I just don't, okay?'

No. It wasn't okay. Kitty didn't want to be by herself when she found them. She needed Lucy with her, because otherwise no one would believe Kitty when she told them. And Kitty was planning on telling everyone.

'Why is it so important, anyway?' Lucy asked.

'Because it'll be fun,' Kitty said. 'And because we're not allowed to go in there and I'm sick of always being told I'm not allowed do anything.'

It wasn't fair, because adults got to do whatever they wanted – even really bad things like Mr O'Brien and her mum – but kids were always being told what they could and couldn't do. Besides, Kitty didn't see why she should do what her mother told her. It wasn't like Mum never did things she wasn't meant to. Kitty knew this because she'd seen her. Seen them. And heard them. Her stomach twisted, remembering it. She thought for a moment she was going to be sick.

'What's wrong with you?'

'Nothing,' Kitty said.

'You look like you're about to spew.'

They were sitting in the tree house at the bottom of Lucy's garden. Lucy's dad owned a hotel, which meant Lucy's family had lots of money. So when the girls played together, Kitty usually came here. Because Kitty's house was tiny, but Lucy had this huge house with a garden and a tree house that her father had built her.

Kitty's stomach hurt and her throat ached from biting down the scream of pure rage that was fighting to get out. She wanted to hurt someone. They were sitting on the wooden floor of the tree house, their legs dangling over the side. Kitty imagined shoving Lucy forward, over the edge, and watching her fall to the ground. Lucy was smaller than she was. Skinnier too, and definitely nowhere near as strong as Kitty. All it would take was one good shove.

She might have done it. She really might have. Except suddenly Lucy took her hand and squeezed it.

'Sorry, Kitty.'

'Why are you sorry?'

'For being scared. It's just, I promised my da, you know?'

Fuck him, Kitty wanted to say. But she knew how bad it was to say that word and she didn't want to upset Lucy, after all. Because Lucy was her best friend and she was holding her hand tight, like she really loved Kitty. And Kitty knew that she loved Lucy too.

'It's okay,' she said.

'No.' Lucy shook her head, her mouth set in a straight line. 'We should do it. They're knocking it down in a few weeks. This will be our last chance.'

'Really?' Kitty looked at her friend carefully, checking her face to make sure she wasn't joking.

'Yep.' Lucy smiled. 'You can come here and say you're having a sleepover. Then, after my parents are in bed, we'll sneak out. We'll get some sweets and cake in the shop during the day. We can have a midnight feast like they do in Mallory Towers. It'll be great.'

'What about Martin Coyne's ghost?'

'That ould fella?' Lucy grinned. 'Sure we both know he doesn't really exist, right?'

Kitty smiled, even though everyone knew the ghost was real. Even Mr O'Brien said he he'd seen Martin's ghost wandering around upstairs when he was at the house last week. Mr O'Brien owned the huge house that had once belonged to the Coyne family. He'd bought it 'for a song' according to Kitty's mother. She would know. As well as having sex with him, she also worked as his PA, which meant she organised all his meetings and things. Mum said he'd bought the house as an investment. He was going to knock it down and build modern houses on the land.

But before it was knocked down, Kitty's mother and Mr O'Brien went to the house when they wanted to have sex. And now Kitty and Lucy were going too. Friday night, when Mum and Mr O'Brien were going to be there. Kitty had heard her mother on the phone, arranging the whole thing.

'Nine o'clock,' her mother had said. 'All you need to do is turn up. You really need to stop worrying, Robert. It's all in hand. No one will ever find out.'

Well she was wrong about that. Kitty already knew. And soon, everyone else would know too.

'Are you okay, Kit?' Lucy asked.

'I'm fine.' It was a lie, but she couldn't tell Lucy about yesterday. Or all the other times when her mother's anger and mood swings made life at home seem like an unbearable nightmare.

She'd finished the last of the milk, forgetting her mother liked milk in her tea.

'You stupid, stupid girl.' Her mother had screamed when she'd found out. She'd screamed lots of other things too, but Kitty couldn't remember all of them. Mum's face scrunched up when she got angry and her cheeks became really red. When she'd grabbed the wooden spoon, Kitty had tried to get away, but Mum had held on tight to her arm, screaming at her while the wooden spoon smacked down on Kitty's shoulders and back, again and again.

'I wish I'd never had you.'

Smack.

'You were a mistake.'

Smack.

'You ruin everything. Why do you have to ruin every single thing?'

Her father was there too, sitting in the corner of the room. Watching, without doing a single thing to stop it. She'd tried to understand why he didn't ever do anything when her mother got like that. At first, she'd thought that maybe because he was drunk he didn't really notice. But then she realised it wasn't that. Because even drunk people could still see what was happening in front of their eyes, couldn't they? No. He didn't do anything because Mum had told him so many bad things about Kitty he'd started to believe them.

That would change after Friday night. When Dad knew what Mum was really like, he wouldn't sit back and let her get away with whatever she wanted. He'd jump in and protect his daughter and keep her safe. He would become the sort of father Kitty had always wanted. Finally.

Ten

It was Sunday morning when Emer returned Dee's phone call.

'Sorry it's taken me so long to get back to you, Dee. Work's been crazy.'

'You're working at the weekends too?' Dee said. 'I hope you'll manage to find some time for sightseeing. London's a great city.'

'Maybe when my contract's over,' Emer said. 'I haven't done a job like this before. That's why I'm putting everything into it. I keep thinking they're going to see through me and realise I'm not up to it. Anyway, in your message you said you wanted to ask me something?'

No time for small talk, then. Fair enough, Dee thought. It couldn't be easy starting a new job in a new city, having to prove yourself to a whole bunch of people who didn't know you. No wonder Emer sounded stressed.

'I wanted to ask you about Lucy Ryan,' she said.

'Anything,' Emer said. 'Do you really think there could be a link between what happened to both of them?'

'I've read everything you sent me,' Dee said. 'And anything else I could find too. It doesn't look as if the police ever thought the two things were connected.'

'I think they did look into it,' Emer said. 'Although, from what I can remember, they never really found anything.'

'Maybe there was nothing to find,' Dee said, not really believing that.

'My mother's always been convinced it was nothing more than a sad coincidence,' Emer said. 'But I know that's not what Lucy's parents thought. Her father, in particular, was convinced Kitty knew what had happened to Lucy.'

'If that's true,' Dee said, 'why wouldn't she have said something?'

'I don't know.'

'It's certainly odd that two girls from the same town both disappeared within a few weeks of each other. Two girls, moreover, who were close friends.'

'They were very close,' Emer said. 'Kitty was completely cut up when Lucy disappeared. It was horrible for everyone. That's why our mother took us on holiday. Because believe me, Dee, we weren't the sort of family who took regular holidays. My parents never had any money. And if they had, they would have spent it on themselves, not a holiday for their daughters.'

'I read that your father stayed behind,' Dee said. 'Is that right?'

'That's right,' Emer said. 'He was offered some work and he couldn't turn it down. He was in and out of work all the time. So I suppose when a job came along, he had to take it. Even if it meant missing out on the holiday.'

'I see.' Dee made a mental note to follow that up, check what job Eamon Doran had been doing and see if she could find anyone who'd confirmed his story at the time.

'What was the hotel like?' she asked.

'Lovely,' Emer said, 'from what I can remember. Why are you asking?'

'I'm thinking aloud,' Dee said. 'Sorry. I'm just wondering how a family with no money could suddenly afford a seven-night holiday in a hotel. Especially if, as you say, it was a nice hotel.'

'Does it matter? Dad probably borrowed the money. He was always borrowing money from people and never paying it back. Maybe that's why he didn't come with us – because they couldn't afford for all four of us to go away. Anyway, I thought you wanted to ask me about Lucy, not how much money my parents had.'

'I'm trying to build up a picture of everything that was going on in Kitty's life,' Dee said. 'Because if you're right, and she didn't drown, then there has to be a very good reason for why she disappeared.'

'Okay,' Emer said, after a moment. 'Sorry.'

'Tell me about Lucy.'

'No one knows what happened to her. She went to bed one night, and the following morning when her mother went to wake her up, she was gone. The Guards had all sorts of theories at the time. Their favourite one was that Lucy's dad killed her and then hid the body. It was bullshit, of course, and they were never able to prove it. But unfortunately, the story stuck. As if the family hadn't already gone through enough, they then had to deal with all the gossip and nasty rumours that started up.'

Emer stopped speaking, clearly upset. Dee didn't blame her. Graham Reed had been the victim of a similar campaign to destroy his reputation, even though he hadn't done anything wrong.

'I assume Kitty was questioned after Lucy disappeared?' Dee said.

'Of course,' Emer said. 'Everyone who knew her was questioned. For all the good it did. They never found her, and after a while they stopped caring.'

'You said Lucy's father believed Kitty knew what had happened to Lucy?'

'He was convinced of it,' Emer said.

'Maybe it was his way of deflecting the attention away from himself,' Dee said.

'I don't think so,' Emer said. 'He didn't kill Lucy. It was the press, more than anyone else, who tried to prove that he had. As far as the Guards were concerned, Kitty didn't disappear. She drowned. Her own mother saw her going into the water that day.'

'What about you?' Dee asked. 'What do you think?'

'The more I think about it, the more convinced I am that the two things are connected. Which is why it's so important we find out who that woman in the pub really is. If she's Kitty, then she might be able to tell us what happened to Lucy.'

'If she's Kitty.'

'I know.' Emer sighed. 'Lucy's family never recovered, you know. Her parents lived out the rest of their lives never knowing what had happened to her... It was a living hell for them.'

'Is that what it's been like for you?' Dee asked.

'Of course.'

'And if I find out that the woman in the pub isn't Kitty?' Dee said. 'What then? Do you think you'll be able to finally accept that she really did drown?'

'I'm not stupid,' Emer said. 'I know there's almost no chance that woman is Kitty. But I have to know for sure.'

Dee thought of Ella. When Dee first got to know her, Ella was living under an assumed identity. Hiding from someone she believed wanted to hurt her. Waking up each day terrified of being found out. If someone had faked

Kitty's drowning and smuggled her out of Ireland, then they must have had a very good reason for doing it.

'Have you found anything more about her?' Emer asked.

'Not yet.'

In fact, Dee had got an email earlier this morning from Leonard. He'd been back to the pub several times and, so far, hadn't seen anyone matching the description of the woman Dee had asked him to look into. He'd keep trying, he told Dee, but she shouldn't hold out hope. When he'd asked one of the other bar staff about Annie, he was told she didn't work there anymore.

'I've got a few more questions,' Dee said, 'about what happened that day on the beach, and also about what life was like in the weeks leading up to the holiday. Do you want to do that now, or would it be easier if I send you an email with all my questions? That way, you can take your time over your answers, making sure you don't leave anything out.'

'Definitely an email,' Emer said. 'Thanks, Dee. For everything you're doing. I really appreciate it.'

'Just one more thing before I go then,' Dee said. 'I read that Lucy had a younger sister. Do you have any idea how I could find her?'

'Maeve? I don't think you need to drag her into all this.'

'It would be good to hear her account of what happened the night Lucy disappeared,' Dee said.

'Okay,' Emer said. 'I know Maeve. I'll ask her if she'll speak to you. But don't hold your breath, Dee. She's a very private person. She may not want to speak to you.'

'But you'll try?'

'Of course.'

'Great,' Dee said. 'And let's try to get together soon. We've got so much catching up to do. Please consider coming to Eastbourne. It really is lovely here.'

'I'm sure it is. Sorry, I've got to go. Send me those questions and I'll take a look at them as soon as I can. You take care, okay?'

After she hung up, it struck Dee how little she still knew about her cousin. She had no idea, for example, where she was staying while she was in London, what friends she had, or even what she planned to do for the rest of the weekend. It was almost as if Emer was deliberately keeping her at arm's length, making sure Dee didn't get too close or find out too much about her.

It wasn't something she had time to dwell on. Ella had asked Dee if she'd look after Jake for a few hours this morning, so she could get some packing done. Dee could hear them now, the crunch of their feet on the shingle as they approached her house.

Putting everything else out of her mind, Dee went to meet them. As always, her spirits soared as she opened the back door and saw Jake's face. He was holding Ella's hand, but when Dee called his name he pulled away from his mother and ran towards Dee.

'Hello!'

She leaned down as he hurtled into her, scooping into her arms for a cuddle.

'What do you want to do this morning, Jakey?'

'Ice cream!'

He started wriggling and, reluctantly, she put him back down.

'You okay if we get ice cream?' she asked Ella.

'Of course.' Ella smiled. 'We're going to Julie's for lunch later. Would you mind getting him back home by twelve thirty?'

That gave her three precious hours. Not enough, but better than nothing.

'Right,' she said to Jake. 'How about we go get some ice cream first? Then we come back here to make pancakes?'

'Yaaay!' Jake turned to go, but Dee called him back.

'What about your mum? Aren't you going to say goodbye to her first?'

'Bye Mummy. Love you.'

'I love you too,' Ella said. Then, to Dee, 'Thanks so much for this.'

'You know I don't mind,' Dee said. 'I want to make the most of the time we've got left together. Heck, if I had my way I'd ask you to let him move in with me until you were ready to go.'

'That's a tempting offer,' Ella said. 'He's been really difficult the last few days. All this upheaval isn't easy for him.'

So why do it to him? Dee wanted to ask. Why not let him carry on living here, where he's happy?

She didn't say that, of course. Instead, she told Ella not to worry, that Jake's difficult moods would pass soon.

'I know that,' Ella said. 'But it doesn't make it any easier when he's having a full-on meltdown and you're looking at all the things you've got to do before we leave. Anyway, I'm sorry. It's not your problem. Have a lovely morning with him, and I'll see you later.'

They did have a lovely morning, but it ended too quickly. At twelve thirty, she was back at Ella's house, hugging Jake goodbye and promising they'd do some more fun things together soon.

'Love you, Jake,' she whispered.

'Love you too,' he said.

Then she had to let him go. She waited for him to turn around and wave, like he usually did, but he didn't do that today. After a moment, she said goodbye to Ella and left quickly, before Ella noticed the tears forming in the corners of Dee's eyes.

Eleven

Later that afternoon, Dee walked back into town to meet Louise. They'd arranged to meet at the West Rocks Beach Bar, one of several bars dotted along the seafront. Like the others, this one had outside seating on the beach. Louise was already there when Dee arrived, sitting at a table outside. Dee ordered a glass of Sauvignon Blanc and went to join her cousin.

The sun was blasting down, and it was too hot for Dee's liking. But Louise was a sun worshipper and, so far, had rejected all Dee's efforts to persuade her to sit inside.

'It's all right for you,' Louise said. 'You can spend your entire day on the beach if you want to. But I'm stuck inside an office most of the day.'

Dee didn't point out that this wasn't exactly accurate. As a local journalist, Louise seemed to spend most of her working life attending events, or driving around the place to interview people for the paper.

'If you're going to make me sit outside,' Dee said, 'then I'm ordering another drink. Can I get one for you as well?'

'Just a water.' Louise pointed at her barely touched glass of wine. 'This will do me for a while longer.'

Dee finished her wine, and went inside to order another glass. When she came back outside, Louise was talking to someone on her phone.

'Martin,' Louise said, when she hung up. 'Wanted to know what time dinner was going to be.'

Dee opened her mouth to say something, then, seeing the warning look on Louise's face, shut it again.

'He'd cook dinner if I wanted him to,' Louise said. 'He's always offering to do it. But the truth is, I prefer doing the cooking. That way, at least, I know I'm going to get something I like.'

'Well more fool you,' Dee said, smiling to take the edge off her words. 'If I had someone willing to cook my meals for me, I wouldn't try to talk them out of it.'

'You had someone more than willing to do that. But you got rid of him, remember?'

'Ouch.' Dee pretended to flinch. 'Can we not talk about Ed for once?'

Because it was a topic Louise refused to let go. In her opinion, dumping Ed Mitchell had been a mistake, and she never wasted any opportunity to remind Dee of this fact.

'How about the menopause, then?' Louise said. 'I haven't had my period for over six months. I thought at first it was stress. You know, after all that business with Derek.'

She was referring to Derek French, a man Louise had had a short-lived affair with. An affair which had very nearly cost Louise her life. Although they rarely talked about it, Dee knew the event had marked both of them in ways they'd probably never fully understand. It had brought them closer, too. Dee's relationship with her cousin was one of the constants in her life. She couldn't imagine a time Louise wouldn't be in her life.

'But I went to my GP last week and apparently it's nothing to do with stress. I'm menopausal, Dee. She checked my hormone levels. Isn't it awful?'

'More awful than PTSD?'

Louise scowled.

'You know what I mean.'

Dee didn't. Not really. She'd started her menopause in her late forties and hadn't had a period in over three years. Apart from the really rubbish symptoms – hot flushes, mood swings and an inability to remember the most basic information – the only reason she'd really cared was because it was final proof that she could never, now, be a mother.

'I think I'm through the worst of it.' Dee said. 'At least, I sincerely hope so. It is horrible Lou, but look on the bright side.'

'What bright side?'

'No more periods.' Dee clinked her glass of wine against Louise's glass. 'Now that really is worth celebrating, don't you think?'

'What about the rest of it?' Louise said. 'How did you cope? You barely mentioned it when you were going through it. Why don't women speak more openly about this stuff? I've been feeling awful recently. Tired, emotional, ratty with Martin and the kids. God, I hate being a woman sometimes. And what happens afterwards?'

'What do you mean?'

'You know.' Louise leaned across the table as she lowered her voice. 'Sex. Is it still the same? I've heard your libido drops to literally zero. What am I meant to do if that happens?'

'Relax,' Dee said. 'It may drop a bit, but it will come back again. You know, when Ed and I first started having sex…'

She was interrupted by Louise, putting her hand up.

'Stop right there, Dee Doran. I do not want to hear about your sex life.'

'You were the one who brought it up.'

Louise pulled a face.

'I didn't expect you to start going into graphic details.'

'Sorry,' Dee lied. 'Listen, Lou, you'll be fine. It's not pleasant while it lasts, but you'll get through it.'

And at least you've been lucky enough to have had two beautiful children, she thought.

'I don't have a choice, do I? Anyway, I'd rather not think about that now. Tell me about Emer. You said meeting her was complicated. What do you mean?'

Dee took a sip of her wine as she considered the best way to answer that.

'She was different to how I expected. Although I don't know how, exactly. I mean, I'd never met her before, but somehow I'd let myself believe we'd have this instant connection.'

'It must have been awkward for her,' Louise said. 'For both of you, I guess. What do you say to someone you've known about all your life but you've never met?'

'It's sad, really,' Dee said. 'She's my cousin. I should have been part of her life before now. But because of some stupid feud between our fathers, we've never had the chance to get to know each other.'

'What happened between your dad and his brother? It must have been serious if they stopped speaking to each other.'

'Dad wouldn't ever talk about it,' Dee said, 'but over the years, Mum told me bits and pieces of what happened. From what I gather, Eamon – Dad's brother – was a bit of a scoundrel. He was a heavy drinker who also had a gambling problem. He was always getting involved in dodgy deals that he thought would make him lots of money. At one point, he stole a lot of money from my grandparents. I don't know how much exactly, but he left them with nothing. They had to sell their house – my dad's family home. He was never able to forgive Eamon for what he'd done.'

'How sad,' Louise said. 'For your dad, I mean. Not Eamon. He doesn't sound worthy of anyone's pity. At least you've got a chance to get to know Emer now. That's a good thing, isn't it?'

'She's had quite a troubled childhood,' Dee said. 'I think she's a bit messed up, to be honest. Not surprising, I guess, with a father like that. And everything else that happened on top of that.'

'Go on.'

Dee told Louise everything, starting with Emer seeing the woman on the Underground, and ending with what Dee had learned about Lucy Ryan – the girl who'd disappeared a few weeks before Kitty.

'Wow,' Louise said, when Dee finally stopped speaking. 'That's quite a story.'

'What do you think?'

'The whole thing sounds bonkers,' Louise said. 'The best way you can help Emer is by convincing her that her sister really is dead.'

'I know that,' Dee said. 'But there are too many things that don't add up. That woman – Annie – she's clearly hiding something. Then there's the strange coincidence of two young girls disappearing from the same town within a few weeks of each other.'

'Except one of them didn't disappear,' Louise said. 'She drowned. The only reason Emer thinks that woman could be her sister is because of the eyes. But heterochromia isn't that uncommon, is it?'

'Not really,' Dee said, remembering the statistic Emer had quoted in the taxi. 'Six in every thousand people, apparently. Anyway, Leonard says Annie's stopped working in the pub. Which means we've hit a dead end. It's probably time to let this go before it gets any crazier, right?'

Louise frowned. 'Dee, I don't mean to pry, but is there something else going on?'

'What do you mean?'

'You've already got quite a lot of work on. Every time we speak you tell me how behind schedule you are with your book. So I don't understand why you haven't already done the right thing and told Emer she needs to accept the truth. All this digging around into her past and trying to prove something that's clearly not true, how is that helping anyone?'

Dee took a sip of her wine as she considered this. Louise was right. This obsession with looking into Kitty's death wasn't helping anyone, least of all Dee herself, who should be focusing on her book and her career and the rest of her life.

Except every time she thought about the rest of her life, every single time, all she could see was the mobile home, a few hundred metres along the beach from her own house, empty and deserted.

Twelve

One month earlier

Emer walked into the bar and looked around, wondering if she'd still recognise Maeve Ryan after all these years. She hadn't been here before. It was one of those new, characterless bars that seemed to be popping up across the city with alarming speed. Full of shiny young things with too much money and no taste. Emer wasn't feeling particularly shiny today, and wished Maeve had suggested somewhere different, somewhere a bit less upbeat. Music pumped from speakers she couldn't see, the sound echoing off the bare brick walls, thumping in time with the throbbing inside her head.

'Emer?'

A petite woman with elfin features and black hair cut into a severe bob was standing in front of her, smiling.

'Maeve.' Emer tried to smile back, not quite managing it. 'God you look fantastic. I barely recognise you. Sorry, that came out wrong. Clearly, you've always been gorgeous.'

'Liar.' Maeve opened her arms and the two women hugged awkwardly.

'Thanks for getting back to me,' Emer said. 'I wasn't sure you'd want to hear from me.'

In fact, she'd almost given up on Maeve. It was almost three months since Emer had found her on social media. Until yesterday, Maeve hadn't reciprocated Emer's follows or shown any sign that she might want to get in touch. Then, yesterday evening, Emer had received a text message from a number she didn't recognise. The sender was Maeve, asking if Emer would like to meet up. Emer had called her immediately and they'd arranged to meet here, in this anonymous bar just off Eyre Square.

Maeve said something, but Emer didn't catch it.

'Is there anywhere quieter we can go?' Emer shouted. 'I can't hear myself think.'

'There's a conservatory through there,' Maeve said. 'No music. You go through and grab us a table. I'll get the first round in.'

The first round, Emer noted. Well, she was fine with that. It wasn't as if she had anything better to be doing this evening. She'd driven to Galway this evening and, guessing the night might involve a few drinks, she'd booked herself into a cheap B&B in Salthill. Even if Maeve didn't want to stay out too long, Emer knew that a night away from her mother's cloying presence would do her the world of good.

Emer gave Maeve her drink order before going into the conservatory, as instructed. She didn't have to wait long before Maeve was back, weaving her way through the crowd, a glass in each hand.

'One G&T,' Maeve said, placing Emer's drink in front of her. '*Sláinte.*'

'I forgot to ask how you got my number,' Emer said, after she'd taken a healthy slug of her drink.

'Robert,' Maeve said. 'We've been doing a bit of work together. He hasn't mentioned it? Well, I suppose there's no reason to, really. I'm thinking about opening a second hotel and Robert's coming in as a silent partner.'

'Wow.' Emer drank some more gin and tonic, trying not to feel woefully inadequate. While she was throwing her life down the pan, Maeve was successfully running one hotel and about to open another one. 'That's impressive.'

'Not as impressive as it sounds,' Maeve said. 'I inherited the Lodge from my parents. When we left Ballincarraig, they had to start over. They built the Lodge up from nothing. It was the only thing that kept them going, really. Now they're both gone, I feel a huge responsibility to keep it going. It wasn't what I wanted to do with my life. I was part of a drama group. I wanted to be an actor, but my parents put a lot of pressure on me to keep the hotel going. I didn't feel as if I had a choice. And it's not so bad, really. I've been doing it for too long to do something different now. So far, things have gone really well. Which is why I'm now in a position to expand.'

Emer remembered the photos of the hotel on Maeve's Twitter feed. A beautiful, waterfront hotel on the banks of the Dunkellin River near Clarinbridge, a small town outside Galway city. It was the sort of timeless, classic place she could see herself and Nikki going for a luxurious mini-break. If they were still together and if Emer had a lot of money which, at the moment, she didn't.

'Well I hope it continues to go well for you,' she said, meaning it. 'I've thought about you so much over the years, you know.'

'I've thought about you too,' Maeve said. 'There were so many times I thought about trying to find you, but I always chickened out.'

'Why?'

'Mam and Dad wouldn't have forgiven me. I don't know how much you remember from the weeks after Lucy disappeared, but they always felt Kitty wasn't telling the truth about what had happened that night. They never forgave her. Or your parents.'

'My parents?'

'My dad thought your mother was protecting Kitty,' Maeve said.

The idea of Emer's mother protecting anyone apart from herself was ridiculous. But even as she thought this, a memory came to her. One of many arguments between her parents during that time. Arguments that got worse in the weeks following Kitty's death. Mostly, those arguments merged together in her memories. Except for one.

Emer had been in bed, her eyes squeezed shut and her hands pressed over her ears, praying to a God she'd already stopped believing in. Begging the uncaring bastard to bring her sister back to life and stop her parents from screaming at each other.

'This is all your fault.'

Her father's voice, cold and angry. And her mother shouting back: 'We didn't have a choice, remember? The girls were there that night.'

The girls.

Sitting here now, in the pub with Maeve, it occurred to Emer that if her mother had been protecting anyone, it was herself, not her daughter.

'Sorry,' Maeve said. 'I didn't mean to upset you by saying that.'

'It's fine.' Emer shook her head, dismissing the memory and the thoughts that hovered around it. Her mother had many faults, but to think she had something to do with what had happened to Lucy Ryan was nothing short of crazy.

'I was gutted when we moved away from Ballincarraig,' Maeve said. 'I didn't know how my parents could do it. I kept thinking, what if Lucy came back and we weren't there? How would she ever find us? But after a while, I realised a fresh start was what we all needed. I wasn't sure I ever wanted to revisit the past.'

'So how did you end up going into business with Robert?'

'We had a chamber of commerce event at the hotel,' Maeve said. 'Robert was the keynote speaker. After the event, he came and found me. We got talking and, somehow, I ended up telling him about my idea to open a new hotel. He was keen to get involved, so we met a few times and before I knew it, we had a plan. Having Robert on board has been great. He's hugely influential, as you know, and it's no secret that you get ahead in this country because of who you know, not what you know.'

There was a lump in Emer's throat that she couldn't get rid of, no matter how often she swallowed, and a sour feeling in the pit of her stomach.

'I had no idea you and he were so close,' she said. 'He never said a thing.'

'He's too kind for that,' Maeve said. 'You know what he's like.'

Emer nodded, but really she was wondering if she did know what Robert was like. Because if he'd been having business meetings with Maeve Ryan and was planning to open a hotel with her, surely he'd have mentioned this to Emer at some point?

'He's really inspirational,' Maeve said. 'I didn't realise he did so much work with the Travelling community. It's rare to meet someone in politics who actually cares about the underprivileged. I mean, I know loads of politicians pretend to care, but with Robert I get the feeling he really believes in the work he does. Did you know that, last year alone, he's secured apprenticeships for sixteen people from Travelling backgrounds? He's even persuaded me to get involved with the programme. We're going to run an apprenticeship scheme when the new hotel opens, recruiting entirely from the Travelling community. I'm a bit nervous about it, but Robert's promised he'll make sure it's a success. Anyway, enough about all that. I'm sure you know way more about that side of his work than I do.'

'I guess I take it for granted,' Emer said. The truth was, Robert rarely told her anything about his charity work. She'd known more about it when she was younger, before Robert and her mother got married. Back then, Ursula had been working as Robert's PA. Emer remembered the steady stream of young women, in and out of the office on work placements. Ursula had done her best to ignore what she called 'Robert's girls', never bothering to hide her disapproval of their presence in her sacred office space. After the wedding, Ursula stopped working, and Emer had barely thought about those young women since.

'I was sorry to hear about your dad,' she said, keen to change the subject.

'Thanks,' Maeve said. 'It was a relief in the end, to be honest. He'd been sick for a long time. Not just from the cancer, which is what actually got him in the end. But depressed, too. He got really bad in later years, especially after Mum died. They never recovered from what happened, you know.'

'Of course they didn't,' Emer said. 'How could anyone recover from something like that?'

'It's the not knowing,' Maeve said. 'It's a form of torture. You don't know how much I'd give to find out what happened to her. And if I ever did find out, I'd make damn sure whoever took her pays for what they did to my family.'

She nodded at Emer's glass. 'Your drink's nearly finished. Let me get you a top-up.'

'You got the last one,' Emer said. 'This is my round. What are you having?'

'Well just one more then,' Maeve said. 'I don't normally drink during the week, but it's worth celebrating being back in touch, don't you think?'

One drink turned into several, as the two women caught up on all the news they'd missed out on over the years. Sharing gossip about people they'd once known, reminiscing about the things they'd got up to before their worlds fell apart and they lost touch with each other.

At some point, Maeve asked about Kitty and Emer found herself telling Maeve everything that had happened in London. It might have been the drink, but Maeve seemed to take the sighting seriously, especially when Emer told her about Kitty coming into her hotel bedroom the night she was supposed to have drowned.

'What did your mother say at the time?' Maeve asked.

'She didn't believe me,' Emer said. 'No one did. They all said I'd imagined it. And that's what Robert and Ursula think now as well. They think I've lost the plot.'

'What will you do?' Maeve asked.

'I've got a cousin in England who's an investigative journalist,' Emer said. 'I wanted to contact her and see if she'd help, but Ursula had a hissy fit. So Robert stepped in and offered to help. He's going to hire a private detective.'

'If he's hired a detective,' Maeve said, 'then he must believe you, right?'

'I think it's more a case of proving me wrong,' Emer said. 'But maybe he thinks there's a chance I might be right.'

'Of course there's a chance.' Maeve nodded at Emer's empty glass. 'One more for the road?'

'Maybe just a soft drink?' Emer said.

'Good idea,' Maeve said. 'Tell you what? Instead of staying here and getting plastered, why don't we go and get something to eat? That way we can carry on speaking for a bit longer. It's so good to see you after all this time. And I'd love to hear more about what you've been doing with your life.'

'That'll be a short conversation,' Emer said. 'But going for something to eat sounds like a great idea.'

They found a tapas bar near the docks and spent the next two hours eating food while they shared memories of the sisters they'd lost. By the time the evening drew to a close, Emer felt if she'd found a part of herself she hadn't realised was missing. As they left the restaurant, Maeve made Emer promise to keep in touch.

'It was so lovely seeing you again,' she said. 'We've both already lost too much. Let's not lose each other again, okay?'

'Definitely not,' Emer said. 'You know, I was scared that you might think I was a freak.'

'Why on earth would I think that?'

'All that stuff about seeing Kitty,' Emer said. 'Most people I've told about it think there's something wrong with me.'

'Well I don't think that,' Maeve said. 'You know what you saw, Emer. Don't let anyone else try to convince you otherwise. Okay?'

'Okay.' Emer's eyes pricked with unexpected tears. Suddenly, for the first time since she'd split up with Nikki, she didn't feel entirely alone.

Thirteen

By the time Tuesday came around, Dee knew she wasn't coping. Her anxiety about a future without Jake was increasing as each day passed. When she woke up, the urge to stay in bed, pull the duvet over her head and hide away from the world was so strong she almost succumbed to it. In the end, she forced herself to get up and have a shower.

This restless anxiety and creeping depression were relatively new. When she was younger, she'd never felt this way. It was only in the last few years, after the break-up of her marriage and the deaths of both her parents, that she'd started to suffer these bouts of blackness. She'd let herself believe that lifestyle changes – drinking less, exercising more, allowing herself to fall in love again – had fixed the problem, but this morning she admitted to herself, for the first time, that this might be something she couldn't fix by herself.

The logical part of her brain knew there was nothing wrong with admitting there was a problem. Especially these days, when every time she opened a newspaper or listened to a podcast she was confronted with some famous person talking about their battles with mental health problems. Despite this, she couldn't help feeling ashamed. As if it was some weakness inside her, and if she was a stronger, more resilient person she would be better able to deal with life's knocks.

She'd grown up believing she could do anything, that she was the sort of person who could achieve whatever she set her mind to. Discovering in middle age that her own mind could refuse to act the way she wanted it to was disconcerting, to say the least.

When she'd spoken to Louise about it on Sunday, Louise had advised Dee to make an appointment with her doctor. At the time, Dee had agreed that was a good idea but, so far, she still hadn't made the appointment. Maybe she'd do that later this morning. First, she needed to get some work done, because the book she was working on wasn't going to write itself.

Somehow, she found the focus to get two solid hours of writing done. By the time she'd finished, she was feeling more upbeat. Her mood improved even further when she checked her emails and saw a new one from Leonard. The email had two photos attached to it. Different shots of the woman called Annie. In the first photo, she was sitting at the bar in the Town of Ramsgate talking to Nick, the landlord. In the next photo, Annie had her head turned away from Nick and was smiling at someone, or something, out of the shot.

Is this her? Leonard had typed beneath the final photo.

Yes, Dee replied, *That's her.*

Leonard's reply came back five minutes later.

What do you want me to do now?

In her mind, Dee could hear Louise's voice, telling her how bonkers this whole thing was. At best, a waste of time. At worst, an unnecessary intrusion into another person's private life. Yet Dee's gut wouldn't let her give it up. Not just yet.

Follow her, she typed. *Find out as much as you can and let me know asap.*

She thought about phoning Emer, then changed her mind. At this time of day, Emer would be working and probably wouldn't be able to answer Dee's call. Besides, Dee didn't see any point in giving her cousin false hope. There was every chance this woman would be exactly who she said she was. It was better to wait until Dee had as much information as possible before giving Emer an update.

Instead, she opened the email she'd received from Emer last night and read it again. Emer had replied to the list of questions Dee had sent her. She'd asked Emer to give her some background information about her parents and stepfather, as well as anything Emer could tell her about Lucy Ryan's family.

In the email, Emer told Dee that her mother had married her second husband in 1999. Which was just two years after Emer's father had walked out on the family. Dee knew that divorce had been very difficult in Ireland back then, but Emer hadn't given any explanation for how her mother had been able to marry again so quickly.

Through an internet search, Dee found an archived story that mentioned the marriage of 'entrepreneur Robert O'Brien to Ursula Doran'. Dee assumed Emer's mother must have got her marriage annulled, and she wondered how much influence the 'entrepreneur' had been able to wield to make this happen.

Emer had also included links to some online articles about her stepfather. Reading about Robert O'Brien was fascinating. A local Ballincarraig boy who'd made his money in property and retail, he was now a prominent member of Ireland's liberal-conservative Fine Gael party.

He was also, according to several articles Dee read, widely considered to be the party's next leader. If that happened, and Fine Gael won a future election, that would make Emer's stepfather the most powerful man in the country.

Most of the articles highlighted the work Robert had done over the years with Ireland's Travelling community. He ran an apprenticeship scheme, creating job opportunities for travellers they wouldn't otherwise have. From everything Dee read, Robert O'Brien seemed that rare breed – a politician who actually cared about something other than himself.

There were also plenty of photos of Robert on the internet. In some, he was alone in the photo, but in most of them his wife was by his side. Several of the articles referred to O'Brien's devotion to his wife. One of them had a direct quote where he described her as 'the love of my life'.

Zooming in on the photos, Dee could see that Emer's mother was a striking woman. She remembered Emer saying she took after her mother's side of the family, but looking at this photo Dee couldn't see the resemblance. Instead, she was struck by how much Ursula O'Brien resembled the woman Emer thought could be Kitty. No wonder poor Emer thought that, Dee reflected, looking at the photo of Ursula O'Brien, taken with her husband at some society event in Dublin.

When she'd finished reading about Robert and Ursula, Dee looked at what Emer had written about Lucy Ryan's family. According to Emer, Lucy's parents never recovered from what happened to them. The family had owned a hotel in Ballincarraig, but they'd sold this and moved to a different town in the years following Lucy's disappearance. During the initial Guards investigation, Lucy's father had been repeatedly questioned about his daughter. Emer said the family had no choice, in the end, but to leave town.

Niall had nothing to do with what happened to Lucy, Emer had written. *But there were so many rumours, so much gossip, the family couldn't cope. They sold the hotel and moved away. It was so sad.*

Dee knew that parents were often the main suspects in cases like this. If Lucy's parents really didn't have anything to do with their daughter's disappearance, she imagined the endless suspicion and scrutiny would be unbearable. Reading up on the case now, she could see how the press had become more balanced over time. She couldn't find anything in the later stories that implied the parents were involved in their daughter's disappearance. Unlike the earlier stories, printed in the weeks following Lucy's disappearance, where almost every article Dee read implied Niall Ryan had killed his daughter and disposed of her body.

A journalist called Shay Flaherty had written extensively about Lucy's disappearance. Unlike everyone else, Flaherty had professed Niall Ryan's innocence from the start. From what Dee had found online, Shay Flaherty was also the only journalist who'd put forward a theory that there might be a link between Lucy's disappearance and what happened to Kitty.

Back in 1997, when Lucy Ryan disappeared, Shay Flaherty was a journalist on a local newspaper called the *Connacht Tribune*. But when Dee looked him up on the internet, she saw he was now working for one of the country's national newspapers, the *Irish Times*. His contact details were on the paper's website. Dee sent him an email, introducing herself and asking if he might be willing to answer some questions she had about Lucy Ryan and Kitty Doran.

After sending the email, Dee decided she needed a break. Closing down her laptop, she spent the next few hours tidying her house, washing clothes and doing all the mundane tasks she always put off for as long as possible. By the time she'd finished, her house was spotless, a row of clothes was blowing in the wind on the line and Dee was ready for something else.

Telling herself she was lucky to be able to do whatever she wanted without having to worry about anyone else, she decided to walk into town and treat herself to an early dinner somewhere nice. Cru, maybe. Or the new restaurant near the train station that everyone said was so lovely. She thought of calling Louise, seeing if she was free to meet up, but decided against it. Instead, Dee was going to prove to herself that she didn't need anyone else to have a good time. She had a decent book to read, and her phone for browsing the internet.

She put on some make-up, something she rarely did these days, threw her faded sweatshirt into the laundry basket, replacing it with the blouse she'd picked up in Phase Eight the previous week, and headed into town.

She walked along the beach. The tide was out so, for most of the way, she was able to walk down on the sand by the edge of the water. The stretch of beach where Dee lived, on the eastern edge of the town, never attracted many visitors, even in the height of summer. As she approached town centre, however, the beach became busier. By the time she reached the pier, she had to slow down to accommodate all the people – tourists mingling with locals – who were out and about, making the most of the warm September sunshine.

She dropped into Bistrot Pierre and, by some miracle, got a table outside facing the beach. She ordered a glass of Chablis and sipped it slowly. This was living, she told herself. Sitting in a nice cafe, drinking decent wine and watching the world pass by. Maybe this life wasn't so bad after all, she thought. Of course, she would miss Jake and Ella. But she would find a way of moving forward. They would keep in touch, and if things kept going the way they were at the moment, Dee would have work to keep her busy.

She thought back over everything she'd read about Lucy Ryan's disappearance and Kitty Doran's death. Two girls, with their whole lives in front of them. One missing, the other dead. That wasn't a coincidence. Something bad happened the night Lucy Ryan disappeared. Because of that, Kitty Doran walked into the sea three weeks later and was never seen again.

Dee imagined a piece of thread, connecting the two events, and connecting her too. Because she was involved now, bound to both those girls and what had happened to them, whether she liked it or not.

Fourteen

One month earlier

Emer was sitting in the conservatory with Ursula and Robert. Emer had done her best to stay out of their way since coming back from Galway this morning, but her mother had insisted she join them for a pre-dinner glass of sherry.

'How was Galway?' Ursula asked, once Robert had handed out the drinks.

Emer took a sip of her sherry, then wished she hadn't. She'd drunk too much yesterday with Maeve. The last thing her body needed now was more alcohol.

'It was fine,' she said.

'Who did you say you went in to meet?' Ursula said.

'I didn't,' Emer replied, 'but if you must know, I went to see Maeve Ryan.'

'Of course.' Robert smiled. 'She mentioned something about getting in touch with you. I'd completely forgotten.'

'You also forgot to tell me you were thinking of going into business with her.'

'I didn't forget,' Robert said. 'I simply didn't think it was worth mentioning. You've never shown the slightest bit of interest in the work I do, Emer. Why would I think you'd be interested now?'

'Because it's Maeve,' Emer said. 'She used to be my best friend.'

'Ah, I see.' The way Robert said it, he clearly didn't see at all. 'Well I'll bear that in mind. I'm glad you two girls met up. She's a very smart young woman. You know, it might be worth having a chat with her about your career options. Someone like that, she'd have all sorts of ideas.'

There were many things she could say to that, and Emer was trying to choose the best one when Ursula decided to make her own contribution to the conversation.

'It's so refreshing to see someone like Maeve making such a success of her life. Most of your generation are lazy, Emer, plain and simple. I know people say Ireland's changed for the better, and I suppose that's true in many ways, but young people today are too soft. You haven't had to work the way we had to. We didn't grow up expecting things to be handed to us on a plate.'

'Is that really what you think?' Emer said. 'Have you seen the state of the economy recently? The Celtic Tiger, the country's big economic success story, is a thing of the past. Look at all the people who've lost their businesses or their incomes over the last ten years. And all the people living in houses they'll never be able to sell because they're in negative equity. How can you think that's easy?'

'People get what they deserve in this life,' Ursula said. 'You haven't seen Robert's business suffer, have you? That's because he's good at what he does and he works hard. It hasn't been easy, but he's weathered the storm, and maybe more people would have done the same if they hadn't given in so easily. Too many people go into business not understanding what it takes to make a success of something.'

'You think the economic crash was because people had poor business sense?'

'I didn't say that, Emer. As well you know. I meant that, for some people, it was a handy excuse, that's all.'

'I don't think that's very fair,' Robert said.

'No?' Ursula said. 'Well why weren't you and others like you affected the same way as all those fools whose businesses went bust? You managed to keep things together during the worst of it.'

'Ah, but not everyone's been as lucky as me,' Robert said. 'They haven't got you by their side, have they? You know yourself how important you've been to my success, darling. All the support you've given me over the years. That goes a long way, you know.'

'I support you because I'm your wife,' Ursula said. 'It's what wives do. But your success isn't simply down to me. You were doing well before I ever agreed to become your wife. No. The simple truth is some people work hard and others don't. Look at Maeve. She's doing so well she's thinking of expanding. Her parents would be proud of her. It's such a shame they haven't lived to see how well she's done.'

'Would you consider a career in the hospitality industry?' Robert asked Emer. 'I'm sure if this new hotel goes ahead we could find a role for you. I think you'd be good at it.'

'It's not something I've really thought about,' Emer said. The truth was, she would rather stick pins in her eyes than work for her stepfather. It wasn't that she had anything against Robert, far from it, but she knew working with him would mean working with her mother as well. As long as there was breath left in Emer's body, she would never let that happen.

'Well maybe you should think about it,' Ursula said. 'You can't drift along the way you have been forever. You need a plan, something to focus on.'

'Actually,' Emer said, 'I was thinking of trying London again.'

A lie. Since losing out on the last London job, she'd lost the confidence to apply for another job there. But now she'd said it, suddenly the idea didn't seem like such a bad one. London was where Nikki was. If Emer wanted any chance of winning Nikki back, it's where she should be too. Plus, if she moved to London she might be able have a second shot at finding Kitty.

'London?' Ursula's eyes latched on to Emer, staring at her as if she was trying to see inside Emer's soul. 'You can't go chasing off to London just because that's where your ex-girlfriend has gone. Unless Nikki's not the reason? Oh, I see.'

'See what?' Emer said.

'It's this nonsense about your sister, isn't it?'

'It's not nonsense,' Emer said. Then, seeing the warning look on Robert's face, she changed the subject. She'd promised him earlier she would avoid talking about this in front of Ursula.

After dinner, which seemed to drag on interminably, Emer escaped to her bedroom. The idea of moving to London for a bit had taken hold. It was great that Robert had hired a private detective, but if Emer was in London then she'd be able to try and contact the woman herself.

She opened her laptop and did an internet search for the Town of Ramsgate pub in Wapping. She'd done this lots of times already and, as she scrolled through the results now, there was no new information here. She'd already looked through the different images of the pub, scanning the faces of the people in the bar, searching for Kitty's face. But no matter how many times she looked, she couldn't see her sister.

The pub's phone number was listed on the website. Several times, she'd called the number. She'd always hung up as soon as someone answered it. Her phone was on the table beside her laptop. She picked it up now and dialled the number again.

'Hello?' A man's voice. The same person who'd answered every other time she'd called.

'Hello?' He said again, sounding impatient. 'Who's calling?'

In the background, she could hear the different noises of the pub – people laughing and talking, the clink of glasses.

'Can I speak to Kitty, please?'

'Sorry, love. No one here called Kitty. You sure you've got the right number?'

'I think so,' she said. 'Kitty. Tall with blond hair?'

A pause before he answered.

'Afraid not,' he said. 'Sorry.'

He hung up before she could say anything else. Had he been telling the truth? She thought so, but she really had no idea. The conversation had shifted something inside her, spurring her determination to take action.

But if she wanted to go to London, she needed money. Which meant she'd have to find a job first. She had been registered with several job agencies for a while now. Apart from that one interview last month, she hadn't heard anything back from any of them.

She thought back to her earlier conversation with Robert. Maybe he was right, and she should have a chat with Maeve. Emer wasn't foolish enough to think Maeve would be able to find her a job at the hotel, but she might have some good ideas. It was worth a shot, at least.

She'd received a text from Maeve earlier, saying how much she'd enjoyed last night and that she hoped they'd meet up again soon. Emer found the text and typed in her reply:

> Really great to catch up. Head very sore this morning. Any chance you're free for a coffee over the next week? I'd like to pick your brain about something.

Maeve's reply was instant:

> Coffee sounds fab. Not sure there's anything worth picking but happy to help. Can't stop thinking about what you said about Kitty. Wd be good to chat x

She'd been mortified earlier when she'd remembered telling Maeve about Kitty. Now, reading Maeve's message, Emer was glad she'd told her. Because Maeve had believed her. Which meant maybe she'd be willing to help Emer find her.

Fifteen

A few nights after the text from Leonard, he called Dee to tell her he'd seen Annie again.

'I followed her this time,' he said. 'Seems she's part of a group of artists exhibiting their work in a gallery near the pub. The gallery is called E-One Art. I'll text you a link. The website has details of all the artists, including the woman you're interested in.'

'Does it give a name for her?' Dee asked.

'Annie Holden, There's a biography and a photo. Says she grew up in Sussex. Nothing to hint that she's really your long-lost cousin, I'm afraid.'

After hanging up from Leonard, Dee went onto the internet and looked up the gallery. The exhibition featured work from a group of artists all local to east London. Scrolling through the list of artists, Dee found Annie's photo and biography. She scanned the text. Annie Holden. Born and raised in Sussex, she now lived in London. After graduating from Central Saint Martins with a degree in fine art, Holden had been slowly building her artistic career and was, apparently, 'one of the rising stars of the East End art scene'.

There was no doubt then. The woman in the pub wasn't Kitty. Even so, Dee wanted to see her one final time, just to make absolutely sure. She decided she would go the next day. The following morning, she got up early and was on a train that arrived into London Victoria train station at 9.35.

Getting off the train, Dee switched to the Underground, joining the bustle of commuters, tourists and other bodies all crammed into a carriage on the eastbound District Line to Aldgate East.

Dee had bought her first flat near Aldgate East, way back in the early nineties, before property prices had gone stratospheric. Today, the neighbourhood was unrecognisable from the scruffy, down-at-heel area it had been back then. Gone were the tatty corner shops, the sleazy pubs and the greasy takeaways, replaced by glossy apartment complexes, trendy bars and high-rise office blocks. Although when she reached Commercial Road, she saw pockets of the area had managed to escape gentrification.

She was pleased to see the Castle pub was still open for business. She'd spent many hours propping up the bar in there, chatting shit with John Doyle, the Irish landlord. Despite a lick of paint and a new sign over the door, the pub looked very much as it had when Dee had lived nearby.

A lot more buildings had been converted into apartments, of course, but the rows of wholesale clothes shops were still here, along with the small kebab houses that sold some of the best meat Dee had ever eaten. And, somehow, Watney Street Market – with its budget shops, Iceland supermarket and one seriously grim pub – had survived the gentrification as well.

The E-One art gallery was on Deancross Street. It occupied the ground floor of a modern, characterless apartment block. Looking through the windows, Dee could see the space included a cafe as well as a gallery and, as she pushed open the door, she was hit with the rich aroma of freshly brewed coffee.

'A flat white please,' Dee said, when the woman behind the counter asked her what she'd like to drink.

'Take a seat and I'll bring it over to you,' the woman said. 'Unless you'd like it in a takeaway cup so you can look at the art while you drink it?'

'A takeaway cup would be great,' Dee said. 'Thanks.'

'Your first visit?'

'Is it that obvious?'

The woman smiled.

'I'm the owner. Spend more time here than I do at home. I recognise people who've been here before. And I don't recognise you. You live in the area?'

'I used to,' Dee said. 'A long time ago. I'm in London visiting a friend today. He told me about the gallery so I thought I'd come and take a look.'

'Everything on display has been done by local artists,' the woman said. 'I'm guessing the area's changed a lot since you lived here. A lot of the artists' studios have been turned into fancy apartments over the last few years. But we've held on to a handful. Most of the artists we're exhibiting at the moment are based in Bow. We have a collective there and, as you'll see, some of the guys are producing pretty impressive work.'

Dee took her coffee and moved around the gallery, taking in the art and the general ambience of the place. It was a lovely space. As well as serving exceptional coffee, there was a decent soundtrack playing in the background – so far she'd heard Van Morrison, Cat Powers and Paul Simon – and plenty of people sitting at tables or, like Dee, moving around the gallery looking at the work on display.

Like most people with little knowledge of art, Dee tended to know what she liked without really understanding why. Some of the work didn't strike her as anything special, but there was a collection of paintings that she kept coming back to. Large, empty landscapes that managed to be both bleak and hauntingly beautiful. Looking at the information sheet on the wall, Dee was surprised to read that these paintings had all been done by Annie Holden.

'Beautiful, aren't they?' The owner had come out from behind the counter and joined Dee as she stood in front of one of the larger paintings. 'Annie's work has sold better than anyone else's over the last few weeks.'

'I can see why,' Dee said. 'They're gorgeous.'

'You interested in buying something?'

Dee hesitated. The last thing she'd had in mind coming here today was to buy some art. But now she was here, it struck her that one of these paintings would look pretty amazing in her living room.

'What can you tell me about the artist?' she asked.

'Apart from the fact she's incredibly talented?' The woman smiled. 'I'm Claire, by the way.'

Dee introduced herself and the two women shook hands.

'She's a bit of a recluse,' Claire said. 'Most artists realise how important it is to push their work. You've got to really get yourself out there in the art scene if you want to be successful. But Annie's not like that at all. I had to practically beg her to let me exhibit her work.'

'How did you discover her if she's so reclusive?' Dee asked.

'Visiting studios is part of the job description,' Claire said. 'Bow Studios, where Annie's based, have regular open days where anyone can go along and view the artists' work. That's how I discovered Annie, and most of the other art here as well.'

'How often do they have these open days?' Dee said. 'I'd love to go along to the next one.'

'I've got some leaflets by the counter,' Claire said. 'They've got all the information you need, including contact details for the artists. Hang on, let me go and grab one for you.'

A moment later she was back, holding a folded leaflet which she handed to Dee.

'This is great,' Dee said. 'Just out of interest, how much do these paintings sell for?'

'This one that you're looking at right now,' Claire said. 'Was sold yesterday for £1,500. In fact, most of Annie's paintings have already been sold, I'm afraid. But if you like what you see here, I'd strongly recommend going to visit the studio. We're only able to display a tiny fraction of the artists' work here.'

'I think I'll do that.' Dee smiled. 'Thanks so much for your time, Claire. I hope this isn't the last time I get a chance to visit your lovely gallery.'

'If you're serious about Annie's work,' Claire said, 'why don't you hang around a bit longer? She normally drops by around this time to say hi. In fact, speak of the devil. Here she is now. I'll introduce you. Annie! Come over here, darling. There's someone I want you to meet.'

Dee watched as the woman from the pub walked across the gallery to them. She walked with a slight limp, barely noticeable unless you were watching her carefully. As Annie drew closer, something flashed across her face, fear or surprise; Dee couldn't tell which.

'Hello,' she said, looking at Dee. 'I think we've already met, haven't we?'

'Dee Morrison.' The use of her ex-husband's name was automatic. Something she'd done time and again in her career, to prevent anyone looking her up on the internet and realising she was a journalist. She hadn't changed her name when she'd married Billy; it had gone against her feminist principles to do that. But using his surname when it suited her, that was another matter entirely.

Dee held her hand out, noticing the hesitation before Annie put out her own hand to return the handshake.

'Dee's just been admiring your work,' Claire said. 'I've suggested she should visit your studio and see what else you've got. As you know, most of the work here has already sold.'

'I have seen you before!' Dee exclaimed, doing her best to sound surprised. 'The Town of Ramsgate, wasn't it?'

'That's right. You seemed to think we'd already met?'

'Menopause brain,' Dee said. 'You look like a friend of mine. Sorry. I really was convinced you were her for a moment. I can see now you don't actually look that much like her at all.'

Annie didn't say anything, leaving it up to Claire to break the awkward silence.

'Dee might be interested in buying one of your paintings. Would you like to tell her a little about the inspiration for the ones on display here?'

'Who are you?' Annie said, ignoring Claire's question.

'I've just told you,' Dee said. 'Listen, I'm sorry if I freaked you out the other day. I only popped in here today because a friend recommended the exhibition. If you don't want to talk to me about your work, that's fine.' She turned to Claire. 'Thanks for your time and the good coffee. I don't want to cause any trouble. Maybe it's better if I go.'

'There's really no need.' Claire scowled at Annie. 'Annie, Dee is interested in your work. That's what you wanted, right? To sell some paintings and make a bit of money for once?'

'Sorry,' Annie said, giving Dee a half-smile. 'I'm a very private person. I find this side of the business difficult – putting myself out there, talking to strangers. It makes me uncomfortable. But that doesn't mean I have to be rude about it.'

'No need to apologise,' Dee said. 'It is a bit of a coincidence bumping into you again like this. I was just telling Claire that I used to live in this area years ago. I only popped into the gallery for a quick look. I'm glad I did. I've fallen in love with your work.'

'Thank you.' Annie blushed. 'That means a lot. It's not easy, putting your art on display like this. I imagine it's a little like walking down a street without wearing any clothes. Not that I'm planning to do that any time soon.'

'Glad to hear it.' Dee smiled before she looked at her watch, pretending to check the time. 'I've got to go, I'm afraid. Is there any chance I could come to your studio some time to see more of your work? I've just bought a new home and I'm looking for some original art to decorate it. I live by the sea and one of your paintings would be perfect for my living room.'

'I'm not sure,' Annie said. 'I don't normally let people come to my studio. It's sort of a private space, you know?'

'Annie Holden,' Claire interjected. 'There is no bloody point showing your work if you're not going to try and sell it to people who want to buy it.'

'Well, if you put it like that,' Annie smiled at Dee, 'how would Saturday morning work for you?'

'I could probably do that,' Dee said. 'Why don't you give me your number and I'll text to confirm?'

'My contact details are on the leaflet.' Annie pointed to the piece of paper in Dee's hand.

'Great,' Dee said. 'Well then, I'll be in touch.'

As she walked away, Claire followed her. 'You'll find the other artists' details there to. Do take a look, some of them are really good. If you see anything you like, I'm sure you could arrange to visit more than one studio on Saturday.'

Promising she'd take a look, although she had no intention of doing so, Dee said goodbye and left before Claire talked her into calling some of the other artists as well.

Outside the gallery, she phoned Emer.

'Hey,' she said, when she got Emer's voicemail. 'It's me – Dee. I'm in London today and was hoping you might be free for a quick coffee. Call me back if you can.'

She hung up, disappointed. She'd sent Emer a text yesterday evening, telling her she'd be in London today and asking if they could meet up. So far, Emer hadn't replied. She thought about hanging around London for a few hours and then trying her cousin again. But then she remembered what Emer had told her the last time they'd spoken. She'd mentioned her stress at doing a job she'd never done before, and how hard she was working to prove herself. The last thing she needed was pressure from Dee to leave work for a coffee.

Maybe it was for the best, Dee told herself, putting her phone away. She had work to do too, and it wouldn't get done while she was loitering in London waiting for her cousin to call her back. The best thing she could do was get back to Eastbourne and spend what was left of her day writing the next chapter of her book.

Sixteen

Dee walked around the studio in silence, taking it all in. She'd never been inside an artist's studio before, but this place was exactly what she'd imagined one might look like. Situated on the second floor of a draughty warehouse, it was a large space flooded with light coming through the huge, industrial windows. An easel stood in the middle of the room. On it was a canvas with an unfinished painting. More canvases, in varying sizes, were stacked against the exposed brick wall.

'Take a look,' Annie said, nodding at the stack of canvases.

Dee flicked through them, pausing every now and then when a particular painting caught her attention. There were more landscapes here, lots of them, along with some striking portrait paintings.

'This is beautiful,' Dee said, lifting one out for a better look.

The painting showed a young woman sitting at the bar of a pub somewhere. The light in the painting was focused on the woman, with the rest of the canvas in muted shades of grey and black. She was sitting sideways, looking over her shoulder, giving Dee the uncanny sense that the woman was staring directly at her. A packet of Benson and Hedges cigarettes and an empty glass were on the bar beside her.

At first, Dee thought the woman was the only person in the painting, but when she examined it more closely, she saw someone else. A shadowy figure in the corner, a young child. The woman was wearing jeans and a tight-fitting T-shirt. She was beautiful, yet there was an expression of such emptiness on her face that Dee couldn't look at her for too long. Somehow, in this single image, Annie had created an almost unbearable sense of something lost. It was incredible.

'Is she you?' Dee asked, because the woman in the painting looked remarkably like Annie.

'What makes you say that?' Annie asked, looking closely at the painting. 'Oh yes, I can see the resemblance, now you mention it. No, she's not me. She was someone I painted from memory. It happens sometimes. I remember a face from my childhood and it gets stuck in my mind until it's almost like I don't have a choice. I have to paint it.'

'My mum used to smoke Benson and Hedges,' Dee said. 'She wasn't a regular smoker, but the odd time when she decided she fancied a ciggie, it was always a B and H.'

'I don't know why I chose Benson and Hedges,' Annie said. 'Do they even exist today?'

'I'm pretty sure they do,' Dee said. 'Although the packaging isn't the same. The painting is perfect. I'd love to buy it.'

'Sorry,' Annie said. 'That one's not for sale. I should have said. A lot of my paintings are commissions. This is one of them. Let me quickly sort through them, so you can see which ones are for sale and which aren't.'

'How do you get commissions?' Dee asked, as Annie rearranged the paintings. A moment ago, Annie had told her she'd done this painting because she didn't have a choice. Now, she was saying someone commissioned it. Dee wondered which version was the truth.

'It's not that hard, actually. We promote our work within the local community and we're incredibly lucky to be based where we are. A lot of the businesses in Canary Wharf like to display original artwork. The collective has a relationship with several of them. When a commission comes through, we all bid for it and one of us gets chosen to produce the work'.

'Is that what happened with this one?' Dee asked, pointing at the one she'd picked out a moment ago.

Annie shook her head. 'That was a private commission. We get those too. Lots of wealthy people living around here. Some banker guy gave me the brief.' She smiled at Dee. 'He hasn't seen it yet. If he doesn't like it, I'll give you a ring and let you know it's back on the market.'

'That would be great,' Dee said.

She was pretty sure Annie was lying, but couldn't see the point in challenging her on it. As far as she was concerned, if Annie didn't want to sell her the painting, all she had to do was tell her that.

'Why don't you carry on looking through these?' Annie said. 'I'll go and make us both a coffee. We've got a kitchen down the hall.'

While Annie was gone, Dee immersed herself in the rest of the paintings. Alongside the landscapes, there were several more paintings that Dee quickly categorised as the 'lonely paintings'. Images of a woman standing by herself in a room or a wide open landscape, looking lost and alone. They were beautiful but not entirely to Dee's taste. Instead, she selected a happier painting to buy – a stunning image of two young girls running across a sandy beach flying a red kite. There was something joyous about this painting and Dee hoped it might cheer her up when Ella, Tom and Jake had gone.

When she heard the studio door opening, she expected to see Annie coming back with the drinks. Instead, an older woman came into the studio, clearly surprised when she saw Dee.

'Hello,' the woman said. 'I was expecting to find Annie. Do you know where she might be?'

'She's gone to make coffee,' Dee said. 'I'm here to look at her art. I saw her work in an exhibition and she kindly invited me to her studio to see some more of her paintings. Are you another one of the artists?'

The woman laughed.

'I wish. The only thing I've ever painted is my front door, and I did a terrible job. I'm Fiona, Annie's mother.'

Something flickered at the back of Dee's mind. A memory. She had seen this woman somewhere before, she was sure of it. But when she tried to focus on the memory, it kept slipping away from her.

Annie's mother was an attractive woman; tall and slender with silver hair cut into a chic bob that reminded Dee of Meryl Streep in *The Devil Wears Prada*. Dressed in navy trousers and a silk white blouse, she oozed money and class.

'You're lucky,' she told Dee. 'Annie's very particular about who she lets into this space.'

'Well I'm glad she's made an exception,' Dee said. 'It's been a privilege to come here today and see the rest of her work. She's incredibly talented, isn't she?'

'I'm so glad you think so. Oh.' She frowned as she looked at something behind Dee.

When Dee turned, she saw Fiona was looking at the painting she'd taken out earlier. The one with the woman sitting in the empty bar.

'Beautiful, isn't it?' Dee said.

'Yes, I suppose it is. I haven't seen it before. I wonder when she did it. Sorry, what did you say your name was?'

'I don't think I've introduced myself. I'm Dee.'

'Nice to meet you. Annie's gone to make coffee, you said?' Fiona looked at her watch, frowning. 'We were meant to be going for lunch, you see. I was expecting Annie to be home half an hour ago.'

'Mum? What are you doing here? Oh God, I'm sorry. Is it lunchtime already?'

Annie had come back into the studio, carrying a mug in each hand, her limp evident again as she crossed the room to hand one of the mugs to Dee.

'Broke my leg when I was little,' she said, when Dee asked about the limp. 'Fell off a swing in the park.'

'She gave us a terrible shock,' Fiona said. 'It healed perfectly well, apart from the limp. Which you only ever see when she's tired. Annie darling, you're not pushing yourself too hard are you?'

'I'm fine, Mum.' Annie rolled her eyes at Dee. 'You'd think at my age my mother would stop worrying about me so much, wouldn't you?'

'Well I know what you're like,' Fiona said. 'Take today, for instance. We were meant to be meeting half an hour ago, but you forgot.' She looked at Dee as she continued speaking. 'She's got a memory like a sieve when it comes to social engagements. Once she gets in here, she forgets about everything else.'

'I hadn't forgotten,' Annie said. 'I just hadn't realised it was so late. The morning's flown by. This is Dee, by the way.'

'Thank you.' Fiona smiled at Dee. 'We've already introduced ourselves.'

'Dee's here to buy one of my paintings,' Annie continued. 'Well, she might – if she finds something she likes.'

'I've found plenty of things I like,' Dee said, 'but I think I've made my decision.'

She pointed to the painting she'd picked out a moment ago.

'Oh.' Annie's face softened as she looked at the painting. 'You've got a good eye, you know. That's one of my favourites.'

'You sure you want to sell it?' Dee said.

'Of course.' Annie smiled. 'I'm glad you like it. I can arrange to get it framed for you too, if want? A friend of mine can do it for half the price you'd pay anyone else. What do you think?'

'Sounds great,' Dee said.

'Let me give her a ring and see if she's free,' Annie said. 'We'll need to go to her workshop so you can choose a frame you'd like.'

'What about lunch?' Fiona interrupted.

'It won't take long,' Annie said. 'You don't mind waiting a few more minutes, do you?'

'There's no need,' Dee said to Annie. 'Can you pick a frame for me? You'll make a better choice than I would.'

'I'm not sure,' Annie said, 'a frame is such a personal choice. What if I choose one and you don't like it?'

'I don't believe that will happen,' Dee said. 'Seriously, Annie. You'd be doing me a favour. I've got a load of work to get through when I get back home. The sooner I can get going, the better.'

'If you're sure,' Annie said.

'I'm certain.' Dee looked at Fiona. 'Sorry I've taken up so much of your daughter's time.'

'I don't mind,' Fiona said. 'Not really. To be honest with you, it's a real pleasure to see Annie finally making money from her art. She's worked so hard at it. We didn't want her to become an artist, you know. She's our only child and we were terribly overprotective. We wanted her to have a career that's a bit more secure. But she's such a stubborn thing. When she decides on something, she goes for it. Doesn't let anyone stand in her way.

'She's always supported herself financially, too. She's never asked us for a penny, working part-time while she built up her portfolio. And now, finally, because of Claire and this exhibition, Annie's able to give up her other work and focus on her art. Which is brilliant, because the more time she's able to spend on her art, the more chance she has of making a go of it.'

And there you had it. A simple explanation for why Annie had stopped working at the pub. Not because she was hiding, but because she'd started making money from the exhibition and she was able to give up the pub job. Suddenly, Dee felt immensely stupid.

It was clear that Fiona and Annie were close. And it was blindingly obvious that Annie Holden was exactly who she said she was. The idea that she was somehow Emer's long-lost sister seemed, suddenly, ridiculous. Dee didn't understand how she'd ever let things get this far. She should have put a stop to it the moment Emer asked for her help.

She took a sip of coffee, then wished she hadn't. Instant coffee, which tasted as if it had been sitting in the jar for years.

'I'd better let you two get to your lunch.' She put the mug down on the single table in the room. 'I've taken up more than enough of your time.'

'It was lovely to meet you,' Fiona said. 'Sorry I interrupted your meeting. I wouldn't have barged in if I'd known you were here. I'm just so used to Annie losing herself when she's here and forgetting she's sometimes meant to be somewhere else.'

'It's not a problem,' Dee said, 'really.'

'Thanks so much for being so enthusiastic about my work,' Annie said, smiling at Dee. 'It means a huge amount. I'll call you as soon as it's ready to be collected. Probably about a week's time, if that's okay?'

Dee paid for the painting and said goodbye to Annie and her mother. After leaving the studio, she called Emer as she walked back towards Aldgate East station.

'I really need to see you,' she said, when Emer picked up.

'Is it to do with Kitty?'

'Sort of,' Dee said. 'But it's not a conversation I want to have over the phone. Can you meet?'

'Not today,' Emer said. 'I know it's the weekend, but I've got a deadline, so I'm working flat out today and tomorrow. Could you do Monday instead?'

'No, I can't do Monday,' Dee said. 'I'm in London now and, believe it or not, Emer, I actually have a life that involves more than running around the place on your behalf. If you want to see me on Monday, come to Eastbourne.'

'Wait,' Emer said. 'I'm sorry. I'm really sorry. This job is a complete nightmare. I'd walk out of it today and never come back, but I've promised myself I'd stick it out, no matter how hard it gets. I haven't always been that good at sticking things out, you see, and I'm trying to get better at it. That's why I can't meet you today. But you're right, I shouldn't expect you to come up to London again on Monday just because it's more convenient. I'll call in sick on Monday and I'll come to Eastbourne. Would that be okay?'

'You don't have to do that,' Dee said, already feeling bad. She was disappointed Emer couldn't meet her, but it was hardly Emer's fault that her new job was keeping her busy.

'I do,' Emer said. 'You've already done so much for me, and I'm really grateful. Just tell me where you want to meet, and I'll be there. I'll work out later how to get to you. I can get a train, right?'

'Emer, stop. I was being a bitch, and I'm sorry. I really don't want you taking a sickie. Your work's important, I get that. I'll come to London. It's really not a problem for me because I can work on the train. Tell me where you work and I'll come to you.'

'Canary Wharf. We could meet at the DLR station.'

'I thought you worked in the City?'

'Isn't Canary Wharf part of the City?' Emer said.

'Not exactly.' Dee smiled. 'You'd better promise me you'll take some time off when all this is done and get to know London a bit better. Okay, I'll let you get back to work for now, and I'll see you Monday. Let's make it around midday. I can treat you to a nice lunch somewhere.'

'Sounds good,' Emer said. 'See you then.'

Seventeen

June 1997

Kitty lay in bed, eyes wide open staring at the familiar grey shadows in the room. Too scared to close her eyes in case she fell asleep, she kept checking her watch as the minutes crawled by. She'd arranged to meet Lucy at half past nine. Kitty was supposed to be at Lucy's tonight for a sleepover, but yesterday Mum had got angry about something and said Kitty couldn't go. It wasn't fair, but there was nothing Kitty could do about it. She'd asked Mrs Ryan if she'd speak to Mum, but Mrs Ryan had sighed and said she didn't think she should interfere. Most of the time, Kitty liked Lucy's mum because she was kind and never got angry, but right now she was raging with her. Mrs Ryan was a coward, just like every other adult Kitty knew. All of them too afraid to stand up to her mother and tell her not to be such a cow.

Dad hadn't come home after work, which meant Mum's mood was worse than usual this evening. It was stupid, because they all knew he was in the pub, and if Mum didn't like that, Kitty didn't understand why she didn't just walk down there and tell him to come home. Instead, she clattered around the house, muttering to herself and shouting at Kitty to get into the kitchen and help her cook tea because did Kitty think her mother was a slave with no life of her own?

Finally, tea was finished and the girls were banished upstairs to their bedroom. Emer had wanted to play a game, and sulked like a baby when Kitty told her she was too tired for anything except bed. Emer had cried for a bit after that and Kitty felt bad then. Normally, she would have climbed into Emer's bed and cuddled her and chatted to her until she stopped crying, but tonight she was too scared to do that in case she fell asleep. Sometimes, it was easier falling asleep in Emer's bed, because it was so warm and cosy when they cuddled up to each other like that.

It felt like she'd been waiting here for ages, and she was starting to wonder if she'd got it wrong. But then she heard the creaking sound the front door made when you opened it, and the click-clack of her mother's heels on the street outside. Kitty threw back her quilt and got up. She'd kept her clothes on when she went to bed, sneaking under the quilt while Emer was brushing her teeth, so her sister wouldn't ask any stupid questions about why Kitty was going to bed with her clothes on.

When she'd eventually stopped crying, Emer had fallen asleep. Now, she was lying on her back, snoring. Kitty wasn't worried about going out and leaving her by herself. Emer never woke up once she was asleep. Kitty thought she could probably have a party in the room when Emer was sleeping and it wouldn't wake her.

Outside, Kitty took in deep breaths of cool evening air, waiting for the bad feelings inside her to quieten down. She was so tired of feeling like this. All the anger that she couldn't shake off, no matter how hard she tried. It burned inside her, eating a big hole in her stomach until there was nothing left of her except this rage. Everything in her life felt so wrong. She wanted things to be different after tonight, but what if nothing changed? No, she couldn't let herself think like that. She had to believe that when her father knew the truth, he would change. He'd stop going to the pub every night and he'd start being the father he was meant to be.

He would leave their mother, and he'd take Kitty and Emer with him. They'd start a new life, just the three of them. And once he was away from their mother, he'd stop drinking because he'd realise he only ever drank to cover up his own unhappiness.

That's why she was doing this, she reminded herself as she ran along the street and turned into the fancy estate at the top of the hill where Lucy lived.

Here, the houses couldn't be more different to the ones on the street where Kitty lived. Tiny two-up, two-down cottages that constantly felt as if the walls were closing in on you. These houses were big, detached, two- and three-storey mansions with double garages and huge gardens with views across town. It wasn't fair that Lucy and Maeve got to live in a big house with a garden and a tree house, when Kitty had to share their tiny house with her parents and Emer. It wasn't fair that Lucy's parents never argued and her mother never, ever told Lucy she was a mistake and she wished she'd never had her. Kitty was starting to realise that nothing in this life was fair.

She'd half expected Lucy not to come. But when she reached the meeting point, behind the tree at the end of Lucy's road, Lucy was already there.

'You're late,' Lucy said.

'Sorry,' Kitty said. 'I had to wait until my mum left. Did you bring the torch?'

Lucy held up the torch.

'Good.' Kitty nodded. 'Don't turn it on yet. Wait until we need it.'

She crossed the road to the woods that divided the town in two, separating Irish Town – the older part of town – from the newer houses where Lucy and Kitty lived. There was a road that ran around the edge of the woods, joining the two sections of the town, but the quickest way to Old Town, and the Coyne house, was to follow the path that ran through the woods. Going through the woods also meant there was less chance they'd be seen by any nosey adults wanting to know what two girls were doing out by themselves this late in the evening.

But even though the sun hadn't set yet, the woods felt dark and scary.

'Better switch that on,' Kitty said.

Lucy did as she was told, but it wasn't long before she was moaning about being scared and telling Kitty she wanted to go home.

'No!' Kitty grabbed Lucy's arm, tugging her forward. 'You promised, Lucy. You can't turn back now.'

'I don't like it in here.' Lucy pulled her arm free. 'And stop dragging me like that. What's so important about doing this, anyway? Don't tell me it's just because we won't be able to do it soon because the house will be knocked down. There's something else going on, isn't there?'

'There's nothing else,' Kitty said. 'I thought it would be an adventure, that's all. Don't you want our lives to be more exciting than they are? You read all those books about kids who do things like this all the time. Why can't you be a bit more like them?'

'They're just books,' Lucy said. 'Not real people. In case you hadn't noticed.'

The light from the torch swept across the lines of trees, creating long shadows that looked like creatures waiting to pounce on them. Angry with Lucy for being such a coward, Kitty kept walking, following the torch light until it started to fade.

'Wait for me!'

The light started moving again, bouncing off the trees and swinging through the darkness. Then Lucy was beside her, taking her hand, and they were walking side by side, letting the light guide them through the woods.

The house stood by itself, on a clearing where the woods ended. There was no wall or fence separating the house from the land around it. All they had to do was cross the clearing until they reached the house. There was a driveway at the front of the property. The gates, at the end of the driveway, were open. Kitty knew if she walked down the driveway and through the gates, she would reach the road that connected the two sides of town.

Several cars were parked outside the house. Kitty recognised her parents' battered Fiat, but none of the others.

'What's your car doing here?' Lucy whispered. 'Your mother will go mad if she sees us. We should leave now.'

She hadn't switched the torch off. As she spoke, she trained the light on the row of cars as if she was trying to see inside them.

'Turn that thing off,' Kitty hissed. 'The last thing we want is anyone inside the house seeing that.'

She crept across the driveway, not bothering to wait for Lucy. Knowing Lucy was too much of a coward to stay out here by herself. They were almost at the house when a movement in one of the upstairs windows caught Kitty's eye. She looked up, saw the curtain had been pulled back and someone was standing there.

She ducked down behind one of the cars, gesturing for Lucy to get down too. She held her breath, her heart beating hard and fast inside her chest. It wasn't too late. They could still turn back, walk away before anyone saw them. But she was here now and she had to go through with it. Again, she remembered pushing open the front door of her house and hearing the noises from the kitchen. It had sounded as if someone was being hurt and she'd been so scared. She should have turned around and gone back outside again, but she hadn't. She'd tiptoed forward, following the noise.

They hadn't even bothered closing the door. It was like her mother wanted someone to see what she was doing. Even though what she was doing was the most disgusting thing Kitty had ever seen in her life and she didn't know how her mother could ever want anyone to see her like that.

'What are we going to do?' Lucy's voice banished the memory.

Kitty peered around the side of the car before she answered. It was getting dark now; the sun had gone for the night and a silver crescent moon had appeared in the grey sky. The lights were on in several of the rooms on both floors. Behind the drawn curtains, she could see the shapes of people moving about. But she didn't care about any of them. All she cared about was the person she'd seen in the upstairs window.

'We're going in.'

She stood up and ran towards house, her feet crunching loudly on the gravelled driveway. The sound echoed in the still night before fading into the darkness, until it was like Kitty had never been there.

Eighteen

'She's not Kitty.'

'Are you absolutely sure about that?'

'Yes, I am. I'm so sorry. I know how much you wanted it to be her.'

'It's okay.' Emer looked down at the table, at the plate of ravioli she had barely touched.

'It's my fault,' Dee said.

'How do you make that out?'

'I shouldn't have let things get as far as they did. I got carried away with wanting to help you.'

Emer picked up a tiny morsel of pasta with her fork and put it into her mouth.

'Who is she then?' she said, when she'd finished chewing.

'Her name is Annie Holden,' Dee said. 'She's an artist. From Sussex initially, but she lives in London now. She used to work part-time at the Town of Ramsgate pub, but she's given that up recently to focus on her art.'

They were sitting in an upmarket Italian restaurant near Canary Wharf. Emer had been waiting for Dee at the DLR station when she'd got off the train, and they'd come straight here.

'I asked my colleagues to recommend somewhere,' Emer had said. 'A few of them said this place is really good.'

And really expensive, Dee had thought, eyeing the menu when they arrived. She'd ordered a plate of osso bucco that she'd almost finished. The veal was tender and delicious and, she'd reluctantly acknowledged, just about worth the outlandish price tag that came with it.

'And there's no way she could be Kitty?' Emer asked.

'I met her mother,' Dee said. 'She's a lovely, ordinary woman who clearly adores her daughter. Talking to her made me realise.'

'Realise what?'

'We both wanted to believe Kitty was still alive,' Dee said. 'You, because it meant your sister hadn't died. Me, because finding Kitty would have been such a lovely thing to be able to do for you. But we were kidding ourselves. Death is the hardest thing in the world to accept. I've lost people close to me and there have been times I'd do anything at all to bring them back to life. But that's not something any of us can do.'

She didn't add that digging into Annie's private life for no good reason wasn't something that sat easily with her. Of course, digging into people's private lives was part of an investigative journalist's job description. But an equally important part of the job was knowing when it was time to stop. And right now, it was time to stop investigating Annie Holden just because she bore a passing resemblance to Emer's dead sister.

'Are you okay?' Dee asked.

'I think so,' Emer said. 'It's a bit difficult to process, that's all.'

'Did you ever get any counselling?' Dee asked. 'After Kitty died, I mean.'

'You think I'm crazy.' Emer smiled.

'I think you're still grieving,' Dee said. 'And maybe you need some help with that. I admire you for refusing to believe your sister was really dead. It takes a lot of courage not to accept something everyone else is telling you has to be true.'

'But now it's time to start accepting it.' Emer nodded. 'You're right. God, it's almost a relief, you know? I spent so long wondering what had really happened. Now I know for sure, I guess.'

'Perhaps this was inevitable,' Dee said. 'Sooner or later, you were bound to see someone who reminded you of Kitty. I wonder if this was what you needed so you could finally let go.'

'Possibly.' Emer placed her knife and fork together on her plate. 'This food is lovely, but I've lost my appetite, I'm afraid. Please let me pay for this?'

'Not a chance.' Dee pulled out her card and gestured to a nearby waiter to bring the bill. 'This is my treat.'

'That's very kind,' Emer said. 'But next time we meet, I'm paying. Okay?'

'You think there'll be a next time?'

'Of course. Why wouldn't there be? You're my cousin. I know I've been too busy to spend much time with you, but hopefully things will change once this contract's over.'

'You want to go for a walk or something before you go back?' Dee asked.

'I'd love to,' Emer said, 'but I really should be getting back.'

'You sure you'll be okay to work?' Dee asked.

In fact, Emer seemed to be handling the news remarkably well. Dee hoped the realisation that her sister really was gone wouldn't hit her later, when she was alone.

'I'll be fine.' Emer smiled. 'Really. And I'm so grateful to you for everything you've done.'

'You're making it sound like a goodbye,' Dee said. 'But we're only starting to get to know each other. I'm still hoping you'll come to Eastbourne soon. What's your work schedule looking like over the next few weeks?'

'Crazy,' Emer said. 'But I'm sure I can squeeze in a trip to the seaside. God knows, I'll need the break soon enough.'

'I've got another cousin, on my mum's side of the family – Louise. She's really keen to meet you. She'll kill me if I don't organise something soon.'

'Sounds great,' Emer said. 'I'll call you over the next few days and sort something out.'

After Dee paid the bill, she insisted on walking Emer back to her office.

'You don't have to do that,' Emer said.

'Nonsense,' Dee said. 'I'd like to see where you work. Besides, it's not like I've got anything else to do.'

They went outside into the warm sunshine and walked along the wide streets lined with glass and concrete skyscrapers, looking for Emer's office block.

'I always get confused,' Emer said, when they'd walked down the same street for the third time. 'Everywhere looks the same, doesn't it? Ah. Here it is.'

She stopped outside one of the skyscrapers which, in fairness, looked pretty much like all the other buildings on this street.

'I'd invite you to come in,' Emer said, 'but I've got a meeting in a few minutes. Thanks again, Dee. For everything.'

'My pleasure.' Dee leaned in to give Emer a hug. 'Promise you'll call?'

'I promise.' Emer extricated herself from Dee's embrace. 'Enjoy the rest of your day. See you soon, okay?'

As she walked through the revolving door and disappeared inside the building, Dee had a sudden rush of panic, fear that she might never see her cousin again. That Emer might simply disappear, just as Kitty had done all those years ago.

Here one minute, gone the next.

–

Later that evening, when she was back home, Dee called Leonard.

'I've been to Annie's studio and met her mother,' Dee said. 'It's pretty clear she is who she says she is.'

'Hardly a surprise,' Leonard said. 'Have you told Emer?'

'Yes. She took it better than I expected, actually.'

'So I can stop following Annie?'

'God yes. I feel bad enough about intruding into her personal life.'

'And the bloke in Stockwell?'

'What bloke?'

'The one I told you about. Annie went to meet him the other night. Old bloke, looked like he could be her dad maybe. I followed her. Didn't you get my text? Hang on, let me check. Oh bugger. It didn't send for some reason. Ah, I forgot. I can't send text messages with attachments. Should have used WhatsApp. My neighbour set me up with that recently. We've got a group thingy so we can share information. Although, if you ask me, all they seem to do is send stupid bloody jokes to each other.'

'Leonard. Stop speaking for one second, could you? It doesn't matter about the man she met in Stockwell. It's none of our business. Don't send me the text, and make sure you delete any photos you've taken. From now on, Annie Holden is nothing to do with us.'

Fifteen minutes later, Dee managed to end the call. Despite what she'd said to Leonard, there was a part of her that still wanted to find out more about Annie and her mother. She couldn't quite forget the flicker of recognition she'd felt the first time she'd seen Fiona Holden.

Opening her laptop, Dee went onto the gallery's website and reread Annie's biography.

> Originally from Sussex, Annie now lives in London and is a member of the Bow Artists' Collective. Following a long tradition of artists inspired by the Sussex countryside, Holden is one of the rising stars of the thriving east London art scene.

The biography didn't state where in Sussex Annie had grown up, but if it was close to Eastbourne, that might explain why Fiona had seemed so familiar. Mystery well and truly solved, then. Dee was tempted to do a bit more searching and see if she could find out exactly where Annie had grown up, but a knock on her back door and the patter of small feet on the outside decking put all thoughts of Annie instantly out of her mind.

Knowing there was only one person in her life who ran along her decking like that, Dee hurried to open the door.

'Surprise!'

Ella and Jake were standing there, big smiles on their faces.

'Thought you might want a bit of company?' Ella held up the bottle of wine she was carrying. 'Tom's away and

Jake's been asking about you all day. I probably should have called first, but…'

'Don't be silly.' Dee leaned down and grabbed Jake. 'I was just thinking of making a peanut butter sandwich. What do you think?'

Holding him tight, she carried him into her house, letting the babble of his little boy voice soothe her. Not allowing herself to think of the time – too soon – when she wouldn't be able to do this any longer.

Nineteen

For the rest of the week, Dee focused on her book. The only time she took a break was Wednesday morning, when she met Louise for an early morning walk. They'd arranged to meet at Holywell, at the western edge of the seafront, beside the white cliffs and the beginning of the South Downs Way.

Louise was already there when Dee arrived, sipping a drink from a brightly coloured reusable thermal mug.

'You're late,' she grumbled, as Dee climbed out of her car.

'Sorry,' Dee said. 'I forgot my bank card and had to go back for it. I'm dropping into the supermarket when we're finished. There is literally no food at all in my house.'

'I don't understand why you don't do a weekly online shop like most normal people,' Louise said. 'I wouldn't survive without Ocado.'

'Most normal people are shopping for an entire family,' Dee said. 'I'm only shopping for myself, remember. It's not worth doing a big shop every week.'

They walked down the hill that led to the beach and turned left, without either of them needing to check this was what the other wanted. They'd been taking regular morning walks together for a while now, and had several routes. This one, from Holywell to the pier and back, was one of their favourites.

As they walked, Dee told Louise about her recent trips to London and her realisation that Annie Holden was exactly who she said she was.

'You can't be too surprised,' Louise said. 'I mean, you didn't really think she was anyone else, did you?'

'I suppose not,' Dee said, 'although of course there was a part of me that wished – for Emer's sake – Kitty was still alive.'

'Does this mean you're letting the whole thing go?'

'I guess so,' Dee said. 'Although there's a part of me that's still wants to know the truth.'

She thought of the conversation she'd had the previous evening with Shay Flaherty, the journalist who'd covered Lucy's disappearance back in 1997. He'd finally got back to her and they'd spoken on the phone for almost an hour yesterday.

Shay had told Dee he'd never stopped believing Lucy's disappearance and Kitty's drowning were connected.

'But I've never been able to prove it,' he said. 'Everyone was so convinced Kitty drowned that day. I wanted to look into it in more detail, but my editor told me it was a waste of time.'

'You think there's a chance Kitty didn't drown?' Dee asked him.

'Maybe,' Shay said. 'But it was never an option anyone properly explored.'

Shay also confirmed that Kitty's father hadn't joined his family on holiday because he'd had a last-minute offer of some work. Although he couldn't now, all these years later, remember who Eamon had been working for. He promised Dee he'd look back over the notes he'd kept from that time and, if he found anything interesting, he would let her know.

'Isn't the truth simple?' Louise said now, dragging Dee's mind from yesterday's conversation to this one. 'Kitty drowned, and that's all there is to it.'

'But what about Lucy?' Dee said. 'What happened to her?'

'Maybe no one will ever know,' Louise said. 'I know it sounds awful, but sometimes there are no easy answers.'

'I know that,' Dee said. But she already knew she wasn't ready to let it go completely. At some point, maybe when she'd finished this book, she was going to go back to Ireland and spend some time investigating the disappearance of Lucy Ryan.

'When do I get to meet Emer?' Louise said. 'Is she planning a trip to Eastbourne any time soon?'

'I hope so. Although I'm not sure she wants to. She's a bit hard to work out, actually.'

'I guess having all that crap to deal with so young has left its mark,' Louise said.

'You're probably right,' Dee said.

She looked out at the sea, rougher than normal this morning because of the wind, thinking about her father's family. She'd hoped meeting Emer might lead to a reunion with her uncle. But Emer claimed she didn't even know if Eamon was alive or dead.

'Her stepfather's someone important,' she told Louise. 'His name is Robert O'Brien. Apparently, he's in with a shot at being the country's next Taoiseach.'

'Next what?'

'Taoiseach,' Dee said. 'It's what Irish people call their prime minister.'

'Wow. Wouldn't that be cool if it happened and you got to meet him?'

'I don't think there's much chance of that,' Dee said. 'Apparently Emer's mother has zero interest in hearing from me. There was a lot of bad blood between my dad and his brother. Some of it obviously rubbed off on her as well.'

'Except she's not married to your uncle anymore,' Louise said. 'Or is she? How long has she been with her new bloke?'

'She married him two years after her husband walked out on her,' Dee said. 'Somehow, she managed to get her first marriage annulled. Divorce would have been practically impossible in Ireland back then. I wonder if she married him for security? You know, after being married to a man like Eamon. Robert's reputation is squeaky clean. He was a successful businessman before he went into politics.'

'What sort of business?'

'Property and retail,' Dee said. 'Probably other things too, but they're the two main areas. He does a lot of charity work as well, most of it around helping Travellers. According to one article I read, he only went into politics because he felt there was no one else representing the needs of Ireland's underprivileged. He sounds really fascinating, to be honest.'

Louise snorted. 'He sounds like a fraud, more like.'

'Why do you say that?'

'He worked in property and retail and now he's a politician? Come on, Dee. I've never met a property developer or a politician who is one hundred per cent squeaky clean.'

'Maybe he's the exception,' Dee said. 'I read an interview with him where he spoke about growing up in a family who had no money and the importance of giving back to the community. He sounded completely sincere.'

'Of course he sounded sincere,' Louise said. 'He's a politician. They're trained to sound sincere even when they're lying through their teeth.'

'It's not like you to be so cynical,' Dee said.

'And it's not like you to believe everything you read about someone. Listen to me, Dee. Isn't it possible that you want to believe all these things about him because it makes it easier for you?'

'How does it do that?' Dee said, not sure she liked where this conversation was going.

'You're such a kind person,' Louise said. 'You want the best for everyone. You know Emer's had a tough time so you're hoping some of that can be helped by having a stepfather who's a good man and who will take care of her. In other words, a stepfather who's nothing like her own father.'

'I don't think that's true,' Dee said. Pointlessly, because Louise was spot on. She had been naïve, believing the one-dimensional profiles she'd read about Robert O'Brien. The simple truth was that, on the whole, people were people – which meant they were neither all good or all bad. Even her uncle, Eamon, had no doubt had his good points as well as his weaknesses. Robert O'Brien was no different. Perhaps his good points outweighed his bad ones, but of course there had to be a dark side to his personality as well. It was there in all of us, no matter how hard we tried to pretend otherwise.

Twenty

Dee spent the rest of the week focusing on her book. By Friday, she had written another 20,000 words. Pleased with the progress she was making, she had emailed her agent and agreed a deadline for when the book would be finished. She was enjoying the process more than she'd expected. At first, the prospect of writing a 70,000-word book had been daunting. She hadn't been sure she'd be able to do it. Now, she was already thinking about other books she might like to write, and could see a future where she divided her time between writing features for newspapers alongside a series of non-fiction books. During the week, she'd come up with an idea for a book exploring the experiences of single women in their fifties and sixties. She'd done a shout-out on social media, asking women to contact her if they were interested in being interviewed. So far, she'd been overwhelmed by the number of women who'd got in touch.

Work helped keep her mind off other matters. Like Emer, who hadn't returned any of Dee's calls or emails. And Ella and Jake, who would be gone by the end of the month. Each time Dee thought of them not being here, it felt like her heart was cracking all over again. She didn't know how she was going to get through the first few weeks after they left.

Annie had called during the week, too. Dee's painting was ready. Annie had got it framed and was keeping it at her house until Dee was able to come and pick it up. Which is how Dee found herself, Friday afternoon, parking her car outside a row of red-brick terraced houses on a quiet street in Wapping, east London. She rang the bell for the address Annie had given her, and waited.

The house was nothing special, but some effort had gone into adding character to the place. The door was painted a deep shade of red that stood out from the other doors on the street. The glass in the front window had been replaced with small square panes of stained glass. And pretty purple flowers bloomed from window boxes on each windowsill.

She didn't have long to wait before the door opened and Annie's mother was greeting Dee and telling her to come inside.

'Your painting's in here,' Fiona said, leading Dee down a narrow hallway into a bright, open living-kitchen area at the back of the house. 'Annie's asked me to check you're happy with it. Anything you don't like just let me know.'

'What's not to like?' Dee said.

The painting had been placed upright, on the stripped floorboards, leaning against the wall so it caught her eye as soon as she came into the room. In its new frame, it looked better than Dee remembered. She couldn't wait to see what it would look like in her living room.

'Annie can't be here, I'm afraid,' Fiona said. 'Something came up in the gallery and she had to go in at short notice. She asked me to pass on her apologies.'

'It's not a problem,' Dee said. 'I'm glad to get my painting. I hope you didn't have to drive up to London just to let me in?'

'I've been staying for a few days,' Fiona said, 'so it's not a problem. Annie's always inviting me to come and stay.'

'That must be nice for you.'

'It is.' Fiona smiled. 'I'm very lucky. And, of course, now that Annie doesn't have to work in the pub, I'm hoping we may get to spend even more time together.'

'I imagine she's got a great future ahead of her,' Dee said. 'She's really talented.'

'I think so,' Fiona said. 'Although I'm biased, as you can imagine. She didn't really take to art until her teens. There was a teacher at her secondary school who really inspired her. By the time she was fifteen or sixteen, creating art had become her life. She studied the subject for GCSE and A-level, then went on to do her degree. She went to Central Saint Martins. I was worried about her coming to London, at first. It was a big change from the village she'd grown up in. But luckily, one of her friends was already living in London and he helped her find her feet. Oh dear, I'm forgetting my manners entirely. Can I get you something to drink?'

Deciding she'd already intruded enough into Fiona Holden's life, Dee declined the offer.

'Although I wouldn't mind using your loo quickly before I go,' she said.

'Bathroom's upstairs,' Fiona said. 'Try to ignore the mess, if you can. My daughter has many qualities, but tidiness isn't one of them.'

The upstairs didn't seem too messy to Dee, but then again tidiness wasn't one of her qualities, either. Unlike Ed, who hated mess of any kind. Another reason they'd been such a mismatched couple.

A huge work of art hung on the landing wall. At first, Dee thought it was an abstract painting. But when she'd finished in the bathroom, she paused to take a closer look and saw it was a photo collage. There must have been over a hundred photos, image after image of Annie at different stages of her life, with friends and family. The longer she looked at the collage, the more Dee realised how much work it had taken to put it together.

It told a story, starting in the middle with a photo of Annie at the age she was now. As you moved out from the centre, there were photos detailing the different stages of Annie's life. Dee would love to get a similar collage done for Jake and Ella. She wondered if Annie might do one for her if she asked her. Of course, Dee would need two copies – one for her, and one for Ella and Jake.

She was about to go back downstairs when one of the photos caught her eye. This one, older than many of the others in the collage, was of two young girls. They were smiling, their arms draped over each other's shoulders. They looked so alike, they could be twins. Except one of the girls was half a head taller and, if you looked closely enough, you could see she had eyes that were two different colours.

The girls were in a garden. A scrap of concrete, edged with a ragged line of yellowed grass. Sun blasting off a piece of rusty metal in the background. But it wasn't the sun or the metal or the grass that had grabbed Dee's attention. It was the girls. She'd seen them before. In the photo she still had on her laptop, showing Emer and Kitty when they were younger. The month before Kitty disappeared from a beach in the west of Ireland one hot summer's day in 1997.

Twenty-one

'What are you doing?'

Fiona's voice, behind her, made Dee jump.

'I was admiring this collage.' She didn't turn around, certain her face would give her away. She pointed at the photo of the two girls. 'This photo, in particular, caught my eye. I didn't realise Annie had a sister.'

'She doesn't,' Fiona said. 'That's some school friend. I'm afraid I can't even remember the girl's name now. The family moved soon after that photo was taken. We lost touch with them after that.'

'Such a shame,' Dee said. She turned around, forcing a smile that wasn't reciprocated. 'They really do look alike, don't they?'

'We need to get your painting into the car,' Fiona said, ignoring the question. 'I've got to be somewhere else.'

Dee didn't like the way Fiona was staring at her, and felt a flicker of fear as she realised they were alone in the house.

'After you.' Fiona pressed her body against the wall, gesturing for Dee to go down the stairs ahead of her. Dee hesitated, before doing as she was told. She descended quickly, tense as she waited for Fiona to shove her hand into Dee's back and push her. Nothing happened, but by the time she reached the bottom of the stairs, Dee was shaking.

'We need to hurry,' Fiona said. 'I didn't realise the time. I've got to get back home.'

'I thought you were staying for a few days,' Dee said. 'Isn't that what you told me?'

'You misunderstood. Today's my last day. I had to wait for you to arrive but now I really need to go.'

'Remind me where home is?' Dee said, feeling calmer now she was back on the ground floor.

'Sussex.'

Dee started to say something about that being a coincidence because she was from Sussex too, but Fiona wasn't listening. She'd walked into the sitting room and was trying to lift Dee's painting by herself.

'Hang on,' Dee said. 'Let me give you a hand.'

Together, they carried the painting outside to the car and, with a bit of difficulty, managed to manoeuvre it until it was lying against the back seats.

'Right,' Fiona said. 'That's all done. Safe journey home.'

She turned to go, but Dee called her back.

'Is everything okay?' Dee said. 'You seem very keen to get rid of me all of a sudden.'

'I've already told you,' Fiona said. 'I need to be somewhere else.'

'Home.' Dee nodded, as if she understood. 'Sussex, isn't it? I'm from Eastbourne. Strange coincidence, isn't it?'

'Sussex is a big county,' Fiona said, 'and lots of people from Sussex end up in London. I don't think it's strange at all. Goodbye, Dee.'

After she went back inside, Dee stood by her car, wondering what to do now. There was no point banging on the front door and insisting Fiona come out and tell her the truth. If she asked Fiona about the photo, she'd say it was a coincidence. She'd tell Dee some story about Annie and the other girl being childhood friends.

As she thought this, Dee wondered if she'd got it wrong. If, somehow, her mind had seen what it wanted to. Except she hadn't wanted to see what she'd seen, had she? She had believed Annie Holden was who she said she was. Part of her still believed that.

But Dee knew what she'd seen today. Just as she knew, too, there had been other signs that something wasn't right. The sense that Annie was hiding something. That moment of recognition when Dee had first met Fiona. That gut instinct that had always driven the decisions Dee made in her life and her work.

She got into her car, making sure she revved the engine so Fiona would hear it, and drove away from the house. As soon as she turned the corner, Dee pulled into the side of the road, jumped out of the car and ran back towards the house. As she came around the corner, she saw Fiona coming out of the house and hurrying along the street in the opposite direction.

Keeping a decent distance between them, Dee followed Fiona as she turned onto Wapping High Street. When Fiona turned left into Wapping station, Dee hurried forward, hoping to catch her before she went through the barriers. But by the time she reached the station, she was too late. Fiona had already passed through the barriers to the platforms beneath the ground.

It took an age for Dee to find her debit card and get through the barriers. Wapping only had one train line, which meant there were just two platforms. Dee tried the westbound platform first. As she ran down the stairs, she was just in time to see Fiona getting onto the train that had recently pulled into the station. But by the time Dee had reached the bottom of the steps, the train had already left the station and Fiona was gone.

Sweating and out of breath, Dee stamped her foot on the ground like a petulant child who wasn't getting their own way. As the wave of anger passed, common sense kicked in. Fiona had already told her Annie was at the gallery. That's where Dee needed to go, instead of chasing after Annie's mother like some hair-brained fool without a plan.

It took her ten minutes to remember where she'd parked her car, and another twenty to navigate the thick east London traffic and find a parking space. By the time she arrived at the gallery, Annie was gone.

'She's had some sort of family emergency,' Claire said. 'She didn't give me the details, just said she had to go right away.'

'You don't know where she's gone?' Dee asked.

'No idea.' Claire frowned. 'Is there something I'm missing here, Dee? First Annie's mother comes running in here, looking as if her world has just come crumbling down around her shoulders. A few minutes later, the two of them leave in a rush, as if someone's after them. Now you're here asking where they've gone – what's going on?'

'I'm not sure,' Dee said. 'Can I ask how long you've known Annie?'

'I remember when I introduced you to her,' Claire said. 'She was wary of you, said you'd already met. What was that about?'

'It was nothing. I'd bumped into her a few days earlier and thought she was someone I used to know.'

'Well, now you know she's not, why do you care how long I've known her? More to the point, what are you doing here now?'

'I wanted to tell her how much I love the painting she got framed for me.'

Even to Dee's ears, the explanation sounded weak. Clearly, Claire thought the same.

'I'll tell her you dropped in,' she said. 'But now I'm going to have to ask you to leave. I've already told you Annie's not here, so there's no reason for you to be here.'

Dee started to say something else, but Claire held her hand up.

'Go. If you refuse, I'll call the police and you can tell them what the hell you're really up to.'

She didn't sound like she was messing around.

'Just tell her I need to speak to her,' Dee said. 'I'd be really grateful. Thanks.'

Back at her car, Dee took out her phone and dialled Emer's number. She'd already called her cousin several times over the last week. Each time, she'd got an automated voice asking her to leave a message. Today, when she dialled the number she got another automated voice. This time, the voice told her the number she'd dialled was no longer in service.

She dialled the number again. And again. Each time she got the same robotic voice telling her the same thing: *I'm sorry. The number you've called is no longer in service.*

For one surreal moment, Dee wondered if she was losing her mind. First Annie, now this. It was starting to feel like one big, elaborate prank. She glanced at the clock on her dashboard. Four thirty. Emer said she worked long hours, which meant there was every chance she'd still be at work if Dee drove over to Canary Wharf now. And if Emer was too busy to see her, Dee would wait. She'd wait all night if she had to. Because she wasn't going home until she got some answers to the questions piling up in her mind.

Finding a space to park was a challenge. In the end, Dee accepted she wasn't going to find anywhere cheap and reluctantly drove into one of the area's overpriced private car parks. By the time she'd parked the car and located Emer's office block, it was almost five thirty.

It had been easier than she'd expected to find the building again. She'd remembered the large sign outside, informing her this was the head office for a company called Pitman and Pace. Dee had simply entered the company name into her phone's internet browser and let Google Maps guide her to the office block. She hadn't heard of Pitman and Pace before, but the information she'd read online informed her they were 'one of the world's pre-eminent law firms'.

A row of women, all perfectly made up and dressed in matching red and blue jackets, beamed at Dee from behind a chrome and glass counter.

'Good afternoon,' one of them chirped. 'How may I help you this afternoon?'

'I'm trying to contact one of your employees,' Dee said. 'She's my cousin and I need to speak with her urgently.'

'Her name?'

'Emer Doran.'

'One moment, please.' The woman looked from Dee to the slimline laptop in front of her and started tapping the keyboard.

One moment turned into several as the woman's smiled slipped into a frown.

'I'm sorry,' she said, looking up from the laptop. 'Could you repeat the name for me?'

'Emer Doran,' Dee said. 'D-O-R-A-N. I don't think she's a permanent staff member. She's on a short-term contract.'

'Okay.' The woman nodded, looking relieved, 'One moment, please.'

Again, the moment dragged on.

'I can't seem to locate her,' the woman said eventually. 'Can you give me another few minutes?'

She picked up a phone and dialled a number.

'Hello, Carly? It's Tracey on reception. Would you mind asking Gerry to pop down for a moment?'

The conversation continued for some time, but Dee wasn't able to catch any more of it, because the woman had turned her head to the side and lowered her voice to a whisper. When she hung up, she asked Dee to take a seat and told her someone would be with her shortly.

With a perfectly manicured hand, she gestured to a row of sofas several miles away on the other side of the lobby.

'I don't understand,' Dee said. 'What's the problem?'

'Oh, it's not a problem.' The woman smiled so hard Dee reckoned her face must be aching. 'I can't find your cousin's name on our list of employees. But you said she's a temp, so that might explain why her name's not on the system yet. Gerry will sort it out for you. Don't worry.'

Dee traversed the marble floor, sat down on a pale grey sofa that was surprisingly comfortable, and waited. Less than five minutes later, a tall, dark-haired man came through the barriers that separated the lobby from the rest of the building and walked briskly across to where Dee was sitting.

'Gerry Boyd,' he said. 'Head of Security. I understand you're looking for your cousin?'

'That's right,' Dee said, wondering why the hell the Head of Security had been called to deal with her.

'And your cousin's name is Emer Doran?'

'Yes. I'm sorry, are you going to tell me what's going on here?'

'I think you've got the wrong building, madam.'

'Absolutely not,' Dee said. 'This is where she works. I saw her walk in here with my own eyes. I'm not making it up. We said goodbye outside and I watched her walk into this building right here.'

'How long ago was that?'

'Last week.'

'That's not possible,' Gerry said. 'I've checked all our records. No one called Emer Doran has ever worked for Pitman and Pace. Not in this building, or at any of our other sites either.'

'She's a contractor,' Dee said. 'Working on some sort of IT project.'

'That may be true,' Gerry said. 'But she's never done that here. I've checked all our records, including the names of every contractor we've had working here over the last six months. Whoever you thought you saw coming in here that day, it wasn't your cousin. It's simply not possible.'

Twenty-two

Emer was alone in the house. Her mother had gone to Dublin for a shopping weekend. Robert was out at a meeting and wouldn't be home until later that night. She'd thought that finally knowing the truth would make a difference. But ever since finding out that Annie Holden wasn't Kitty, Emer had felt more adrift than ever. She knew she had to accept what she'd been told. But she couldn't let go of how she'd felt that day on the London Underground. The moment of absolute certainty when she'd realised she was looking at her sister. She still didn't know how she had got it so wrong. How could you believe something so completely when it wasn't true?

Earlier, Robert had tried to talk to her, find out what her plans were. When Emer told him she didn't have any plans yet, he'd offered to speak to 'some people' and see if he could find her some short-term work. Not for the first time, Emer wondered how a man as kind as her stepfather had ended up with someone as selfish and self-centred as her mother. But maybe that was the only way it worked. Because she couldn't think of anyone else who would be able to put up with her mother as patiently as Robert had done over the years. And despite her mother's difficult personality, it was clear Robert adored her. A devotion Ursula took entirely for granted.

In the kitchen, Emer poured herself a glass of wine and carried it into the sitting room. Her laptop lay open on the sofa, Annie Holden's face filling the screen. Annie's eyes that looked so like Kitty's. Emer had spent the last hour reading everything she could find about Annie. There wasn't a lot, but she hoped seeing the facts of the woman's life, laid out in black and white, would help her to accept this new truth. So far, it hadn't worked. Because each time she looked at Annie's photo, the doubts crept back in. No matter how many times she told herself the facts spoke for themselves, she wasn't able to completely believe it.

Shutting down her laptop, she went over to Robert's stereo – an old style Bang and Olufsen stereo with top-class speakers. Her stepfather had one of the best collections of vinyl Emer had ever seen. Earlier in the week, she had unearthed his John McCormack albums and was planning to work her way through them over the next few days.

She chose a record and sat back down. Pushing her laptop to one side, she reached for the photo album on the table in front of her. With McCormack in the background, singing about his love down by the Salley Gardens, Emer flicked through the pages, looking at the different snapshot moments from her family's life. Despite being a rubbish mother, Ursula had loved taking photos of her children. Emer was still young when she'd worked out the photos were a pretence – her mother's way of trying to demonstrate she was an adequate and loving parent.

The first few pages contained photos from 'before' – when Emer still had a sister who she loved and who'd loved her back. She was already familiar with all these photos. She'd scanned the images and stored them on her laptop so she could see them whenever she wanted to. But looking at them on a screen was never quite the same as looking at the print versions of the images.

Too quickly, these pages ended, replaced by the rest of her life – the lonely, unhappy time that had begun the day Kitty drowned and had never really ended. Looking at her face in the photos, Emer imagined she could see the changes. A sadness behind the eyes and a hardness around the lips that weren't evident in the earlier photos.

She flicked back and forth through the pages, spending longer each time on the earlier pages and the photos of Kitty. On one page, there was a space where someone had removed a photo. Emer rubbed the blank rectangle where the photo should be, trying to remember what had been there. But the image wouldn't come to her, and after a moment she gave up and turned to the next page.

She lifted her glass of wine, then put it back down again without drinking from it. She was tired of being like this. Tired of feeling crappy all the time, of messing up every good thing that ever happened to her. Tired of holding on to the past and refusing to move on with her life. She'd messed things up with Nikki, but there was still time to fix it if she really wanted. First thing tomorrow, she would call their family doctor and ask him to refer her for counselling.

The decision triggered an unfamiliar surge of optimism. She could do this. Get sober, get sorted, get Nikki back. Her very own three-step programme to recovery. But she could only do if she accepted, once and for all, that Kitty was gone.

She closed the album, took her glass into the kitchen and poured the wine down the sink. Pleased with herself, she went upstairs to brush her teeth and get ready for bed. She had just switched off her bedroom light when the landline started to ring. Whoever was calling, they wouldn't be looking for her, so she decided not to bother answering it. After ten rings, the phone stopped and Emer snuggled down under her duvet. Her eyes closed. Like it always did, her mind started drifting back to that night in the hotel. Tonight, she withdrew from the memory and forced herself to think about something else. Like getting Nikki back.

Her body relaxed, her breathing grew deeper. And then the phone started ringing again. Grumbling and cursing, Emer threw back the duvet and ran to answer it.

'Hello?'

'Ursula?' A woman's voice. English accent.

'I'm afraid she's not here right now,' Emer said. 'Can I take a message?'

'It's actually her daughter, Emer, I'm looking for.'

Something was wrong. She could feel it, a tingling sensation down her arms, an icy shiver down her spine. She should hang up. End the call and go back to bed, safe in the illusion that all was well in her world. She thought back to earlier, her decision to let the past go and move forward with her life. Somehow, she knew if she continued with this call, none of that would happen. But even as she thought this, she knew she didn't have a choice.

'This is Emer,' she said. 'Who are you?'

Twenty-three

Every Friday night, Dee and her neighbours got together to share pizza and catch up with each other. Tonight, it was just Dee and Ella. Tom had gone to Ireland a few days earlier to visit his parents and he'd taken Jake with him. The two women sat out on Dee's deck, sharing a bottle of wine and watching the night creep in across the sky after the sun had disappeared beneath the horizon.

'Tom and Jake are back tomorrow evening,' Ella said. 'We were wondering if you'd like to come over for dinner on Sunday.'

'That would be lovely,' Dee said. 'You sure you want to, though? Won't you be busy packing up?'

They were leaving on Wednesday. Five days from now. Impossible to imagine.

'I've done most of it,' Ella said. 'We really want to cook dinner for you, Dee. You're like family to us. Please? It would mean a lot. To Jake, especially.'

'In that case,' Dee said, 'how can I say no?'

She would have if she'd been able to. The thought of sitting around a table, chatting and having to pretend everything was fine, was unbearable. But Ella was right. It was important they did this for Jake, which meant Dee would have to go through with it.

'I'm going to miss all this,' Ella said, gesturing at the beach.

'No you won't,' Dee said. 'Canada's meant to be stunning, isn't it?'

'I guess. But we'll be living in the city, so we won't wake up to this view every morning.'

'Are you okay about the move?'

It hadn't occurred to Dee, until now, that moving to Canada might not be something Ella wanted.

'I am now,' Ella said. 'I didn't want to move, at first. You know how much I love living here. But now I've got used to the idea, I'm excited.'

'Of course you are. It's a wonderful opportunity. And God knows you deserve a fresh start after everything you've been through.'

'There are days I don't think I deserve anything,' Ella said.

Dee knew she was referring to the incident twelve years earlier that had driven Ella to run from her old life, turning up here in Eastbourne pretending to be someone else. But the person she'd been running from had found her eventually, with near-fatal consequences for Ella and Jake.

'You'll continue with your counselling when you move?' Dee asked.

'Definitely. Neil – that's who I see at the moment – he's given me some recommendations. I'm not too worried about that.'

'So what are you worried about?'

'How I'm going to cope without you. I still can't believe we won't be able to see each other whenever we feel like it. I'm going to miss you so much, Dee.'

'I'll miss you, too.' Understatement of the bloody year. Dee's heart already felt shredded, and they hadn't even gone yet. 'But we've got Skype and FaceTime. And I'm already planning my first visit. I'll probably visit so much you'll be sick of seeing me.'

'Never.' Ella smiled.

She looked like she wanted to say more, but Dee cut her off. Unable to bear it.

'Will you work when you're there?'

'At some point I'd like to get back to my music, maybe do a Masters. But my priority at the beginning will be getting us all settled.'

On the table, Dee's mobile started ringing.

'Take it if you want to,' Ella said. 'You know I won't mind.'

'It's Leonard,' Dee said, diverting the call. 'I left him a message earlier because there's something I need to speak to him about. But actually, I'd like to pick your brains first. If you don't mind?'

'Anything that will take my mind off packing,' Ella said. 'I'm all ears.'

Dee told Ella everything that had happened with Emer, starting with their first meeting in Gordon's Wine Bar, right up to her visit to Emer's workplace earlier that day.

'So now I'm thinking, what if Emer was right all along?' Dee said.

'About Annie being her sister?' Ella frowned. 'You can't really believe that, Dee.'

'I know it sounds crazy,' Dee said. 'But what if I'm right? And even if that's not what's going on, something is. Where the hell has Emer disappeared to? You know, I'm really tempted to fly to Ireland so I can find her myself and ask her what the hell is going on. I feel as if I'm the victim of someone's practical joke.'

'Isn't it possible you made a mistake?' Ella said.

'I know what I saw.'

'You know what you *think* you saw. A photo of two girls that looked a bit like the girls in the photo your cousin sent you?'

'More than a bit.'

Even to her ears, Dee sounded pig-headed, but she couldn't help it. In that moment, she'd been so certain.

'Well, so what if they looked like your cousins?' Ella said. 'You've already told me that Annie looks like Emer's sister. It makes sense she'd have looked like her when she was a kid as well.'

'Maybe,' Dee said. 'But what about Emer? Why did nobody at her work know who she was? And why has her phone been disconnected?'

'It's Canary Wharf,' Ella said. 'I've got completely lost every time I've been there. Isn't there a chance you simply went to the wrong building?'

'Are you suggesting I'm losing my marbles?'

'I wouldn't dare.' Ella smiled. 'But I think you could be overcomplicating things. I know what you're like, Dee. You want to fix things. So when your cousin came into your life asking for help, of course you said yes. And of course that big Dee Doran heart wanted to fix your grieving cousin. As for believing Annie really could be someone else, surely that's my fault?'

'How do you work that out?'

'When you first met me, I was pretending to be someone I wasn't. Maybe that's made you more suspicious of people than you'd be otherwise.'

'I don't think that's the case,' Dee said, 'but maybe you're right. The truth is, I don't know what to think.'

'Well I'll tell you one thing,' Ella said, 'Taking on another person's identity is a tough thing to pull off. Changing your name and having to forget every bit of your past life, cutting ties with people you care about… it's hard work, Dee. There's an emotional aspect to it that saps your energy and makes you doubt yourself, all the time. If Annie really is your cousin, then she's got a damn good reason for not wanting anyone to find out. She's running away from something, and if you're going to pursue this, you'd better make sure you know what you're dealing with.'

—

After Ella left, Dee was too restless to go to bed. She opened her laptop and checked her emails. On the train back from London earlier, she'd sent Emer an email. So far, Emer hadn't replied. But there was an email from Shay Flaherty. Dee had emailed him earlier as well, telling him they needed to speak. He'd replied with a phone number, asking her to call him tomorrow morning.

Opening Facebook, Dee checked Emer's account, thinking she might have posted an update. Again, there was nothing. Dee knew she should let it go, forget about Emer and Annie and Kitty and focus on the book she was writing. Emer clearly didn't want to stay in touch and, if Dee had an ounce of good sense, she would accept that decision and move on with her life. But good sense had never been Dee's strongest point.

Giving up on the internet, she went into the room that used to be her mother's office. In the months following her mother's death, Dee had spent a lot of time in this room. It had been her mother's private space, where she came when she wanted some peace and quiet. Opening the door now, Dee realised with a shock that it had been months since she'd last come in here. The room smelled musty and everything was covered in a layer of dust. Including the old address book on the desk in the middle of the room.

Dee sat down in the chair her mother used to sit in each day to do the *Times* crossword. Opening the address book, she flicked through it until she found the name she was looking for. Dee's father might have stopped speaking to his brother, but nothing in the world would have stopped her mother keeping tabs on his family over the years. Ursula Doran's name, address and telephone number were all here, recorded in the neat handwriting Dee remembered so well.

It was only ten o'clock. Most people, Dee reasoned, would still be up at this time. There was a landline phone on the desk. Using this, Dee dialled the phone number in the address book and waited. She listened as the phone the other end rang. Ten rings later, she got a recorded message, asking her to leave her name and a number.

She hung up without speaking. Then, a few seconds later, changed her mind. Redialling the number, she waited, preparing the message she was going to leave when she got the answering service. Except this time, someone picked up.

'Hello?'

'Ursula?' Dee said.

'I'm afraid she's not here right now,' the woman said. 'Can I take a message?'

'It's actually her daughter, Emer, I'm looking for,' Dee said.

'This is Emer.'

'Emer, thank goodness. It's Dee. I've been trying to call you the last few days but your phone's been disconnected.

You didn't tell me you were going back to Ireland. Is everything okay?'

'Excuse me, I think there's been some mistake. What did you say your name was?'

'Dee. Your cousin.'

'And how am I meant to know you?'

'Because we've met,' Dee said. 'In London.'

But she already knew it was pointless. This woman sounded different. Her voice was deeper, her accent stronger.

'I think I must have dialled the wrong number,' she said. 'Sorry.'

'Hang on,' the woman said. 'You said your name is Dee?'

'Dee Doran. Your cousin.'

'I do have a cousin called Dee,' the woman said. 'But I've never met her. Which means she wouldn't be calling here asking to speak to me, pretending we'd already been in touch. So maybe you can start again. And this time, tell me who the hell you really are.'

Twenty-four

'I doesn't make any sense,' Emer said.

'But you were in London in July?' Dee said. 'And that incident on the London Underground really happened?'

'That's right.' Emer could still feel it. The shock of recognition when the woman had looked up from her book. 'But it's not her. My stepfather hired a private detective who told him she's definitely not Kitty.'

'What else did you stepfather tell you?'

'He said she's not Kitty. Her name is Annie Holden. She's an artist from Sussex.'

'Which is right,' Dee said. 'But it wasn't a private detective who found this out, Emer. It was me.'

Emer didn't reply, because she had no idea what to say.

'Are you okay?' Dee asked.

'Not really,' Emer said. 'If what you're telling me is the truth, then that means Robert has been lying to me.'

'When did your stepfather tell you about Annie?'

'Tuesday,' Emer said. 'Why?'

'On Monday, I went for lunch with the woman who was pretending to be you. That's when I told her that Annie Holden wasn't Kitty. Then the next day – the very next day – your stepfather told you the same thing.'

'So the woman who was pretending to be me,' Emer said, 'she was the detective hired by Robert?'

'I don't think so,' Dee said. 'Why would a private detective need me to do their dirty work for them?'

'Robert didn't want you involved,' Emer said. 'That's why he hired the detective. But maybe she contacted you without him knowing about it.'

Or maybe Robert had been spinning her a load of bullshit. It wasn't cold in the house but Emer was shivering. Her body was reacting faster than her brain to what she was being told.

'How do I know you're telling the truth?' she asked. Because now she thought about it, the person making this phone call could be anyone.

'You don't,' Dee said. 'But what possible reason could I have for making any of this up?'

Good question.

'And this woman,' Emer said. 'She sent you a photo of me and Kitty?'

'You were standing on a street somewhere,' Dee said. 'You had your arms around each other's shoulders and you were both smiling. It's a lovely photo.'

Emer remembered the empty space in the photo album. And she remembered the photo that used to be there. There were only two people who could have removed that photo – Robert or her mother.

'I found another photo of you both in Annie's house,' Dee said.

'My mother's idea of playing happy families,' Emer said. 'Taking photos of us. Most of the time, we hated it. Although we never told her that. We always played along, because we were too scared not to. There were always a lot of photos. It would have been easy for Kitty to take one and keep it for herself. No one would notice one photo was missing.'

Emer felt giddy, light-headed. Was it really possible that she'd been right all along?

'You really think Kitty's still alive?' she said.

'I'm not sure,' Dee said. 'But I think she might be, yes. Do you remember a girl called Lucy Ryan?'

'Of course I remember Lucy. What about her?'

She remembered other things too. Lucy and Kitty whispering secrets to each other, planning something in the weeks leading up to Lucy's disappearance. Lucy's father, banging on their front door, screaming for Kitty to come out and tell him what had happened to his daughter. Mum, Kitty and Emer cowering in the kitchen, hands over their ears, praying for him to go away. Her parents arguing. Her father telling her mother they didn't have a choice. A choice about what?

The girls were there that night.

Is that what her mother had said, or had Emer misheard her? She couldn't trust anything, not even her own memories.

Outside, she heard Robert's car pulling into the driveway. He'd been like a father to her. Better than her own father had ever been. Solid, reliable, calm. A positive presence in her life. If there was anyone she could trust, it was Robert. Wasn't it?

'Dee, I've got to go. But first, tell me why you asked me about Lucy.'

'It's complicated,' Dee said. 'And I'd rather not say anything until I'm sure. I'm going back to London tomorrow to try to speak to Annie again. I'll let you know how I get on.'

'Brilliant, thanks. I'll speak to you tomorrow evening.'

She hung up, just as the front door opened.

'Hello?'

She heard the steady sound of his footsteps walking down the hall towards the kitchen. She crossed the room, so she could be closer to the knife rack. It was ridiculous to think of taking one of those knives and using it against him. But everything felt ridiculous and wrong suddenly.

'Emer.' He smiled when he saw her. 'I wasn't sure you'd be still up. How's your evening been?'

'Weird,' she said.

'Weird how?'

He walked over to the fridge and took out a beer. Only one. Every night, the same routine. A single beer at the end of his working day. Except who worked until almost eleven o'clock on a Friday evening?

'Where have you been?'

She watched as he carefully poured the beer into his glass before answering.

'Dinner with some of the people I'm hoping will invest in my campaign.' He took a sip of his beer. 'Ah. That's better. They're a boring lot, but schmoozing is an important part of my job, as you well know. So, what happened tonight that was so weird?'

He crossed the room until he was standing opposite her, on the other side of the oversized island in the oversized kitchen.

'A woman phoned the house.' Emer watched him closely to see how he reacted. 'She said she was my cousin.'

'What cousin?'

'You remember, my uncle Frank's daughter, Dee. The journalist.'

'And she just called tonight out of the blue? Any idea what she wanted?'

He took another sip of his beer. Was it her imagination, or did he seem to be drinking more quickly than normal?

'Both her parents have died,' Emer said. 'I think she's lonely.'

'Doesn't she have family of her own?'

'I don't know.'

She hadn't asked Dee any of the questions she should have asked. Instead, the entire conversation had focused on both women trying to understand who had contacted Dee, and why they'd done it.

Robert cleared his throat.

'So let me get this straight. Your cousin – someone you've never spoken to until this evening – phoned because she's lonely, or she's missing her dead parents, or whatever. But she didn't actually tell you anything about herself? Are you sure it wasn't some sort of prank call, Emer? People can be very cruel, you know.'

'It wasn't a prank,' Emer said. 'She knew too much about me and my family.'

Even as she said this, she started to have doubts. Because why should she trust some stranger instead of Robert, who had loved her and taken care of her better than her own father ever had?

'Emer…'

'What?'

'I'm a high-profile politician, love. You need to be careful when strangers call the house. There are all sorts of people who'd love nothing more than to dig up a bit of dirt on me.'

'But if you've nothing to hide,' Emer said, 'then you don't need to worry, do you?'

He drained his beer and put the bottle down carefully on the island.

'What's that supposed to mean?'

'Nothing,' she said. 'Just what I said. I don't think you need to worry, that's all.'

Robert opened the fridge door and took out another beer.

'Friday night treat.' He winked at Emer. 'Don't tell your mother. This can be our little secret.'

Apart from the second beer, he was exactly the same as always. Solid and reliable. If he was freaked out by hearing that Dee had called the house, he was doing a good job of hiding it. Then again, he was a politician. Hiding what he really thought was a key requirement of his job.

'She had a photo,' Emer said.

'What do you mean?'

'Dee had a photo of myself and Kitty when we were young girls.'

'So?'

'So how did she get hold of it?'

'Jesus, Emer, how the hell do I know? She was probably lying.'

'She wasn't lying. She described it in detail. It's a photo from one of the albums in the sitting room. Except when I was looking through the album earlier, that particular photo was missing.'

'This is getting ridiculous.' Robert took another sip from the bottle before he continued. 'This woman – what's her name?'

'Dee.'

'Right. So she called tonight and said hi, I'm your long-lost cousin and I'm calling now because my parents are dead and I want to know more about the rest of my father's family. Is that right?'

Emer nodded.

'Did you exchange phone numbers?'

'Well she already had our number,' Emer said. 'She called here, remember? But yes, we did exchange numbers. I gave her my mobile number and she gave me hers.'

'Where does she live?'

'Eastbourne.'

'Okay.' Robert nodded. 'Shouldn't be too difficult to find out if there really is a Dee Doran who lives in Eastbourne.'

Suddenly, Emer didn't want to be here. She needed time to process everything she'd learned tonight and work out who she could trust. Robert or Dee. Or neither of them.

'You're right.' Emer pretended to yawn. 'I'll look her up tomorrow. Right now, I'm exhausted. I think I'll go to bed if you don't mind.'

'Sleep tight.' Robert lifted his glass in a mock salutation. '*Sláinte.*'

She was midway up the stairs when she knew she couldn't let it go. Turning around, she went back down the stairs and into the kitchen, stopping just inside the door, so she could leave quickly if she needed to.

'I nearly forgot,' she said. 'You told me the woman I saw in London definitely wasn't Kitty.'

'That's right.' He sounded guarded now, less relaxed.

'Because that's what the private detective told you?'

'Yes, because it's what he told me. How else would I have found out?'

Robert's face had hardened and when he spoke, his voice was razor sharp, devoid of any trace of kindness. 'What are you playing at, Emer? There's something you're not telling me. You'd better not be playing me for a fool, or there will be consequences.'

'Is that a threat?'

'Excuse me?'

'You heard me.'

'How dare you.' Robert slammed his bottle on the marble worktop. 'You ungrateful little so-and-so. I have done nothing but protect you and love you and support you ever since you and your mother moved in with me. You haven't always made it easy, but I've done my very best. For you to stand here now, in my house, and accuse me of... actually.' He took a step towards her. It took all her strength to stand her ground. 'What exactly are you accusing me of, Emer?'

'Lying.'

'Get out of my sight.' Then, when she didn't move, he roared at her: 'Now! Get the hell away from me, you hear? I've had a long day and the last thing I need right now is to have to deal with your craziness. Your mother's right, you know. You need help, Emer. Proper, professional help.'

She should have left it, but she was angry now, and she'd never been very good at being sensible when she was angry.

'You lied,' she said. 'Or if you didn't lie, then the detective you hired wasn't very good at their job. Because Kitty's still alive, Robert. That's why Dee called tonight. To tell me she'd found Kitty.'

'Bullshit.'

Suddenly, she couldn't bear the thought of being in the house with him a moment longer. She stepped back into the hallway, grabbed her car keys from the table and ran outside.

'Emer, don't you dare run off on me. Come back here this instant.'

She heard his footsteps, hard and fast on the stripped wooden floorboards as he came after her. She pulled open the front door, ran outside and climbed into her car. Fumbling with the keys, she managed to get them into the ignition and switch the engine on, just as he reached the car. She released the handbrake and the car shot forward. The last thing she saw as she turned out of the driveway, was Robert's silhouette in the rear-view mirror, shaking his fist in the air as he shouted at her to turn around.

Twenty-five

June 1997

The front door was locked. They'd walked around the house, trying to find a way in. Kitty had been thinking of giving up when she noticed one of the kitchen windows was open.

'Here.'

It was an old sash window and, when she pushed it, nothing happened.

'Let's leave it and go home,' Lucy said. 'We shouldn't be here.'

But Kitty wasn't going home. She tried the window again, using every bit of energy she had, and it moved. Not far, but enough so that she could wiggle through the gap.

'Come on.'

She jumped onto the ledge and squeezed through the small space. She went head-first, half her body dangling inside the window, half out.

'Push me,' she said. 'Hold on to my feet and shove me forward.'

Lucy grabbed her legs and pushed and suddenly she was falling. She landed hard, pain shooting up her hands and arms as they hit the ground first. She jumped up, ignoring the pain, and went to help Lucy.

'What now?' Lucy asked, when they were both inside.

It was dark and smelly in here. The door was closed but Kitty could hear voices in other parts of the house. Taking Lucy's hand, she went across to the door and slowly opened it.

Light from the hallway flooded into the kitchen and the noise of people speaking and laughing grew louder. She could hear music now too, and the clink of ice in glasses.

They crept forward into a hallway that was bigger than Kitty's entire house, with high ceilings and a sweeping staircase that curved up through the house. Different rooms led off the hallway. All the doors, except one, were open. The noises Kitty could hear were coming from behind the closed door.

Lucy's eyes were like plates they were so wide as she looked around. Kitty put her finger on Lucy's lips, warning her to stay quiet. Because she could hear something else. This noise was coming from one of the rooms upstairs.

She moved towards the sweeping staircase, drawn to the sound. The need to see what was up there was far greater than the need to stay safe and get the hell out of there.

'No,' Lucy whispered.

Ignoring her, Kitty put her foot on the first step and started climbing. She was halfway up when she realised the sound was a woman crying.

'I don't want to,' the woman was saying. 'Please. I'm begging you. No.'

There was something about the woman's voice, a familiarity that Kitty couldn't place no matter how hard she tried. She continued up the stairs, ignoring the voice inside her head, telling her to turn around and get the hell out of here before it was too late. She'd just reached the top of the stairs when the woman started screaming. Kitty froze.

It was dark up here, apart from a sliver of yellow light beneath a closed door at the end of the corridor. That's where they were. The woman and whoever was hurting her.

Kitty knew she should keep going, walk to the end of the corridor, open the door and rescue the woman. But she couldn't move. The sounds coming from the room mixed with other sounds in her head. The ones Mr O'Brien and her mother had been making when they were in the kitchen.

The door swung open, and someone was standing there. A man. Behind him, there were three other men in the room and two women. One of them was lying on the bed, crying. The other woman was standing at the end of the bed, her face hidden behind a video camera. The light from the overhead bulb was reflected in the shiny tip of her black, high-heeled shoe.

'Hey!'

The man in the doorway had seen her.

Kitty turned around and ran. She could hear him shouting at her to stop, chasing after her. His footsteps were loud and heavy on the bare floorboards. She skidded down the stairs and raced across the hallway towards the front door that Lucy was trying to open.

'Hurry up!' Kitty said.

The door was bolted. Lucy was trying to pull the bolt back but nothing was happening. Behind her, Kitty could hear the man getting closer. Pushing Lucy out of the way, she grabbed the bolt and pulled it with every bit of strength she had. At first nothing happened. The bolt didn't budge. Groaning, she put everything she had into tugging it one final time. It moved. Just a little at first, then a little more, until suddenly the bolt was pulled back and she was able to open the door.

A flood of cold air hit her as she raced outside, along the driveway, through the gates and onto the road. There wasn't a pavement so they ran along the edge of the road. When Lucy tried to stop, Kitty grabbed her hand and tugged her forward.

'Please, Kitty. Stop. Just for a minute.'

Lucy had never been good at running. Not like Kitty, who was able to run faster than any of the other girls in her class. And most of the boys too.

'I can't breathe.'

There was a whiny tone to Lucy's voice that Kitty couldn't bear. She wanted to press her hands over her ears and tell Lucy to shut up. Shut up, shut up, shut up so Kitty could think. But she wouldn't shut up, because she never did. Not even now, after they'd seen what they'd seen and they were running away from it before the men caught them.

Behind them, somewhere in the dark night, Kitty could hear them. The men's voices, shouting to each other as they scanned the countryside, searching for the two girls who'd run out of the house. The roar of a car engine as it started up. She knew the men weren't going to stop until they'd found the two girls who shouldn't have been there.

Her stomach heaved. Vomit rose up her throat but she swallowed it down. Images she didn't want to think about stuck inside her head. If she had a knife right now she'd slice her head open and scoop it all out until there was nothing left.

'Was that sex?' Lucy asked. 'Is that what they were doing up there?'

'Don't be stupid.'

'I'm not stupid.'

'Yes you are.' She felt the rage burning through her. 'Shut up.'

'You shut up,' Kitty snarled. 'Or I'll make you.'

'Why are you being so mean to me?' Lucy said.

'Because you're stupid! You're a stupid little crybaby who never stops moaning. Your parents let you get away with it because they spoil you and they're scared of doing anything to upset you, so they let you do whatever you want.'

'That's not true!'

Lucy shoved her and she stumbled backwards, just managing not to fall.

Vaguely, she was aware of the car coming towards them. Flashes of light illuminating the countryside in the distance. The rumble of the engine, getting closer.

'My parents love me, that's all. But you wouldn't know what that's like, would you? Your mother has sex with Mr O'Brien and your father's a loser who spends all his free time in the pub. And I know she hits you because Emer's told Maeve that your mother doesn't love you, not even a tiny little bit.'

The rage roared up inside her, she couldn't help it. She ran forward, screaming loudly, and shoved her hands into Lucy's stomach. Lucy flew back and, just for a moment, it was the best feeling to watch her friend fall and know she'd pushed Lucy harder than Lucy had managed to push her.

But the moment passed. Bright lights appeared around the bend in the road. Lucy's body, captured in the lights so she looked like an angel as she fell. A thud as her body landed on the ground and the startling, shocking collision of noises. The roar of the car's engine, the screeching of the brakes, and the unforgettable crunching sound of a body being crushed under the weight of the car.

Twenty-six

That night, Dee barely slept. Each time she closed her eyes, her mind raced off in multiple directions, trying to make sense of everything. As the first fingers of grey light started creeping into her bedroom, she gave up on sleep and got up, groggy and grumpy. Over a pot of coffee, she made a plan. She was going to go back to London to find Annie, and she wasn't leaving until she got some answers to the questions that had kept her awake during the long night.

An hour later, she was at the train station. Even on Saturday, the price of a return ticket to London was jaw-droppingly expensive. At least, Dee consoled herself, taking the train was faster and less painful than driving into the city.

Following her long conversation with Emer on the phone last night, Dee had sat down on her sitting room floor with a sheet of A3 paper, creating a mind map that gradually filled the page. This was how she'd always liked to work. Noting down everything she knew about a story. Then, once she had all the facts written down, she was able to see the bits of information still missing.

The facts were easy enough. On 5 June 1997, Lucy Ryan said good night to her parents and went to bed. The following morning, when Lucy's mother went to wake her daughter, Lucy's bed was empty. Her daughter was gone. To this day, Lucy's sister, and the Guards investigating her disappearance, didn't know what had happened to her.

Three weeks later, on 27 June 1997, Kitty Doran disappeared, supposedly drowning in the sea while on holiday with her family in the west of Ireland. Her body was never discovered but a coroner's inquiry concluded that Kitty had drowned. According to her parents, Kitty had always been afraid of water and had never learned to swim. Shortly after Kitty drowned, her father walked out on the family and was never seen again.

Fast forward twenty-three years to the day Emer saw a woman on the London Underground that looked like her dead sister. The woman couldn't be Kitty because she had a different name, and a different family. But she also had a photo of Kitty and Emer as young girls in the collage upstairs in her house.

At some point after Emer had seen Annie on the train that day, someone pretending to be Emer had contacted Dee, asking her to find out if there was any possibility that Annie Holden could be Kitty Doran.

Those were the facts. Alongside them, Dee had noted down her list of questions:

What happened to Lucy Ryan?

Why was Kitty's body never found?

Why did Eamon Doran abandon his wife and remaining child, and where did he go?

Did Annie actually have a photo of Kitty or Emer? Or had Dee made a mistake?

If it wasn't a mistake, did that prove that Annie was Kitty?

Who was the woman who'd contacted Dee, and why did she do it?

And, importantly, how did she know about Emer seeing Annie Holden on the London Underground?

With no way of finding answers to the last two questions, Dee decided to focus on the things she could do. Like getting back inside Annie's house and taking another look at the photo of the two girls.

On the train, she sent Emer a text, repeating what she'd said on the phone last night – that she hoped they'd stay in touch and she'd love to meet Emer in person sometime soon. When her phone pinged a few seconds later, she assumed it was Emer's reply. But when she checked her texts, the message was from Ella, reminding Dee about the dinner invitation for tomorrow evening. Their last meal together before Ella and her family left for Canada.

Looking forward to it x

The reply sent, Dee put her phone back in her bag and spent the rest of the journey looking out the window and trying not to think about how soon it was until they left.

To get to Annie's house, Dee had to change trains at Whitechapel for the East London line to Wapping. But the gallery was close to Whitechapel station, so it made sense to go there first just in case that's where Annie was this morning.

Coming out of the underground station, Dee called Shay Flaherty.

'Dee,' he said. 'Your message yesterday intrigued me. What was it you wanted to talk to me about?'

'What would you say if I told you there's a chance Kitty Doran is still alive?'

'You think that's a possibility?'

Dee updated him on everything that had happened since they last spoke. When she'd finished, he let out a low whistle.

'That's some story you've got there, Dee.'

'It's only a story if Annie really is Kitty,' Dee said.

'I always knew something wasn't right about that,' Shay said. 'I was never able to prove anything, but I felt it. If I'd stayed in Galway, maybe I'd have continued to look into it. But that was around the time I got the job at the *Irish Times*. Assistant political correspondent. My dream job, at the time. Twenty-something years later I'm still in Dublin, still writing about politics.'

'You're the political editor now,' Dee said. She remembered seeing his job title on the paper's website. 'I'm guessing that means you know a thing or two about Robert O'Brien?'

'Squeaky Clean O'Brien,' Shay said. 'Future leader of our great country, if you believe what people are saying about him.'

'And you?' Dee said. 'What do you think?'

'I think no one's as clean as O'Brien pretends to be,' Shay said. 'Although if he's got any dark secrets, he's done a damn good job of keeping them hidden. The country adores him.'

'He married Kitty's mother two years after Kitty drowned,' Dee said. 'How did he manage that if she was already married to someone else?'

'Ireland's no different to any other country,' Shay said. 'Even back then, O'Brien was well-connected. I assume he pulled a few strings and got the first marriage annulled. Word on the ground is they were seeing each other long before her husband disappeared. Although to be fair, that's exactly the sort of thing people would say. I've never found anything to prove that's true. Why? You think it's relevant to what happened to Kitty?'

'Probably not,' Dee said. 'I'm just thinking aloud. If Kitty really didn't drown that day, then someone went to a lot of trouble to pretend she did.'

'So what do we do now?' Shay said.

'You mean you'll help me?'

He laughed.

'Fine Gael's current leader will be stepping down next month,' Shay said. 'At the moment, O'Brien's the number one candidate to take over. If that happens, and the party win the next election – which everyone thinks they will – then he's in line to become the country's next Taoiseach. I don't like the man. I think he's a fraud. So if I can find something that proves I'm right, about him and about what happened to Kitty, that would make me a very happy man indeed.'

'And if I'm wrong?'

'No shame being wrong,' Shay said. 'You could be right too, don't forget.'

'I'm going to try to speak to Annie today,' Dee said. 'I'll let you know how I get on.'

'Great. In the meantime, I'll do a bit of digging this side. Lucy Ryan's parents are dead, but her sister's still alive. Maybe I'll see if she'll talk to me.'

They said goodbye, and Dee ended the call. By now, she was on Deancross Street and she could see the gallery up ahead. When she went inside, it was clear from Claire's frosty reception that she wasn't too happy to see Dee back again so soon.

'Annie's not here,' she said.

'Any idea how I can get hold of her?'

'Listen to me,' Claire said. 'Annie's told me who you really are. You're a journalist, aren't you? If I'd known, I would never have let you anywhere near Annie. I genuinely don't understand what you're playing at. Don't you think her family has already been through enough?'

'I have no idea what you're talking about.'

'You can lie all you want,' Claire said. 'But if you've come here trying to get me to dish up gossip about Annie, you might as well leave. Because hell will freeze over before I tell you anything about her.'

'Annie's mother looked you up on the internet,' Claire went on. 'She found lots of Dee Morrisons, but none of them were you. But she also found a journalist called Dee Doran who'd been married to someone called Billy Morrison. That's you, isn't it?'

Dee recognised a brick wall when she hit one. Leaving the gallery, she used her knowledge of the area to walk from Deancross Street through Shadwell into Wapping.

She didn't know what she'd expected when she got to Annie's house. Maybe that Annie would refuse to open the door, or that there'd be no one at home and Dee would have to wait. But when she rang the doorbell, she hardly had to wait at all. The door was opened by a man in his thirties. Tall and thin with dark curly hair, heavy-framed glasses and a goatee beard, he looked like a typical east London hipster. Which possibly explained Dee's instant aversion to him, before he even opened his mouth.

'Can I help you?' he asked, looking expectantly at Dee.

'I'm looking for Annie,' Dee said.

'Who?'

'Annie Holden. She lives here.'

The man frowned.

'Annie? Sorry. You must have got the wrong house.'

'Bullshit,' Dee said. 'I was here yesterday in this very house talking to Annie's mother.'

'Hold on a second.' He held up a hand, and Dee had to fight an urge not to slap it back down. 'You're telling me you were here in this house yesterday?'

'That's right.'

'Well I'm afraid you've made a mistake. I was here all day yesterday. I work from home, you see. If there was anyone else in the house, I think I might have known about it.'

He had a strong Yorkshire accent. Vaguely, Dee remembered reading somewhere that people found northern accents more trustworthy than southern ones. Maybe so, but right now this guy was bullshitting her. Because Dee knew she wasn't losing her mind, which was the only other explanation for what was happening right now.

'These houses all look pretty much the same along here,' Hipster Bloke said. 'I'm sure if you try some of the others, you'll find the person you're looking for.'

'No. This is the house. I'm sure of it.'

Even as she said this, she was stepping back to take another look at the house, just in case she'd got it wrong. But everything was the same – the red front door; the stained glass panels in the front window; the purple flowers in the window boxes. This was the same house.

'I think you should go now.' He started to close the door but Dee put her hand on it, stopping him.

'If you won't let me in, then maybe you could pass on a message. Tell Annie she doesn't need to be afraid of me. I want to help her, that's all.'

But Hipster Bloke wasn't listening and was pushing the door closed again. Dee might have put her foot out, preventing him from shutting it fully, but a voice behind her made forget all about the door.

'Dee?'

She froze. The voice wasn't real. It couldn't be. Which meant maybe none of this was real, either.

'Dee. Is that you?'

Slowly, she turned around. Scared of what she'd see, in case there was no one there and all of this was her mind playing tricks with her.

But this wasn't any trick. He was here. Standing on the street, frowning at her the way he did when she'd done something he disapproved of. Which, as it had turned out, was a lot of the time.

'Ed?'

'What the hell is going on?' he said.

She opened her mouth to speak, but no words came out.

Ed Mitchell, a detective inspector with East Sussex Police. She hadn't seen him since their break-up six months ago. Since then, she'd invested a lot of energy in trying hard not to think about him. And if she did still think of him from time to time, and imagined bumping into him, it was never like this.

Twenty-seven

'I'm going to England to meet Dee and find out for myself what's been going on.'

'I'm not sure that's a good idea,' Maeve said. 'How can you trust someone you barely know?'

'That's the problem,' Emer said, 'I don't know who I can trust anymore. Until last night, I'd have said I trusted Robert.'

She was walking with Maeve in the grounds of Maeve's hotel in Clarinbridge.

She'd driven here last night, unable to bear staying in the same house as her stepfather. She'd been halfway to Galway when she realised she had nowhere to go. There was no Nikki to run to anymore. So she'd pulled into the side of the road and called Maeve, who'd insisted Emer come straight to her cosy little house in the grounds of the hotel. This morning, after breakfast, they'd gone for a walk by the river while Emer tried to work out what to do.

'You can still trust Robert, surely?'

'He lied to me, Maeve. He told me he'd hired a private detective. Instead, he hired someone to pretend to be me so he could make contact with my cousin.'

'You don't know for sure that's what he did.'

'Robert knew what happened in London, and he knew I was thinking of getting in touch with Dee. Ursula didn't want me to contact Dee. I don't know why, but Robert did what he always does. He stepped in to fix things; making sure I didn't do anything his dear wife didn't want me to.'

'But this is Robert we're talking about. He's one of the most straight-up men I've ever met.'

'Maybe he's just better at fooling people.'

'That's not true,' Maeve said. 'You need to speak to him, Emer. He's worried sick. I told you he called earlier, asking if I'd heard from you.'

'You can't tell him I'm here.'

'Don't worry,' Maeve said. 'I won't say a word, even though I think you're wrong. But before you make plans to run off to England, can we at least think this through together?'

'There's nothing to think through,' Emer said.

'Of course there is. You've decided Robert hired this woman, but what if there's another explanation?'

'Like what?'

'Like Dee is lying to you. Or the woman she met has nothing to do with Robert. Think for a second. Who else did you tell about seeing Kitty when you were in London?'

'Hardly anyone,' Emer said. 'Robert and Ursula. You. Nikki. That's about it.'

'So why not suspect me or Nikki?'

'Because you didn't know about Dee,' she said. 'You didn't know I have a cousin who's an investigative journalist. Robert, on the other hand, did. I'd told him I was thinking of contacting Dee, and he talked me out of it. He persuaded me to let him handle the whole thing. And because I trusted him, that's what I did.'

'What about Nikki?'

'Why would Nikki have anything to do with this?'

'You could ask the same question about Robert,' Maeve said. 'So tell me, does Nikki know about Dee?'

Emer thought of the emails she'd sent. The ones that remained unanswered. She'd assumed Nikki was ignoring her. Was it possible there was another reason she hadn't replied to any of Emer's emails?

'Nikki has nothing to do with this,' she said.

'You told me she's living in London,' Maeve said. 'It would be easy for her to get in touch with Dee and pretend she's you.'

'Stop it,' Emer said. 'I don't want to talk about Nikki, okay?'

Maeve shrugged.

'Your choice. If you say she's not involved, then I'm sure you're right. I'm just saying you need to consider every angle. It makes as much sense as blaming Robert.'

'Not if Robert had something to do with Kitty's disappearance.'

'You think that's possible?'

'I don't know. Maybe.'

Maeve stayed silent for a moment, before shaking her head.

'What reason could he have for doing that?'

Again, Emer heard her mother's voice.

We didn't have a choice. The girls were there that night.

'He'd have done it if my mother asked him to.'

Maeve started to say something, but Emer held her hand up.

'Stop,' she said. 'Don't ask me about it. I shouldn't have said anything because I may have got it wrong. We shouldn't talk about it until we know the facts. That's why I need to see Dee.'

'How are you going to do that? I assume you didn't bring your passport with you?'

Good point. She'd brought nothing with her except her purse, her mobile phone and the clothes she'd been wearing.

'I can go back and get my passport,' she said. 'And a change of clothes. My mother's in Dublin for the weekend and Robert will be spending most of today at the golf club, like he does every Saturday.'

'It's nine thirty,' Maeve said, checking her watch. 'What time will he be heading to the golf course?'

'Round about now.'

'Okay.' Maeve nodded. 'You drive back home and pick up whatever you want. I'll book the flights.'

'Flights?'

'That's right. If you're going to England, I'm coming with you. Don't look so worried, Emer. I won't intrude on your meeting with your cousin. I'm sure you'll want to do that by yourself. But if Kitty really is alive, then I want to be there when you find her. Kitty's my last connection with Lucy. She's the only person who might be able to tell me what really happened to my sister.'

'What about the hotel?'

'The hotel will be fine without me for a few days. I've got a great team who are more than capable of running the place.'

'Well, if you're sure,' Emer said, 'it would be nice not to have to do this by myself. Thanks, Maeve.'

'You don't need to thank me. I'm doing this for myself, remember?'

'Last night,' Emer said, 'right before Dee called, I'd decided to let it go. I was going to focus on getting my act together and trying to move forward with my life.'

'You can't move forward until you know the truth. Neither of us can do that.'

Before Emer could answer, Maeve's phone started to ring.

'A private number,' she said, frowning. 'Hang on a second. Let me see who this is.'

She walked away from Emer to take the call. While she was gone, three white swans appeared around the bend in the river, sailing grandly past as if they didn't have a care in the world.

'A journalist,' Maeve said, when she came back. 'He says he wants to speak to me about Lucy. Said he might have some new information about what happened to her.'

'Oh my God,' Emer said. 'What are you going to do?'

'He said he didn't want to tell me over the phone. He's asked if we can meet up this weekend.'

'What are you going to do?'

'I told him I'd see him when I got back,' Maeve said. 'If Kitty's still alive, then the chances are she'll know more about what happened to Lucy than some journalist who never knew her.'

Maeve nodded at the swans.

'Beautiful, aren't they? They've been here almost two weeks already. We normally don't see swans here until mid October. They'll be here for the winter, but they'll head north again around April.'

'Wouldn't that be lovely?' Emer said. 'Imagine being able to head off wherever you wanted when you got fed up of being somewhere.'

'You think that's what happened with Kitty?'

'No. Kitty left because she was scared of something.'

The girls were there that night.

What if it was Robert her mother had been arguing with? That wasn't how Emer remembered it, but she wasn't sure she could trust her memory after all this time. She'd read stories of people with fake memories. The psychologist Jean Piaget famously remembered being kidnapped in a park as a small child. The memory had been created by a story his nanny told about the kidnapping, which subsequently turned out to be false. Is that what was happening here? Was Emer's mind creating false memories to help her better make sense of her past?

There was so much she didn't understand. But there were four irrefutable facts. Fact Number One: Lucy Ryan disappeared one night and was never seen again. Fact Number Two: three weeks later, Kitty disappeared. Fact Number Three: two months after Kitty disappeared, Emer's father walked out on his wife and remaining child. And finally, Fact Number Four: two years after her father abandoned her, Robert O'Brien got what he'd always wanted – Ursula Doran as his wife.

Twenty-eight

'Do you want to tell me what's going on, or do I have to try to guess?'

'I have absolutely no idea,' Dee said. 'I'm happy to tell you what I'm doing here, but only if you're going to do the same.'

'Go on then,' Ed said. 'Because I'm really looking forward to hearing this one.'

They were sitting on the terrace at the back of the Prospect of Whitby – the pub closest to Annie's house. Or what had, until yesterday, been Annie's house.

The pub had been Dee's idea. As far as she was concerned, they could have stayed in the street and sorted everything out. But she knew Ed Mitchell, and she knew the best way to get him onside was to buy him a cup of coffee and pretend she was taking his well-meaning, but so often patronising, advice seriously.

The problem was, it was difficult to take him seriously when he spoke to her like that. As if he'd already decided to disapprove of her explanation, before she'd even got a chance to give it. So far, the best thing about this encounter was how it was helping her to remember all the reasons they hadn't been right for each other. Which was a hell of a lot less painful than remembering those moments when she'd felt as if she'd finally found her soulmate.

'Okay,' she said, swallowing her irritation. 'A woman called Annie Holden lives in that house. I came to London today because I want to speak to her.'

'About what?'

'Does it matter?'

'Of course it matters,' Ed said. 'You're a journalist, Dee. There's only one reason you're trying to speak to someone who clearly doesn't want to speak to you. It's a story you're working on, isn't it?'

'No, actually. That's not why I'm here. Besides, how do you know she doesn't want to speak to me?'

He smiled, and Dee's stomach did that irritating flip-flop thing it did whenever he looked at her the way he was looking at her right now.

'Do you really need a detective to work it out for you?'

Dee smiled back. She couldn't help it.

'You mean if she's got someone to lie about her living there, the chances are she's avoiding me.'

'I'd say that's a pretty reasonable assumption.'

'If I tell you why I'm really here,' Dee said, 'do you promise – I mean absolutely promise, so you can't change your mind no matter what I tell you – to just hear me out without interrupting and giving your opinion?'

'I'll do my best.'

'Good. Although the truth is, I don't even know where to start. It's so complicated.'

'When isn't it complicated with you?'

'Shut up.'

'Sorry.' He sat back, crossed his legs and said he was ready to listen.

She told him everything, starting with meeting the woman she thought was her cousin in Gordon's Wine

Bar, ending with the conversation she'd had with Emer on the phone last night.

'So?' she said, when she'd finished, 'What do you think?'

She expected him to jump right in and tell her the whole thing sounded every bit as crazy as she'd warned him it would. Instead, he remained very quiet, as if he was carefully considering everything she'd told him. Unless, of course, the account had left him so lost for words he didn't know what to say.

'Ed?'

'Sorry,' he said. 'I'm trying to make some sort of sense of it, that's all.'

'That's the problem,' Dee said, 'it doesn't make any sense.'

'No,' Ed said. 'But I know you. I don't think you'd be pursuing this crazy story unless you really believed there was something in it.'

It was so far from the reaction she'd expected, Dee wasn't sure how to respond. A painful lump had appeared in her throat and she needed to swallow several times before she could speak.

'What do I do now?'

'Any chance you could let me look into this before you do anything else?' Ed said.

'You mean you want to help me?'

'I mean, I'd like a bit of time to look into Annie's background. Would that be okay?'

'I guess.'

'Great.' He looked at his watch. 'I've got to get going. I'm working the late shift today and I need to get back for that. Did you get the train? I can give you a lift if you want to?'

'It's okay,' Dee said. 'I've got a few more things to do before heading home.'

'Promise me you'll take care of yourself?'

'Scout's honour.'

'You'd better.' When he leaned down and kissed her cheek, it was all she could do not to grab him and hold him tight.

'Hang on,' she said, as he turned to go. 'You never told me what you're doing here today.'

'You're right.' He smiled. 'I never did. See you around, Dee.'

'Hey!' She shouted, but he kept walking. She didn't bother chasing after him, knowing it was pointless. He'd already decided not to tell her, and nothing she did would get him to change his mind. Thankfully, the irritation replaced the vague sense of loss she'd felt right after he'd kissed her cheek. By the time he was out of sight, she was able to convince herself she was glad he was gone.

A few minutes later, she was back outside Annie's house. This time, when she rang the doorbell, no one answered. Deciding to try some of the other houses, Dee walked along the terrace to the first house in the row and rang the doorbell.

An elderly man answered, peering suspiciously at Dee from behind a pair of the thickest glass spectacles Dee had ever seen.

'I'm trying to find my cousin,' Dee said. 'I know she lives in this neighbourhood, but I've lost her address so I'm trying all the houses on this street until I find hers.'

'Sounds a bit dodgy if you ask me,' the man said. 'My daughter's always telling me not to trust people who turn up at the house unannounced. Scammers, she calls them. How do I know this isn't some scam?'

'It's no scam,' Dee said. 'Her name's Annie. She's early thirties, with short blond hair. Does anyone who looks like that live on this street?'

'People on this street come and go all the time,' he said. 'Wasn't always like that, but most of these places are buy to let properties. Rental market is a fluid one. I hardly know any of them. Don't think I can help you, love. Sorry.'

He started to close the door, but Dee put her hand out, stopping him.

'The man who lives at number thirty-two, do you know him?'

'Like I said, I don't know any of them along here these days. Now do me a favour and sod off, would you?'

She tried a few more houses with no luck. Most of the properties were empty and the few people who opened the door weren't able to help her. Dee thought back to her own time in London, trying to remember if her neighbourhood had been as anonymous as this one. She didn't remember it like that, but maybe she viewed that time of her life through rose-tinted glasses.

Giving up on the neighbours Dee crossed the road, found a place where she could see Annie's house, and waited. Two hours later, she was still waiting and no one had come in or out of the house. Her throat was dry and a gathering of grey clouds in the sky warned of rain on the way. Frustrated and fed up, Dee started walking back along Wapping High Street towards the Underground station. But passing a wine bar, she saw a woman inside with bleached blond hair. Thinking her luck had changed, she pushed the door open and went inside.

The wine bar was busy, with couples and groups of people sitting at tables, drinking glasses of wine and sharing plates of cheese. Dee scanned the faces, searching for Annie's distinctive eyes. There were several women in here with blond hair, but none of them resembled Annie. After a moment, Dee went back outside. As the door gently closed behind her, the buzz of conversation disappeared. A gust of wind blew in from the river, a clap of thunder grumbled in the distance and the rain that had been threatening came pouring down, soaking her within seconds. Autumn had arrived with a bang. By the time she reached the Underground station, she was soaking, freezing and utterly miserable.

Twenty-nine

Back in Eastbourne, there was no sign of the rain that had soaked her in London. After a hot shower and a supper of cheese on toast, Dee poured herself a glass of wine, put her jacket on and carried her laptop onto the deck.

On the horizon, the sun was sinking closer to the surface of the water. The sky and sea were streaked with shades of red and burnt orange; the grey and white shingle seemed to glow. Dee soaked it all in, telling herself that whatever else was wrong in her life, she'd got this bit right. Living here, on this deserted beach, was something she'd always be grateful for.

Earlier, she'd had an email from Shay. He'd managed to speak with Lucy's sister, Maeve, and had arranged to meet her next week. He told Dee he'd also remembered that, at the time Kitty drowned, both her parents had been working for Robert O'Brien.

Ursula was his PA, Shay wrote. *Robert didn't employ Eamon full-time but he gave him odd jobs every now and then. Looking back over my notes, it seems Eamon was doing some decorating work for Robert when Kitty drowned. It's why Eamon wasn't on holiday with the rest of the family. Since speaking to you this morning, I'm more convinced than ever there's a story here. One other thing that may interest you. According to several people I've spoken to, Robert is devoted to Ursula. So, whatever else he may or may not have done, I think you can rule out an affair. Let me know how you got on in London today?*

So far, she hadn't got back to him because she didn't know what to tell him. On the train back to Eastbourne, she'd resisted the urge to go onto the internet and search for information on Annie Holden. She knew it was better to give her mind time to process everything that had happened. She didn't want her own feelings – frustration, confusion, anger – to blur the facts.

Further along the beach, she could see Ella and Jake with a group of friends. They looked like they were having a picnic. Their voices and laughter travelled along the beach to where Dee sat. She knew she could go and join them if she wanted. She'd met Ella's friends before and they were a friendly bunch – other young mothers like Ella, with children and families of their own – but Dee had little in common with them. She didn't think she could face an evening smiling and laughing and acting as if everything was okay, when inside she felt like shit.

One question kept niggling her. Why had Ed been there? The more she thought about it, the more Dee realised his sudden appearance outside Annie's house wasn't a coincidence.

She typed three names into her internet browser: Ed Mitchell, Fiona Holden, Annie Holden. Almost immediately, the results came back. Over 1 million of them, but Dee saw immediately she wouldn't have to scroll far to get the information that she needed. It was all there on the first page. The shock of it being this easy took a moment to sink it. Once it had, Dee clicked on the first result and started reading.

By the time she'd finished, night had drawn in. The sky was a pitch black blanket, broken by the twinkling lights of faraway stars and the silver sliver of a crescent moon. Several times, while reading the different news stories, Dee had had to stand up and pace back and forth along the deck. The adrenaline rush of discovering so much at once made it impossible to sit still.

Eventually, she pushed her laptop away, and went inside to call Leonard.

'Hear me out,' she said when he answered, 'and don't interrupt until I've finished.'

'Good evening to you too,' Leonard said.

'Annie Holden has a photo of Kitty and Emer when they were children. I was at her house yesterday and I saw it. But when I went back there today to ask her about it, a man told me no one called Annie had ever lived there. Now, I know that's not true, because I met her mother there the day before.

'Plus, I tried to contact Emer yesterday. When I couldn't get hold of her, I phoned her mother's house in Ireland. A woman called Emer answered the phone and said she'd never met me before. When I told her we'd already met, she didn't know what I was talking about.'

Leonard started to speak, but Dee interrupted him.

'Shh, Leonard. Please. I need to work this out, and the only way I can do that is by talking about it. Do you remember Ed Mitchell? Yup. That's him. Good. While I was outside Annie's house – which, just to be clear, is in London – Ed turned up asking me what I was doing there. And do you know what's really weird? When I told him why I'd been looking into Annie, he seemed to take me seriously. I expected him to tell me the whole thing was ridiculous, but he didn't do that. Which got me wondering… What did he already know about her?'

'And you've worked that out?'

'Damn right.' Dee was so pleased with herself she didn't even mind the interruption. 'Get this, Leonard. Ten years ago, a man called Michael Holden was charged with murder. The murder took place in a village called Alfriston, which is about ten miles from Eastbourne.'

Dee paused, making sure she got all the facts right and didn't forget anything. Going back onto the deck, she scrolled through the different news stories about the murder.

The unnamed body of a man had been found buried in a shallow grave in the countryside surrounding the village. A local dog walker had discovered the body. The victim was never identified, but the police found the killer following an appeal to the public. A local man, Michael Holden, was arrested and charged with the murder. Witnesses had seen him near the scene of the crime, and there were enough traces of his DNA on the victim's body for the CPS to bring a case against him. Michael Holden served ten years in prison for manslaughter.

The story had been widely covered, and Dee had vague memories of reading about it at the time. What had particularly interested people was the killer's motivation. According to everyone who knew him, Michael Holden was a quiet, unassuming man who'd never committed a crime before in his life. Yet for reasons no one had ever been able to work out, he had gone out one night in October 2010 and killed a man he claimed he'd never met before. The police had never been able to find anything to link Michael Holden to his victim. In the intervening years, several journalists had revisited the story, but had never found out what had motivated Michael Holden to kill a complete stranger.

'He's Annie's father,' Dee said. 'She was in her early twenties when the murder happened. There are plenty of references to Fiona in the stories about the murder, and photos of her at the trial. But there's nothing about Annie.'

'You know, this goes a long way to explaining why she was so reluctant to speak to you,' Leonard said. 'Something like that in your life, it's bound to make you wary of strangers.'

'I suppose so,' Dee said.

'What about Ed Mitchell? Where does he fit into this?'

'I was wondering when you'd ask.' Dee clicked on one of the stories, searching until she found the sentence she wanted:

> Standing outside the court after the senten-cing, Detective Ed Mitchell, who led the investigation into the murder, gave a brief statement.

'He was in charge of the investigation,' Dee said, 'which means he knows Annie and Fiona.'

A photo of Ed accompanied the story. Ten years ago, he had more hair and less bodyweight. Apart from that, he'd barely aged at all since the photo had been taken. Seeing him today had shaken her more than she wanted to admit. She'd spent the past few months doing all she could to forget about him. Then today... Wham! The old feelings she'd had for him had resurfaced, as sharp and strong as ever.

'We need to find Annie,' Leonard asked. 'She's the key to all of this. Whatever *this* turns out to be.'

'How?'

'There's something I didn't tell you,' Leonard said. 'Do you remember that old bloke she was visiting in Stockwell? You told me not to go back, but I couldn't help myself. I went to the pub where she'd met him and he was there. I followed him back to his flat. I didn't get a name for him, but I know where he lives.'

'Good,' Dee said, glad for once Leonard had ignored her advice. 'Let's go there tomorrow, see if we can get him to speak to us.' She paused, as a thought occurred to her. 'Could he be Eamon, do you think?'

'Emer's father? Possibly. He's about the right age, I imagine. Depends whether or not Annie turns out to be your cousin. Best not to go jumping to any conclusions just yet, okay?'

'You're right.' Dee wondered what it would mean to discover her father's brother was alive after all this time.

'If she really is Kitty,' Leonard said, 'then she must have a damn good reason for not wanting anyone to know about it.'

'I know.' Ella had said more or less the same thing. 'But what am I meant to do? Just forget everything I've found out?'

He laughed. As so often happened, the laugh turned into a hacking cough.

'You're like me, Doran. A hack through and through. We've started this, and now we'll have to finish it. One way or the other.'

On the road at the front of the house, Dee heard the sound of a car approaching. Light from the headlights swept across the shingle, briefly illuminating the beach, before the world plunged into darkness again.

'I've got to go,' she said. 'Call me tomorrow after you've been to Stockwell.'

'I'll do that. And Dee?'

'Yes?'

'Promise me you'll be careful.'

'Cross my heart.'

She hung up, listening to the sound of a car door slamming and the crunch of footsteps as someone approached her house. Leonard's words echoed through her head and suddenly she felt afraid. She rarely had visitors, especially this late in the evening. As the events of the last few days came rushing back, Dee realised that digging into Kitty's disappearance might mean putting herself in danger.

The front doorbell rang, the sound making her jump. As she went to answer it, she picked up the poker from the fireplace. Just in case. It crossed her mind the visitor might be Ed. She wouldn't put it past him to drive over and check up on her. But when she opened her front door, it wasn't Ed standing on the doorstep looking at her expectantly.

'Dee?'

A woman Dee had never seen before, yet she knew immediately who she was. A series of images played through her head, some real and some imagined. Annie Holden, smiling shyly when Dee complimented her paintings. Two little girls playing together on a beach in the west of Ireland on a hot summer's afternoon. Dee's father, his face shutting down each time she asked him about his family in Ireland. Kitty Doran and Lucy Ryan, two little girls caught in the middle of something too big for either of them.

'It's me,' the woman said. 'Emer. Can I come in?'

Thirty

Sunlight streaming through the windows woke Emer up. She put her hand over her face, trying to block out the light, but there was too much of it. Groaning, she rolled onto her side and cracked her eyes open just enough to make out her surroundings. That's when she saw the view. Eyes wide open now, she got out of the bed and wandered across to the window. On the other side of the glass, a sweeping expanse of clear blue sky, a sea as flat and still as a plate of glass, a shingle beach of grey and white stones polished and bright beneath the morning sun.

She'd known Dee's house was near the beach but last night, arriving in the dark, she hadn't realised how near. Dee had explained that her father had bought this plot of land and designed and built the house for his wife and daughter. Emer had already seen how beautiful the inside was. But she'd had no idea just how stunning the location was. It was strange to think her uncle – her father's brother – could have created a house like this. It was proof, not that she needed it, of how different the two men were. If her own father ever had enough money for a project like this, he'd have wasted every penny of it in the pub.

Her phone pinged with an incoming text. It was from Maeve, asking how she was getting on.

All good here, Emer typed, *how are things in London?*

They'd flown into Gatwick together yesterday afternoon. On the plane, they'd agreed that Emer would go and see Dee by herself, and Maeve would book into a hotel in London. The hotel had been Maeve's idea, and Emer was grateful to her for thinking of it. Meeting Dee for the first time was bound to be emotional, and it wasn't a moment Emer wanted to share with anyone else.

I'm going for a wander, Maeve replied a few seconds later, *call me later and let me know if you're able to meet up.*

The smell of fresh coffee and cooked bacon wafted into the room. Sending a quick reply to Maeve, Emer got dressed and went downstairs. In the sitting room, she paused to look again at the painting Dee had shown her last night. If she'd had any doubt that Annie Holden might not be Kitty, this painting had eliminated it. She'd recognised the moment recreated in the painting. The first day of the only holiday they'd ever had. They'd bought a kite and taken it to the beach, where they'd spent the afternoon trying to make it fly. They'd almost given up, when Kitty suddenly worked it out. One moment, the kite was lying on the ground, the next it was soaring into the air and the two girls were racing after it along the white sand.

'Bacon sandwich?' Dee's voice interrupted the memory, dragging Emer back. 'Or are you vegetarian?'

'Bacon sandwich would be great,' Emer said. 'And that coffee smells fantastic.'

They ate breakfast on the deck at the back of the house, which overlooked the beach.

'How are you feeling this morning?' Dee asked.

'Still trying to take it all in.' Emer took a sip of the coffee, which was excellent, and pushed her plate away. She'd eaten half her sandwich but couldn't finish it. Unlike

Dee, who was tucking into her second sandwich and her fourth cup of coffee.

'What did she look like?' she asked. 'The woman who pretended to be me.'

'Nothing like you,' Dee said. 'Smaller frame. Shorter hair. Very different.'

The description matched Nikki, who was small-framed as well. But Nikki wouldn't ever do something like that.

'Sound like anyone you know?' Dee asked.

'My ex-girlfriend,' Emer said. 'But before you ask, it wasn't her.'

'You're sure?'

'Positive.'

She'd considered the possibility it could be Nikki. Of course she had. But every time she thought about it, the more certain she became that whatever was going on here, it had nothing to do with Nikki.

Dee nodded. 'Okay. So if it's not her, then who is it?'

'Robert lied to me. My mother didn't want me to speak to you. I don't know why, but I know if she'd asked Robert to intervene and stop me getting in touch, he'd have done it.' She frowned. 'It's a weird feeling, you know? Finding out that someone's been going around pretending to be you.'

'Is it worth calling your mother?' Dee asked. 'She has a right to know what's going on.'

'No.' Emer shook her head. 'That's definitely not a good idea.'

'Kitty's her daughter. Surely she'd want to know if she's still alive?'

214

'It's not that simple,' Emer said. *The girls were there that night.* 'I think Kitty and Lucy saw something they weren't meant to.'

'Something to do with Robert?'

'I don't think so,' Emer said. 'Unless it had something to do with my mother and Robert got involved by accident.'

'Why do you say that?'

'He's crazy about her,' Emer said. 'If she was involved in anything dodgy, maybe she asked him to help her.'

'What's she like?' Dee asked.

'Ursula?' Emer's stomach tightened, the way it always did when she thought about her mother. 'She's not a very nice person. I know it sounds terrible to say that about my own mother, but it's the truth. She's a narcissist. Completely self-obsessed. Selfish.' She paused, smiling. 'Sorry. You did ask.'

'And your stepfather puts up with that?'

'He adores her,' Emer said. 'She's very beautiful, you see. He told me he fell in love with her the first time he saw her. She was already married, and Robert never thought he was in with a chance. But then my parents split up, so I guess he saw his opportunity and took it. Why?'

'I'm just interested,' Dee said. 'How did they meet? Robert and your mother, I mean.'

'Ballincarraig's a small town,' Emer said. 'They probably knew each other for years. But they grew close when Ursula started working as Robert's PA. There've been a few rumours over the years. You know, that they got together before Dad left. I have no idea how true that is. I wouldn't put it past my mother, but I'm not sure Robert would have risked his reputation, even back then.'

'I've been reading up about your stepfather,' Dee said. 'He's an interesting man. He's also got a reputation for decency and honesty. What if the girls saw something that could damage Robert's reputation? He'd want to make sure the girls never told anyone what they'd seen, right?.'

'You think he killed Lucy?' For a moment, Emer thought she might throw up. 'Absolutely not. He's... Robert's not like that. He's not a violent person. Besides, if Robert knew what happened to Kitty, why would he get you involved in trying to find her? He'd already know Kitty was still alive.'

'Kitty was eleven when she disappeared,' Dee said. 'If she didn't drown, then she didn't disappear by herself. The most logical explanation is that at least one of your parents helped get her out of the country.'

Emer's brain was exhausted from trying to rethink every aspect of her life until this moment. She didn't know what was true, or who she could trust. For all she knew, Dee was lying to her too. Maybe Robert had paid Dee to call the house the other night. Or maybe her mother had, or... Emer felt her mind spinning, knew how dangerous that could be. Because one moment you felt in control, and the next you started doing all sorts of crazy shit.

'I can't sit here and do nothing. My brain feels as if it's been fried. My whole life, the people I trusted most have been lying to me. Do you have any idea what that feels like?'

'Stop.'

Dee stood up and put her arms around Emer.

'It's okay,' Dee whispered. 'We're going to work it out. Together. Okay?'

Emer nodded and Dee squeezed her harder.

'That's the spirit, Emer. Come on, let's tidy up here and we'll get going.'

'Going where?'

'London.' Dee let her go. 'Annie was visiting an older man in south London. I think there's a chance he could be your father. My friend Leonard knows where he lives. I've already arranged to meet him there this morning. Why don't you see if Maeve wants to join us? You can text her the address.'

They drove to Stockwell, a part of the city Emer wasn't familiar with. At the beginning of the drive, Dee did her best to keep the conversation going. Until Emer asked her to stop. She couldn't cope with talking. All she wanted to do was close her eyes and give her brain time out. On top of everything else she was trying to process, she now had to deal with the shock of discovering her father might still be alive. That she might actually see him this very day.

They drove to a soundtrack of country music. Artists Emer was already familiar with, like Johnny Cash, Dolly Parton and Willie Nelson. And some new music that she hadn't heard before. A man whose broken voice was so full of raw emotion, Emer found herself holding her breath as he compared romantic love to a glass of smooth Tennessee whiskey.

'Chris Stapleton,' Dee said, as she came off the motorway and started navigating the busy south London streets. 'I'm hoping to see him live next year when he comes to the UK.'

'My dad loved all that country stuff,' Emer said. 'Mum hates it. I guess Robert must hate it too, because we never listened to anything like that when I was growing up. Come to think of it, after Dad left we never really had music playing in the house. Robert has a great vinyl collection but he never seems to listen to it.'

'What a shame. We always had music on in our house. My dad loved country. Mum preferred classic, but they seemed to find a good balance of listening to both.'

'You were lucky,' Emer said.

'I know. And if you're lucky, maybe one day I'll tell you how I got to be called Dee.'

'One day?' Emer looked across and saw Dee was smiling. 'How about now?'

'I'll give you a hint,' Dee said. 'Dad was a huge Tom Jones fan.'

'I'll need more than that.'

Emer looked out the window at the grey streets and greyer buildings. Even in the blazing hot sunshine, everything looked washed out and run down. It made her sad to think her dad might have ended up living somewhere like this.

'Think of some of his better known songs.'

'I can't think right now,' Emer said. 'I've already told you that.'

'Sorry,' Dee said, sounding anything but. 'Delilah.'

'Delilah? You mean that's what Dee's short for?' Despite herself, Emer smiled. 'Oh my God, that's funny.'

'Glad you think so. Look, we're almost there. Now all I have to do is find a parking space. Which isn't going to be easy, by the looks of it.'

It took a while to find a parking space. Eventually, she found a space on a quiet, residential street that was less scruffy than some of the others Emer had seen. Instead of high-rise concrete blocks, this one had Victorian terraced houses running along either side. The houses were small, but most of them were well-tended.

'It's not this street,' Dee said, as if she knew what Emer was thinking. 'Just a short walk, though.'

A short walk and another world away, Emer realised as they arrived at the correct street. Here, there were no pretty terraced houses. Instead, they'd entered a dark, claustrophobic street that shouted poverty from every corner. Row after row of concrete council blocks, many of the windows boarded over. A gang of young men stood guarding the entrance to one of the buildings, their eyes boring into Dee and Emer as they passed. The air was thick with the smell of fried food and marijuana.

At the last block of flats, a tall, painfully thin man stood at the entrance smoking a cigarette. Despite the heat, he was wearing a long coat and when Emer shook his hand after Dee had introduced them both, his skin was icy cold.

'Took your time,' Leonard said.

His voice was thick and gravelly, as if someone had driven a tractor over his vocal chords.

'Traffic was terrible,' Dee said. 'Sorry.'

She looked up at the high-rise block of flats behind Leonard.

'Is this it?'

'Only block on the street that hasn't been emptied by the council,' Leonard said. 'They're selling off all these buildings to private developers. Which means the poor people who've lived here all their lives are being dispersed to whatever part of the city will take them.' He looked at Emer. 'Which means if the fella living here is your old man, we're lucky. Another few months and he wouldn't be here.'

'You really think it could be him?'

Leonard started to answer, but his words turned into a cough.

'No idea,' he said eventually. 'All I know is Annie Holden met up with him several times. Could be all sorts of other reasons for that, of course.'

'But he's about the right age?' Emer asked.

'Yes, love.' Leonard gave her a smile, so unexpectedly warm and sweet her eyes filled with tears. 'He's definitely about the right age. But before we go in there, I need to tell you. He's not looking the best. I know that's rich coming from me, but this geezer looks like he's already lived several lives, and none of them have done him much good.'

'That make sense,' Emer said, unable to control the wobble in her voice. 'My dad was a big drinker. If he's drinking as much as he used to, it's a miracle he's still alive.'

'You ready?' Dee put a hand on Emer's arm, steadying her.

Emer took a deep breath and nodded.

'Ready.'

Inside, the building was all bad smells and angry sounds. People's voices echoed off the concrete walls and metal doors. There was a lift, but when Leonard pressed the button to call it, nothing happened.

'Bastard was working earlier,' he said. 'Flat's on the sixth floor. No way I'll manage that on the stairs. You both okay if I stay here?'

'Actually,' Emer said, 'I'd rather go on my own.'

'You sure about that?' Dee asked.

Emer nodded. She really was sure. On the drive up to London, she'd thought she wouldn't be able to go through with it. But now she was here, she felt strong. Whatever she faced when she climbed those six flights of stairs, she was ready for it.

She got the flat number from Leonard, told them she'd be back soon and promised Dee she'd phone if she needed her at any point. And then she was alone, pushing open the swinging glass doors that led to the stinking stairwell.

It was at the side of the building, encased in glass that was filthy from years of neglect. Despite the dirt, Emer was able to catch glimpses of the city, stretching out as far as the horizon, as she ascended the building.

Several times on the way up, she thought she heard someone following her. But each time she turned around, there was no one there. Even so, as she continued up the stairs she couldn't shake off the feeling that she was being followed. At one point, the feeling was so strong she stopped and shouted at whoever was behind her.

'Hello?'

Silence. She held her breath, listening for any sign they'd heard her, but there was nothing. After a few minutes, when the heat had become almost unbearable, she turned back and continued up the stairs.

By the time she reached the sixth floor, she was sweating and out of breath. At this time of the year, the stairwell was like an oven – sun streaming through the dirty glass, baking the steps and the metal handrail. Each time she'd put her hand on the handrail to steady herself, she'd pulled back with a yelp as her skin connected with the hot metal.

Pushing through the door at the top, she stepped out of the heat into a long, dark corridor. The doors to the flats were all numbered. As she looked along the line, she again had that sense that someone was behind her, watching. When she swung around, she saw a shadow behind the glass door to the stairwell, as if someone was quickly stepping back, out of sight. She waited a moment, but no one came through the door and the shadow had disappeared, so she continued along the corridor.

It didn't take long to find the flat she was looking for. Pressing her ear against the door, she heard the faint sound of a TV or radio, the shuffle of footsteps and a man's phlegmy cough.

She pulled back, her heart racing. He was in there. Her father. Memories slammed into her, image after image from the first few years of her childhood. Sunny afternoons on the beach in summer; Christmas Day, her father asleep in the armchair in the sitting room, mouth open as he snored; her parents shouting at each other while Emer and Kitty lay in bed, sheets pulled over their heads to block out the noise.

And the last time she saw him. A sunny afternoon, three weeks after Kitty had drowned. Emer was sitting in the back garden, seeing how many stones she could balance on top of each other. Doing anything not to think about what had happened. Her father had come out and sat beside her. For once in his life, he was clean-shaven and his breath, when he leaned in to kiss her, didn't stink.

'I'm not a bad man, Emer. Remember that, won't you? I always tried to do my best for you girls.'

She didn't know why, but his words made her angry. She'd pulled away from him, screamed that his best hadn't been good enough. Kitty was dead and they all knew it was his fault because he hadn't loved them enough to come on holiday with them. If he'd been with them, she'd screamed, Kitty would never have drowned. She ran back into the house, and when she came back outside later, her father was gone.

When she found out that he wasn't coming back, she'd blamed herself. And hadn't stopped blaming herself in the years that followed. The guilt she already felt about Kitty intensified to include guilt at letting her father leave. Until, eventually, guilt became the thing that defined her. Something she couldn't escape, no matter how hard she tried or how many glasses of wine she drank to block it out.

She had spent so much time wishing she could find her father one day and apologise. Maybe now that moment had finally arrived. Emer lifted her hand and knocked on the door.

Inside the flat, the voices from the TV or radio stopped. She waited for him to come and open the door, but nothing happened. She knocked again.

'Hello?' she called. 'Dad?'

At first, she thought he wasn't going to respond. But then she heard the shuffle of his feet, getting closer. She held her breath, listening to the rattle of the door being unlocked. Time stood still as she waited until, eventually, light from the flat flooded into the dark hallway as the door slowly started to open.

Thirty-one

It wasn't him. She knew right away, but the knowledge – followed by the sharp stab of disappointment – took a moment to sink in.

'Can I help you?' He peered at her through the gap in the open door. A tall man, stooped over and old before his time. White hair that stuck out at odd angles, skin that looked like dried-out paper, and a face made for regrets.

'I'm sorry,' she said. 'I must have got the wrong flat.'

She turned to go, but he called her back.

'Wait a moment.' He stepped into the hallway and came closer. So close she could smell him – stale sweat and old clothes. He wasn't her father, this strange, broken man. She should have been pleased, but she wasn't. She was heartbroken. It was only now, standing here in this dark corridor, that she realised how much she'd let herself believe she'd find him today.

'I know why you're here,' he said.

'Sorry?'

'You're looking for Annie.'

'How do you know that?'

He smiled. But even his smile was sad.

'Isn't it obvious? When I opened the door and saw you, I thought for a second you were her.'

Tears pricked her eyes. She wiped them away, but more tears came and suddenly she was properly crying.

He put a trembling hand on her arm.

'You won't find her. I'm sorry, love. But Annie's gone. You're too late.'

'Where is she?' she said, between sobs. 'I just want to see her and know she's okay. Is that such a bad thing?'

'Here. Take this.'

He pulled a filthy-looking handkerchief from the pocket of his trousers and held it out for her.

'It's okay,' he said, when she hesitated, 'it's freshly washed. Just old, that's all.'

'Thanks.' She took it and used it to wipe her face, thinking she'd worry later about whether or not he was telling the truth.

'And now you need to go.'

'Will you tell her I'm looking for her?' she said.

'I can't do that.'

'What do you mean?'

'I already told you, love. She's gone. Too many people looking for her. You'd do well to do the same. Because you won't find her, but if you keep trying, you'll end up dead.'

'Who are you?' Emer asked.

But he'd already gone back into the flat and closed the door.

'Hey!' She banged on the door, shouting at him to open up. But he stayed behind the closed door, ignoring her.

–

'She's been too long,' Dee said. 'I'm going up there.'

They were waiting outside the building. The smell had started to get to Dee and she'd suggested they stand outside. She kept an eye on the entrance to the stairwell, watching the people going in and coming out. She'd seen plenty of people but, so far, none of them were Emer.

'No need,' Leonard said, nodding at the entrance to the block of flats. 'Look, here she comes now. Although judging by her face, she didn't have the joyful reunion she'd been hoping for.'

He was right. Emer looked devastated as she walked towards them.

'What happened?' Dee asked.

'Can we go somewhere else?' Emer said. 'I can't bear to spend another second here.'

'There's a pub a few streets away,' Leonard said. 'Not too bad, considering the neighbourhood. We can go there.'

Emer waited until they were in the pub and had ordered their drinks. They found a table in the small beer garden outside and, once they were all sitting down, she told them about her encounter with the elderly man.

'The weird thing is,' she said, 'I got the impression he knew who I was.'

'But you didn't recognise him?' Dee asked.

Emer shook her head.

'Maybe you just remind him of Annie,' Leonard said. He looked at Dee. 'They're the spitting image of each other, aren't they?'

'You do look a lot like her,' Dee agreed.

'So what?' Emer said. 'Looking like her isn't going to help me find her. He told me she's gone and she's not coming back. Too many people looking for her, he said.' She glared at Dee. 'He meant you, didn't he?'

'Possibly,' Dee said. 'But I only started looking for Annie because someone asked me to, remember? God, what a bloody mess. Is it worth trying to speak to him again?'

'He refused to answer his door the second time,' Emer said. 'I kept trying until one of his neighbours came out and threatened to call the police if I didn't go away.'

Emer was about to say something else when her phone started ringing.

'It's Maeve,' she said, 'hang on.'

She picked up her phone and moved away from the table.

'What do we do now?' Dee asked Leonard.

'We go back there,' he said. 'And we don't leave until we get him to talk to us. Your cousin there, she's not a journalist. You and me, on the other hand, we've got years of practice persuading people to talk to us.'

'Okay,' Dee said. 'But I've got something important on later, Leonard. I'll need to be heading back by mid afternoon at the latest.'

She felt a flash of joy, tinged with pain, as she thought about dinner later with Ella, Jake and Tom. As well as being home in time for the dinner, she'd have to give herself time to prepare emotionally. No easy task.

'That shouldn't be a problem.' Leonard nodded at Emer, putting her phone into the pocket of her jeans as she walked back to them. 'Think she'll want to stick around while we try again?'

'Maeve got lost,' Emer said, coming back to the table. 'Apparently, she couldn't work out how the Underground works. I know that must sound stupid, but she's never been to London before. I think she's feeling a bit overwhelmed. I've arranged to meet her back at her hotel. After that, I was wondering, Dee...'

'Of course,' Dee said, anticipating the question before Emer asked it. 'You're both welcome to stay. There's plenty of room, as you know. The only thing is, I'm going out this evening. Are you okay getting the train to Eastbourne and a taxi to the house? Here.' Dee rooted around in her bag until she found her keyring. Pulling off the front door key, she handed this to Emer. 'Make yourselves at home.'

'What about you?' Emer asked.

'My neighbour has a spare key,' Dee said. 'I can use that. Just text me and let me know what time you'll be back.'

'Penny for them,' Leonard said, after Emer had left.

'Sorry,' Dee said. 'I was thinking about Maeve. Trying to work out why she came to London with Emer.'

'She wants to find out what happened to her sister,' Leonard said. 'Nothing strange about that.'

'Maybe,' Dee said.

'No maybe about it,' Leonard said. 'Besides, you'll be seeing her later. You can ask her yourself. In the meantime, let's try the old bloke again. Who knows? Maybe he can shed some light on this whole bloody mess.'

'You really think there's any point going back there and trying again?'

'I don't think we've got a choice. We need to get him to speak to us. Find out who he is and what he knows about Annie.'

–

Back at the building, Leonard decided to try the stairs. But by the time they'd reached the second floor, it was clear he wasn't going to make it to the sixth. His breathing had become laboured, his face red from the effort of making it this far.

'Sorry,' he wheezed.

'It's okay.' Dee put a hand on his shoulder. 'Really. Head back down to the ground floor when you've got your breath back. I'll be down as soon as I can.'

As she continued without him, she became aware of the smell. A rich scent of ginger, citrus and sandalwood. It reminded her of something, although she was almost at the top before she realised what it was. Her father, when he was still alive, had always had a thing for expensive colognes. That's what she was smelling now. Dee wondered how someone living in a place like this could afford expensive scents. Then she realised the person wearing the cologne was most likely a visitor to the building, just like she was.

By the time she reached the top, she felt ready to collapse. The heat in the stairwell hadn't helped. Sweating profusely, she pushed open the door and stepped into the relative cool of the corridor.

It was a dank, dingy space. Narrow and long, with doors so close together she guessed the flats behind them were tiny. The only break in the gloom was the light coming from the open doorway of one of the flats further along the corridor.

When she'd got her breath back, Dee started walking, using the numbers on the doors as a guide. She was almost at the open door now. Counting the numbers, she realised the open door belonged to the flat she was looking for.

Her fight or flight instinct kicked in, flight winning over as every nerve in her body screamed at her to turn around and get the hell out of there. Somehow, she kept going, driven by the urge to find the truth – however terrible it turned out to be.

'Hello?'

She'd reached the door. It wasn't fully open, but enough for her to glimpse the flat inside. A TV, sound muted, was playing in the corner of the dirty room. The single window in the room was open. The light coming through it cast an unflattering glow over the place, highlighting the layer of dust, the stains on the thin carpet, the damp patches on the walls.

Here at the entrance to the flat, she got that scent of cologne again; although it seemed fainter now. Either the air blowing through the open window had dispersed it, or else there was no smell and Dee was just imagining it.

Using the tip of her index finger, Dee pushed the door open wider and stepped inside. The silence screamed back at her; faces on the TV speaking words she couldn't hear; the only movement in the tiny flat was the flickering of the thin curtains in the breeze coming through the open window. Her mind and body seemed to separate, until she was watching herself, crossing the room to the open window and the flapping curtains.

The flat was at the back of the building. Looking out the window, Dee could see a stretch of wasteland and a deserted construction site. The contrast with the bustling street at the front of the building was remarkable.

A single scream broke the silence, followed by voices. Lots of voices. All of them coming from outside, six storeys below. Dee already knew what she'd see when she leaned out of the open window and looked down.

She knew, but she couldn't stop herself doing it, her eyes travelling down to all the people coming around the side of the building to see what the commotion was. And there, directly below the window, lying face down on the concrete, the broken body of the man Dee had come to speak to. The man who, one hour earlier, had told Emer she'd end up dead if she continued trying to find Annie Holden.

Thirty-two

'I took the Tube in the wrong direction,' Maeve said. 'Before I knew it, I was in Camden. I might not know much about London, but I know that Camden is north London, not south.'

'It doesn't matter,' Emer said. 'It wasn't him.'

'Who was he, then, if he wasn't your dad?'

'I don't know. He could be anyone. You want to know something? I'm starting to think we should stop this whole thing now. It's bullshit. I don't know who to trust anymore, or what to believe. I'm worried if I keep going with this, I'll lose my mind.'

'We can't stop now,' Maeve said. 'If Kitty is alive, she's my only chance of finding out what happened to Lucy.'

They were sitting outside a cafe in Covent Garden, near Maeve's hotel. Maeve had suggested a pub, but Emer had opted for this place instead. Alcohol was the last thing she needed right now, and she didn't trust her ability to abstain if she went to a pub.

She was on edge, anxious and tense and finding it difficult to focus. None of these feelings were new. The difference now was she wasn't trying to block them out with alcohol. Maeve wasn't helping her mood, either. She kept questioning everything Emer said, as if she didn't believe what Emer was telling her.

'I'm going to head back to Eastbourne,' Emer said. 'There's no point staying in London. We can't do anything here. You should come with me. There's plenty of room at Dee's, and she's already said you're welcome to stay.'

'Does this mean you're not giving up then?'

'I don't know what I'm doing,' Emer said. 'But we've come this far, it doesn't seem right to just turn around and go home. Besides, it's not all about me, is it? You've got a say in this too. You deserve to know what happened to Lucy.'

'Thanks.' Maeve reached out and squeezed Emer's hand. 'That means a lot, Emer.'

'It's okay,' Emer said, some of her bad mood evaporating. The truth was, this was an impossible situation for both of them. She'd have to try harder to keep her emotions in check and get on with Maeve as best she could.

'I'm not sure about going to Eastbourne, though,' Maeve said.

'Why not?'

'It's like you said, we don't know who we can trust. It makes more sense for us to do this alone for now. Until we know exactly what's going on.'

Emer didn't say anything. She'd liked Dee so far, and trusted her. But maybe Maeve was right.

'So if we don't go to Eastbourne,' she said, 'what do we do?'

'I guess we need to make a plan,' Maeve said.

'Dee told me last night that Annie's father was convicted of murder,' Emer said. 'Let's go online now and see what we can find out. The family live somewhere near

Eastbourne. I can't remember the name of the town, but it shouldn't be too hard to find.'

'Eastbourne's in East Sussex,' Maeve said, taking her phone out of her pocket. 'We can start by looking up *Holden* and *East Sussex* and *murder*. Do you know the father's first name?'

Emer felt some of the tension draining from her body. It was good to finally feel that she and Maeve were together in this. Dee had been great, but Maeve and Emer had a shared history, a shared sense of loss, that united them in a completely different way.

'I've got it.' Maeve looked up at Emer. 'The village is called Alfriston. Get your phone out and look up *Michael Holden* and *Alfriston*.'

Emer took her phone out of her bag and typed into her browser. The results came back almost immediately and she started reading. When she'd finished, she looked up at Maeve, frowning.

'It doesn't make sense.'

'I know,' Maeve said. 'It's such an odd story. Why would anyone kill a complete stranger for no reason?'

'We don't know the victim was a stranger,' Emer said. 'Holden never said why he killed that man, but clearly he had a reason.'

A photo of Michael Holden accompanied most of the stories. On her phone screen, the photo was too small to see his face clearly. Now, Emer enlarged the photo, examining his face in more detail. He was wearing a shirt with the sleeves rolled up. He had sandy, blond hair that hung down almost to his shoulders. He was grinning at the person taking the photo, a big happy smile that made you want to smile back at him.

He'd changed a lot, and certainly hadn't been smiling like that the last time she'd seen him. But Emer was in no doubt. The man in the photo was the same man she'd met at the flat in Stockwell earlier that morning.

Thirty-three

The dark shadows were creeping closer. Each time they threatened to pounce, Dee refilled her glass and drank some more wine. She was too weary to try to fight it. She felt wrung out, done in, finished. All she sought now was oblivion, and past experience had taught her that this was the fastest route. It had also taught her that drinking tonight would make it harder to manage the darkness the following day. But that, she reflected, draining her glass and savouring the taste of the cool wine on the back of her throat, was a problem for tomorrow, not now.

Further along the beach, she could just make out the glow of light through the sitting room curtains inside the mobile home. She should have been over there earlier this evening, having dinner and spending precious time she would never get back with the little boy who'd become the centre of her world over the last few years. But by the time she'd got back home from London, it was too late for dinner and Jake was already in bed.

The hours when she should have been driving home and getting ready for dinner had been spent inside Brixton Police Station. When she'd finally got out, it was already dark and she knew her dinner would have to be cancelled.

'We'll find some time over the next few days,' Ella had said, when Dee called to tell her she wasn't going to make it.

Dee had said yes, of course they would. But she knew, even as she said it, that it wouldn't happen. How could it, when there were only five days remaining until they left?

She'd been expecting Emer and her friend to be here, but there was no sign of them when she arrived. When she'd gone to get her spare key, Ella had invited her in for a glass of wine, but Dee had declined. All she wanted was to be by herself. It was a relief when she got Emer's message, telling Dee they'd decided not to come to Eastbourne this evening. It meant Dee didn't have to pretend to be okay, when the truth was she was anything but.

The image of the dead man had haunted her all day, and continued to haunt her now she was back home. The sheer waste of a life. The police, who had questioned her repeatedly throughout the afternoon, had implied more than once that the death was murder, not suicide.

She'd thought they were going to keep her there, locked up in that place. Two detectives had interviewed her. She couldn't remember either of their names, but one of them had given her a business card in case she later remembered anything else she could tell them about the dead man.

She'd already told them everything she knew, but it was clear they thought she was hiding something from them. She couldn't blame them. Her account of how she'd ended up inside the flat sounded ridiculous – searching for a girl who didn't technically exist because she'd drowned over twenty years ago.

When she'd come in earlier there'd been a message on the landline from Emer's mother, asking Dee to call her as soon as she could. Dee hadn't been able to face calling her back right away but now, fortified with wine, she went inside and dialled the number she'd found in her mother's address book.

'Ballincarraig 24696.'

'Hello? Is this Ursula?'

'This is she. Who's calling, please?'

'Ursula, it's Dee Doran. Frank's daughter. You left me a message.'

'I need to speak to you about Emer,' Ursula said. 'Robert's told me you called here on Friday night and filled her head with some story about her sister still being alive. As Kitty was my child, the least you could do is tell me what the hell is going on.'

If anything dodgy was going on, it would have involved my mother, not Robert.

Emer's voice, like a warning.

'I'm not quite sure myself,' Dee said. 'What did Robert tell you?'

'Some cock and bull story about you telling Emer that her sister is alive and well and living in London. It was very irresponsible of you. Emer is fragile, you see. She suffers from poor mental health. I think the conversation she had with you has tipped her over the edge. She ran off somewhere after speaking to you and we've no idea where she is.'

'She didn't strike me as fragile when we met,' Dee said. 'When did you meet my daughter?'

'She was with me this weekend,' Dee said.

'Put her on to me right away. She's my daughter and I need to speak to her.'

'I can't do that,' Dee said.

'Why not?'

'Because I don't know where she is. The last time I saw her was in London this morning. She was on her way to meet a friend.'

'Nikki. I knew it. That's the real reason Emer's there. To try persuade that odious woman to take her back.'

'I don't know who she's with,' Dee said. 'Sorry.'

She hoped she was doing the right thing. The logical part of her mind knew that Ursula deserved to know where her daughter was. But Dee couldn't forget the way Emer had looked when she spoke about her mother. A closing down behind her eyes, like she was blocking out things she didn't want to think about.

'Sorry? Is that all you've got to say? This is your fault, Delilah. You had no right – absolutely no right – calling my house and speaking to Emer without consulting me first.'

'Emer's an adult,' Dee said. 'If she wants to speak to me, or come and visit me, that's her business. I don't mean to be rude, Ursula, but I think it's probably better if I hang up now.'

'Wait. Please. Don't hang up just yet. I apologise if I seem rude. I'm worried, that's all. I've already lost one daughter. I can't bear to think of something happening to Emer was well. Surely you can understand that?'

'Of course,' Dee said, relenting slightly. 'All of this must be very difficult for you.'

'This isn't the first time, you see. There have been other times before this, too many to count, when Emer has seen someone she thinks is Kitty. Each time, she becomes obsessed. It's taken its toll over the years.'

'Would it help if I told you I think this time she may be right?'

'I think what would help,' Ursula said, 'is if you could tell me how you got involved in all of this in the first place? So far, all I've had is a garbled, second-hand account from my husband. Maybe if I hear it from you I'll be able to make some sense of it.'

As quickly as she could, Dee updated her on everything that had happened since her first meeting with the woman pretending to be Emer in Gordon's Wine Bar. She figured she might as well tell Ursula the truth. If she had been involved in her daughter's disappearance, then she already knew Kitty was still alive. If, on the other hand, she'd had nothing to do with it, she certainly deserved to know the truth.

'But you've got no actual proof that this Annie person might be my daughter?' Ursula said, when Dee had finished.

'She had a photo of Kitty and Emer,' Dee said. 'And when I went back the next day to speak to her, she was clearly hiding from me.'

'That doesn't mean anything,' Ursula said. 'If that's all you've got, then I'm sorry, Delilah. I simply cannot believe such a far-fetched story.'

'I know it sounds ridiculous,' Dee said, deciding now wasn't the time to tell Ursula she couldn't stand to be called by her full name. 'But I'm telling the truth about everything that happened.'

'I only have your word for that. I should never have called you. I can see that now. I'd hoped you might be different to your father, that you might actually want to help my family. Clearly, I was wrong. Please don't try to call me back. I won't pick up.'

She hung up before Dee could respond. Which was probably just as well, because anything Dee wanted to say right now was probably best said to an empty room. Dee understood it would be upsetting – devastating, in fact – for a mother to learn that a child she'd thought had died over twenty years ago might still be alive. But she couldn't excuse Ursula's immediate insistence that everything Dee had said was a lie. As for the way she'd spoken about Dee's father, the less Dee dwelt on that the better.

Deciding to put the conversation out of her mind for now, Dee refilled her glass and went back out to the deck. Staring into the black night, she listened to the growling waves as they rolled in and out across the shingle, thinking back to that moment inside the flat, staring down at the crumpled body six floors below.

The police hadn't confirmed the dead man's identity, but she'd worked it out from the questions they'd asked. He was Michael Holden. Annie's father. Which explained, at least, why Annie had been visiting him. Dee had given the police the address she had for Annie and she wondered if they'd managed to find her yet. If they hadn't, how long before Annie even knew her father was dead? Twice since coming home, Dee had tried the mobile number she had for Annie. Both times, she'd got Annie's voicemail. She'd left a message, telling Annie she needed to speak to her urgently. So far, Annie hadn't called her back.

Dee's laptop was open on the table in front of her. Until now, she'd put off searching for the inevitable news story about the man thrown from a block of flats in south London. But three quarters of a bottle of wine had given her the courage she needed to look it up. So far, only the local south London news had picked up the story, although Dee guessed it would hit the national news within the next twenty-four hours.

There was nothing on the news sites that she didn't already know. The victim, not yet formally identified, was a sixty-five-year-old man who'd been living alone in his flat. Police had confirmed they were treating the death as 'suspicious' and there was one 'significant witness' helping with their enquiries.

That would be me, Dee thought, draining what was left in her glass and going inside to refill it. As she put another bottle in the fridge, she felt it. The flicker of something at the furthest edges of her mind. What was it? She tried to focus on it, but it kept slipping out of reach.

She went back over everything she knew about Kitty and Lucy and Annie. Two girls in a small town in Ireland. Another girl in a small town in Sussex. A town ten miles from where Dee was standing right now. Annie Holden, who might be Kitty Doran – Dee's cousin. Her father's niece.

And there it was. The thing that had been staring her in the face all along. Her father. She hadn't seen it before, because she hadn't wanted it to be true. But it was the only thing that made sense. Because Dee knew her dad. No matter how he'd felt about his brother, he wouldn't have been able to sit back and do nothing if his niece needed help.

Carrying her glass outside, Dee paced back and forth along the deck, needing to move because her mind was racing and her body couldn't sit still. Her footsteps were hollow and loud on the wooden boards as she reworked Kitty's story in her mind.

In June 1997, Lucy Ryan disappeared. Whatever happened to Lucy that night, it had involved her best friend, Kitty Doran. Three weeks later, Kitty's parents faked her drowning and managed to get Kitty out of

Ireland. At some point, Eamon Doran asked his estranged brother, Frank, to help him hide his daughter. Somehow, Frank – Dee's father – had persuaded Michael and Fiona Holden to take the eleven-year-old girl and pretend she was their daughter.

Was that really what had happened? After the last few weeks, it seemed too simple an explanation. Dee sat down, went back onto her laptop and scrolled through the stories she'd found about Michael Holden, trying to find out when the family had moved to Alfriston. That had to have happened after Kitty/Annie came to live with them. Alfriston was a small town, the sort of place where everyone knew everyone else's business. If a childless couple suddenly appeared with a daughter they'd not previously had, it would have sparked all sorts of gossip and speculation.

Dee had almost given up searching when she found it. A single sentence that confirmed everything:

> Holden, former landlord of the Victoria pub in Eastbourne, had been living in Alfriston with his wife and daughter since October 1997.

The Victoria pub. The name triggered a barrage of memories from Dee's early life. Sunday roasts in winter time. Dee and her parents gathered around one of the wooden tables by the fire. Sitting at the grand Victorian bar with her father and her ex-husband on one of their frequent visits back to Eastbourne when she was living in London. Sunny afternoons in the small beer garden at the back of the pub. Watching Ireland win the Five Nations rugby tournament in 1985, when she was sixteen. And again in 2009 after it became the Six Nations. Her father taking her to 'the Vic' for a drink after the break-up of Dee's marriage; sitting beside her at a small table in the corner, his concern for her written all over his face, as he told her Billy Morrison was a fool and she was better off without him.

The Victoria had been her father's local after he'd moved to Eastbourne in 1961. There were other decent pubs in the town, especially back then, but her father rarely drank in them. He'd never been a big drinker, but when he went out to meet friends, those encounters invariably took place inside the Victoria. It was the sort of boozer where the locals all knew each other and you could wander in on your own at any time of the day or night and know you'd find someone to have a chat with.

And in that moment, Dee realised why Fiona Holden's face had seemed so familiar. Dee remembered Fiona and Mike from their time running the pub – a laid-back, happy couple who'd always made a point of giving Dee a treat whenever her parents took her with them to the pub.

Other memories now. Her mother, whispering to her father after Fiona had come over with a bar of Dairy Milk for ten-year-old Dee.

Such a shame they can't have kids of their own. They'd make such lovely parents.

Her body started to tingle, a fizzing sensation beneath her skin that happened when a story came together. Her fingers itched with the need to do something. She picked up her phone to call Emer, then put it back down again. First, she needed to check her facts. Instinctively, she knew she was on the right track. But in journalism, instinct only got you so far. Every story you wrote, every word you committed to paper, had to be backed up with facts.

She went back onto the internet, looking for an address for Fiona Holden in Alfriston. She didn't find one, but wasn't about to let that put her off. Alfriston was a small place. If she drove over there tomorrow morning, Dee was confident she'd find someone who could tell her where Fiona lived.

Her phone buzzed with an incoming text. Her stomach fluttered when she saw the sender's name. Ed, his message short and to the point, as always:

Just checking you're okay?

She missed him. Even now, six months after their relationship had ended. She missed him and hated herself for it. She should be stronger than this. Damn it, she *was* stronger than this. She put the phone down without replying to the text, lifted her glass and drank some more wine. She wasn't going to let herself get drawn back into that. They'd broken up because, ultimately, they weren't a good match. She'd do well to remember that. Now, and in the future.

Thirty-four

As it turned out, Dee didn't need to resort to walking around asking strangers if they could tell her where Fiona Holden lived. A quick phone call to Louise and she had all the information she needed. The only problem was, when she told Louise why she needed the address, her cousin insisted on coming with her.

'You don't know what you'll find when you get there,' Louise said. 'I'm not about to let you go over there by yourself.'

'Haven't you got work to do?' Dee said.

'I'll call in sick,' Louise said. 'Let me get the kids to school and I'll pick you up right after that.'

'Can't we go separately and meet there?'

'Do you know how bad that is for the environment?' Louise said. 'And don't suggest taking your car. We both know I'm a better driver than you are.'

This 'fact' was new information to Dee, but she let it go. Louise had, potentially, saved her a lot of time by finding the address so quickly.

While she waited for Louise to pick her up, Dee called Emer.

'It's me,' she said, when she got Emer's voicemail. 'I'm heading out for a few hours this morning, but I'll be home later. Let me know if you're coming to Eastbourne today. I can pick you up from the station.'

Dee didn't mention that the police were also keen to speak to Emer. Apart from Michael Holden's killer, Emer was probably the last person to have seen him alive. If anyone had been hanging around the stairwell or near the flat, Emer may have seen them.

Hanging up, Dee called Shay Flaherty. He'd left her a voicemail while she was being interviewed by the police yesterday. By the time she'd got out of the station, she didn't have the energy to call him back.

'I may have something on O'Brien,' he said. 'So far, it's nothing more than a rumour, but I'm going to follow it up today and see if there's anything in it.'

'In what?' Dee said.

'Someone who's worked with O'Brien told me his wife and her ex-husband were swingers. This source, who was very cautious about speaking to me, says there's a woman in Loughrea who might be able to shed some light on this. I'm driving down to see her today. She's from the Travelling community. One of O'Brien's favourite causes, in case you weren't aware of that.'

'Oh yes,' Dee said. 'I've read all about his charitable endeavours. This woman you're going to see, any idea what she'll be able to tell you?'

'Not yet. But I'll keep you in the loop. How about you? Anything you'd like to share with me?'

'I'm getting closer,' Dee said. 'Hopefully I'll have more news by the end of today.'

She saw Louise's red SUV turning into the narrow road that led to her house. Telling Shay she'd speak to him later, Dee ended the call and waited for Louise's car to pull up alongside her.

'We covered the murder trial,' Louise explained, as Dee clambered into her car. 'That's why I know where they live. Of course, she may have moved since then.'

'It's worth a shot though,' Dee said. 'Jesus Lou, you can't really lecture me about the environment when you drive around in this thing.'

'I have a family,' Louise said.

'So do lots of people,' Dee said, 'but they don't all have cars like this.'

'Only because they can't afford it.'

Dee knew when to give up so she changed the subject before the conversation became any more ridiculous.

'What do you remember about them?' she asked.

'It was a weird one. Actually, I remember your dad being really upset about it. Of course, I assumed it was because he knew Michael from the pub. It never occurred to me there could be any other reason.' Louise shook her head. 'This story about your dad helping to hide his niece. Do you really believe he'd do something like that?'

'I think he'd have done anything to keep a child safe. Although I'm struggling to accept that there might be this whole other part of his life I didn't know anything about.'

'How could you have known?' Louise said. 'You were living in London then, weren't you?'

'1997. The year I got married. I had a job I loved and a husband I adored. The truth is, I didn't give much thought to what was going on in my parents' life back then. I was so caught up in my London life. Do you think my mum knew? I hope so. I'd hate to think of him keeping secrets from her.'

'All couples keep secrets from each other,' Louise said. 'It doesn't mean there's something wrong with their marriage.'

'You said the trial was weird,' Dee said, once again moving the conversation onto safer ground. After the catastrophic end to the affair that had almost ruined Louise's marriage, Dee wasn't ready to hear about any other secrets her cousin might be keeping from her husband. 'What was weird about it?'

'Everything,' Louise said. 'Mike Holden had never been in trouble in his life. Then out of the blue, he killed a man but never gave a reason for why he did it. He had psychiatric assessments but I don't think anyone was ever able to find anything wrong with him. He always claimed he didn't know the victim, and the police were never able to prove otherwise.'

'There must have been theories about why he did it.'

'Lots of theories,' Louise said. 'Most of them that Mike was involved in something dodgy. But I never really believed that. If he was, it would have come out sooner or later, and it never did. What about you?'

'What about me?'

'Oh come on, Dee. You must have your own idea of why Mike killed that guy.'

'Maybe,' Dee said, 'but for now that's all it is: an idea. I don't want to jinx it by talking about it just yet.'

'Even though I got you the address and now I'm driving you to Alfriston?'

'Sorry.' Dee smiled. 'So, if you didn't think he was involved in something dodgy – what did you think?'

'All right,' Louise said. 'But remember, I want to hear your clever idea as soon as you're ready to share it.'

'You'll be the first to know,' Dee said. 'I promise.'

'I thought he was being blackmailed. It's the only thing that made sense. I don't believe he suddenly turned into a psychopath and killed a random stranger for no reason.'

'Being blackmailed about what?'

'I assumed he was having an affair, something like that. But now I'm wondering, if you're right and Annie isn't really their child – that would be a good reason for blackmail.' She glanced across at Dee. 'How am I doing?'

'Not bad,' Dee admitted.

In fact, Louise's theory was pretty close to Dee's. The only difference was that Louise hadn't made the jump to working out the identity of the man Michael Holden had killed.

'By all accounts they were a really close family.' Louise frowned. 'You know, all the time I covered that story, I never once got any hint that Annie wasn't their child.'

'They'd been out of Eastbourne a long time by then,' Dee said. 'Annie would have been = what? – twenty-one at the time of the murder? From the articles I read, journalists barely mentioned her in their stories.'

'They had no reason to,' Louise said. 'Although now you mention it, I vaguely remember someone telling me Fiona and Mike didn't always have a daughter. Who was that? God, it was so long ago… It probably doesn't matter. I'm sure they said Annie was adopted. That would make sense, wouldn't it? They adopted Annie and moved to Alfriston soon after that.'

'Of course,' Dee said. 'People adopt older kids all the time. It's the perfect cover. And, as you say, if they moved to Alfriston soon after, there'd be fewer people to ask difficult questions about the adoption.'

'If someone was looking for Kitty,' Louise said, 'I doubt they'd make the connection with Mike and Fiona. It's too tenuous. Who would even know they were friends with your father?'

'I don't think they were friends exactly,' Dee said, 'not really. Dad drank at the pub they ran, but that's as far as it went.'

She thought of the painting she'd seen in Annie's studio. The woman sitting at the bar with a packet of cigarettes in front of her, and a child hiding in the corner. At the time, she'd thought it was a self-portrait. But over the last few days, Dee had pored over every news piece she could find about Robert O'Brien and his wife. She'd seen enough photos of Ursula O'Brien to work out she was the woman in Kitty's painting. The only question now in Dee's mind was whether the child in the painting had been Kitty or Emer.

They'd arrived in Alfriston by now, Louise navigating her way slowly down the high street that was too narrow for two cars to pass each other at the same time.

'I want to move here when we retire,' Louise said. 'I love Alfriston.'

'They were pub landlords,' Dee said, looking out the window at the timber-framed buildings and flint-fronted terraced housing. 'Alfriston's an expensive place to live. How did they afford that? Did they even work after they moved here?'

'They sold the pub,' Louise said. 'It was a freehold back then. That probably gave them enough money to buy a house somewhere like this. They ran their own catering business after they moved here. You could probably make a lot of money in catering somewhere like this. Imagine all those wealthy people having dinner parties but not wanting to do the cooking themselves. Plus the fancy weddings and christenings and birthdays you could cater for. It could be quite lucrative.'

She indicated and turned left into the driveway of a classic, flint and red-brick two-storey house set in its own grounds on the outskirts of the village.

'Wow,' Dee said, taking in the house. 'It must have been very lucrative.'

Louise switched off the engine and they got out of the car.

'Looks pretty quiet,' Louise said.

'There's a car here,' Dee said, pointing to the cream-coloured Mini Clubman, 'maybe someone's home.'

But when she rang the doorbell, no one came to answer it.

'What do we do now?' Louise asked.

'We have a look around.'

Dee walked around the outside of house, peering through the windows. Inside, the house was every bit as lovely as the outside. Large, high-ceilinged rooms with plenty of original features, all tastefully furnished and decorated. The back of the house had been extended to create a huge kitchen-diner with doors leading to the well-tended back garden.

'What's that?' Louise pointed at a low stone building at the end of the garden.

'Looks like an old ice house.'

Intrigued, Dee wandered over to take a closer look.

Built entirely out of stone, the little building resembled a stone igloo. It had a thick, wooden door, with an old-fashioned lock. A rust-covered key was in the lock which, after a few attempts, Dee managed to twist around. She pushed her weight against the door and it creaked open slowly. Dee guessed this was the first time it had been opened in years. She stepped forward, into the pitch black and icy cold. A stale smell wafted out and she wrinkled her nose as she switched on the torch on her phone and looked inside.

'Amazing,' she whispered to Louise, standing behind her. 'Probably been here since the seventeenth century. They wouldn't use it today, of course.'

'It's horrible,' Louise said. 'Come away, Dee. I don't like it in there. It gives me the creeps.'

Dee was about to tell Louise not to be such a sissy, when she remembered what had happened to her cousin at the beginning of the year. She'd been attacked and locked inside the boot of her car. It was no wonder a dark space like the inside of the ice house would freak her out.

'There's nothing in there, anyway.' Dee stepped back and pulled the door closed. 'Come on, let's try the house one more time.'

She walked around the outside of the house again, looking into the rooms and banging on the windows, even though she knew it was pointless. Wherever Fiona and Annie were hiding out, they weren't here.

'We could wait,' Louise said. 'I've taken the morning off so I don't have to be anywhere else.'

'We could,' Dee agreed. 'But I don't think there's much point.'

At the front door, she crouched down to peer through the letterbox. She got a partial view of a large hallway with pale blue walls and ornate cornicing on the ceiling. And on the tiled floor, a piece of white paper, folded over, with Annie's name hand-written across the front.

'Someone's dropped a note through the letterbox,' she said. 'Here, take a look.'

She stepped back from the door, making space.

'It's too far away to reach,' Louise said, 'if that's what you're thinking.'

'There must be some way we can get it,' Dee said.

She remembered seeing a shed in the back garden, but when she went to see if she could find something she could use to retrieve the note, the door was locked.

In frustration, she kicked the shed. But all that succeeded in doing was sending a shot of pain through her toes and into her foot.

'What about breaking into the house?' she said.

'No,' Louise said. 'We're not breaking the law, Dee. Come on. There's nothing else you can do here. Besides, that note could have been from anyone.'

'It's from someone trying to get in touch with Annie,' Dee said. 'Which means we're not the only people trying to find her.'

'Yeah, but you already know that,' Louise said. 'Isn't that why she's hiding? Because she knows someone is looking for her?'

'I want to know who,' Dee said, 'and why.'

'Well you're not going to find that out by staying here. Come on. Let's grab a coffee in the village. We can ask around about Annie and Fiona, see what we find out.'

Leaving the car where it was, they walked into the village and stopped at the first coffee shop they found.

'You're the second person in as many days to ask me about Annie,' the young woman behind the counter told Dee. 'You want to tell me why you're so interested in trying to find her?'

'Annie's my cousin,' Dee said. 'I was in the area today so I thought I'd see if she was at home. Except we've just been to the house and there's no one there.'

'Annie doesn't have any cousins.'

'How do you know that?' Louise asked.

'She's my mate,' the woman said. 'Now if you don't mind, ladies, I've got other customers to serve. Enjoy your coffees.'

'Hang on,' Dee said. 'I really think Annie might be my cousin. I'm not lying about that. I swear to you.'

'I've already told you. Annie doesn't have any cousins. Both her parents are only children.'

'But they're her adopted parents,' Dee said, 'aren't they? I think Annie's birth father is my uncle.'

'How do you know she's adopted?'

'Because my uncle had a daughter who was given up for adoption. But later, he had another daughter, and now she's an adult and she's trying to find her sister. And she thinks that sister could be Annie.'

'This sister,' the girl said, 'she's not Irish, by any chance?'

'She is, actually. Why?'

'She was here yesterday. Asking about Annie just like you. But she didn't say anything about being Annie's sister.'

'Tall with dark hair?' Dee said. Then, when the girl nodded, 'Her name's Emer. I don't suppose you know where she is now, do you?'

'Sorry.' The girl shrugged. 'I told her where Annie lived and she left. I haven't seen her since then.'

Thanking her, Dee went outside and called Emer.

'It's me,' she said, when she got her cousin's voicemail again. 'I know you've been to Annie's house. I've just come from there, but it's empty. Call me as soon as you can. I really need to speak to you.'

'Everything okay?' Louise had followed Dee outside, holding two paper cups. 'I got your coffee to take away. Here.'

'Thanks.' Dee took the cup and drank some of the coffee. 'I've just called Emer but she didn't pick up. Can you drop me home? If she was in Alfriston yesterday, maybe she'll turn up in Eastbourne today. If she does, I want to be there.'

Except when Louise pulled up outside Dee's house, it wasn't Emer who was waiting on Dee's doorstep.

'Looks like you've got a visitor,' Louise said.

'What the hell…?' Dee unstrapped her seatbelt, then changed her mind. 'Can you drop me in town, Louise? I really can't face this right now.'

'Don't be such a coward,' Louise said. 'Go on.'

Dee rolled her eyes, but did as she was told, making sure to slam the door hard when she got out so Louise would know she was annoyed with her. She waited until Louise had turned the car and driven away. Then she walked slowly towards her house, where Ed Mitchell stood waiting for her.

Thirty-five

Emer stood in the small art gallery, across the road from the coffee shop, watching Dee. She was speaking to the woman Emer had talked to yesterday afternoon. Part of her wanted to cross the road and tell Dee she was here, but she couldn't bring herself to do it. Maeve was right, it was better not to trust anyone until they knew exactly what was going on.

A moment later, Dee came outside and made a phone call. The sudden sound of Emer's phone ringing made her jump. When she saw Dee's name on the screen, she thought her cousin must have seen her. She diverted the call and waited for Dee to cross the road and confront her. Instead, Dee stayed on the phone – leaving a message, Emer guessed. By the time Dee had finished, another woman had joined her and handed Dee a disposable cup.

Emer watched as they crossed the road, holding her breath until they'd passed the gallery and were out of sight again.

'Are you sure I can't help you?'

The man running the gallery was clearly getting fed up with her lurking in here with no intention of buying one of the overpriced paintings on display.

'I'm sure,' Emer said. 'Thanks.'

She stepped outside, checking up and down the street to make sure Dee was really gone. After listening to Dee's message, she headed back to the fourteenth-century inn on the high street where Maeve was waiting for her.

They had travelled down from London the previous day, taking a train to Polegate and a taxi to Alfriston. Finding Annie's house was easier than they'd anticipated. A quick chat with the woman running the coffee shop had given them the information they'd needed. Maeve had waited outside, while Emer spun the woman a story about being an old university friend of Annie's. The woman had become quite animated, telling Emer how often Annie spoke of her uni friends and how happy she'd be to see one of them turning up in Alfriston. Except when they arrived at the house, it was empty.

At that point, Emer had wanted to give up and go to Dee's house in Eastbourne. But Maeve had persuaded her to spend the night in Alfriston and try Annie's house again the following morning. So they'd found a place to stay and spent the evening working out what to do next.

This morning, after breakfast, Emer had gone back to the house to try again. Before leaving the hotel, she'd written a note to put through the letterbox, giving 'Annie' her phone number and asking her to get in touch. When she arrived at the house, there was a car parked in the driveway – a cream-coloured Mini Clubman. But when she rang the doorbell and knocked on the front door, no one answered. Frustrated, she'd slipped the note through the letterbox and walked back to the village. She'd been passing the art gallery when she saw Dee walking into the coffee shop across the road.

'We should leave,' Maeve said, when Emer got back to the room and told her about seeing Dee. 'If your cousin's here, it's only a matter of time before she sees you. There's only so long you can hide in place this size.'

'Go where?' Emer asked.

'Eastbourne,' Maeve said. 'There's a nice hotel near Polegate – I looked it up while you were out. We can stay there without anyone noticing us, and get back here quickly if we have to. I'm going to look into hiring a car as well. Makes more sense than taking taxis everywhere.'

'How much will the hotel cost?' Emer said. 'My money's running out faster than I can spend it.'

'I'll pay for the hotel,' Maeve said. 'Really, it's okay. What else am I going to spend my money on? My parents were loaded. I inherited everything when they died. If this woman really is Kitty, and she can tell me what happened to Lucy, then I'd happily spend every penny of my money trying to find her.'

'Only if you let me pay you back when I'm working again,' Emer said. 'Make sure you keep track of everything you spend.'

'You don't need to worry about that,' Maeve said. 'Come on. Let's pack up.'

'You sure it wouldn't it be better to stay here?' Emer asked.

'Cooped up in this room all day? No thanks. If Dee's in Alfriston, that means we can't even risk going downstairs and having a drink at the bar in case she comes in and finds us.'

'So what if she does?'

Emer did her best not to sound annoyed, but it was difficult. Letting someone else take charge was harder than she'd expected. The fact that Maeve was now paying for everything didn't help. It made Emer feel as if she had to go along with whatever Maeve wanted.

'You can't trust her,' Maeve said. 'I thought we agreed about that.'

'You agreed about it,' Emer said. 'Dee's never given me any reason not to trust her.'

'Emer, she told you the most ridiculous story about meeting someone who was pretending to be you. Surely you don't really believe that's why she got in touch with you?'

'Yes,' Emer said. 'That's exactly what I believe. You haven't met her, Maeve. She's lovely, and she seemed to really care about helping me find Kitty.'

'You think I don't care about that?'

'I'm not saying that. Sorry. How did this suddenly turn into an argument?'

'None of this is easy,' Maeve said. 'It's a big crazy mess and we've got caught up in it because we're both so desperate for Kitty to still be alive. For you, it means you haven't lost your sister. For me, it means finding out – finally – what happened to Lucy. I'm starting to wonder if it might be healthier for us both to accept we'll never get the answers we want and walk away from this before it's too late.'

'Too late how?'

'I'm not sure.' Maeve frowned. 'It just seems we've lost sight of what we're actually doing.'

'We're trying to find the truth,' Emer said. 'That's all that matters, and I'm going to see this through to the end.'

'Even if you find out that Annie Holden is exactly who she says she is?'

'Yes.'

Maeve rubbed her face with both hands.

'Okay. If you trust your cousin, give her a ring and arrange to meet her. See if she can help us find Annie.'

'Brilliant.' Emer hugged Maeve and grabbed her phone. 'I'll need to go outside to call her. I can't get a signal in here. Thanks, Maeve.'

Outside, she had to cross the road and walk up a narrow side street until she finally got three signal bars on her phone. She tried Dee's number, but Dee didn't answer and Emer hung up without leaving a message. She wanted to speak to Dee in person, not to her voicemail.

She started walking back towards the inn, and was about to cross the road, when two things happened.

A silver Lexus came along the high street, driving slowly enough for Emer to get a clear view the driver's face in profile as the car passed. She put her hand over her mouth, and jumped back, terrified he'd seen her. But he hadn't looked at her as he'd passed and the car drove on without stopping.

She was trying to convince herself she'd made a mistake, that the driver couldn't be the person she thought it was, when her phone started to ring. Still in shock, she answered it without bothering to check the caller ID.

'Hello?'

Silence.

The silver Lexus was gone, but in her mind, she could still see it. She thought this was him, the man driving the car, calling to say he'd seen her.

'Emer?'

The voice triggered a flood of memories from long ago, before Kitty disappeared and Emer's life changed forever. They rolled over her like waves, until she was drowning, slipping back into the past while the walls of the houses on either side of the narrow street closed in on her.

'Emer, it's me. Kitty.'

The phone fell from her hand. As the darkness crept closer, she felt it again, that shock of recognition when she'd seen the silver car and realised the man driving it was her stepfather, Robert.

Thirty-six

'Any chance I could come in for a coffee?'

'Do I have a choice?' Dee remembered when she'd first got to know him. Back then, Ed was investigating the murder of a young woman whose body had been discovered by Dee. He used to regularly drop in like this, unannounced, looking for coffee and information.

In the kitchen, when he offered to make the coffee, Dee reminded him that this was her house and she'd make her own coffee, thank you very much. Which at least shut him up for a bit.

'We'll sit outside,' she said, once the coffee was made. 'It's just about warm enough. And before you ask – no, I don't have any biscuits.'

She carried the tray onto the deck, put it on the table and poured coffee for both of them before he had a chance to do it for her.

'I assume this has something to do with what happened in London the other day?' she said.

'Sort of.' Ed shifted in his chair, looking uncharacteristically uncomfortable.

'What is it?'

'I heard what happened yesterday, and I wanted to check you're okay.'

'How did you hear about that?'

'A friend of mine working at Brixton station got in touch asking questions about you. What the hell were you doing there, Dee?'

'I already told your *friend*,' she used her index fingers to make imaginary speech marks, 'exactly why I was there.'

'You were looking for Annie,' Ed said. 'The same reason you were in Wapping on Saturday.'

'That's right.' Dee took a sip of her coffee, trying to work out what she'd missed. Because she knew Ed better than he realised. He was here because he wanted information.

'Michael Holden,' she said, as she worked it out. 'You want to know if I've found anything out about the murder he was convicted of. You were part of the original investigation, weren't you?'

'My first case as SIO,' Ed said. 'Senior Investigating Officer. It was a frustrating case from the outset and I was never really happy with the outcome. Don't get me wrong – there was no doubt that Mike had killed the guy. But it always bugged me that we never found out why he'd done it, or who the victim was. We got the conviction we wanted and I had to move on, but it was always there, a niggle at the back of the mind. This last week, it's all come back to me, and I've been trying to work out what we missed back then.'

She wanted to tell him. But she had no proof. Not yet.

'I can't help you, I'm afraid,' Dee said. 'Until yesterday, I'd barely given Annie's father a second thought. She's been my whole focus, not him.'

'Except if Annie turns out to be someone else, then that might explain Mike's actions. Because I'm telling you, Dee, that murder was completely out of character. In this job, you get a feel for who the real crooks are, the bad ones who deserve what's coming to them. Mike Holden was never one of those. He was a decent man who did a terrible thing. Now he's dead and I know, in my gut, that those two events are related. We missed something during the investigation ten years ago. Because of that, a decent man was sent to prison. Now he's dead and I feel as if I've failed him all over again.'

'You can't blame yourself,' Dee said. 'Whatever his reasons for killing that man, it was still his decision to do it. That's on him, not you.'

Ed spread his hands open in a gesture she remembered. It was his way of saying he didn't know what to do.

'Did Annie call you?' she asked. 'Is that why you were in London that day?'

'Fiona called me,' he said. 'Annie's mother. She said a journalist had been harassing Annie, trying to get her to do an interview about the murder. She was quite upset, but there was something not quite right about the conversation. I felt as if she was asking me to do something without coming right out and saying what it was. So I decided to take a few hours off work and go and see Annie myself.'

'But when you arrived at her house, you found me instead.'

'Lucky me.'

Dee felt the rush of heat to her cheeks. When she glanced at Ed, he was smiling. She looked away quickly, the heat intensifying.

'Sorry,' he said. 'I didn't mean to embarrass you.'

'I'll get over it. Listen, Ed, I think Annie might be in danger. And I think it might be my fault. I was so stupid. I let that woman dupe me into believing she was my cousin. I practically handed Annie to her on a plate.'

Ed started to speak, but Dee interrupted him.

'Hang on a second. If you came to London to speak to Annie, then I wasn't mistaken, was I? That's her house. You could have bloody told me that. I've spent the last few days wondering if I'm losing my mind.'

'I suppose I could have told you. Sorry.'

The second time he'd apologised since he'd been here, Dee noted.

'I was so surprised to see you there,' he continued. 'I wasn't sure what to tell you.'

'And the person who answered the door? Who was he?'

'Louis Haynes. He's married to an old school friend of Annie's, apparently.'

'Nick,' Dee said, remembering the conversation she'd had with the Australian woman at the pub. 'Landlord at the Town of Ramsgate.'

'And you know this how?'

'It doesn't matter,' Dee said. 'Annie clearly asked Nick and his partner to cover for her.'

'I can understand she might not have wanted to speak to you about her father and the murder,' Ed said. 'But to pretend she didn't live there? Doesn't that seem a bit extreme to you?'

'Not if she's hiding other secrets as well,' Dee said.

'Maybe.' Ed didn't sound convinced. 'I've kept in touch with Fiona over the years, you know. I told myself it was because I hoped she might tell me the real reason Mike did what he did. But the truth is, I felt sorry for her. She's a lovely woman, and she had such a terrible time during the trial. Keeping in touch seemed the decent thing to do.'

And there you had it. Decency, kindness, intelligence. Three things that, coupled with a wicked sense of humour and chocolate brown eyes, made it impossible to forget her feelings for him and get on with her life.

'I've been trying to get in touch with her,' Ed continued. 'I don't want her to hear about Michael from a stranger. But she's not answering her phone and when I drove out to the house yesterday evening, there was no one there.'

'So what do we do now?'

When she said this, she saw a trace of the old Ed. The one she'd fallen for so hard and so fast. A twinkling humour behind his eyes that sent her stomach somersaulting.

'We?'

'Yes, we. You came here today because you're looking for answers. I've told you as much as I can, so what happens now?'

'We could have another pot of coffee. I know you said you don't have any biscuits but, by my reckoning, it's almost lunch. Maybe you could whip up a round of sandwiches while you're at it?'

She should tell him to get lost and make his own bloody sandwiches. Except now he was smiling and – God help her and forgive her – Dee found herself smiling right back at him.

Thirty-seven

Emer stood on the Eastbourne seafront, her back to the ocean, staring at the façade of the Cavendish Hotel. Her sister was in there. Just a few metres from where Emer stood. Ever since getting the phone call earlier today, it was all she'd been able to think about. She should have felt vindicated for all those years when she'd refused to believe Kitty had died. Instead, she felt nothing but a profound sadness for the years they'd lost and would never get back.

Kitty had made it clear she'd only meet Emer if she came by herself. So Emer had lied to Maeve and told her she was going to meet Dee. Luckily, Maeve was happy for Emer to do that alone. Emer had left her at the hotel in Polegate and taken the train to Eastbourne town centre. From there, it was only a ten-minute walk through the town to this hotel, where Kitty had said she'd be waiting for her.

She crossed the road, and walked up the steps into the hotel lobby. Groups of people sat on the sofas and armchairs scattered around the large space. Emer scanned the faces, searching for Kitty. There was no one who looked like the woman she'd seen on the train. She looked around again, searching more intently, panicking now because Kitty wasn't here. Which meant she'd changed her mind and wasn't going to turn up. Or something had happened to her in the two hours between speaking to Emer on the phone and now. Or…

'Emer!'

Kitty's voice. Not here in the lobby. Looking down at her from the staircase that curved up through the centre of the hotel. Emer's breath caught in her throat. For a moment, she didn't think she could go through with it. The urge to turn around and run away was surprisingly powerful. She didn't understand. This was what she'd wanted, wasn't it?

And then, as if she had no control over her actions, she was walking towards her sister, her vision blurring as she started to cry. Tears pouring down her face as she climbed the stairs, moving faster now, taking the steps two a time, running towards her past.

'Emer. Oh Emer.'

Kitty grabbed her and was hugging her, holding her tight as she kissed her face over and over.

'Is it really you?' Emer managed, between sobs. 'Is it you, Kitty?'

'It's me.' Kitty squeezed her so tight Emer couldn't breathe. She didn't care if she never breathed again. All that mattered was this moment.

At some point, Kitty released her and Emer was laughing now. Joy and hysteria poured out of her, mixing with all the other emotions she couldn't control. Grief and anger and relief. Her sister was alive and all the things that had been wrong in Emer's life could be mended. Finally.

Taking Emer's hand, Kitty led her up to the next floor. Kitty talked non-stop, asking questions Emer didn't have time to answer before Kitty moved on to the next one. It was strange hearing her speak with an English accent. Emer hadn't expected that.

'This is us.' Kitty stopped outside one of the hotel bedrooms. She opened the door with a card key and they entered a big, airy room. Two double beds. High ceiling. A separate seating area with four armchairs and a walnut coffee table. French windows leading out to a small balcony with sea views. An older woman, tall and slender with blond hair and grey eyes, smiling at Emer as if they were old friends.

'I found your note,' Kitty was saying now. 'I drove back to the house this morning to pick up my passport, in case I needed it. When I read what you'd written, I knew I couldn't leave without seeing you first.'

'You were there this morning?' Emer asked. She remembered seeing the Mini Clubman parked outside the house. She should have tried harder to get Kitty to answer the door.

'Only for a few minutes,' Kitty said. 'I saw you. I was upstairs and I saw you on the doorstep. I almost went down to you, but you were gone so quickly. I was wondering whether or not to go after you when someone else arrived at the house. Two women. I could hear them but I was upstairs and I was afraid to look out the window in case they saw me. They were there for ages. At one point I thought they were going to try to break into the house, but they left eventually. As soon as they were gone, I went downstairs and I saw the note you'd left me.'

'You didn't see anyone else?'

'Like who?'

'I thought I saw…' Emer stopped speaking. Right now, she wasn't sure she could trust what she'd seen. Was it possible she'd made a mistake and it wasn't Robert driving that car? No. She knew what she'd seen. Which meant Kitty must have missed him by minutes.

'You're so clever,' Kitty continued, 'finding the house and everything else. You always were the clever one. I was so scatty and disorganised, do you remember? You had all the brains.'

That wasn't how Emer remembered it, but she wasn't going to argue the point.

'I'm Fiona.' The woman with the grey eyes had come over and was pulling Emer into a warm hug. 'So lovely to meet you. I've heard a lot about you, Emer. Coffee?' She let Emer go and nodded at the pot of coffee on the table between the armchairs.

Emer shook her head. She wasn't here for coffee. She was here for answers. She looked at Kitty.

'Why did you leave us?'

'It was never what I wanted,' Kitty said. 'I swear.'

'So why?' The anger was becoming a full-on, burning rage – about everything she'd lost; the mess her life had become and the lies, the endless lies from people she'd trusted. Her mother, her sister, her father, Robert.

'Does anyone else know you're here?' Fiona asked.

'No. And who the hell are you? I came here to see my sister. Not anyone else.'

'Emer, it's okay.' Kitty patted one of the armchairs. 'Come and sit down. I'll tell you everything.'

Thirty-eight

Kitty could barely believe she was sitting in a room with her sister. So many times, she'd imagined this moment. Now, finally, it had happened. She kept wanting to reach out and touch her, make sure she was really here.

'I'm so sorry,' she said. 'I can't imagine how hard this is for you.'

Emer still looked as if she wasn't sure whether to stay or go.

'Please sit down?' Kitty said.

'I'll sit down if you tell me why you ran away from me that afternoon on the Underground.'

Kitty had been in town, having lunch with Louis and Nick to celebrate Nick's birthday. She'd left the boys in Soho and was heading back to Wapping for her shift at the pub. She'd had a tough few weeks. The summer months were always difficult. An annual reminder of the night her life had changed forever. Some years were better than others. This year had been one of the bad ones. If it hadn't been for Fiona's steady presence, she wasn't sure she'd have made it through this time.

She'd been reading a book but something, some sixth sense, made her look up. And there she was. Emer. The sister she'd missed so much in those agonising early years when she'd first left Ireland. The longing to be with her again had been physical, an ache deep inside her that no amount of painkillers could ease.

'I was scared,' Kitty said. She looked across at Fiona, the woman who'd taken her in and raised her as if she was her own child. The woman whose life had been devastated by that single decision. Not that Fiona would ever admit that. Even now, after everything, she still insisted that taking care of Kitty had been the single best thing she'd ever done.

'Scared of what?' Emer said, sitting down on the empty chair.

'Everything.'

The memories from that night never left. They filled her mind until she felt as if her head would explode. The guilt was the worst thing. Guilt at pushing Lucy, guilt at lying about what had happened, guilt at leaving her sister. Endless, suffocating guilt that became such a part of who she was she couldn't remember what it felt like to live without it. She should have had counselling, professional help to give her strategies for coping. Instead, she'd had two adults – Fiona and Michael – who'd done their best to love her and keep her safe. Kitty remembered all the self-help books Fiona had made her read, the mindfulness sessions that Kitty had hated at first but now, as an adult, were one of the props she used to get her through each day. None of it was enough, though, because no matter how hard she worked to control the dark thoughts inside her head, they kept coming.

'Annie, you don't have to do this,' Fiona said now, dragging Kitty back from the darkness like she always did.

'Yes I do,' Kitty said. 'And let's stop with the Annie now. I can go back to being Kitty again.'

'Whatever you want,' Fiona said. 'You know that.'

Fiona's face blurred as Kitty's eyes filled with tears. She was able to recognise how lucky she'd been. In many ways, coming to live with Michael and Fiona had saved her. Because they were kind and loving and not messed up and cruel like Kitty's own parents.

'I never stopped thinking about you,' she said to Emer. 'I've kept track of you over the years. Well, as much as I was able to.'

'What do you mean?'

'Social media mainly,' Kitty said. 'Your Facebook and Instagram accounts are private, but it still wasn't that hard to find you. You're friends with lots of people from Ballincarraig. On Facebook, all I did was set up a fake account and send them friend requests. Lots of people will accept a friend request without even checking how they know the person. I did the same on Instagram. Started following people you know first, then you.'

She stopped speaking, thinking of all the hours she'd spent, poring over her sister's social media posts. Trying to work out if Emer was doing okay without her. It wasn't just Emer, either. Using her fake account, Kitty had also been able to find Maeve Ryan on social media. For a long time, she'd followed Maeve's stories too. Until the compulsion to contact Maeve and tell her the truth about her sister became too strong and Kitty had to block Maeve's accounts so she couldn't see them any longer.

'I have lots of Facebook friends,' Emer said. 'Half of them, I barely remember how I know them.'

'You're getting married?' Kitty said, remembering Emer's post about her girlfriend proposing to her. 'Nikki, isn't it? She looks lovely.'

'I don't want to talk about Nikki,' Emer said abruptly. 'Not now. I want to talk about you, and why you left.'

'How did you cope?' Kitty asked. 'Growing up with our mother must have been hell.'

'It wasn't easy,' Emer said. 'But she was never as bad with me as she was with you. And she got a lot better after we moved in with Robert. Oh God. You probably don't even know, do you? Dad left and Mum remarried Robert O'Brien. Remember him? But I can tell you about that later. First, I want to know what happened.'

The cold clutch of fear when she heard his name. Even now, all these years later.

'I knew,' she said, when she could trust herself to speak. 'I've read about Robert's progress over the years. And seen the photos of the two of them together. I can't imagine what it must be like, having that man as a stepfather.'

'He's been great,' Emer said. 'More than great, in fact.'

'Really?'

'Yes, really.' Emer frowned. 'Why wouldn't he be?'

'Because…' Kitty paused. 'Sorry. This isn't easy. They were having an affair. Mum and Mr O'Brien. Did you know that?'

'I've heard rumours,' Emer said. 'But even if they were, so what? Ursula's been a lot better with Robert than she ever was with Dad.'

'Ursula?'

'It's what she likes to be called,' Emer said. 'Anyway, that's not important. I want to know what happened, Kitty. Why did you leave?'

'They didn't give me a choice,' Kitty said. 'Lucy was dead and I knew who killed her. They told me if I went to the Guards, you'd be next.'

Thirty-nine

June 1997

'Kitty! I know you're in there. Open the door and let me in. All I want to do is talk to you. Please, Kitty.'

She squeezed her eyes shut and put her hands over her ears. But she wasn't able to block out the sound of Lucy's father banging on the front door, or the desperate edge to his voice as he shouted up to her.

The temptation to get up, go downstairs and speak to him was hard to resist. Because she liked Mr Ryan. He was kind and funny and he was always nice to Kitty when she was at Lucy's house. He deserved to know the truth. That Lucy was dead because Kitty had pushed her in front of a car. And later, after Kitty was dead, the man who'd been driving the car had carried Lucy's body into the woods and buried it. She wanted him to know she was sorry. That she'd tried to stop the man taking Lucy's body, but he'd forced her inside the boot of the car and locked her in there until he was finished.

The problem was, if she told all this to Mr Ryan, he would want to know who the man was, and Kitty wasn't allowed to tell him that. Because if she told anyone – even Mr Ryan, who deserved to know the truth – she would be in worse trouble than she already was.

Outside, she heard a car pull up. Doors slamming, the clatter of her mother's heels on the pavement. The sound triggered another memory from that night, something else she didn't want to think about but it was there, inside her head, and she couldn't get rid of it no matter how hard she tried.

'Niall, you need to leave the girl alone.'

Her mother's voice, sharp and unsympathetic like the rest of her.

'How can I do that, Ursula? My child is missing and Kitty's refusing to tell anyone where she is. Have you tried speaking to her?'

'She doesn't know anything. I've already told you that. I want you to leave now. If you don't, I'll have no choice but to call the Guards.'

He said something that Kitty didn't catch. Then the front door opened and slammed shut and Mr Ryan was gone.

'Kitty?'

'I'm in my room.'

The whisper of voices followed by the creaking of the stairs as her mother came up to see her.

'You didn't let him in,' Mum said, coming into the room without knocking and standing over the bed. 'Good girl.'

'He deserves to know the truth,' Kitty said.

'And what's the truth? That you killed his daughter? You'll go to prison, Kitty. Is that what you want?'

'It's not me you're worried about.'

Mum leaned down, her face so close Kitty could smell coffee on her breath. Resisting the urge to draw back, Kitty stayed still, waiting.

'What's that supposed to mean?'

'You don't care about me,' Kitty said. 'All you care about is making sure no one knows what was going on in the house that night.'

She didn't see her mother's hand until it hit her. A slap across the side of her face that knocked her head sideways and left a ringing sound inside her head so that when Mum started speaking again, Kitty had to struggle to hear the words.

'You need to watch your mouth, young lady. You have no idea the amount of trouble you're in. Your father and I, we're doing everything we can to protect you, but you don't make it easy for us. You're lucky you didn't end up dead that night as well. If you tell anyone – and I mean anyone – what happened that night, you are putting all of us in danger. Think about that. It's not just your own life that's at risk anymore.'

'What do you mean?'

'The men who were at the house that night are very powerful. If you speak to the Guards, two things will happen: one, you will be arrested and sent to prison for pushing your friend in front of a car; and two, our family will be punished.'

'You're lying!' The words burst out of her mouth before she could stop them. She jumped off the bed and faced up to her mother, rage making her reckless.

'You don't care about me or Emer or Dad or what happens to us. You only care about him. Does Dad know about the two of you? No. Of course he doesn't. Well maybe it's about time he knew the truth.'

'That's enough.'

She hadn't heard him, hadn't even realised he was here in the house. But now he was standing in the doorway of her bedroom, blocking out all the light from the corridor.

Bigger and wider than her father, and stronger. The bruises on her arms were proof of just how strong he was.

'Can I speak to her for a moment, Ursula?'

Kitty looked at her mother, eyes begging her not to leave. But Mum ignored her, just like she always did. And then her mother was gone and the bedroom door was closing and he was walking towards her.

She screamed, as loudly as she could, and when he reached out to grab her, she tried to dodge past him. But she wasn't fast enough. His hand wrapped around her arm and his other hand wrapped around her neck. And when he leaned his face close to hers and started telling her what would happen to Emer if Kitty ever spoke to the Guards, she lost control of her bladder and the rush of urine on the inside of her legs was the last thing she remembered before she passed out.

Forty

Dee had promised Ed she would stay away from Annie Holden. But even as she'd made the promise, Dee knew she wouldn't be able to keep it. The memory of that note in the hallway of the empty house had stuck in her head. Which was why, a few hours after Ed left, she got in her car and drove back to Alfriston.

As she approached the house, she noticed a silver Lexus parked on the road a few metres from the entrance. She drove past it and parked further along, beyond the next curve in the road, so her car couldn't be seen from the entrance to the house. Walking back, she looked inside the Lexus, trying to work out why someone would park all the way out here. Apart from a few houses, all with their own driveways, there was nothing here except miles of rolling green fields. She supposed someone might park there if they'd driven out here for a walk. Although, Dee knew there were plenty of better places to park if you fancied a walk on the downs near Alfriston.

It was a hire car. A sticker with the name of the hire company was on the back window. There was no one inside the car. Dee looked up and down the road, but she was the only person here. Peering through the driver's window, there was nothing inside the car to give any indication of who had driven it here.

It was possible, she supposed, that the person driving the car was visiting one of the other houses along this stretch of road. Possible, but unlikely. The most logical explanation was that the driver of the silver Lexus had done the same thing she was doing now – parking a few metres along the road from Fiona Holden's house so she could approach the house without anyone inside knowing about it.

At the entrance to the driveway, Dee paused, checking the house and the garden for any sign there was someone else here. But everything seemed unchanged from earlier today.

This time, she'd brought a wire coat hanger with her. She hoped it would be the perfect tool for reaching inside the letterbox and retrieving the note. She'd unwound the hanger before leaving her house. Clutching it now, she approached the front door and rang the bell.

When no one answered, she crouched down, just as she'd done earlier, and peered through the letterbox. But the tiled floor was bare. The piece of paper, with Annie's name handwritten across the front of it, was gone.

'Who's taken it?'

Dee looked at the wire coat hanger in her hand, as if it might have the answer.

'Damn it.'

She straightened up and was considering what to do next when a voice behind her made her jump.

'There's no one at home.'

Turning around, Dee found herself face to face with a man about ten years older than her. His accent, she'd already noted, was Irish. His face was familiar, although it wasn't until he stretched out his hand and introduced himself that she realised she recognised him from the photos she'd seen of him on the internet.

'Robert O'Brien. I'm here looking for my step-daughter, Emer Doran. Don't suppose you've any idea where I could find her?'

'What makes you think she's here?' Dee asked, ignoring the outstretched hand. Quickly, she ran back over the bits of information she'd gathered about Emer's stepfather. Squeaky Clean O'Brien, the small-town politician with big aspirations and left-leaning views that matched the mood of twenty-first century Ireland. The man Shay Flaherty hadn't been able to find anything bad to write about.

According to Emer, Robert was the person who'd sent someone to contact Dee pretending to be Emer. Which is why, right now, she wasn't inclined to shake his hand. After a moment, he let his hand drop back down and shrugged.

'I'm trying everywhere I can think of,' he said. 'Her mother is worried sick about her. We both are. Emer's never been the most stable person, you see. She watched her sister drown in the sea when she was a young girl. The experience traumatised her. She should have had counselling, of course. But in those days… well, let's just say I'm glad people are a bit more open-minded about that sort of thing today. Sorry.' He gave Dee a sheepish smile that she bet worked a treat with his constituents. 'I'm talking too much. A terrible habit, but one you fall into easily in my line of work. I'm a politician, you see. We all talk too much. We're constantly trying to argue for something or another. Turns us into fierce chatterboxes, altogether.'

He held his hands up and took a step back, away from her.

'I'll let you get back to whatever you were doing. If you do know Emer, would you just tell her to give us a ring and let us know she's okay.'

'Hang on,' Dee said, as he turned to go. 'You still haven't told me why you think Emer might be here.'

'You're right.' He smiled. 'And you still haven't told me your name or whether or not you know where she is.'

'Emer's my cousin.' Dee didn't see why she should give him any other information about herself. 'She came to see me a few days ago, when she first arrived in England. But I haven't seen her since yesterday. I really don't know where she is.'

'Cousin?' He sounded surprised. 'My word. You must be Dee – Frank's daughter. Is that right?' He was smiling properly now, a big happy grin that made it difficult not to smile back. 'Your dad and myself were great pals at one time. We lost touch over the years, but I have so many happy memories from before he left. I was terrible sorry when I heard he'd passed away. He was a grand fella, old Frank.'

When she'd first seen him, Dee had thought Robert was in his sixties. But if he was friends with her father then he was in his early seventies, at least. She tried to remember if any of the articles online mentioned his age, but nothing came to her. Maybe he was lucky and was one of those people who never looked their age.

'He was indeed grand,' she said, swallowing the lump in her throat.

Robert nodded.

'A lot better than that brother of his, I can tell you. Do you know Eamon, at all? No, I suppose you wouldn't.

They had a serious falling out, those two. All Eamon's fault, of course. He stole from your grandparents. Conned them out of a huge amount of money. They lost their home because of it. They lost everything. It was your father who looked after them, you know. Eamon was a walking disaster, so he was.

'Truth be told, it was a relief for Ursula when Eamon finally left. He made her life a misery. I never blamed your dad for cutting him out of his life. Eamon was like a cancer, destroying everything he touched. Ah, I'm sorry. He's still your uncle, isn't he? I should have kept my big mouth shut.'

'No.' Dee shook her head. 'It's okay. My dad never spoke about the row with Eamon, but my mother told me the bare bones of it. I just think it's sad, that's all.'

Robert nodded.

'You're right there, Dee. It's very sad indeed.'

'What makes you think Emer could be here?' Dee asked, recognising she was being schmoozed by a man who clearly knew a thing or two about schmoozing.

He paused, as if he was weighing up how much to tell her.

'You said Emer got in touch with you a few days ago,' he said eventually.

'That's right.'

'And if you're here, I assume she told you that she believes the daughter of the people who live here is her dead sister? Well, it's like I already said, Emer has problems. Mental health problems. Her sister, Kitty, drowned when Emer was a child and she's never got over it. She hasn't ever been able to accept that Kitty's dead. It's not the first time something like this has happened. She's probably not told you that, but there's a pattern to this.

'She sees some stranger and convinces herself the person is Kitty. Then she spends the next few months throwing herself heart and soul into proving that person is her dead sister. Every time, of course, it turns out the person really is who they say they are. And, after a bit, Emer gets over it and moves on. Until the next time.'

'You really think that's what's happening here?'

'Isn't it obvious?' Robert said. 'Listen, Dee. When she started up this time, I intervened early. I hired a private detective to investigate the woman thoroughly. Turns out Annie Holden is exactly who she says she is. No surprise there. When I told Emer, I thought she believed me. In fact, I'm pretty sure she did until you called the other night and stirred it all up for her again. I hope you don't mind me saying this, but it was a bit irresponsible of you. Her mental health is very fragile, and I think this has tipped her over the edge completely.'

Ursula had said something similar about her daughter. Dee wondered why her and Robert were both so keen to portray Emer as someone with mental health problems.

'She seemed pretty strong to me,' Dee said, 'especially considering everything she's been through.'

'She's good at pretending when she wants to be,' Robert said. 'But this woman, Annie, she's not Kitty.'

'How can you be so sure?'

'She's the niece of the couple who adopted her. Her parents died in a car crash when she was eleven. There's a whole police report on the crash. Fiona and Michael adopted her through the proper channels. I'm happy to share everything with you if you'd like. Although I've just remembered – you're a journalist, aren't you? You're not planning to write about any of this, are you?'

Dee's head was spinning. She had lots of questions she wanted to ask, but he was already speaking again.

'Emer's a very mixed up young woman. That's why I'm so desperate to find her. I'm worried she's unstable enough to do something stupid.'

Dee didn't reply, uncomfortable with his insistence on emphasising Emer's mental health problems. The Emer Dee had met didn't show any signs of being unstable or at risk of doing something stupid.

Robert frowned.

'Sorry if you think I'm being indiscreet. I'm worried about her, that's all. She's put us through a lot these last few years. It's hard to start trusting her again. I'll tell you what, Dee. Can I give you my number, at least? If she gets in touch, maybe you could let me know she's okay? I know I'm not her real dad, but I love that girl as if she was my own child. I can't bear the thought of anything happening to her.'

'Of course,' Dee said, after a moment. Because how could she refuse? She thought of Jake and the time he'd disappeared last year. The terror she'd felt not knowing whether he was okay or not. She wouldn't wish that feeling on anyone.

'Thanks so much, Dee. I've booked into Dean's Place for the night. If I can't find Emer by tomorrow I'll have to go back home. I really hope it won't come to that.'

Dee knew Dean's Place. She'd been to several weddings and other events at the hotel on the other side of Alfriston. She put Robert's number into her phone and sent him a text, so he'd have her number as well. She promised she'd be in touch if she had any news about Emer.

'Right then,' he said. 'I'll be getting off. When I get home, I'll see if I can dig out some old photos of me and

286

your dad. If I can find them, I'll make copies and send them to you.'

'I'd like that very much,' Dee said. 'Thank you.'

As he walked past her, a memory flickered at the back of her mind. Something about him felt familiar to her. It was more than the fact she'd recognised his face from the research she'd done on him. It was something else. A feeling that she'd been close to him recently. But when she tried to focus on the memory it kept sliding away from her until she let it go.

She decided to take one last look around. Maybe as she did, she'd remember why she was so sure she knew him from somewhere. Again, she walked around the outside of the house, peering through the windows. Everything looked the same as it had done yesterday. No sign of anyone hiding behind the stylish furniture in the living room, or beneath the polished wooden table in the dining room. No half-drunk mugs of coffee or dirty plates in the kitchen.

It was only when she reached the back of the house that she saw something had changed. A pane of glass in one of the doors to the extended kitchen had been broken, and the patio was covered in shattered glass. Tentatively, Dee pushed the door and it creaked inwards.

Sunlight streamed through the glass roof and a wave of heat hit her as she stepped inside. She paused, her ears listening out for noises inside the house. But when she heard something, the sound came from behind her. She swung around, but she was too slow. He had already grabbed her, his fingers digging into the soft flesh of her arm as he shoved her forward, towards the granite-topped island in the middle of the room.

She started to scream, but he clamped a hand across her face, blocking out the sound.

'Shut the fuck up.'

Irish accent. Robert O'Brien. The charming politician with the twinkling eyes that had reminded her of Ed. The heat in the kitchen was intolerable, especially with his body pressed against her and the thick stink of his expensive cologne clogging the air. The cologne, she recognised it now. It was why she thought she'd been with him recently. She'd smelled it as he'd walked past her. The same smell she'd got inside the block of flats in Stockwell. Panic flared inside her. He'd killed Michael Holden. And now he was going to do the same thing to her.

Pressing his hand into the back of her head, he shoved her face down onto the worktop. Behind her, she could feel him moving. For one terrible moment, she thought he was going to rape her.

There was a knife rack just in front of her face. She saw his hand wrap around one of the knives. The silver blade glinted in the sunlight as he pulled it towards her face. Cold metal against her cheek. The blade of the knife, right beneath her left eye.

'If you try anything,' he hissed. 'I'll cut your eye out. Is that clear?'

She tried to nod her head but he was holding it too tight.

'Is that clear?' he repeated, louder this time.

'Yes,' she managed. 'I won't try anything. I swear.'

She could feel his breath, hot against the side of her face. He pressed the blade deeper, cutting the skin. Warm blood trickled down her cheek. Her stomach contracted.

He pulled her up by the hair and pushed her through the kitchen towards the garden. A shock of cold air hit her as he opened the door. Outside, across the patio, down the steps, onto the grass. Towards the ice house.

Dee screamed, her body jerking and struggling against him.

'I told you to shut up.'

The tip of the blade pierced her skin again. More blood. She tried to pull her head back, but he had her in a grip so tight it was impossible to move. Impossible to do anything except allow herself to be forced forward towards the stone igloo.

'Please,' she begged, too scared to do anything now except plead for her life. 'Don't do this. The police know where I am. I called them right after you left. They're on their way. They know you killed Michael. You were seen at the flats that morning. You won't get away with this.'

'Bullshit.'

They were at the entrance to the ice house now. The door was open. He must have opened it when he saw her arriving at the house. A black gaping darkness lay in front of her. Every fibre in her body was protesting at having to go in there.

'Wait,' she said. 'You don't need to do this.'

'You know too much,' he said. 'I should have shut this mess down earlier. I would have done, if she hadn't lied to me.'

'Who lied to you?'

'What the fuck does that matter now? I need to fix this, and I can't do that with you sticking your nose in. I'd never have involved you if I thought you'd take it this far. But you couldn't let it go, could you? Do you know how hard I've had to work to get where I am today? No, of course not. No one knows what it takes to do what I've done. And I can tell you now, there's no way I'm going to

289

let some interfering nobody take it all away from me. No one will hear you in here. Walls so thick you can scream as loudly as you want to. The only person who'll ever hear you is yourself.'

He shoved her, hard, and she fell forward into the darkness.

Behind her, the door slammed shut and suddenly there was nothing except the darkness and the sounds of her own screams, bouncing back at her off the stone walls.

Forty-one

'It was Robert?' Emer said, when she was finally able to speak.

'I don't think he meant to hit Lucy,' Kitty said. 'That was my fault. But it suited him to have her out of the way. We'd both seen things we shouldn't have in that house. By the time the car had stopped, Lucy was already dead. I remember wanting to run away, but I couldn't move. I didn't recognise him at first, but as he got out of the car I saw his face. I think I tried to scream, but he was fast. He grabbed me and put his hand over my mouth and bundled me into the boot.

'I thought I was going to die, Emer. I was sure he'd kill me. Instead, he drove me back home. Mum was already there. Dad was in the kitchen, passed out like always. After Robert left, Mum sat me down and made me swear not to tell anyone I'd been out that night. I was so scared I did everything she told me to. I told the Guards I hadn't been with Lucy that night; said I'd been home in bed like I was supposed to be.'

Emer stood up, went to the window and looked out at the sea. It was rough and grey today. Waves lashed the shore, splashing against the sides of the gold-domed pier. She wished she could open the window and fly out, over the sea, across to the silver line on the horizon where the sky and ocean met. And when she reached it, she would keep flying.

She thought of Kitty and Lucy. Two little girls, both so innocent, walking in on that scene in the bedroom. The shock and the horror as they tried to comprehend what they'd seen: how could any child cope with something like that?

'Emer?' Kitty's voice dragged her away from the horizon and back into the room. It had seemed so big when she'd first come in, but felt too small now because there wasn't anywhere she could hide away and pretend none of this had happened.

She wished she'd never seen Kitty on the train that afternoon in June.

'Are you okay?' Kitty asked.

Emer shook her head, keeping her back to the room, her eyes fixed on the horizon.

'Robert's been like a father to me,' she said. 'I thought he really cared about me. But all this time, he's been lying to me.'

'He paid Mum and Dad to get rid of me,' Kitty said. 'I'm pretty sure they would have killed me, if they thought they'd get away with it. But maybe faking my drowning was an easier solution. No body, no evidence of any wrong-doing. Or maybe Dad realised, even then, that keeping me alive could be a way of getting extra money further down the line.'

'Why involve Dad at all?' Emer asked. 'Wouldn't it have been easier to keep him out of the picture?'

'Robert was in love with our mother,' Kitty said. 'It suited him to get Dad out of the way at the same time. So he paid Dad to make both of us disappear. I didn't want to go. All I wanted was to go to the Guards and tell them everything that had happened. But Robert threatened me. He said the people who'd been at the house that night knew I'd been there. He said if I ever told anyone what I'd seen, they would kill me. Not just me, he said they'd kill you as well. So he gave me a choice. Keep my mouth shut and you'd stay safe, or speak up and let you get killed.'

'No.' But she knew Kitty was telling the truth. The only person in her fucked-up family who hadn't lied to her.

'How did they get you out of the country without anyone noticing?'

'Robert paid for us to go on holiday,' Kitty said. 'That day, when Mum took us to the beach, Dad was hiding in the dunes, waiting for me. Mum had already told me what to do. I was to start a row with you and pretend to be angry. Then I had to wander off by myself. When no one was looking, I had to take off my shorts and let them drift into the water. After I'd done that, I ran back up the dunes to where Dad was hiding. We sneaked into the hotel through a fire escape at the back of the building. No one saw us. Then I hid in their room. No one even thought to search the room. Isn't that remarkable? They all believed our mother that I'd gone into the water and been pulled out by the current. When it was time to go, I knew I couldn't leave without seeing you one last time. I came to say goodbye, do you remember?'

'Of course I remember,' Emer said. 'It's why I was never able to believe you'd died. I thought it was my fault. We'd had a row and you went to a different part of the beach. When they told me you'd drowned, I blamed myself.'

'But the row was my fault,' Kitty said. 'Don't you remember? I'm sorry, Emer. I was only doing what Mum had told me to.'

The relief was overwhelming. And so was the rage that followed. All these years, her mother and Robert had convinced Emer it was her fault Kitty had drowned that day on the beach.

'We left the hotel in the middle of the night,' Kitty continued. 'Out through the fire escape again. We drove to some town – I can't remember what it was called – and Uncle Frank was there, waiting for us. Dad told me Frank was his brother and he was going to look after me. I didn't want to go. I was terrified, but Dad insisted. So I got into the car with Uncle Frank and we drove to Belfast, where we got the ferry to Liverpool. From there, we drove to Uncle Frank's home in Eastbourne.'

'Your father's brother was a friend of mine,' Fiona said, picking up the story. 'Somehow, Eamon persuaded Frank that Kitty's life was in danger. Together they came up with a plan for keeping her safe. Michael and I weren't able to have children of our own. When Frank asked us to help, it felt like a gift. Don't get me wrong, it wasn't easy taking on a traumatised child, but it was worth it.' Fiona smiled at Kitty with such genuine love, Emer felt a sudden, unexpected pang of jealousy. 'She was the best thing that ever happened to us.'

A wave of nausea washed through Emer. The room started to spin. Somehow, she managed to get back to her chair before her legs gave way. She put her head down between her knees, waiting for the worst of the dizziness to pass. As soon as she was able to, she looked up at Kitty.

'And that was it,' Emer said, 'you started a new life and forgot all about me.'

'I never forgot about you,' Kitty said.

'I know how hard this is to hear,' Fiona said to Emer. 'But your father wasn't a good man. After we took Kitty in, after we'd begun to love her as if she was our own child, Eamon started blackmailing us. We paid him as much as we could for years, but he was so greedy... no matter how much we gave him, it was never enough. We should have gone to the police and told them everything, but we were scared. We were already in too deep. We knew if we told anyone what was going on, we'd lose Annie. And we couldn't bear that.'

She stopped speaking and a silence descended. Emer could hear her own breathing, loud and fast. Seagulls screeching outside the window. People in the corridor outside the room. Normal people going about their normal lives. While in here, Emer's whole world was falling apart.

'The man your husband killed,' she whispered.

Fiona looked at her, and didn't look away when she said it. 'Eamon.'

Her father was dead. Now she knew, with absolute certainty. And the knowledge was harder to bear than she'd imagined.

'I thought finding you would make everything better,' she said to Kitty. 'But it hasn't. It's done the opposite.'

'Isn't it better to know the truth?' Kitty said.

'No.'

Until this moment, she hadn't realised how important Robert was to her. She'd loved him and believed he'd loved her too. She'd talked to him and told him things about herself that she would never tell her mother. She'd trusted him. But now she knew the truth. Even if he hadn't meant to kill Lucy, he had hidden her body so her family would never know what had happened to her. He was a manipulative, cold-blooded killer.

Forty-two

'He's here,' Emer said, 'in the UK. It's my fault. I told him you were still alive. You said you were in the house earlier. You must have missed him by minutes. But I still can't believe…'

Her voice trailed off. There was no other reason for Robert to be here. He'd found out that Kitty was still alive, and he'd come to kill her. So she could never tell anyone the sort of man he was. Because if people realised what he was really like, that would properly ruin Robert's plans to become Ireland's next Taoiseach. And not just Robert's plans, but Ursula's as well.

'What about Uncle Frank?' Emer asked, remembering Dee's beautiful house on the beach. 'Did he know what Eamon was up to?'

'He knew all right,' Fiona said. 'He tried to warn Eamon off, more than once, but Eamon just ignored him.'

'Uncle Frank always kept in touch,' Kitty said. 'He was wonderful.'

'And Dee? You never met her?'

'Uncle Frank didn't think it was safe,' Kitty said. 'Don't forget, he really believed my life was in danger. The only way to keep me safe was for as few people as possible to know who I really was.'

'But you changed your name, your whole identity. How is that even possible?' Emer asked. 'How can you get a national security number or a passport if you're not who you say you are?'

'We ran a pub,' Fiona said. 'You meet all sorts of people through that job. It was easier than you'd imagine to pay someone to arrange a new identity.'

'So Kitty became Annie and I was told to accept my sister was dead.' Emer shook her head. 'I can't believe it was that easy.'

'It didn't feel easy,' Kitty said. 'It still doesn't. Fiona and Michael were brilliant, but I was a difficult kid. I was pretty messed up.' She smiled. 'Most people would say I still am.'

'That makes two of us then.' Emer leaned over and squeezed her sister's hand. The contact gave her strength. She looked at the two women sitting opposite her.

'What happens now?'

'We do what we should have done years ago,' Fiona said. 'We go to the police. If I'd been brave enough to do that earlier, we might not be where we are today. Michael would never have gone to prison.' She looked at Emer. 'And you'd have had your sister back. I'm so sorry.'

'I met Michael,' Emer said. 'I went to visit him yesterday morning. I thought he might be Dad.'

'What made you think that?' Kitty asked.

'It's a long story,' Emer said, 'and it doesn't matter now, anyway. He was very kind to me.'

'He's okay then,' Kitty said. 'Thank goodness. I tried to call him yesterday but he didn't pick up, which is unusual.'

'When he got out of prison,' Fiona said to Emer, 'I wanted him to move back home. He refused. He's never been able to forgive himself – or me – for what he did to your father. It destroyed our marriage.'

Emer wanted to tell the woman she wasn't surprised. Michael Holden was a murderer and his wife was complicit in that murder. They didn't deserve a happy marriage after what they'd done.

Instead, for the first time since she'd stepped inside the room, Emer felt in control.

'Maeve is here,' she said. 'She's in a hotel in Polegate, waiting for me to call her. She doesn't know I've come to meet you. We should go and see her so you can tell her what happened to Lucy. She deserves to know the truth.'

-

Forty-five minutes later, Kitty was parking her Mini Clubman in the car park of a boutique hotel just off the A27.

'I've heard of this place,' Kitty said, getting out of the car. 'But I haven't been before. Maeve must have money if she can afford to stay here.'

The hotel was in the grounds of an eighteenth-century coaching inn. A plaque on the wall informed visitors that the inn had been 'sensitively' restored and converted four years ago.

'I hope she's here,' Emer said, as they approached the elegant building. 'She sounded a bit funny when I spoke to her earlier.'

'You're absolutely sure she wants to see me?'

'I think so,' Emer said. 'It was just the shock, you know? But you're the reason she's here, Kitty. She's spent her whole life wondering what happened to Lucy. Now she's finally got a chance to find out. I can't imagine what that must feel like.'

They were inside the hotel now, standing in the lobby.

'She said she'd be in the bar,' Emer said. 'That looks like the bar over there.'

They found Maeve sitting at a table by the window that overlooked the grounds at the back of the hotel. Emer stood back, letting Kitty approach her first.

'Hello Maeve.'

Maeve stood up, but when Kitty leaned forward to give her a hug, she stepped sideways, avoiding contact.

'It really is you.' She frowned. 'I don't think I fully believed it when Emer called to tell me.'

'Are you okay?' Emer asked. Maeve seemed tense, and she looked as if she wanted to scratch Kitty's eyes out.

'Of course I'm not okay,' Maeve said. 'You can't be okay, either. This is… this is fucked up.' She looked at Kitty. 'You know why I'm here. Do you know what happened to her?'

'Yes,' Kitty whispered.

'Jesus. Oh Jesus. Okay. Emer, do you mind if I do this alone?'

'If that's what you want,' Emer said. 'Of course. Kitty, is that okay with you?'

In truth, she was relieved not to have to listen to it again. Once had been more than enough. So, when Kitty said she was happy to speak to Maeve by herself, Emer told them to call her when they were ready and she got out of there as quickly as she could.

Outside, a milky sun was just visible behind a layer of pale grey clouds. Walking through the grounds, Emer found a gate that led to the open countryside at the back of the hotel. She spent the next hour tramping across the rolling green Sussex hills, giving her mind the time it needed to process everything Kitty had told her.

There were too many gaps, more than she'd realised. She started making a list of all the questions she had, but she couldn't focus, jumping from one piece of information to another, trying to make sense of the incomprehensible.

It was a lonely feeling, realising the only family you'd ever known weren't who you thought they were. She could feel the self-pity creeping up on her and it was tempting – so tempting – to give in to it. How easy it would be to blame everyone else for the mess she'd made of her life. Her parents, Kitty, Robert – they'd all deceived her in different ways. But she'd done a pretty good job of deceiving herself, too. Convincing herself that all the problems in her life were because of what had happened to Kitty. Refusing to take any responsibility for her own actions, constantly – tediously – laying the blame elsewhere.

Because of that, she'd lost the best thing that had ever happened to her. Nikki's absence was a constant ache in her chest. An ache, she realised now, she wouldn't be able to live with. When this was all over, she was going to do whatever it took to get Nikki back. She could do it. She would do it, because she'd already lost too much. A lot of that had been outside her control, but not this. If she lost Nikki for good, she would only ever have herself to blame.

She'd done a circular walk and could see the hotel ahead of her in the valley below. She wondered how the conversation was going. At one level, Maeve would be relieved to finally know the truth. But what good, Emer wondered, was the truth to her now? Lucy's disappearance had destroyed Maeve's family. Her father's reputation had never recovered from the cloud of suspicion that hung over him. Her family had had to move to a new town and do what they could to start their lives over. Both her parents had died without knowing what had happened to their oldest child.

As Emer was thinking about this, she remembered something: Maeve sitting across from her in the bar that afternoon in Galway, telling Emer what she'd do if she ever found the person responsible for what had happened to her family.

Emer speeded up, walking faster and faster until, by the time she reached the grounds of the hotel, she was running. There was no sign of Kitty or Maeve in the bar. She checked the toilets and the smoking area outside. Nothing. And when she dialled their numbers, both calls went straight to voicemail.

'Can I help you?'

She looked around, saw the man working behind the reception desk was speaking to her.

'I've lost my friend,' she said. 'Her name's Maeve Ryan. She's staying here, but I don't know what room she's in.'

'I can't give you her room number,' the man said. 'But I can look it up and call the room, tell her you're here.'

'Would you mind?' Emer said. 'That would be brilliant. Thank you.'

It felt like an age for him to check the computer in front of him. Emer had to resist the urge to swing the screen around and look for herself. How long could it take to find someone's room number?

'I'm sorry,' he said, eventually. 'Could you repeat your friend's name?'

'Maeve Ryan,' Emer said. 'Maeve is spelt M-A-E-V-E.'

He tapped something else into the keyboard while he looked at the screen, frowning.

'We don't have anyone with that name staying here,' he said.

'That's not possible,' Emer said. 'I was with her here earlier.'

The man didn't say anything, clearly waiting for Emer to accept that there was no Maeve staying at the hotel.

Emer ran outside to check the car park. Maeve's hire car was still there. So was Kitty's car. Which meant wherever they'd gone, they hadn't gone far.

Back in the bar, she scanned the faces again, certain they had to be here and she'd missed them. But they weren't there. Ignoring the shouts from the guy on reception, she ran up the stairs that led to the higher floors.

She ran along the corridors, shouting Kitty's name. But it was like history repeating itself. Kitty was gone, almost as if she'd never been here at all.

Forty-three

Dee couldn't breathe. The walls were closing in on her. She couldn't see them, but she could feel the space around her getting smaller as the walls edged towards her. It was impossibly dark. A blanket of pitch black that crept down her throat, blocking her airways until she knew she would die. No. She couldn't die. She wouldn't die. She had to focus. Stay calm. Breathe. She tried to suck air in, but nothing happened. Flares of panic shot through her. She was cold. Too cold. Her teeth were chattering, her body shaking. The darkness was inside her now. Crawling into her lungs and pushing its way inside her brain, blocking out all her thoughts and memories, consuming her. She would die in this place and it would take days, months, years before anyone found her body.

Then, just as suddenly, it was over. She was still here, trapped in the freezing darkness, but she was breathing again. Cool air was rushing into her lungs, the roaring inside her head was subsiding, and the burning sensation at the back of her throat was easing.

She wrapped her arms around her body, doing all she could to warm herself, but it wasn't enough. Space was the problem. Or, more specifically, lack of space. She couldn't stand because the roof was too low. She'd tried moving about in a semi-crouch, until the pain in her back and neck became unbearable. Since then, she'd sat here, in the darkness, trying to think of a way to get out of here.

He'd fooled her. Classic politician. Full of empty charm and bullshit. He wasn't here for Emer. He was here to finish off whatever he'd started in Ireland twenty-three years ago. He was here for Kitty.

Foolishly, she'd left her phone in the car. She doubted she'd get a signal in here, but at least she'd be able to use the torch to check there were no rats or other creatures hiding in the corners waiting to pounce. Instead, she had to sit here in the dark, ignoring the scratching sounds she heard every now and then. Trying not to imagine what could be making them.

Breathe. She had to remember to breathe. In and out. Slowly. She'd started practising mindfulness a few months ago. Hadn't kept it up, but she tried now to remember the basics. Counting her breaths, feeling the rise and fall inside her body.

Her face. He'd cut her face. She'd been bleeding. She touched her cheek now and felt the scab. It was huge. Maybe it wasn't as bad as it felt. Scarface. Stupid, macho film full of noise and hysterical acting. She'd hated it. One of her ex-husband's favourites. Billy Morrison. Her first love. Until he stopped being someone she loved and became a man she barely recognised. Bloated and angry and sad.

Breathe. Focus. Thoughts were clouds that came and went. She closed her eyes, found it helped not to be looking at the darkness. She continued breathing. In and out. One, two, three. Counting the breaths. Bringing her mind back to the breathing.

She was in control again. The panic had been replaced with something else. Strength. She opened her eyes, and this time she didn't see the darkness. Instead, she saw the tiny cracks of light coming through the gap at the top of the door.

She wasn't going to die. Not today, not any time soon. She was going to find a way out of here. And when she did, she was going to find the bastard who'd cut her face and locked her in here, and she was going to make him pay for what he'd done to her.

Forty-four

Someone was crying. Kitty wanted to find them and comfort them. But when she tried to move, she couldn't. She was lying on her side, looking at furniture she didn't recognise. A throbbing pain at the back of her head made it difficult to concentrate. Something was badly wrong. Her hands had been pulled behind her back, her wrists bound together. When she tried to move them, the ties cut into her skin.

She wanted to call for help, but thick material had been stuffed into her mouth. When she tried to spit it out, she couldn't. Panicked, she started struggling, pulling against her ties, screaming into the material inside her mouth.

A face appeared in her line of vision, triggering the flicker of a memory and a surge of fear. She was in a hotel bedroom. Maeve's room. She'd told Kitty she didn't want to talk in a public area. Kitty had understood. Was glad, in fact, because she'd known what she was going to tell Maeve would be painful. So they'd come here instead.

'How could you have kept it to yourself all these years?' Maeve was crying. Tears running unchecked down her cheeks. Her face so close Kitty could feel the heat of her breath. She twisted her head, trying to get away from Maeve's grief and anger, but Maeve grabbed her chin, forcing Kitty to look at her.

'You weren't there. You didn't see what it did to my family. It destroyed us. Can you imagine? Can you? My parents never got over it. My father... do you know that everyone assumed he'd killed her? They thought he'd killed his own child. It wasn't enough to have to deal with the grief of losing her, never knowing where she'd gone or what had happened to her. My parents had to cope with all those rumours as well. We had to leave Ballincarraig altogether. Leave the only home I'd ever known, the only friends I'd ever had.

'They imagined the worst, you know. My mother would wake up screaming. I'd hear her. Screaming in the middle of the night before rushing into the bathroom to throw up. The grief ate into her, month after month, year after year. She died never knowing what had happened. And all the time... all this time, you knew and you could have changed everything. But you didn't, did you?'

Maeve stopped speaking. Her face disappeared as she moved to another part of the room. Kitty looked around, trying to see what Maeve was doing. But Maeve had disappeared.

She'd shown no reaction at all when Kitty first told her.

'Are you okay?' Kitty had asked. Maeve hadn't responded, and then... what? Kitty had gone to switch the kettle on. Tea, she'd thought. Tea is what she needs. She might have even said it aloud, she couldn't remember. She couldn't remember anything after that moment.

She'd been hit. On the back of her head where the pain was worst. Had Maeve hit her? Or was someone else here too? The question sent shockwaves of panic surging through her body. The slamming sounds from the bathroom were getting louder and more frequent. Maeve was saying something. Repeating the same words, over and over.

'Do it, do it, do it.'

Kitty fought to pull her wrists and ankles free, but all she succeeded in doing was cutting her skin until she bled. It felt like she'd been tied up with wire or cable ties.

'Kitty!'

She was hallucinating. Had to be. Thought she'd heard Emer. A memory. That's all it was. A memory from that night, all those years ago, when she was running down the hotel corridor and Emer was running after her.

'Kitty!'

No. Not hallucinating. This was real. Emer was outside the room. Kitty struggled harder, her screams muffled and inaudible behind the towel in her mouth.

'Shut the fuck up!'

Maeve. Not Emer. Leaning over her again.

She had a pillow. Holding it up for Kitty to see.

'I'm going to kill you.'

Kitty shook her head, struggled harder. Outside the door, Emer's voice faded and disappeared as Maeve rolled Kitty onto her back and the pillow came down. Blackness and unbearable pressure. She couldn't breathe. Her lungs screaming for air as she bucked and thrashed and did everything she could to push back. But Maeve pushed harder, the pillow pressing down on her face. A flare of pain across her chest. Her heart was beating too fast, trying to keep her body going. Blue and white dots danced toward her through the darkness.

The dots faded and so did the darkness, until there was nothing left.

Forty-five

Dee didn't have a phone in her bag, but she had a nail file. Not a fancy Leighton Denny crystal nail file like the one Louise had. A bog-standard metal file with a pointed edge to it. An edge that fitted perfectly into the old-fashioned lock on the heavy wooden door. Now, all she had to do was get the stupid thing to twist and unlock the door so she could get the hell out of here.

She didn't know how long she'd been in here, but she was pretty sure it felt longer than it actually had been. Anger kept her focused. Each time her arm started to ache from the length of time she'd spent trying to unlock the door, and the voices started inside her head, telling her it was pointless and she was never going to get out of here, she would picture Robert O'Brien's face when he was arrested for murder and whatever other crimes he'd committed.

While she worked on the lock, Dee went back over everything she knew about Lucy Ryan and Kitty Doran, trying to piece together the different bits of information into a single narrative. She knew for certain now that Robert O'Brien had played a role in whatever happened to both girls. And he was doing his best to make sure no one else found out what he'd done.

That's why he was here. To cover his tracks. Or someone else's? A line from Shay Flaherty's email lodged in Dee's head:

Robert is devoted to Ursula.

Ursula who, according to her daughter, was a deeply unpleasant woman. In 1997, when Lucy disappeared and Kitty supposedly drowned, Ursula had been working as Robert's PA. So Ursula and Robert were in this together. Lucy Ryan and Kitty Doran had seen something they shouldn't have. Maybe both girls were meant to have been killed, but Ursula couldn't face killing her own daughter. So she'd sneaked Kitty out of the country and given her a new identity. A plan which had worked perfectly until Emer spotted her sister on the London Underground earlier this summer.

Dee wondered if Robert O'Brien knew Kitty hadn't drowned that afternoon. If he didn't, if he'd spent all these years believing Kitty was dead, that would explain why he'd offered to help Emer find out about the girl she'd seen on the Tube. It would have come as a shock to realise his wife had been lying to him all this time. More of a shock to discover that the one person with the power to topple his political career was still out there.

So he'd hired someone to contact Dee and get her to do his dirty work for him. And once he'd learned the truth – that Kitty was still alive – he'd come to London to finish off what he'd started twenty-three years ago. He was going to get rid of Kitty, and anyone else who knew she was still alive. Starting with Michael Holden.

There were still gaps in what she knew, but Dee was getting closer to the truth. She could feel it. Now, all she needed to do was get out of here and find out the rest of it. She jiggled the nail file some more, twisting it one way, then the other. Several times, she thought she'd done it. The file caught the lock at just the right angle and, with soaring spirits, she would twist it a tiny bit harder. But the lock wouldn't budge.

'God damn you, stupid door.'

She slammed the door with her fists, shouting for someone to come and let her out. But there was no one out there and, after a while, she stopped shouting. The urge to slump onto the ground and simply give up was strong. But she wasn't going to do that. Besides, it wasn't as if she was never going to be found. Sooner or later, someone would notice she was missing. And her car was parked on the road outside the house. It wouldn't take a genius to work out where she was.

Except that could take days. The only people who would notice she was gone were Louise and Ella. Louise was going on holiday tomorrow, and Ella was moving to the other side of the bloody world in four days' time. Which meant Dee couldn't sit around waiting to be found. She had to get out before then.

Grabbing hold of the plastic handle on the nail file, she twisted with all her force. A snapping sound and the resistance she'd encountered every other time she'd tried disappeared. She thought she'd done it, that she'd finally managed to twist open the lock. But when she lifted her hand, she realised the sound she'd heard wasn't the lock opening. It was the sound of the nail file snapping in two, leaving the plastic handle trapped between Dee's fingers, and the metal part of the file stuck in the lock.

Forty-six

Back outside the hotel, Emer called the Cavendish Hotel and asked to be put through to Room 204. Thankfully, she'd noted the room number when she'd been at the hotel earlier. She hoped Fiona was still there. If she wasn't, Emer had no way of contacting her. At first she thought Fiona wasn't going to answer, but after the eighth ring someone picked up.

'Hello?'

'Fiona, thank God. It's Emer.'

'Has something happened?'

'Kitty's disappeared.'

'What do you mean?' Fiona said. 'How can she have disappeared? I thought you were with her.'

'I left her with Maeve, and when I came back to the hotel, I couldn't find them. Maeve never checked into the hotel. I've no idea why. Her car's still here, though. So is Kitty's car. Unless they got a taxi, they haven't gone far.'

She'd walked around the grounds, checking everywhere for any sign of Kitty and Maeve.

'Your stepfather,' Fiona said. 'Do you think they're with him?'

'How would he know they're here?'

'Maeve must have told him. You saw him in Alfriston, didn't you? How would he even know to go there if someone hadn't told him?'

'He killed Maeve's sister,' Emer said. 'Why would she want to help him?'

'What about your cousin – Dee? As far as I can see, this is all her fault. If she'd kept her nose out of our business, you'd never have found us. Annie would be safe.'

'And I'd never have known my sister was still alive.'

When Fiona didn't reply straight away, Emer guessed the comment had upset her. She didn't care. Because if anyone was to blame for this mess, it was Fiona herself. She should have gone to the police years ago and told them everything.

'You're right,' Fiona said. 'You have no idea how sorry I am. I've been so focused on not losing Annie, it took over everything. I'd spent so long wanting a child of my own. When we had the chance to care for Kitty, it felt like a gift. Michael wasn't sure, at first. We both knew Kitty was being hidden from something dangerous and Michael was worried about what would happen if the people she was running from ever found her. He was right to be worried. I know that now. But once she was living with us, he loved her as well. That's why he killed Eamon. It was the only way he could think of to keep her safe.'

Emer tried to imagine what it would be like to deliberately plan to kill someone, the mindset it would require and what it would do to you afterwards.

'He didn't plan it,' Fiona said, as if she'd guessed what Emer was thinking. 'He'd arranged to meet Eamon to tell him we weren't going to pay him any more money. Eamon threatened to tell your stepfather that Annie was still alive, and Michael lost it. Something he's spent the rest of his life regretting.'

It was all so sad, Emer thought. When this was over, she was going to do two things: she was going to get her shit together, and she was going to make sure her mother and Robert paid for all the damage they'd caused.

'Are you still there?' Fiona asked.

'I've got nowhere else to go,' Emer said.

'I'm coming to get you. Annie… Kitty… took the car, but I can get a taxi.'

'Where are we going?'

'Alfriston. That's where you saw Robert, so we go there first. If we can't find them, then we'll think about where to go next.'

'What about the police? Shouldn't we call them and tell them Kitty's in danger?'

'They won't take us seriously,' Fiona said. 'Kitty hasn't been missing for long enough. But I'm friends with the detective who led the murder investigation. I think he might be willing to help. I'll call him on my way to pick you up. Wait outside the hotel. I'll be with you as soon as I can.'

Fiona seemed distracted when she arrived in the taxi to pick up Emer.

'Something's happened,' she said, once Emer had climbed in beside her and put her seatbelt on. 'The detective I told you about has just called. He says he needs to speak to me urgently.'

'Any idea why?'

'He said he didn't want to tell me over the phone,' Fiona said. 'But I think it's Michael. Kitty's been trying to contact him since yesterday. He's not answering his phone.'

'But I saw him yesterday,' Emer said. 'I told you that. I spoke to him at his flat. He seemed fine.'

'So why isn't he answering Kitty's calls?'

'I don't know,' Emer said.

The truth was, she didn't want to think about Michael Holden. She wanted to focus on the anger raging inside her. She was angry with everyone, including the woman sitting beside her in the back of the taxi. Because if Fiona had done the right thing years earlier, Emer would have known that her sister was still alive. And maybe if that had happened, all the other bad things in her life could have been avoided. The jobs she'd lost, the relationships she'd ruined, the God-awful mess she'd made of everything – how different things might have been if she'd only known the truth. And it wasn't just herself she was angry for. There was Lucy's family too. Her parents had gone to their graves never knowing what had happened to their daughter. All of it because Robert O'Brien had cared more about his reputation than doing the right thing.

By the time the taxi dropped them off at the house in Alfriston, Emer was ready to kill Robert with her bare hands when she found him. Jumping out of the taxi, not bothering to wait for Fiona, she ran to the house and started banging on the door.

'Robert,' she shouted. 'Are you in there?'

'Wait,' Fiona said, coming to join her. 'I've got a key. You don't need to break the door down.'

She opened the door and they stepped into the house. Silence greeted them. Emer stood in the hallway, listening for any sign there was someone else in here. But apart from the sound of birdsong outside, she couldn't hear a thing.

'They're not here,' she said.

'They have to be somewhere.' Fiona moved through the house, opening the doors and looking inside every room. When she went upstairs, Emer didn't bother following her. She knew it was pointless. Kitty wasn't here.

The rage that had kept her going until now had died away, leaving a weary exhaustion it its place. She went into the kitchen, turned on the tap, leaned down and let the water flow into her mouth. She'd just finished, and was wiping her lips, when she saw a flash of movement in the garden outside. Moving to get a closer look, she noticed the broken pane of glass.

Opening the door, she stepped onto the patio. A large, landscaped garden stretched out in front of her. Tidy beds on either side of a neatly mown lawn. The entire space was enclosed by a red-brick, ivy covered wall. Emer stepped off the patio onto the grass, scanning every corner of the garden, but she couldn't see anything out of the ordinary.

She stood for a moment, listening to the sounds of the countryside – birdsong and the rustle of wind through the leaves of the magnolia tree in the centre of the lawn, the occasional car passing on the road at the front of the house.

And suddenly, something else. Footsteps crunching over broken glass. The sound had come from behind her. She swung around, but not quickly enough. Someone grabbed her, dragging her across the grass towards the front of the house. She opened her mouth to scream, but a hand clasped over her mouth, blocking the sound. Breathing through her nose, the smell hit her. Ginger and citrus, an undercurrent of sandalwood. As her panicked brain recognised the smell, she heard his voice, close to her ear:

'Stop fighting me. I'm here to get you out of here before you get hurt.'

Forty-seven

Emer tried to pull free, but she'd forgotten how strong he was. Sixty-five years old and he still worked out every day. Muscles like steel and the strength of two men half his age.

At the side of the house, he stopped.

'I just want to talk,' he said. 'That's all. If I let you go, will you at least listen to what I've got to say?'

She nodded, too scared to do anything else.

'Good girl.'

He removed his hand from her mouth and let her go.

'What the hell?' She stepped away from him, needing to put some space between them both. Her arms hurt where he'd held her too tight. She imagined she could still feel the imprint of his hand across her face.

'I'm sorry,' he said. 'I saw you and I panicked. I've been worried sick. Your poor mother's going out of her mind. You've no idea the hoops I've had to jump through to find you. We need to leave, Emer. There are things you don't know about the people living in this house. You're putting yourself in danger just being here. I need to get you away right now.'

'No.' She shook her head. She wasn't going anywhere with him. 'I know what you did, Robert.'

'Jesus Christ.' He rubbed a hand across his face, a gesture she recognised. One he used when he wanted to show his vulnerability. 'Would you just listen to me for once in your life, Emer? I don't know what stories they've filled your head with, but none of it's true. Kitty killed Lucy. I had no idea about any of it. Your mother finally told me the truth when I drove to Dublin on Saturday morning and asked her what the hell was going on.'

'Bullshit. You killed her. You hid her body so no one would ever know what happened. And you paid my father to disappear and take Kitty with him.'

'None of that is true,' Robert said. 'Kitty was jealous of Lucy and she killed her. Plain and simple. Your parents knew Lucy's family wouldn't let Kitty get away with what she'd done. So they came up with a plan to get her out of the country. Your father did his best, God help him, but the people who took her in were monsters. They filled her head with lies, turned her against him. Then, when he refused to give up, they killed him. And now they'll kill you. That woman, Fiona, she'll do anything to keep you away from Kitty. Now come on, Emer. We need to get out of here.'

She saw his hand reaching out and jumped back. But her foot caught on something and she stumbled. Robert caught her before she fell, his fingers digging into her upper arm as he dragged her towards the driveway at the front of the house.

'No.' She screamed, and tried to pull her arm free, but again his grip was too strong.

'Shut the fuck up.' He shook her, so hard her teeth rattled. She didn't know what shocked her more, the sudden violence or the swearing. She didn't think she'd ever heard him swear before. Tears pricked her eyes. This was Robert. He wasn't meant to behave like this.

'Sorry,' he said. 'I shouldn't have done that. I just want to get us both out of here.'

He was walking alongside her as he pulled her towards the end of the driveway. As he continued talking, she turned to look at him so she could see his face.

'I understand why this is confusing for you. I was in the same boat until Friday night. After you left, I was distraught. I'd suspected for a while that your mother hadn't been honest with me. She'd been acting strangely ever since you told us about seeing Kitty in London. That's why I hired the private detective. I wanted to find out what was really going on.'

'But you didn't hire a detective,' Emer said. 'You paid some woman to contact Dee pretending to be me. And then you told me the woman I'd seen wasn't Kitty. You said she was Fiona and Michael's niece, that they'd adopted her after her parents were killed in a car crash.'

'I didn't pay any woman anything,' Robert said. 'As for the rest of it, I was going to tell you the truth when the time was right. But I was trying to protect you. And yes, I was trying to protect your mother, too. That's why I'm here. I came because I knew you were putting yourself in danger and I couldn't bear that. My car's out here. We'll drive to the nearest police station and tell them what's going on. After that, we'll find a quiet place where we can try to work out what we do next.'

She'd started crying, although she wasn't sure what had triggered it. The pain in her arm where he was holding her too tight, or the knowledge that he was a psychopath and her whole relationship with him had been based on lies.

'There's no need to cry, love. We'll get through this. I'm sure that woman has filled your head up with all sorts of nonsense, but that's all it is, Emer – nonsense. You've no idea how worried I've been. I thought… well, I'm just glad you're okay. Now come on. Look, we're almost at the car. It's just out there, on the road outside. You'll be safe now, I promise.'

His voice was soft, cajoling – the voice he used when he wanted her to apologise to Ursula or agree not to 'cause a fuss' about something, or tidy up after dinner because 'your poor mother's had a tough day and she could do with a bit of help from you every now and then.' The voice he used when he wanted to control her. Because that's what he'd been doing. All these years, when she'd thought he was caring for her and loving her as if she was his own child, he'd been controlling her.

'No.' She stopped walking, only moving when he dragged her forward and she didn't have a choice. 'I'm done with the lies, Robert. I know what you did. Kitty didn't kill Lucy. It was you. You were driving the car that night. And you were at that party where that poor girl…'

'Emer, listen to me. You're confused. Everyone knows that. You have complex mental health issues which have never been properly treated. That's probably my fault – I should have faced up to the problem earlier, but I'm facing up to it now. We're going to get you back home and get you the help you need.'

'You're nothing but a fraud,' she said. 'You pretend you're this decent man who wants to help others. But the only person you're interested in helping is yourself. Kitty told me what happened. You were driving the car that hit Lucy and killed her.'

'Stop that right now.'

His voice had changed, hard and angry now. His fingers dug deeper into her arm as he swung her around so she was standing in front of him. He leaned his face close to hers as he continued speaking. The stink of his cologne filled the air around her, clogging her nose and lodging in the back of her throat.

'You are a stupid, spoiled little brat who has no idea what you've got yourself involved with. I am doing my best to keep a lid on this thing, trying to keep you and your mother safe. But you're not making it easy for me. I told you not to go sticking your nose in, didn't I? It's not my fault your parents lied to me. All these years living with your mother, believing your sister had died. Can you imagine what it's been like for me to find out that the woman I love has been playing me for a fool?'

'You paid my father to make himself and Kitty disappear.'

She tasted vomit at the back of her throat, as she realised something else.

'Oh Jesus. When they told you Kitty had drowned, you believed them. You thought they'd actually killed their own child just to protect your stupid reputation.'

'Why wouldn't I believe it?' he said. 'Your father was a greedy bastard and I paid him well enough to get the problem sorted. It wasn't what we'd agreed. The plan had always been for your father to take Kitty to England. But when your mother told me she'd drowned, well, how was I to know she was lying to me? She's spent the weekend trying to convince me it was all your father's idea, but we both know that's bullshit, don't we Emer? Your father didn't have the brains to orchestrate something like that. Ursula lied to stop me asking too many questions, that's all.'

He'd dropped all pretence now. There was only one reason for that. He was planning to get rid of her. He'd stopped caring about what he said because he thought she wouldn't get the chance to tell anyone.

'What happened to Lucy was an accident,' he continued, 'but it was hardly my fault. Those girls shouldn't have been out that night. And they certainly shouldn't have been sneaking into a house that didn't belong to them, seeing things they weren't meant to see.'

'Why did you drive after them?' Emer said. 'If you didn't mean to kill them?'

'I needed to find out how much they'd seen. They were young girls – easy for them to misinterpret things.'

'What things, exactly?' Emer said, remembering the scene in the bedroom that Kitty had described to her.

'It was a networking event,' Robert said, 'Your mother organised them for me. It's never easy for important people to get together and let their hair down a bit. There's always someone watching you, ready to judge or jump to the wrong conclusion. Your mother came up with the idea of organising some private events, away from prying eyes. They were very popular for a time, until those stupid girls turned up and ruined everything. Because, of course, they had to stop after that.'

'What about Lucy?' Emer said.

'You mean what happened to her? Well, she was already dead. It was an accident, like I said. There was no need for anyone else to know what had happened. I buried her in the woods.'

'You sick bastard.'

Emer leaned her head back then threw it forward, her forehead smashing into his face. With a roar, he let her go and staggered back, hands over his damaged face. She twisted away from him but his hand shot out, grabbing her and pulling her back. His hand wrapped around her neck, blocking the air.

She struggled against him, kicking and lashing out with her hands. She heard him say something, but she didn't catch the words, and suddenly he was falling backwards, taking her with him.

He hit the ground first, cushioning her fall. She rolled off him, scrabbling to get away but she wasn't fast enough. He grabbed her and suddenly he was on top of her, the weight of his body pressing into her, his fists punching her shoulders, her head, her back.

She was lying on her stomach, face down in the gravel. Stones in her mouth as the punches kept coming. She tried to crawl forward but she couldn't move. He was too heavy, making it impossible for her to breathe. Her hands flailed on the gravel, trying to find something she could hold onto to pull herself forward. Darkness was creeping in from the outer corners of her eyes. The world fading out as the punches kept coming.

And then, just as suddenly as it began, it was over. The punches stopped, and she was able to breathe as his body slipped off her and slumped onto the gravel beside her.

'Emer?'

Fiona was standing over her, an iron poker in her hand.

'Oh God, Emer. I'm so sorry. I should have acted faster. Are you okay?'

On the ground beside her, Robert groaned. He was still alive. She didn't want him to be alive. She wanted to stand up and grab the poker and smash it down on him, again and again, until she'd killed him.

She might have done it, too. Except, as she pushed herself off the ground, a car turned into the driveway, screeching to a halt in front of them. A man Emer didn't recognise got out of the car and came towards them.

'Fiona, I came here as soon as I could. What the hell is going on?'

He had kind eyes, Emer noticed. Fiona said something, but Emer couldn't hear her. The words were muffled, as if they were speaking through a wall of cotton wool. Emer could see Fiona's mouth moving, and her hands, pointing at Emer and Robert, but Emer couldn't make out what she was saying.

Something was wrong with her ears. Her legs had stopped working as well. She wobbled, trying to keep upright, but she couldn't do it. Her legs collapsed and she fell forward, straight into the arms of the strange man with the kind brown eyes.

Forty-eight

At first, Dee thought the sounds were part of the stories unfolding inside her head. She was somewhere between sleep and wakefulness. Drifting through memories from years ago and moments in the future she'd never get to experience. Imagining Jake at different stages of his life, wondering how long it would take for him to forget her completely. Somewhere, in the middle of it, the voices had started. She thought they'd go away; part of her wanted them to go away so she could get back to Jake's imaginary future. But the talking continued. She pressed her ear against the door.

There was nothing, at first. Then, when she was starting to give up hope, she heard footsteps. Feet crunching over the broken glass on the patio. The murmur of voices, followed by a scream.

She started banging on the door, shouting until her throat was raw, making as much noise as possible. But no matter how loud she was, no one came. How was it possible she could hear them but they couldn't hear her?

The tips of her fingers were raw and bloodied from trying to scrape away some of the wood at the top of the door. She'd thought if she could just make enough space to press her mouth against it, she might be able to shout loudly enough to be heard. But the wood was hard and thick and all her efforts hadn't made the slightest bit of difference.

Every part of her was exhausted. And cold. So cold. She'd stopped feeling her feet some time ago. She tried to keep stamping them, moving around to keep the blood flowing around her body, but trying to move in this cramped space was exhausting. Now, all she wanted to do was lie down and give up. Because what was the point of fighting and trying to keep going if no one was going to come? She didn't know how long she had left, but it was hours, surely, not days. The cold would get her eventually. One by one, her organs would shut down and her body would simply give up. It would be over.

She thought of the mobile home that would soon be empty, and all the long, lonely days she had to look forward to. Maybe it was better to go now. She'd already lived the best years of her life. She'd been young once. Young and attractive and in love. She'd had a job she loved, a husband she loved even more, and a whole heap of ambition raging inside her, driving her to achieve more and more.

It had all ended, of course. You could only sustain that way of living for a limited amount of time. Working hard and playing harder – it wasn't a long-term life plan, but she'd loved it too much to give it up voluntarily.

And afterwards, when her world had come crashing down, she'd had to find a new way of living. A simpler existence that brought its own precious rewards. Like the joy of watching a little boy grow up and letting him become a part of her life until she could barely remember what it had been like not to have him around. But now that was coming to an end, what did she have left? Nothing.

She pulled her knees up against her chest, her head and back resting against the door because it was slightly less cold than the stone wall. She let her eyes close, and the pleasure that came from not trying to keep them open was beautiful. It was time to go. She'd found her peace with that now.

The sound of a car, braking suddenly, brought her back. Her eyes shot open, a surge of adrenaline putting all her senses on high alert. She could hear more voices now. At least one woman and one man, possibly more.

She started banging the door, screaming as loudly as she could. She didn't know who was out there, or even if they'd want to let her out. Maybe they'd rather keep her locked up in here until she died, but she had to try. Because despite everything, she wasn't ready to die just yet.

At first, she thought it would be like the last time and no one would hear her. But then a miracle happened. A man was outside, shouting through the door, asking who was in there.

'My name's Dee,' she said. 'I'm a friend of Emer's. Is she with you? Is she okay?'

'Dee?'

'There's no key.' A woman's voice, this time. 'You won't get inside without a key.'

'Give me that,' the man said. 'I should be able to use it to prise the door open. Dee! Get away from the door while I open it.'

It took an age, but eventually he managed to crack open the door. And then he was pushing it and light was flooding in, too bright. Dee put an arm over her eyes, protecting them. She stumbled forward and he caught her, putting his arm around her as he guided her outside.

'It's okay,' he said. 'You're safe now.'

Gradually, her eyes adjusted, and when she was able to take her arm away, he was staring at her, his brown eyes creased with concern.

'Ed,' she said. 'What the bloody hell are you doing here?'

'I was about to ask you the same question,' he said.

–

Time passed in a blur of activity. The man who'd attacked her – Robert O'Brien – was in custody. Before rescuing Dee, Ed had handcuffed Robert to the door handle of his car so he couldn't get away. Then he'd called for back-up, which arrived shortly after in the form of a squad car with two uniformed officers and Ed's partner, Rachel Lewis. The two officers had taken Robert to the custody suite in Eastbourne. Rachel stayed behind to help Ed try to make sense of the mess Dee had found herself in the middle of.

First, though, Ed had to tell Fiona Holden that her husband was dead. Dee remembered the shock of hearing her ex-husband had been murdered. It had devastated her, even though she'd spent the years prior to Billy's murder convincing herself she hated him. Turned out that wasn't true. After he was dead, she realised it was possible to still love someone long after you stopped wanting to share your life with them.

'It's all my fault,' Fiona said, when she'd stopped crying enough to be able to speak. 'I've ruined everything.'

'It's because of Annie,' Ed said, 'isn't it? All this time you've been protecting her. From what, Fiona? You need to tell us, because right now we've got one dead man, one abduction, and a prominent Irish politician who's caught up in all of this for reasons I don't yet understand. Robert's in custody at the moment, but there's going to be hell to pay if we're not able to explain very soon to the Irish authorities why he's been arrested.'

Together, Emer and Fiona told Ed everything they'd worked out so far about Kitty Doran's disappearance.

'Robert killed Michael,' Dee said, when they'd finished. She looked at Emer. 'He wears a distinctive cologne, doesn't he? I smelled it at Michael's flat on Sunday morning when I discovered his body.'

'He's gone into crisis management mode,' Emer said. 'He's a great man for sorting out a mess. Normally it's other people's messes and he hires people to help. With this, he's had to do it by himself. Because Kitty's his weakness. Until today, Kitty was the only person left alive – apart from my mother – who knew that Robert killed Lucy and hid her body. Ursula's not going to say anything, but Kitty might. He's decided he can't risk that, so he's come here to sort it out himself.'

'I should have stopped it years ago,' Fiona said.

'You had your reasons,' Ed said. 'Although if we'd known everything earlier, Michael may have got a more lenient prison sentence.'

'But we'd have lost Annie,' Fiona said.

'Kitty,' Emer said. 'Her name's Kitty.'

They were sitting in the elegant sitting room Dee had seen through the window earlier. If someone looked into the room now, they'd think it was five friends sitting around sharing a pot of coffee and some biscuits. So far, Ed had managed to avoid pointing out that Dee had broken her promise about staying away from Alfriston. Although Dee was sure it was only a matter of time before he cracked and said something.

She reached up to touch the wound on her face, remembering the fear she'd felt as the blade had cut her skin. Rachel had already examined the cut and told Dee the wound was superficial. She'd offered to take Dee to A&E to get it properly checked out, but Dee had refused. She wanted to see this through to the end.

'What will happen to Robert now?' she asked.

'Depends.' Ed looked at Fiona. 'Do you think Kitty will be willing to tell the Irish authorities the truth about Lucy?'

'If we ever find her, then yes, of course she'll want to tell them what she knows,' Fiona said. 'The only reason she hasn't already done that is because I didn't want her to.'

'Because you wanted to protect her,' Ed said. 'You shouldn't blame yourself for that.'

Dee had forgotten how kind he could be. Or how good it felt to sit beside him on a sofa, like now, knowing he was here and he'd do whatever it took to keep all the people in this room safe.

'My colleagues in London will want to interview you again too,' he told Dee. 'The post-mortem results confirm Michael was killed. Which means, for now, you're the last known person to have seen him alive.'

'What about Robert?' Dee said.

'There's a window of about an hour between Emer speaking to Michael at the flat and you finding his dead body,' Ed said. 'Of course we'll be questioning him about the murder. Before we do, it would be helpful to under-stand how he knew where Michael lived. Emer, can you shed any light on that?'

'Maeve,' Emer said. 'I sent her the address that morning, remember Dee? So she could meet us there.'

'But you didn't tell her what flat Michael lived in,' Dee said. 'You only gave her the building number and street name. It's a huge block of flats. There's no way Robert could have knocked on every door until he found Michael. I was back at his flat no more than an hour after you left him.'

'When I was going up to the flat,' Emer said, 'I thought someone was following me. But each time I stopped and looked around, there was no one there. Is it possible Robert had come to the flats and followed me up the stairs?'

'We can look into that later,' Ed said. 'If Robert killed Michael, we'll find a way to prove it. For now, let's concentrate on finding Kitty.'

Rachel cleared her throat, a signal Dee recognised. She was about to say something others would find uncomfortable.

'Fiona and Emer, I know this is difficult, but I think you need to accept the possibility that Kitty's sudden disappearance is her own choice.'

'What do you mean?' Emer said.

'Isn't it possible all of this simply became too much? Maybe she just wanted to get away. Make a fresh start somewhere else.'

'No,' Fiona said. 'That's not what's happened. She wanted a chance to go back and do the right thing – to tell the truth, regardless of the consequences.'

'It wouldn't do any harm to put a call out,' Ed said. 'Have you got a recent photo you can give us?'

'Only on my phone,' Fiona said.

'That's fine,' Ed said. 'I'll give you my phone number and you can send it to me.'

'What about the other girl?' Dee said. The fog in her mind was lifting. Replaced with a moment of startling clarity. 'You said she never checked into the hotel, but her car was still parked outside?'

'And Kitty's car,' Emer said.

Finally, the different pieces started to make sense, and Dee could see how they all fitted together.

'So if both their cars are there,' she said, 'then the chances are they're still at the hotel, right?'

'They're not,' Emer insisted. 'I checked everywhere, and the guy on reception was adamant – Maeve never checked in.'

'What if she used a different name?' Dee said. 'All she'd need to do was check in with a false name and you'd never know she was there.'

'Why would she do that?' Ed said.

'Have you got a photo of Maeve?' Dee asked Emer.

'I don't think so.' Emer scrolled through her phone, frowning. 'Hang on, we're friends on Instagram. Just a sec. Here.'

Dee took the phone and looked at the photo on the screen. A young woman with bobbed hair and elfin features. It was difficult to make out the colour of her eyes from the photo, but Dee already knew they were an unusual shade of pale blue.

'That's her.' She handed the phone back to Emer. 'The girl in that photo is the same girl who contacted me pretending to be you.'

Forty-nine

The darkness lifted and suddenly she was breathing. Just. One nostril was blocked, but she was able to suck air through the other one. Red dots were floating in front her eyes, blurring her vision. A loud noise inside her head, like gushing water, blocked out any other sounds. She could see Maeve. Her mouth was moving, as if she was speaking, but Kitty couldn't hear her. Then the rushing water stopped and the words started trickling through.

'Can't do it... wrong... want to but I can't. Stop it! Shut your eyes. Don't look at me. I can't stand it.'

The words sounded strange, as if she was having problems controlling her tongue. Kitty thought the problem was her ears, that the lack of air had damaged them, somehow. She imagined the sudden rush of blood to her brain bursting her ear drums, damaging her hearing forever. But then she saw the bottle of vodka in Maeve's hand and realised that's what was causing the problem with her speech. She was drunk.

The knowledge triggered another surge of panic. Kitty closed her eyes, forcing herself to breathe as slowly as she could – not easy under the circumstances – while she waited for the worst of the panic to pass. But it was impossible with Maeve screaming at her.

'Why, Kitty? You could have sent a letter, done something to let us know. But you did nothing. Not a single thing. Do you know what you've done? Do you have any fucking idea the damage you've caused?'

Maeve paused to drink from the bottle. When she'd finished, she leaned in, fumes of boozy breath invading the little bit of air Kitty was able to breathe.

'You're a psycho. A fucking psycho. You and your whole family. Your parents used to organise sex parties, did you know that? My dad told me about it when she got married to Robert. I suppose your mother stopped all that when she got married again. She wouldn't have needed the money.'

Kitty remembered cars in the driveway, and the voices drifting from behind the closed door. Robert O'Brien standing in the doorway of the bedroom. Her mother's face hidden behind the video camera. Lucy's body illuminated in the car's headlights. The roar of the engine drowning out the sound of her screams.

'Fuck it.' Maeve leaned forward and pulled the flannel out of Kitty's mouth. 'But if you make a sound I'll smash your face in.' She lifted the bottle and Kitty nodded, letting her know she understood.

She breathed in mouthfuls of beautiful air. Her mouth was unbearably dry, her tongue swollen and thick.

'Water,' she croaked. Then, when Maeve didn't move, 'Please.'

The dryness was beyond anything she'd ever experienced. She tried to repeat her plea but she couldn't get another word out.

'Jesus.' Maeve stood up. Kitty listened as she went into the bathroom and turned on a tap, the sound of water like a dream.

'Here.'

Maeve's hand movements were jerky. The glass clinked painfully against Kitty's teeth and water ran down her chin and neck, but she didn't care because she was drinking and she'd never tasted anything this beautiful in her entire life.

'Thank you,' she said, when Maeve finally lifted the glass away.

'I wanted to kill you,' Maeve said. 'But now I've got the opportunity, I can't do it.'

Maeve leaned towards her and Kitty shrank back, thinking Maeve was going to try the pillow again. She didn't have the strength to survive that a second time. Instead, Maeve reached behind Kitty's back and started playing around with whatever she'd used to tie her wrists together.

'Cable ties,' Maeve said. 'I got them earlier, when I knew I was going to be seeing you. But I forgot to get scissors, so now I can't untie you.'

'I'm so sorry,' Kitty said. 'If you only knew how sorry I am. I've thought about Lucy every day since. I've gone over it so many times, wishing I could go back to that night and change what happened.'

'You should have told the Guards.'

'I know.'

The guilt of it all weighed on her chest and shoulders. Something she knew she would always carry with her.

'I should have killed you,' Maeve said.

'Part of me wishes you had,' Kitty said. 'It's been unbearable, Maeve. Living with the guilt all these years. I'm so glad you finally know the truth.'

'Well I'm glad too. But don't think this means I forgive you, Kitty. I'm not ready to do that just yet.'

'I don't blame you,' Kitty said. 'I'd feel the same way if I was you.'

'Well, you've done the right thing now. That's got to count for something, I suppose.'

'What would you have done if you'd killed me?' Kitty asked.

'I don't know.' Maeve shrugged. 'I hadn't thought that far ahead. All I could think about was making you suffer.'

'I'm so sorry,' Kitty said. 'I know how pointless it is to say that now, but it's the truth. I wanted to contact you, Maeve. There were plenty of times when I almost got in touch.'

'What stopped you?'

'I was scared. It's no excuse, I know. I'm sorry.'

'You're right,' Maeve said. 'It's no excuse.' She nodded at Kitty's legs. 'You're going to have to stay like that until I can find something to cut you loose.'

'I've got a nail clipper in my bag,' Kitty said. 'Try that.'

'Maybe I'm not ready to untie you.' Maeve walked over to the window, stood with her back to Kitty for several minutes.

'Oh, to hell with it,' she said eventually.

She crossed the room, out of Kitty's eyeline.

'Got them,' Maeve said. She came back to Kitty, nail clipper in hand, and set about cutting the ties. It took a while but eventually Kitty's wrists were free and she was able to sit up while Maeve started on the cable ties around her ankles.

'I'd been thinking about going into business with Robert,' Maeve said, as she worked on the cable ties. 'We'd been talking about opening a hotel together. I was keen to expand to another part of the country, and Robert was looking for a sound investment. I know it's a risk going into business with someone else. But I really thought I could trust Robert.

336

'We'd arranged to meet at his house to discuss next steps. When I got there, he was in the garden with your mother. They were talking about you. Emer had told them about seeing you in London, and Robert was asking if it was possible you could still be alive. Your mother kept insisting it wasn't. She said you'd drowned that day, and that was the end of it.

'I must have made a noise then, because suddenly they stopped speaking. So I went around the corner and pretended I'd just arrived. But later, during my meeting with Robert, I told him I'd overheard some of their conversation. And I told him if there was any chance you might be alive, I wanted to help find you.

'Robert knew if you were somehow living in England, there was a good chance your uncle Frank had helped your father. He thought speaking to Dee was a good starting point. It was easy for him to check that Emer and Dee had never met. So he suggested I come to London and contact Dee and tell her I was her long-lost cousin.

'It was obvious she didn't know anything about Kitty, but when I asked her to help me find you, she said yes immediately. It was the perfect solution. She could do all the hard work. We could sit back and wait for her to tell us if Annie Holden really was who she said she was.'

'Weren't you worried she'd find out you were lying?'

'A little,' Maeve said. 'But I kept our face-to-face meetings to a minimum. I even set up a fake Facebook account, calling myself Emer Doran, and sent her a friend request. She had no reason to think I was anyone else. I'd already met up with Emer and found out exactly what had happened on the Underground that afternoon, so I knew what to tell Dee. It worked perfectly.'

'Until Dee realised you weren't Emer.'

'Well, yeah. But by then everything else had pretty much fallen apart as well. There.' Maeve cut through the last of the ties on Kitty's ankles. 'You should feel better now.'

She lifted the bottle of vodka and held it out. 'Want some of this?'

Kitty took the bottle and drank some. It burned her throat and stomach, warming her body.

'Thanks.'

'Keep it,' Maeve said. 'I've already had too much. I'm sorry, by the way.'

'It's okay,' Kitty said, meaning it. 'I can't blame you for hating me.'

'It's all so messed up,' Maeve said. 'Are you absolutely sure it was Robert driving the car that night?'

'Positive. Later, he paid my parents to clear up the mess. I think they told Robert I really had drowned.'

'How did you work it all out?' Maeve asked.

'Some of it I pieced together,' Kitty said. 'Some of it I found out later.'

Because after Michael was charged with murder, Fiona had told her the truth about her father. The lies he'd told and the lengths he'd gone to so he could line his own pockets.

'I didn't come to England to kill you,' Maeve said. 'I just wanted answers. But then, when Emer called… when I found out you were still alive, and you knew, you'd known all this time, something snapped. All I could think about was making you pay for the damage you'd caused by never speaking up.

'We had a hamster when I was little. I remember one winter it got sick and my dad had to smother it with a cushion. He said it was an act of kindness because the hamster wouldn't survive, anyway. I thought I could kill you the same way, not as an act of kindness but as an act of revenge. I went onto the internet and found there was an IT store in Polegate. I drove there and bought a packet of cable ties. Then I bought the vodka, because even though I hated you, I knew I wouldn't be able to do it unless I was drunk. And I did so well, but I couldn't finish it. I couldn't even do that.'

She'd started crying again. Kitty wanted to give her a hug, but she wasn't sure Maeve would let her. Before she could work out the best course of action, someone knocked on the door.

'Kitty?'

Relief flooded through her at the sound of her sister's voice.

'It's Emer,' she said to Maeve. 'Are you okay if I let her in?'

Maeve nodded, and Kitty stood up. As she walked to the door, she thought of the other time she'd been in a hotel with her sister. And her heart filled with joy that this time she was walking towards her, not running away.

Fifty

Three days later

'It's the deceit I can't get over. All those lies. And you, my beautiful child, those precious years we'll never get back. I've been robbed of so many moments we should have had together.'

'You really had no idea?' Kitty said.

Ursula dabbed the corner of her eyes with a tissue, looking every inch the heartbroken mother she was trying hard to portray. She'd have to try a hell of a lot harder, Emer thought, before she convinced either of her daughters.

They were sitting in the conservatory – a huge space overlooking the landscaped grounds of the old coaching house. Kitty and Emer had flown into Dublin last night and driven down to Ballincarraig first thing this morning.

At some level, Emer had always known her mother had never really loved Robert. She'd married him for his money and the lifestyle he'd promised her. She suspected Robert had known it too, but his slavish devotion to the woman he regularly described as 'the most beautiful creature on God's earth' meant he was willing to overlook her inability to love in exchange for being able to call her his wife.

'Of course I had no idea. How could I? Your father and Robert orchestrated the whole thing between them. That's what men do, isn't it? They take all the big decisions, and the women have no choice but to go along with them. I shouldn't be surprised by your father's part in this. He was always a crook. But I thought Robert was different. You know the British police are saying he killed that poor man? Threw him out the window of his own flat. I've spent all these years married to a man I barely know.'

Kitty's face was blank, betraying nothing, but Emer knew this wasn't easy for her. Robert had been charged with murdering Michael Holden. Traces of his DNA had been found on Michael's body and in his flat. In his arrogance, it had never occurred to Robert that he'd get caught.

Ursula paused to dab her eyes some more.

'It's your fault, Emer. You told Maeve where that man lived and she passed the information on to Robert. He told me he'd gone to London for a business meeting. That was a lie too, wasn't it? He'd gone there to clean up the mess he'd made of everything. I thought I was married to the future leader of our country. Instead, I've wasted the best years of my life with a liar and a crook.'

Emer hadn't seen Robert since he'd been arrested, but Ed Mitchell had kept her updated. Robert had eventually confessed to killing Michael Holden, although he claimed the death was an accident. His story was that Maeve had told him Emer would be at the block of flats that morning. He'd gone there to try to persuade her to come back home. When he'd seen her go into the building, his curiosity got the better of him and he followed her. Then, when he'd asked Michael where he could find Emer, Michael got aggressive and Robert had no choice but to defend himself. It was clearly a load of bullshit but, for now, that was Robert's story and he was sticking to it.

'I feel utterly betrayed.' Ursula looked at Emer. 'You remember, don't you darling? I was a mess after we lost your sister. You were the only thing that kept me going. My reason for getting up and dragging myself through day after endless day. And all the time, my baby girl was alive.'

'Mum,' Kitty said. 'Robert is saying the whole thing was your idea. He's claiming he didn't even know, until recently, that I was still alive.'

'Of course he's saying that,' Ursula snapped. 'And I do wish you'd call me Ursula. *Mum* is such a dreary world. Robert had to have known. He was driving the car that hit Lucy, wasn't he? You were there. Robert killed that poor girl and he buried her body in the bog. And you lied about it, Kitty. I know you were only a child, but think of the damage that's been caused by your lies. I thought I'd raised both my children to be honest and truthful. But the first bit of trouble you found yourself in, you tried to lie your way out of it. Nature over nurture, I fear. You're your father's daughter, after all.'

'You've just told us you didn't know what happened,' Emer interrupted. 'If that's the case, how do you know he buried her in the bog?'

'Don't you think I've had enough time over the last few days to piece things together?' Ursula said. 'I do have a brain, you know.'

'So you're just guessing that's what he did?' Emer said.

'How dare you?' Ursula said. 'Kitty, do you see what she's like? It's been a challenge raising her. She's got a mean, nasty side to her. You, on the other hand, were always such a good girl. That's why it's so wonderful to have you back, finally.'

Their mother's ability to reimagine the past was astonishing, Emer thought. The truth was, she'd always been harder on Kitty than she'd ever been on Emer. Probably because Kitty had been braver than Emer, more willing to stand up to their mother. Something Emer had always been too scared to do.

'I saw you,' Kitty said, her voice low and hard.

'I don't know what you're talking about.'

'You know exactly what I'm talking about.'

The tension between them was tangible. The room fizzed with it. Emer couldn't take her eyes off her mother, waiting to see how she'd react. There was a pattern with Ursula, a woman who didn't see anything wrong with lying and cheating or doing whatever was needed to get her own way. Whenever she was called out on a lie, or a wrongdoing, she always responded in the same way. First, she'd act wounded, as if she couldn't believe anyone would ever doubt her. This would rapidly become a defensive anger, until it eventually became too exhausting for the other person and, inevitably, they would back down.

That wasn't going to happen now, though. This time, there was no Robert to intervene on his wife's behalf and do everything he could to smooth the situation over as quickly as possible. This time, Emer wasn't alone.

'You were in the house that night,' Kitty said. 'Upstairs in the bedroom, filming what was being done to that poor girl. And later, you brought Robert to the house and let him threaten me. Do you remember that, *Ursula?* He came into my bedroom and put his hands around my neck and told me he would kill me if I ever told anyone what had happened.'

Ursula frowned.

'I really have no idea what you're talking about. It was such a long time ago, darling.'

'I saw you.'

'Please.' Ursula held up a hand. 'Whatever you think you saw, you need to stop. Losing you destroyed me. But you're back now. We should be celebrating, not finding ways to blame each other for what happened. I thought you were dead, Kitty, and I can't bear for you to think I was in any way involved with what happened to you. How could you? I'm your mother. I would have done anything to protect you and keep you safe.'

'Bríd Keenan.'

Something flickered across Ursula's face. Fear. For the first time since they'd been here, she was frightened of where this conversation was going.

'It took me a while to work it out,' Kitty said. 'But I've had nothing but time to think about everything. Twenty-three years of it. You used to take me into work with you sometimes. I remember Bríd. She was doing work experience for Robert. A fifteen-year-old girl from the Travelling community. It was part of his persona, wasn't it? Doing his bit to help the Travellers. Except what people didn't know is that the young girls who did work experience were expected to do a few other things as well, weren't they?'

Ursula stood up.

'I refuse to stay here a moment longer and listen to any of this. How dare you come into my house after all these years and start throwing accusations at me? I am not the villain here, Kitty. Oh, I'm sure your sister's done a fine job of filling your head with lies about me. But that's all they are. Lies! I am a decent woman who has had to endure more than any mother ought to. On top of that,

I've just discovered both my husbands lied to me. It's too much. Can't you see that?'

She started to leave, but Kitty called after her.

'I've been to see her.'

Ursula stopped walking, but kept her back to them so Emer couldn't see the expression on her face. She could imagine it, though. Cold and angry, her mouth set in a straight line, as she thought of a way to wiggle her way out of this one.

'I remember her,' she said, after a moment. 'A lying little bitch. We had to fire her, as I recall. We discovered she'd been stealing money from the petty cash. I tried to warn Robert, told him there would always be problems with those sorts of people. But he wanted to help, despite my warnings. Well, this just shows how misguided he was.'

She turned around, smiling now because she thought she'd found her way out.

'People like that are always looking to tell lies about men like Robert. They're jealous of him. Plain and simple. I'm sure she's never forgiven him for letting her go, even though she's lucky that's all it was. He should have reported her to the Guards, if you ask me. She'll say anything she can to sully his reputation. But that's all this is. A bitter young woman lying to get revenge on a man who only ever wanted to help her.'

'Christ almighty,' Emer burst out. 'You're not even being consistent with your lies. Are you trying to convince us Robert is a crook who killed Lucy and then made Kitty disappear? Or that he's a good man who's dedicated his life to helping people?'

'I wouldn't expect you to understand,' Ursula said coolly. 'People are complex. It's perfectly possible for a good person to make a mistake. That's all Lucy was. A silly

345

mistake that he's going to have to pay for. And I'm glad, because it's good that everyone finally knows the truth. As for what your sister thinks she saw, we were having a party. Powerful men like Robert and his associates, they have big appetites. A real zest for life that so many people are lacking. My job was to make sure those appetites were satisfied. That may sound distasteful to you two, but everyone at that party wanted to be there. Those girls used to beg me to let them come along. Why? Because they were little scrubbers who didn't think twice about opening their legs in exchange for cash. And believe me, they got paid handsomely for anything they did at those parties.'

She stopped speaking, as if realising she'd already said too much.

'Three days after Lucy was killed,' Kitty said, 'you took me into work with you. Bríd wasn't there. When I asked you where she was, you told me Robert had fired her because she'd been stealing from you.'

'That's right.' Ursula nodded her head. 'You see? I've been telling the truth all along.'

'I recognised her voice,' Kitty said. 'At the time, I didn't know where from. It was only later, years later, that I worked it out. I've never been able to separate out what happened that night with poor Bríd getting fired.'

'I'm not sure what to say.' Ursula shrugged. 'People get fired from their jobs all the time.'

'But she wasn't the sort of person to steal,' Kitty said. 'She was kind and funny and decent. I remember all those things about her, even now. So I decided to track her down and ask her if she was the woman I'd seen in the house. Finding her was easier than I'd thought. There's a charity in Loughrea that helps traveller women across the county. I went there a few days ago and asked about Bríd. Turns out she set up the charity herself. Using the money you gave her to keep quiet about what happened to her that night. Except she's not going to keep quiet any longer. She's already told a journalist what happened, and he believes her. The story's going to be all over the press in the next few days.'

'No.'

The word came out like a whisper. The colour had drained from Ursula's face. For a moment, Emer thought she would crack and confess. Instead, her mother turned and walked out of the room without another word.

'Let her go,' she said, as Kitty stood and went to follow her.

Outside, a car was turning into the driveway. A navy blue sedan that pulled up beside Ursula's BMW convertible. Two men in dark suits climbed out and started walking towards the front door.

'The Guards are here,' Emer said. 'I'll go and let them in. They can deal with her now.'

'What about us?' Kitty said. 'What do we do?'

'We're taking a trip to Galway,' Emer said. 'There's someone I want you to meet. Her name's Nikki. She's already heard a lot about you. I called her last night and it turns out she's home this weekend. She can't wait to meet you.'

Fifty-one

'So this is it then.' Ella took a step forward, and Dee grabbed her. Held her tight then let her go and twisted her face into a smile.

'Text me when you get there?'

'Of course.' Ella turned and called for Jake, who was sitting on the beach, stacking stones one on top of the other. 'Come and say goodbye, Jakey.'

He stood up and walked over, his little face scrunched into a scowl.

'I don't want to go.'

Dee knelt down on the stones so her face was level with his.

'Of course you don't want to go,' she said, 'because it's something new. And sometimes new things are scary. But it's going to be brilliant, Jake. Canada is beautiful.'

'Daddy's going to teach me to ski.' The frown disappeared, replaced by a smile so wide and perfect what was left of Dee's heart shattered into tiny pieces.

'And you can teach me when I come to visit.'

She opened her arms and he jumped into them, just as he'd done countless times over the last few years. She buried her face in the top of his head, breathing in his unique Jake smell, wondering how she was ever going to find the strength to let him go again. But somehow she managed it. As she stood up and watched him run towards the waiting car, part of her hated herself for not fighting harder to make them stay. She knew it wouldn't have made a blind bit of difference, but right now, she couldn't help blaming herself, her mind finding all the reasons why – if she'd only tried harder – they might never have left.

'Are you okay?' Ella asked, as Jake climbed into the car and slammed the door shut without looking back.

'I'm fine.' Dee shook her head. 'Well, I will be fine. I'm going to miss you like hell, but I'll get used to it.'

'We'll FaceTime every week,' Ella said. 'I haven't worked out the time difference yet, but we can still do our Friday get-togethers, even if we do them at a different time. And I meant what I said about you coming for Christmas. It would be the best present ever for Jake. And for me.'

'Of course I'll come,' Dee said. As soon as the car pulled away, she was planning to go inside and check out plane fares. She was pretty sure flying anywhere at Christmastime cost the earth, but so what? She would sell the house if it meant spending Christmas with Jake.

'Dee, I don't think I've ever told you this,' Ella said, 'but I would never have got through the last few years without you. I don't know how I can ever thank you for everything you've done for me.'

'You don't need to thank me,' Dee said. 'Having you all in my life, it's been a joy.'

'I love you, Dee.'

'I love you too. Now go on. Get the hell out of here before I make a fool of myself and start crying in front of you all.'

Ella looked as if she was going to say something else, but Dee waved her away. She had never been one for long, drawn out goodbyes. The longer Ella and Jake were here, the harder it was getting to hold it together.

'Bye, then.'

Ella turned and walked across the shingle to the car, where Jake and Tom were waiting. The rumble of the engine, a puff of dust as the car started down the narrow track away from the mobile home, a flash of waving arms, a final glimpse of Jake's face mouthing goodbye through the car window. And just like that, they were gone.

–

Dee sat on the deck, watching the sun slowly sink beneath the horizon. She had a glass of chilled white wine in front of her, and Johnny Cash in the background, singing about missing a girl in Tipperary town. Along the beach, the mobile home stood empty. No lights on, no voices drifting through the still air, reminding her that she wasn't alone out here on this quiet stretch of beach.

Work had got her through the rest of the day. At four o'clock this afternoon, she'd finished the book and emailed it to her agent. Later, she'd driven to the wine shop in Meads and treated herself to a single bottle of Tokaji Furmint – Hungarian, dry and very expensive.

Today had been hard, but she'd expected that. Gradually, she would adjust to their absence, as she'd adjusted to so many other things. Adjusting to change was part of life. And while she adjusted, she would focus on the positives. Like the fact that she'd just written her first book, and knew she'd done a good job with it. Better than she'd ever have thought possible. Her agent would, doubtless, suggest some improvements, but nothing Dee couldn't manage.

Then there was Dee's growing relationship with her newly found cousins. Dee had spoken to both women yesterday. They were in Ireland at the moment, tying up the final loose ends in a story that had started twenty-three years earlier. Robert O'Brien was being held in custody in England and looking at a long jail sentence. The only question left unanswered was whether he served that in the UK or Ireland. Via video link two days ago, he'd told the Irish Guards where he'd buried Lucy Ryan. Her body had been recovered yesterday morning. So Maeve finally knew what had happened to her sister, and the people responsible were going to get the justice they deserved.

Ursula O'Brien had also been charged with a number of offences and was on remand awaiting trial for her role in the rape of Bríd Keenan. Shay Flaherty's story would be front page news in tomorrow's *Irish Times.* Twenty-three years after Lucy Ryan disappeared, Shay had finally got to write about what had happened to her.

The wound on Dee's face, where Robert had cut her, was healing well too. Soon, there would be no trace of the wound at all. But no matter how many times Dee listed her reasons to be happy, she couldn't feel it. Instead, there was nothing but this dreadful emptiness.

The sun was disappearing beneath the horizon, the kaleidoscope of pinks and oranges and reds fading to grey, when she heard a car coming towards her house. When the car stopped and the driver got out, the sound of the door closing echoed through the quiet night air.

Dee listened to his footsteps, crunching over the shingle, as he walked around the side of the house towards the deck. She thought about standing up and going inside. Closing the doors and blinds, and not answering if he knocked at the back door. But she already knew she wasn't going to do that. Because despite everything she'd tried to tell herself over the last six months, she still missed him. And when he finally appeared around the corner, a bottle of wine in his hand and a stupid grin on his face, she pulled out the chair beside her and motioned for him to join her.

Acknowledgements

Thanks to my lovely agent, Laura Longrigg; the amazing team at Canelo – Louise Cullen, Francesca Riccardi, Nicola Piggott, Siân Heap and Miranda Ward; my fellow crime writers Lorraine Mace, Marion Todd and Chris Curran for keeping me sane in times of crisis! A big shout-out to book blogging community who do so much to support and promote authors. Thank you Chris Simmons for just being fabulous in so many different ways and continuing to be my friend even when I disappear off the radar for months at a time. Thanks also to Maureen Webb for being such a meticulous reader! Finally, a very special mention for the brilliant group of people who run the UK Crime Book Club – you guys have created something very special. Your book group is a wonderful online community for all lovers of crime fiction. I am privileged to be part of it.

Do you love crime fiction and are always on the lookout for brilliant authors?

Canelo Crime is home to some of the most exciting novels around. Thousands of readers are already enjoying our compulsive stories. Are you ready to find your new favourite writer?

Find out more and sign up to our newsletter at canelocrime.com